"MORGAN!"

She was screaming his name, over and over, a litany to the heavens above. After a brief hesitation, Morgan burst into the room, just in time to see the candle on the nightstand sputter out. The bedchamber was plunged into darkness. He fumbled his way down the bed to the sobbing invalid, and managed to capture her flailing hands in the darkness.

"I'm here. 'Tis Morgan. Ssh, you're safe now."

His own heart thumped when she threw herself against his chest, frantically clutching at him.

"A dream! Fire. Water. Blood . . ." She shivered and moaned, a white wraith. Morgan closed his arms around her.

"Hush," he said. " 'Twas just a bad dream, dear. The storm has upset you. Granted, they can be wild here on the Welsh coast. Falcon's Lair is a veritable fortress, though. You are safe here."

"Morgan?" Her curious hands found and molded his face in the darkness. He flinched, then remembered the room was pitch-dark. She could not see him.

As her cool, calloused fingers traced his jaw, nose, and lips, Morgan steeled himself against the bittersweet emotions slamming through his tense figure.

"Who are you?"

FIRE RAVEN

Patricia McAllister

Zebra Books
Kensington Publishing Corp.
http://www.zebrabooks.com

FIRE RAVEN is dedicated to friendships, old and new. With love to all my friends in Southern Idaho Chapter RWA. Special thanks to mega-talented fellow authors Charlene Raddon, Linda Sandifer, Fela Dawson Scott, Vicki Scaggs and Pat Tracy for their support and encouragement.

Cyberhugs to my new friends on the Undernet, who help weave Lasairan's dramatic adventures and cheer her on. To all my ire kith and kin at #Celtic_Realm—we've weathered many a 'sian' together, m'friends. With special affection to Sionnach, Valaquar, ShadowFox, Pryme, Jamie and Criostoir . . . thank you for magically transforming gloomy times into those full of laughter with your own blend of Celtic magic. (Las grins and says, "Bless ye all!") And with love to Joshua Standen, the 'real life' chivalrous hero behind a wolf called Faolan . . . who reminds me that the most important rule in life is to always "follow your heart."

ZEBRA BOOKS are published by

Kensington Publishing Corp.
850 Third Avenue
New York, NY 10022

First Printing: March, 1997
10 9 8 7 6 5 4 3 2 1

Printed in the United States of America

O let the solid ground
Not fail beneath my feet
Before my life has found
What some have found so sweet;
Then let come what come may,
What matter if I go mad,
I shall have had my day.

Let the sweet heavens endure,
Not close and darken above me
Before I am quite quite sure
That there is one to love me;
Then let come what come may
To a life that has been so sad,
I shall have had my day.

—Alfred Lord Tennyson

Prologue

May, 1598
The Irish Sea, off the coast of Wales

"Captain! Look out!"

The first mate's cry spun Kat around on the balls of her feet. She was just in time to deflect the savage downswing of the Spaniard. Sparks flew when their blades met and clashed.

She staggered back against the mainmast, every muscle in her sword arm screaming for reprieve. She saw the mad gleam in the Spaniard's dark eyes and knew he meant to kill her. England's old enemy was now her own.

Her mind grappled to understand the motive behind the attack, even as she struck a defensive posture in preparation for the next blow of her assailant's sword. *Fiach Teine* was a merchant ship. She was peacefully crossing the Irish Sea. Transporting goods for the Eastland Company was her trade—not war. This unprovoked, savage attack made no sense.

When Kat first heard the lookout—Corby, reporting another ship coming astern upon them—she'd paid him no heed. Not until he added the fact that the ship flew Spain's colors.

Even then, she had not been unduly concerned. Perhaps the other ship was in trouble. It appeared to be listing to one side. As the galleon drifted closer, Kat saw she was right. The Spanish crew waved to them and signaled that they needed help. Kat ordered her own men to ready the grappling hooks and boarding planks.

Normally she was not a trusting sort, but she had been raised somewhat unconventionally at sea by her parents, and her father, in particular, had always stressed the need for rules governing civility and formalities, even on the high seas. Besides, the Armada was long past. King Philip was on his deathbed. There was no reason for Spain to attack a lone merchant vessel.

How wrong she had been! Kat's temper burned with the memory of her folly. The Spaniards turned on her crew the moment the ships were linked together. The bloody pirates came streaming across the boarding planks, swinging over on the ratlines, like the dirty rats they were. Half Kat's crew had been murdered before her eyes, and only Rory, bless him, had managed to buy her a moment of reprieve—time enough to dash to the captain's cabin and retrieve a weapon.

Sweet Jesu! Rory! She dared not glance at his inert figure, lying silent and too still on the deck near the mainmast. If she did, Kat knew she would lose her concentration, and hence her life.

Damme, she was weakening. The Spaniard hacking so gracelessly away at her seemed enraged that he could not best a mere female. His blows became wilder, undisciplined. Inch by inch, Kat felt herself losing ground on the slippery deck. Soon she was trapped, pinned against the mainmast, her disciplined slash-and-parry style was ineffective against the Spaniard's reckless assault.

Skkkreee . . . their swords met again, grappled, then slid apart again with a too-human shriek and the mournful echo of steel. For a moment, the two combatants paused, panting, staring at each other with a mixture of hate and grudging respect.

Kat was the first to break eye contact. Rory's body came

into her sweeping line of vision instead. Did he stir, or
had she only imagined it? *Oh, Sweet Jesu, please!* she prayed,
and to her astonishment, the red-haired man moaned
slightly. She faltered. Only for a second. 'Twas enough.
Her sword flew from her hand with a metallic clatter and
skidded across the deck.

Just before her triumphant attacker lunged, a male
voice rang out from the melee.

"*Halte 'la!*"

Kat's head snapped around to find the source of the
order. Wind whipped her dark hair back from her face,
and she stared in shock as a man jauntily stepped over
dead bodies on the deck, headed in her direction. He
was dressed like a court dandy, in a black doublet and
fine Venetian hose. His velvet breeches were lined with
gold braid and silk panes. It seemed incongruous: he was
so elegantly attired while his crew wore little more than
rags. Even more mystifying was the fact that he spoke
fluent French instead of Spanish.

He stopped before Kat, elbowing her former adversary,
the Spaniard, out of his way. A low chuckle rose to the
Frenchman's lips as he gazed at Kat defiantly facing her
death.

"*Bonjour,* Mademoiselle Katherine. May I compliment
you on your fine swordplay? You almost make me regret
my duty."

Kat felt a nameless terror rising to clutch her by the
throat. The other pirates were mere rabble, but there was
something truly frightening about this man's emotionless
black eyes, his small moustache so carefully groomed and
waxed, his precise and dignified speech.

She swallowed hard and finally found her voice. "How
do you know my name?"

He smiled. 'Twas a perfunctory smile. It stretched his
lips into a thin, bloodless line, yet never quite reached

his glittering black eyes. He waved his hand in a dismissing fashion.

" 'Tis of no importance now. What matters is I have found you, and at last I shall have my revenge."

Revenge? Kat had never seen the man before. She opened her mouth to tell him so, as he reached down to pluck up a rapier from one of her dead crew.

"I will not be denied the satisfaction of killing you myself," he said pleasantly, as he straightened and hefted the weapon in well-manicured hands. *"Je regrette;* you are more intriguing a woman than I ever imagined."

Kat flicked a desperate glance at her own lost sword, lying some feet away. There was no way she might reach it before he moved. She braced her hands against the mainmast, her nails scoring the wood. The wind sent the rope ladder swinging in the breeze, and she felt it brush against her sweaty hands.

The crow's nest! 'Twas her only chance. Kat prided herself on being able to climb quickly and nimbly. She had no fear of heights. Somehow she had to bolt up the mainmast and fend off her attacker long enough to attract the attention of another passing ship. *God's nightshirt!* she almost swore aloud. 'Twas a difficult feat, if not downright impossible. Kat had always been known for her reckless nature, though. Hadn't the O'Neill always teased her she should have been born a man? Mayhap if she had, she could have saved them all. . . .

She forced the agonizing thought aside before it clutched her in its iron grip. She had no time to grieve now, and if she succeeded in eluding these murderers long enough for Rory to recover, perhaps all was not lost.

This reckless gamble appealed to Kat as well as any. While her mind made some quick calculations, perspiration broke out on her brow, and she desperately tried to outwit her unknown enemy.

"Forgive me, Monsieur, I cannot grasp your motives.

Why would you want to harm me or my crew? I've never seen you before in my life." She spoke perfect French, the better to surprise and disarm him. She hoped, in his fascination with her, he might not note the fact that Rory was rousing. She saw the redheaded man out of the corner of her eye; he appeared to be clutching the wound in his side. Coming round, slowly but surely. *Sweet Mother and Mary, Rory, hurry!*

"If I must die by a stranger's hand, Monsieur, I deserve to know why," she added, stalling for more time.

The Frenchman seemed reluctant to answer her demand. "You might say this is a family matter, Mademoiselle. Or may I be so bold as to call you *Petite Chatte*, as does your crew?"

"My men are dead, thanks to you. You are no more than a coldblooded murderer."

He ignored her fury. "Such a pity," he said, reaching out to toy with a lock of the silky dark hair blowing across Kat's face. She snarled and jerked her head away. His laughter was thin and cold, like the sea wind biting through her canvas shirt. "You even hiss like an angry kitten. Are your claws as sharp?"

"D'you wish to find out?" Her challenge caught the Frenchman by surprise. She deliberately made her tone seductive, her steady gaze locked with his and smouldered with promise.

His momentary hesitation was enough. Kat reached for her right boot and snagged up her *scian*, an ornate Celtic dagger. The gift from her Irish grandfather had served as little more than a letter-opener until now. It molded to her tight fist like a lover, and she clutched it fiercely as she lunged for the Frenchman.

He raised his arms to block her bold attack, stumbling back with visible shock. He was not a physical sort, as Kat already surmised. She scored his sleeve, shredding the fine silk, and leaving a trail of bloody beads on his left forearm. To his credit, he recovered rapidly, lashing out with his own foil as she leapt deftly out of range.

Kat knew she had but moments to choose her course. She clamped the *scian* between her teeth and flung herself up on the rope ladder tied to the mainmast. She shimmied up the sagging steps, not daring to look down. She heard the Frenchman's bellow of frustrated rage below her.

Safe for the moment in the crow's nest, Kat peered down and saw him ordering one of his crewmen to pursue her. The other little fellow looked spry and agile as a monkey. He was halfway up the ladder before Kat's trembling hands sawed her dagger's blade through the final knot anchoring the ladder to the crow's nest. With a scream, both man and ladder fell and hit the maindeck below. The sickening thud made Kat shiver. She heard the Frenchman curse again.

A moment later he chuckled, a cunning sound. It raised the hair on the back of her neck. " 'Twill do you no good, *Petite Chatte!*" he shouted up at her. There are other ways to . . . ah, how do the English say . . . skin a cat?"

Kat's eyes widened as she watched him remove a small case from his doublet. Humming merrily, he opened the silver box and removed a flint stone. With calm, deliberate precision, he struck a spark and lit a cigar.

Mesmerized by his movements, Kat nervously licked her lips. Fire at sea meant death, as everyone knew well. She cried out when a bit of burning tobacco dropped to the wooden deck. He carelessly let it smoulder there.

The Frenchman glanced up at her in faux surprise, once again speaking English. "You must forgive my clumsiness, Little Cat. I shall take care to dispose of this properly." He moved to place the still-burning cigar atop a wooden casket. Kat's hands whitened where she gripped the rail. The keg was full of whale oil!

He ignored her furious cries and pleas as he crossed the deck to the boarding planks still linking his ship to the *Fiach Teine*. Pausing only once, he turned to eye the smoking casket, then raised his malignant gaze to the tiny figure huddled atop the mainmast.

"Au revoir," he called out, with a peculiar mixture of triumph and regret. The unmarked Spanish galleon drifted away on the evening tide, while the *Fiach Teine* began to burn.

Several weeks later, on the Continent, the Frenchman relayed the success of his journey to another. The woman seated before the blazing hearth listened without comment, but as he continued the tale, her gloved hands clenched in her lap. She wore a rich gown of tawny velvet, long sleeves slashed to show cloth-of-gold inserts, the hem and neckline trimmed with pearls. Her garb was beautiful, the height of Paris fashion. Her figure was exquisite, judging by her tiny waist and the slender hands clutched in her lap.

Her face remained averted while he relayed his news, but he heard her soft intake of breath when he described the fire.

"Are you certain the ship was destroyed?" she asked. Her voice was low and throaty, almost as enticing as her generous display of snow-white cleavage.

"*Oui*. I waited just long enough to watch the *Fiach Teine* and her dead crew sink beneath the cold black waves."

She shivered. He knew it was from excitement, rather than horror. "At last!" she whispered, her husky voice trembling. "At long last I have found a way to revenge myself upon those who ruined my life."

She looked at him directly then. Pale blue eyes gleamed above the yellow silk facial veil covering the rest of her face. "When Slade Tanner gets word of his precious daughter's death, he will doubtless be prostrate with grief. We must strike again, Adrien, while the iron is still hot."

"As you wish," he replied. He could deny her nothing. He adored this woman, the only family he might claim. Long ago, an English cur named Slade Tanner had stolen this lady's famous beauty, and hence her life. She had been banished to France, poor creature, to live in penury for many years, but in compensation, she had raised Adrien with a thirst for vengeance, nourished him on the heady milk of revenge.

He sensed her smile, though he saw only the faintest outline of her lips through the opaque veil.

" 'Twill be so easy," she whispered. "So easy to destroy Slade's life as he did mine; to take from him everything he holds dear and to make the rest of his days a living hell."

"You have already begun," Adrien reminded her.

"Aye." There was bitter satisfaction in her husky voice. "So I have. I could not have done it without you, *ma doux.*" The smile reached her eyes this time, and her gaze visibly softened on him. Adrien felt a familiar frisson of anticipation and stepped forward to stroke her hair. Once, she told him, her hair had been silvery as the moon, the envy of all Englishwomen. Now it was pure white, another lingering legacy of Tanner's evil act.

Suddenly a vision of hair dark as night crept across his mind. Green eyes, the color of the Irish sea she sailed. Those damned eyes! Sea-green, tinged with blue foam. He had planned to kill the Englishman's daughter without a qualm. Kat Tanner was too much a woman to be so lightly dismissed, however. Adrien felt a fleeting regret. Too late. She was gone forever. Only one possession remained to him now. Or was *he* the possession, in truth?

He bent and fervently pressed his lips to Gillian's pale hair. Her quick intake of breath excited them both. They were in each other's blood, in more ways than one.

"You know I would do anything for you, *ma chère* Gillian," he whispered in her ear, emboldening himself to caress her half-bared breasts.

"*Oui,* my darling boy." She reached up to stroke Adrien's face. Her gaze was both wicked and inviting. "Aye, little brother, I know."

One

"Easy, boy."

Morgan Trelane calmed the fractious black as he rode the stallion down the rocky slope to the seashore. The sound of his voice soothed the blooded animal. Idris responded with alacrity when Morgan pressed his heels to the horse's ebony flanks.

Soon they were galloping along the Welsh coastline, Morgan's wool mandilion snapping behind him in the breeze. 'Twas still cold in the early spring, and he was glad he'd taken the short cloak at the last minute. He clamped his thighs against the saddle, letting the exhilaration of the wild ride wash over him as the horse's hooves sprayed sand in every direction. Idris thundered across the low plateau, extending his neck for more speed.

Abruptly, the stallion veered away from the waves rushing in about his ankles, and bugled in alarm. Morgan fought for control. Despite his efforts, the black reared up and pawed the air. *Horses are as unpredictable as women,* Morgan thought wryly. He gathered the animal up. After several minutes of alternate coaxing and scolding, Idris was calm enough for Morgan to dismount and make sure the horse hadn't injured himself.

"What spooked you, boy? The water?" Morgan knelt and examined each of his steed's trembling legs in turn. One was twisted, perhaps, but not broken. He let out a sigh as he straightened up again. Out of the question for him to ride the animal now. 'Twas a good five leagues back to Falcon's Lair.

Absently patting his stallion's sweaty neck, he glanced out over the water. Today the Irish Sea seemed even moodier than usual, slate-gray foam rushing up to curl with a hiss around his riding boots. His attention focused on several wooden boards being dashed against some shoreline rocks. His gaze narrowed as he recognized several kegs bobbing along in nearby tidal pools. Had there been a recent shipwreck?

'Twould not be the first time. Cardigan Bay was dangerous even during mild weather, and the coastline looked deceptively benign. As local fisherman knew, however, deep waters became shallow in a second, and hidden rocks could pierce a ship's hull like parchment in the wrong tide.

Idris shifted restively again and pawed the sand. Morgan retrieved the reins, preparing to walk his mount back home. He stiffened and froze. He was sure he'd heard a slight moan.

He was sure it wasn't the wind or water. He'd lived beside the tempestuous sea long enough to know her every sigh and sound, as one lover might recognize another. He pivoted, noticing Idris's ears also flattened back against his head at the noise.

"Whoa, boy." Morgan rolled a sizable rock over the stallion's reins, pinning him to the sand. He got out of the way of the prancing hooves. "I think I'll just take a look around for your spook."

There was a lightness to Morgan's step. It disappeared when he caught sight of a boot sticking out from behind a lichen-covered boulder. Curiously enough, his first reaction was outrage. He lived alone by choice as well as necessity, and the thought of finding anyone on his private shore—shipwrecked sailor or not—made him angry.

After the briefest of hesitations, he approached the boot and the body belonging to it.

His gaze traveled up a pair of legs. Pale white flesh gleamed under the late afternoon sun where the seaman's canvas trews were torn. Long, bloody gashes adorned two tanned arms splayed across the victim's face. Morgan felt a pang of pity.

If God was merciful, the ill-starred sailor was long dead. Even as he thought this, the lad stirred. Again Morgan heard a pained moan. A flicker of indecision gripped him.

Damme! The tide was coming in. Slowly but surely, the advancing waves rolled up against the shore, this last one just reaching the tips of the boy's boots. Morgan cursed again as he knelt and scooped a hand under the lad's shoulders. Why, the stripling barely weighed a hundred stone. He rose, cradling the injured youth in his arms.

His eyes widened. The wet hair belonging to his sea burden unfurled to reach the sand. His surprised gaze dropped to the white shirt gaping at the sailor's neck. He had an unobstructed view of two creamy-pale mounds rising and falling with each breath. No lad this!

Framed between those enticing peaks, lay a magnificent golden amulet. 'Twas a primitive, pagan thing, Morgan noted, etched with what appeared to be ancient symbols and a flying bird of some sort. The metal cast a warm hue on the young woman's skin, painting it a rich redgold beneath the sunlight.

He was startled to find his traitorous body responding to the unfamiliar feel of a woman in his arms. He carried her a few more paces to the shelter of some nearby trees and knelt there, supporting her with one arm behind her shoulders as he unfastened his wool mandilion with the other. He wrapped it snugly about her, revealing his dark blue velvet doublet and the matching jerkin beneath.

Her cracked lips moved. Dark crescents of lashes trembled upon her cheeks. Morgan gently lowered her head to the ground, felt the damp tendrils of her hair slide like watered silk through his fingers. He wondered how her mane might look, dry and spread out on the sand. Magnificent, no doubt, the hue of a raven's wing, with the texture of spun silk.

He grimaced and closed his eyes, banishing the forbidden image. When he looked at her again, he forced himself to concentrate more objectively upon her features. Her tanned skin perplexed him. Surely she had not been lying unconscious on his beach long enough to be browned by the sun. He rode here every day, and he was certain he would have seen her before this.

She would die without his help. Perchance too quickly, Morgan realized, if he left her much longer to the mercy of the cold wind and the incoming waves. There was no question about it—'twas simply too dangerous to move her without a wagon. He must return to the keep, and send several of his staff back to bring her to shelter. He dare not take the chance of her awaking and seeing him instead.

She moaned. Morgan stiffened, prepared to depart. Then he saw a single tear seep from beneath her closed lashes. This moved him more than the finding of her washed up, almost dead, upon his shore.

She never opened her eyes. Instead, she whispered something. He was forced to bend close to catch the word.

"*Uisce.*"

Morgan recognized the Gaelic word for water. She repeated it several times, and he felt helpless to console her.

"Soon," he said. The deep rumble of his voice seemed to comfort her. "Rest now." He tugged the cloak higher about her face, shielding her eyes from sight of him if she should open them.

"Rory?" she asked faintly, coming around now. She used the word as a proper name. " 'Tis you?"

"Nay." Morgan laid a broad hand upon her glistening dark head and felt himself tremble at the action. Touching her at all created a most distracting sensation. His breathing quickened when she spoke again.

"Who, then?"

"Morgan," he said. He sounded hoarse. It occurred to him that he rarely offered his Christian name to anyone.

"Oh." The tiny word accepted him, as Morgan knew she never would, if she knew anything of the man behind the name. He rose to his feet, studying the woman curled in his cloak.

Morgan's fingers rose to touch the mark covering the left half of his face. The crescent moon on his face had labeled him doomed from birth, but in the ultimate jest, God had seen fit to make the other side perfect. Viewed from the right side alone, Morgan was handsome enough. He had inherited the lustrous, wavy black hair of his Spanish mother, though 'twas ironic she had taken one look at her infant son and hurled herself from Falcon's Lair's seaside precipice on the same midwinter night he was born.

Morgan's jaw clenched. Better he should have gone with his mother. Because of this damned devil's mark, the locals dubbed him Satan's Son. *Oh, himself? He bears the devil's mark, did ye nae ken?* they eagerly informed those passing through the village. Mayhap Lady Elena had consorted with Satan and so produced this son; a man who was fair on the right side, tragically demonic on the left. 'Twas quite understandable, local gossip reasoned, that poor Lady Trelane had killed herself rather than live with such shame upon her mortal soul.

On and on the stories went. As a lad, Morgan came to resent his father, as well. Rhys Trelane ignored the stares and whispers whenever they rode through the village. Rhys had accepted his son. But in Morgan's opinion, his father went too far. Rhys had acted as if his son's blemished face didn't exist, daring others to remark upon it. Lord Trelane had boasted of the fact that his only child excelled at hawking, horsemanship, and running the estate.

All those things were important, of course, for they served to occupy Morgan's mind during those painful, early years. His father was dead now; Falcon's Lair was his sole burden and responsibility. The ancient keep took a great deal of time and effort on his part to maintain. By absorbing himself in his inheritance, Morgan sometimes forgot the jarring reality of his face.

Seeing another person, a stranger, brought all the memories flooding back with a painful rush. How the village girls shrieked and scattered whenever he rode through town. The children's mocking, sing-song taunts. The way their parents hastily crossed themselves, making the sign of the Evil Eye whenever they saw or spoke about Lord Trelane.

Morgan rarely went to town anymore. He sent his servants instead: a small, handpicked lot who had been loyal to his father and asked to stay on. He treated them generously, feeling somehow obliged to pay more by virtue of the fact that they must look at him each day.

He turned from the young woman and went to retrieve Idris. 'Twas a long journey back to Falcon's Lair, and he wanted to arrive at the keep before dusk.

"Duw! Had you no more sense than to leave the mite out for so long?" Wynne Carey scolded Morgan as she exited the guest chamber, banging it shut in its frame.

"Why, the poor thing is frozen clear through. 'Tis a blessing, it is, she survived the day at all. And a righteous miracle, indeed, she's no broken bones to show for it."

As his housekeeper shook her head, cinnamon-colored

curls bouncing around her freckled face, Morgan couldn't help but smile.

"Is she awake yet, Mrs. Carey?"

"Hardly, with the bump the size of a goose egg she's got on her head. Pumped half a keg of seawater from her lungs, too." Winnie clucked her tongue like a mother hen as she bustled past him, her wide fustian skirts sweeping the Turkish carpet. She paused on the landing above the stairs to look back at him, hands planted on her ample hips.

"Mind you, milord, give the girl half a chance to come 'round before you boot her out the door."

Morgan started, feeling guilty. He demanded, "How did you know 'twas what I intended to do?"

Winnie sniffed. "Did I not wet-nurse you myself when Lady Elena left us?" Winnie never referred to the suicide; she always made it sound as if Morgan's mother had merely gone out for a pleasant jaunt in the countryside and never returned.

"Faith, milord, you can't toss the poor moppet out without so much as a by-your-leave. There's her kin to be found, and mark my words, they'll be having some questions for us, too."

" 'Tis what I'm trying to avoid," Morgan said as he studied the door shielding the young woman from his view. "Perhaps I should have left her for the sea to reclaim instead."

Winnie pressed a freckled hand to her heart. "La! You can't be serious, milord. I've never known you to turn your back on those in need, and this wee one needs you right now."

"This is different, Mrs. Carey."

"How so? You slip your tenants food from time to time and wipe out their debts so they can care for their families. Does this poor dear deserve any less?"

"You forget those in my demesne know not where

those little kindnesses come from. If they did, you and I both know they would refuse such aid. I am Lord Satan to them, nothing more and nothing less."

Morgan's words were as bitter as wormwood. Winnie's bright blue eyes glistened with emotion. She lifted a corner of her apron to dab at them. "They don't know you as I do."

"Nor do they wish to," he said dryly, but at her hurt look, he walked over to pat her plump shoulder. "Why don't you go check on Cook. See about the evening meal?"

Winnie stopped sniffling at the mention of food, reminded of how much she enjoyed experimenting in the larder and planning their daily repasts. She brightened as she turned for the stairs.

"Oh, Mrs. Carey," Morgan called out as if by casual afterthought. "I request that you and the others not reveal my true identity to our unexpected guest. Not yet, anyhow. 'Twould only serve to frighten and confuse her further. I am simply 'Morgan' to her now. I prefer it remain so."

"Very well, milord." Winnie glanced back at him, disapproving but willing to let it pass for now.

"Another thing: You must not address me as 'milord' in the young lady's presence. Please instruct the other staff to remember I am to be addressed as 'Morgan' from now on."

Winnie sighed, then nodded. "As you wish, milord . . . Morgan. Mind you, I won't have any more talk about sending the girl away for at least another week," she called out over her shoulder, as she descended to the first floor and disappeared around a corner.

Morgan turned and eyed the closed door again. It mocked his weakness. He'd been unable to get the young woman out of his mind. 'Twas as if by saving her life, he had created a bond of some sort he was helpless to deny.

He wanted to. Jesu knew he wanted nothing more than to see her immediately removed from Falcon's Lair and from his life. He didn't need this kind of complication. Mrs. Carey was right: the girl's kin would demand to know what role he had played in their daughter's rescue. How honorable a gentleman he had been.

Honor was the last thing on Morgan's mind when he caught an inadvertent glimpse of those firm, rosy-peaked breasts beneath the white linen shirt she wore. He'd been startled by the frank stirring in his loins. At eight and twenty, he'd all but given up hope of ever finding a woman who might endure his touch. She had felt so good in his arms. Good and . . . and right.

Sweet Jesu, there must be a storm coming in, Morgan thought, as he rubbed his jaw. Sudden changes in weather always made him fanciful; now was no exception. The mysterious wench, whoever she was, must be carted away from Falcon's Lair the minute her health was restored.

Morgan had assumed by her darkness she might be Spanish or French, but her Gaelic tongue betrayed her. An Irish beauty would be even more deadly to his already wounded pride. All the Celts had sharp tongues, God knew. Once she caught a glimpse of his face, this one would doubtless be seized by shrill hysterics.

Morgan started to move past her door. Then he saw a sudden flash of lightning through the east hall window and heard the low rumble of thunder rolling through the Welsh hills. A moment later, he heard the scream.

"Morgan!"

She was screaming his name, over and over, a litany to the heavens above. After a brief hesitation, Morgan burst into the room, just in time to see the candle on the night-stand sputter out. The bedchamber was plunged into darkness. He fumbled his way down the bed to the sobbing invalid, and managed to capture her flailing hands in the darkness.

"I'm here. 'Tis Morgan. Ssh, you're safe now."

His own heart thumped when she threw herself against his chest, frantically clutching at him.

"A dream! Fire. Water. Blood . . ." She shivered and moaned, a white wraith. Morgan closed his arms around her, inhaling the fresh scent of lavender from the nightrail she wore. Mrs. Carey had gotten rid of her patient's mannish clothes at once, and the young woman felt clean and warm to the touch.

A moment later he pried her away from him.

"Hush," he said. Morgan found he could not bring himself to be any harsher with her. " 'Twas just a bad dream. The storm has upset you. Granted, they can be wild here on the Welsh coast. Falcon's Lair is a veritable fortress, though. You are safe here."

"Morgan?" Her curious hands found and molded his face in the darkness. He flinched, then remembered the room was pitch-dark. She could not see him.

As her cool, calloused fingers traced his jaw, nose, and lips, Morgan steeled himself against the bittersweet emotions slamming through his tense figure.

"Who are you?" she whispered, her hands falling at last to her sides.

"My full name is Morgan Trelane."

She went rigid. Had a flash of lightning revealed his grotesque birthmark?

"Is't a French name?" she asked him, recoiling back against the pillows.

Morgan was puzzled by her sudden terror. He knew she could not see him. Lacking knowledge of his face or family history, what had she to fear?

"Nay. 'Tis Welsh. I'm a Welshman born and bred, I assure you. Why?"

"I . . . I don't know why. It just frightened me to think of you as French for some reason," she murmured. By another flash of lightning, he saw her hands raise to tentatively touch her bandaged face. "I've been hurt, haven't I?"

"Aye. You were in a shipwreck of some sort. Surely you remember it?"

She thought a moment and shook her head. "I remember nothing." Her tone turned timorous, frightened. "I don't even remember my name."

Morgan's soothing murmur cut off her mounting panic. " 'Twas the blow on the head you took. I wager you drank your share of seawater, too. No matter, it shall come back to you by and by. In the meanwhile, you are safe here."

"Morgan." Her terrified whisper echoed off the stone walls at him. "D'you know who I am?"

He hesitated, remembering the amulet Mrs. Carey had removed from her patient's neck and given to him earlier. He had examined it in the privacy of his library for some time. 'Twas a beautiful, old, and valuable thing, but it held few clues to her identity. He had decided to set it aside for now and worry about it later.

"Nay," he answered her at last. "I found you on the beach. You were unconscious. But I believe you might be Irish. You spoke a few Gaelic words."

"What were they?"

"*Uisce.* 'Tis the Gaelic for water. You asked for someone named Rory." He didn't mention the amulet. 'Twould only confuse her further at this point. Although his curiosity was piqued by the strange object, 'twas far more so by the beautiful invalid occupying his guest room.

She shook her head, upset by his words. "I don't remember anything." He heard tears starting when her voice caught. "Oh, Jesu, how my eyes burn!"

"The saltwater injured the tissues." He grasped her arm in an attempt to make her lie down again. "You need to rest and keep them closed. I'll have Mrs. Carey examine them in the morning."

"Mrs. Carey?" she repeated sleepily. Instead of lying back on the pillows, she propped herself against Morgan instead. "The lady who was here earlier?"

"The same one. She's the housekeeper here, known far and wide for her hospitality. Now get some sleep, or she'll scold us both quite soundly. In the morning we'll worry about who you are and how you got here."

Moments later Morgan heard her even breathing and realized she had fallen asleep from sheer exhaustion. He lowered her to the bed, tucking the covers up over her still form. He bent and tentatively touched his lips to her brow. He left the room, wondering why he had felt the compelling need to kiss her.

In the welcome seclusion of his library, Morgan poured himself a generous goblet of warm golden brandy and watched the violent storm at the window. The flashes of white and blue lightning and the drumming roll of thunder suited his mood. 'Twas on just such a night as this he had been born, or so the old legend went.

The brandy went untouched as he contemplated the many ironies of his life. Descended of Rhodri Mawr, the Great, and Hywel Dda, the Good, his prominence in Wales as a Trelane had been assured from the moment of his birth. Heir to half the lands in Cardiganshire, as well as three private residences, and acting as overlord of several villages, Morgan was unlike the other land-poor barons who populated the Tudor Court. Only because his father favored a quiet, countrified existence had he been spared the humiliation of mixing with his peers in London. Morgan was also aware of the fact that Rhys Trelane had not avoided Court so assiduously before his son's birth.

Yet he did not blame his father for his secret shame and disappointment. Rhys Trelane's heir was imperfect, with something much more damning than a simple scar or limp. One might be had by honorable battle, the other obtained through unfortunate illness. This hideous birthmark was attributable to neither. It had not helped, of course, when Lady Trelane felt obliged to take her own life so soon after her son's birth.

Morgan often wondered why his father had not remarried and thus secured a line of more promising—and unblemished—boys. He had never asked Rhys, sensing somehow the topic was forbidden. Perhaps his father had feared the taint of the terrible birthmark would be passed on to other sons or daughters through his blood. Although the scourge might have issued from Elena's bloodlines instead, such uncertainty was enough to assure Rhys Trelane would never father another child. Morgan well understood such caution. He himself had sworn never to wed, never to force upon any hapless female the same tragic fate which had befallen his own mother.

She awoke with a start, the muslin gown in twisted, sweat-soaked folds about her thrashing figure. For a terrifying moment she remembered nothing at all. The panic mounted when she saw nothing but a shifting field of black.

"Morgan!" she wailed, calling the only name she remembered. The one word that brought comfort to her blank, helpless mind. Her hands scrabbled on either side of her. Feeling the contours of a bed, she was marginally comforted. The sound of wind and rain howling outside her dark prison brought back the fear again. She was not aware of screaming until a pair of hands took her own, and a motherly voice with a thick accent cut off her gasp for more air.

"There now, Dearie, everything is all right. Winnie Carey is here with you now; you're not alone."

She took several deep breaths, tears streaming down her cheeks, as she listened to the croon and clutched the plump hands with their comforting warmth.

"Morgan," she repeated in a sob-choked voice. "He didn't come."

"He couldn't hear you," Winnie said. "He rode out at the wee crack of dawn, he did. He has a great deal of work to do this time of year. 'Tis the shearing season."

The younger woman raised her hands to touch her face. "I thought 'twas still night. 'Tis so dark in this room."

Winnie hesitated, glancing to the lead-paned windows. Morning sun streamed in. 'Twas dim, to be sure, but only because of the clouds. She saw her patient clearly enough.

"Methinks your eyes may be a bit weak," Winnie said, as she moved to tuck the heavy eider quilt closer about her patient. " 'Tis not to be unexpected after such a griev-ous swim in the sea. I'd best examine them straight away."

The patient stayed silent. Her hands clutched the blan-kets to her chest while Winnie carefully examined her eyes up close.

" 'Tis as Morgan thought," Winnie murmured when she had finished. "The seasalt has inflamed the tissues. No wonder your eyes are sore. I'll have to make some ointment for them. 'Twill be best to bandage them up for a time, too."

A shudder coursed through her patient. "Please . . . no. I don't want to be in total darkness."

"Child, you'll need to let my compresses do their work. Rest is what you need, plenty of rest and warmth and quiet. You'll strain your eyes further, perhaps do some permanent damage, if you don't listen to me."

"Are you a doctor?"

"A lady-doctor? Whoever heard of such a thing?" Win-nie laughed merrily at the notion. "I ken I'm the closest thing in these parts, though. I tend the fevers and set the broken bones and deliver the wee ones when 'tis time. My man, Lloyd, works in the stables."

"Have you any children, Mrs. Carey?"

"Winnie, please, dear." The woman patted her hand again. There was a moment of silence, and Winnie said with forced cheer, "I had a daughter. Mary Katherine was her name. She would be about your age now, had she lived."

"Oh, Winnie, I'm sorry."

" 'Twas the blight, dear. It happened long ago. She was but two and ten. A bonny girl, my Mary Kate, with her dark hair and bright blue eyes. Your hair reminds me of hers."

"Are my eyes blue, too?"

"Nay, dear, yours are a beautiful sea-green. You remind me of my daughter in other ways, though. She had the same shaped lips. Her teeth were straight and white, too. She was so bright, was my Katie, curious and impatient about nigh everything. I can see the same trait in you." Winnie was pleased when her patient smiled at the compliment.

The young woman's eyes blindly sought Winnie's. She wanted so desperately to see the face belonging to Falcon's Lair's housekeeper.

Winnie was as wonderful as he was. Just the memory of Morgan's deeply timbered voice brought a wash of comfort over her now. How rich and musical his voice was, soothing as a salve. She wished he was here to care for her again, and realized 'twas selfish. But she remembered the calming effect his voice and touch had on her.

"There, now," Winnie said briskly as she rose from the bedside, "you just rest while I visit my little apothecary and mix up some healing ointments for your eyes. I'll bring up a breakfast tray for you as well. 'Tis best to keep your eyes closed until I can bandage them shut."

Obediently, she closed her eyes, hearing the rustle of

the housekeeper's skirts as she moved to leave. "Winnie?" she called out before the older woman left.

"Aye, poppet?"

"Until we find out what my real name is, would you mind calling me Mary Kate, as well?"

Judging by her little sniffle, Winnie was pleased and touched by the request. "I would fain do so," she said. "It seems to suit you somehow. Mary Kate. Katie. Aye, it surely does."

Two

" 'Twill never do, Renfrew."

Morgan rose from inspecting the wool stores, and brushed his palms on his broadcloth breeches. "You've been slighting the animal's feed again. 'Tis showing quite clearly in their wool."

"Milord," the heavyset, thick-jowled steward whined, " 'tis too time-consuming to drive them to higher pasture this time of year. I already spend enough hours trying to find the special feeds you want. The local peasants cheat me at each turn. I'd have to go all the way to Aberystwyth every fortnight or so."

"Then do it," Morgan snapped. He had lost all patience with the man. Renfrew had inherited his father's position after the elder steward had died, and proved to be a lazy, slothful worker—something Morgan would not abide did he not have such a difficult time getting any of the villagers to work for him. Were it his choice, Morgan would have sent the man packing long ago.

"As you say, milord." Though his tone was meek, Renfrew's pale eyes fixed with hatred on Morgan's back as his master turned to leave.

"Oh, and Renfrew—" Sensing the malignant stare, Morgan pivoted about and eyed the sullen steward one last time. "Don't forget to bring back the change this time. I shall be counting each groat."

Renfrew almost choked. How'd the high and mighty

Trelane guessed he'd been pilfering the spare coins for the past few months? With the size of his coffers, the great Lord Satan shouldn't be pinching each ha'crown! With a resentful mutter, Renfrew bobbed his head and ducked past Trelane out into the pouring rain.

Morgan shook his head after the man departed. Decent help was almost impossible to come by in the remote reaches of Wales. Except for the few faithful retainers he employed in the keep, the rest were a surly lot he dared not trust with his life. He was certain most were afraid to cross him only because of his unsightly face. In a way, it provided some small advantage. Being the Devil Baron did have its benefits.

Chuckling at the thought, he left the storehouse and headed back to the keep. The rain still streamed down. He took his time, enjoying the cool sensation of droplets spattering across his skin where he had rolled up the sleeves of his white linen shirt.

Reaching the keep, Morgan dashed up the curving, narrow stone staircase. He slipped through the servant's entrance, arriving in the rear of the huge kitchen where delicious baking smells wafted down the open hall.

Morgan peeked around the corner and spied Cook, her homespun skirts swishing furiously from side to side, as she removed the soiled rushes into a corner with a broom. With a quick sleight of hand, his fingers darted out to snatch a berry tart, but before he spirited it away, something hard smacked across his knuckles.

"Ow!" Morgan nursed his injured hand. Cook set aside her broomstick and plunked the tart back on the trestle table.

"Shame on ye, milord," the big woman said mildly, rearranging the pastries to suit her fancy. "Ye know yer nae to sample dessert before the main course."

"Ailis, when will I ever get the best of you?" Morgan

complained. "You caught me every time when I was a lad, too."

Cook smiled, pleased with herself. " 'Tis said a mum sprouts an extry set of eyes in the back of 'er 'ead for each babe. I've bore eight, ye know."

"Ahh, that explains it," Morgan muttered, but flashed Mrs. Taggart a good-natured grin before continuing on his journey. In his own home he never thought to hide his disfigurement; now a stranger had been brought to Falcon's Lair, and he realized he should take some precautions.

Morgan hesitated in the great hall, wondering where he might hide for the rest of the day, just as Mrs. Carey appeared in her cloak and hood. As if reading his mind, she gave him a determined look.

"Oh, there you are, milord." Winnie waylaid Morgan before he could escape again. She tugged on a pair of thick wool gloves as she spoke. He eyed her warily in return.

"Morgan," he reminded her.

"Aye, milord. Now, I just finished giving our patient a good scrubbing and now I need your help. 'Tis as you thought. The girl's eyes were burnt by seawater. I don't have the proper herbs to make the salve I need. I'll have to go find some fresh."

He shrugged. "You have my permission, Mrs. Carey."

"Lud, I know it. The girl needs nourishing broth in the while. I've prepared a tray in the kitchen. You can take it up to her."

Morgan felt a flush rising on his neck. Irritation made him speak more curtly than usual. "Surely 't'won't be necessary, Mrs. Carey. Where are Gwynneth and the other girls?"

"Remember, milord, you gave them permission to attend the Beltane celebrations at Cardigan this year. They'll be gone a whole week, they will."

"Damme. I forgot." Morgan was chagrined by the reminder. "Well, what about Cook?"

Winnie clucked her tongue and shook her head. "By now Mrs. Taggart's elbow-deep in lamby pies for our supper. 'Twill only take a moment for you to feed the child, milord. She's as weak as a newborn kitten and won't eat more than a bird would."

Morgan knew when he was beaten. He sighed and said, "You'd best pray my demonic face doesn't scare her into becoming a halfwit, Mrs. Carey."

The housekeeper sniffed her disapproval of his comment. "First of all, I doubt 'twould, for she's more common sense in her little finger than you have in your whole head. Second, she can't see a thing yet, poor mite. I'm sure 'tis probably temporary, but she's awful scared, is our Kate."

"Kate?" Morgan was surprised. "Did she remember who she is, then?"

Winnie seemed abashed. "Forgive me, milord. She just reminds me so of my own Mary Kate. She asked if we might call her Kate until she remembers her own name."

"Well, if you've no objections, I guess 'tis acceptable for now."

Winnie flashed him a grateful smile. "Now get along with you, milord."

"Morgan," he reminded her, for the hundredth time in less than a week. Too late, he saw the mischievous twinkle in her eye.

"Go along then, *Morgan* my boy. The poor waif must be starving. I'll be back shortly, rain permitting."

"You'll be soaked," he warned her. "Don't catch a chill. I don't know what I'd do without you."

"Oh, go on with you."

Still, Winnie beamed at the praise.

* * *

"Who's there?" Kate cried out. She heard solid footsteps ringing across the stone floor of the chamber, and her head jerked in Morgan's direction.

" 'Tis Morgan again. How are you feeling?"

At the sound of his voice, Kate relaxed. She sat up against the pillows, looking lovely to Morgan's aching eyes. Her freshly washed hair spilled over the white muslin gown like a tempestuous dark sea. The same sea held the truth of her identity and teased Morgan with its secrets whenever he looked out over the shimmering water.

"I've brought you something to eat," he said, tearing his gaze away from her heart-shaped face. He hadn't taken a good close look at her before. Aye, she was beautiful. Flawless, in fact. Despite the fading scratches and bruises, he knew her to be a beauty. He felt a nervous tic start in his left cheek as she turned her eyes toward him. Was Mrs. Carey certain her patient couldn't see?

A moment later, Morgan had his answer. Kate blinked her emerald green eyes as if to clear them, but no revulsion showed on her face—yet. Morgan set the tray down on a table beside the bed with an audible clatter.

"Oh!" Kate exclaimed, starting with surprise. She looked abashed. "I'm sorry. The noise frightened me."

"Forgive me. I'm a man, you know. We're renowned for being clumsy." Morgan forced a smile into his voice, even though smiling was the last thing he wished to do. He was anxious to escape the room and the disturbing presence of the beauty in the bed.

"Please, won't you have a seat? At least, I assume there's a chair somewhere in the room."

"Several," he confirmed, pulling one up to the patient's bedside. "I can only stay a moment. I'm headed out again to the pastures."

"Winnie mentioned something about shearing. Have you many sheep to tend?"

"Aye, several thousand." Morgan read the genuine interest in her expression and was taken aback. No women he knew even pretended an interest in agriculture. Was she the daughter of a local serf? Unlikely. He had spoken to her in Welsh once or twice, yet she seemed not to understand him.

"Have you crops to look after, as well?"

"Little enough. This part of Wales is mostly grazing land, fit for pasture rather than food." Morgan wiped his moist palms on his breeches. 'Twas getting harder and harder to effect a quick escape.

"I would fain see everything," she whispered. "The land, I mean. I hope my sight comes back soon."

"I've no doubt 'twill. Winnie knows all about the healing ways of plants."

"I adore her. She's so kind and funny. Pray tell, what does she look like?"

"Well, let me think a moment. She's plump and fussy, rather like a mother hen in manner. She has bright red hair and a great many freckles."

Kate clapped her hands. " 'Tis exactly how I pictured her in my mind!"

Despite his mood, Morgan couldn't help but chuckle at her obvious delight. "How d'you imagine me?"

The minute he asked the idle question, he regretted it, but then 'twas already too late. Her bandaged brow was already furrowed in thought.

"Why, you're tall, of course. Quite muscular, but lean." At her quizzical, waiting look, Morgan shifted uneasily but remained silent. Her guess was uncannily accurate.

"My coloring?" he asked her.

"Dark. Quite dark. I don't know why, but I'm sure your eyes and hair must be almost black."

"Are you sure you can't see me?" he teased, his gut twisting at the thought of her staring horror-stricken at his face.

She shook her head. "Then I'm right? How odd. 'Tis

almost as if I can see you with my mind, rather than my eyes."

Count your damned blessings, Morgan thought. He changed the subject. "You must be famished. Here, I'll set the tray on your lap."

Carefully, he settled the silver salver in place. He guided her hand to the utensils but she remained frozen, not even attempting to eat.

"What's wrong?" he inquired.

"I'm afraid I'll make a mess of things. 'Tis meat broth I smell, isn't it? I'll spill it all over the bed."

Devil take you, Wynne Carey, Morgan thought as he picked up the spoon for her. His housekeeper must have known the girl wouldn't be able to feed herself, either.

"Here," he said, setting aside the tureen lid and lifting a spoonful of broth to her lips. "I'll help you."

"Thank you," she whispered and opened her mouth to swallow the broth.

This continued for several minutes until the broth was gone. Morgan smiled in satisfaction to see her appetite.

"You'll be good as new in no time. There's some fresh bread here as well. Would you care for a wedge?"

"Oh yes, please. It smells heavenly."

As he buttered one of the thick slices and handed it to her, their fingers inadvertently brushed together across the sweet cream butter.

When she raised her hand and licked each finger free of butter, Morgan almost groaned aloud. Sweet Jesu, 'twas such a sensual movement, though unconscious on her part. As she sank her straight white teeth into the soft bread, he rose to leave.

"I must go," he muttered, scraping back the chair.

Kate swallowed and set aside the bread. "Are you sure, Morgan? I mean . . . I thought you'd stay with me until Winnie returns."

"I would," he began, ashamed of the lie that must

needs follow, "but I fear the lambs won't wait much longer."

"Oh, of course. Thank you for everything." Her sightless eyes tracked the sound of his footsteps retreating across the floor. "Is there anything else I can get you?" he asked her from the doorway. "D'you wish me to stoke up the fire again?"

"Fire?" A visible shudder went through her at the word. Her face drained to chalk white in seconds. Morgan rapidly crossed back to her bedside again.

"What is it?" he demanded. "Did you remember something?"

Her lips formed each shivering word. "Fire. Flames. Smoke." She moaned and clutched at the bed sheets in a spasm of terror. Morgan removed the tray and set it aside. In another moment he grasped her shaking hands in his own.

"I'm here," he said. "Hold tight."

"Oh, Morgan!" she suddenly sobbed, shuddering and clutching his hands in return.

When she was calm again, he said, "There must have been a fire at sea. 'Twould explain much." He hesitated, then confessed, "I also found a peculiar amulet around your neck. I would fain describe it for you, then let you feel it, to see if it stirs some memories. Tomorrow, perhaps, when you're feeling stronger. Meanwhile, I'll ride down to the shore again and try to find some more clues. Right now, you mustn't think of anything but getting well. You require much quiet and rest to recover."

"I can't help it," she whispered, her blind gaze seeking his. "If I was on a ship which burned and sank, there must have been others who were with me. Friends. Relatives. Oh, Sweet Jesu, what if my whole family was aboard that doomed vessel?"

"Ssh, little one, 't won't do any good to fret about it now." Morgan reached out and stroked her head until she calmed down again. She took a deep, shuddering breath, and leaned against him. His arm curled around her shoulder; he marveled at her instinctive trust of him. Even as he exulted in their closeness, he knew it could never materialize into anything more. He felt a pain greater than anything he had suffered before, a searing agony deep as his wounded soul.

"Morgan," she begged him, turning her damp face into his linen shirt, "Oh, Morgan, don't leave me yet. Please."

There was no question of it. He held her tightly, safely, in his protective embrace, till at last she slept.

"There, that should do it," Winnie proclaimed with satisfaction, securing the last of the compresses in place and stepping back from her patient. "There now, Katie love, I want you to keep the ointment in your eyes. Blink as little as possible. We'll change the dressings twice a day."

" 'Tis soothing," the newly christened Kate admitted, raising a hand to touch the soft linen wrap over her eyes. "What's in it?"

"Eyebright, Golden Seal, and Witch Hazel. 'Tis an old Welsh remedy for sore eyes. A week or so and you should be right as rain again." Winnie wiped her hands on her apron and observed her patient with a motherly air. "In the while, I want no undue moving about. You're bruised enough as 'tis."

"Aye, Mum," Kate agreed, with a grin for the scolding undertone in Winnie's voice. "I hope your order doesn't rule out any calls of nature. After all the tea you've brought me, I'm nigh close to bursting!"

A short time later, Winnie saw her patient settled for the night, and departed for her own cottage nearby. Kate lay in bed listening to the gentle drizzle of the rain outside, wondering why she couldn't sleep. She knew the answer. *He* was in her heart, and he also had a name: Morgan Trelane. She rarely stopped thinking about him. She must admit she was fascinated by the man. His voice, his hands, the rugged contours of his face. She remembered how his face had felt to her touch: the proud aquiline nose, the high cheekbones, the thin yet sensuous lips. Morgan was smooth-shaven. She liked that, too. She almost saw him in her mind's eye right now: his brown velvet eyes gazing down at her in the bed; an ebony lock of hair spilling boyishly over his brow. He was smiling . . .

"*Faeilean?*"

The deep male voice seduced her from the edge of consciousness, and she murmured with sleepy pleasure:

"You called me *Faeilean*. Is't my name?"

Morgan chuckled. "Nay. 'Tis the Gaelic for 'seagull.' 'Twas what you reminded me of when I carried you upstairs, looking for all the saints like a wee, drowned bird washed up with the tide."

She smiled, and Morgan's heart contracted in his chest. A hoarseness entered his voice.

"I'm sorry, I shouldn't disturb your rest. I'll leave—"

"No! I . . . I mean, please stay. I'm glad you came up to see me again."

Morgan swallowed hard and pulled up a chair. 'Twas a mistake to linger, he knew. All the while his mind reasoned, his gaze devoured Kate in the bed. Tonight Mrs. Carey had dressed her patient in a deep blue nightrail. The color brought out the lustrous highlights in her dark hair.

"I've brought the amulet along, as I promised. Here, hold out your hand." She did so, and he placed the cold disk in her palm, curling her fingers about it.

" 'Tis red-gold, well-crafted, and looks ancient," Morgan informed her as she explored the object with her fingers. "It is strung on a simple cord, one rather well-worn, from what I can tell. I imagine 'tis a talisman, either meant for protection or some sort of identification. I believe the bird carved in it might be an eagle, mayhap a raven."

" 'Tis a raven," Kate whispered, not even aware of such knowledge until she spoke. Startled from her reverie, she clutched the amulet to her breast. It comforted her, somehow, just knowing 'twas a part of her mysterious past, whatever her past was—a link to an unknown family. Morgan made no move to take it back from her. Instead, he offered:

"I wondered if you wish me to read you a story. I thought a familiar book might bring back pleasant memories to you."

"Aye, I should welcome it very much."

He reached out, found, and held her left hand, while the other still clutched the amulet. He found her fingers every bit as calloused as his own. He drew her hand along with his to rest atop the leather cover of the book he had brought.

"Let's see if you can guess what I have here."

She smiled at the challenge. " 'Tis thick. Is it the Bible?"

"Ah! Our first clue. You were raised in a Christian household. This is working even better than I imagined."

She shook her head, puzzled. "You said the amulet appears to be pagan in design. What does it mean?"

"Mayhap nothing. Often the two are combined. For instance, many here still celebrate Beltane and Samhain, the old Celtic festivals, as well as Christmas and Lent."

She relaxed, then tensed with excitement again. "Let's see if I know how to 'read' the letters, as well." She drew her fingers over the gold leaf in the leather. Counting out the spaces, she concentrated a moment and then laughed with triumph. *A Midsummer Night's Dream!*"

"Correct," said Morgan. Her laughter was so sweet and

spontaneous, Morgan could not resist joining in. "I take it, then, you're acquainted with Shakespeare. Shall I read a bit?"

Kate nodded eagerly and leaned towards Morgan as he began to read from the book. 'Twas one of her favorites. She knew it somehow, just as she knew Morgan's rich, deep voice was suited to reading aloud:

> *I know a bank where the wild thyme blows,*
> *Where oxlips and the nodding violet grows,*
> *Quite over-canopied with luscious woodbine,*
> *With sweet musk-roses with eglantine:*
> *There sleeps Titania sometime of the night*
> *Lull'd in these flowers with dances and delight,*

For almost an hour, she sat mesmerized as he recreated the scene of Shakespeare's fairy kingdom. Its queen, Titania, chose a flowery woodland bank for her bed, whereupon she seduced her lover, Nick. It mattered not that fairy magic transformed Nick into a lower creature; the same blissful magic blinded Titania to her lover's defects. Bedecking Nick's crown with flowers, Titania murmurs love words in his ear. Kate imagined two twining vines, the pair of entangled lovers on their grassy bank beneath a swaying canopy. Her heart beat faster, as Morgan leaned close and murmured Titania's words from another time, another place:

"*Sleep thou, and I will wind thee in my arms . . . so doth the woodbine the sweet honeysuckle gently entwist.*"

She closed her eyes, wishing she might confess her growing feelings for Morgan, praying he might somehow sense her need and thus respond. A moment later Morgan shut the book.

"You must get some sleep. I didn't mean to keep you up overly late."

"Oh, I loved every moment. I wished we didn't have

to stop," she said wistfully. "I dread the thought of going to sleep again. Whenever I do, I have the same nightmare."

"The fire?" His voice held obvious concern.

"Aye, and something more. There's cold water rising around me. I'm trying to swim, yet I can't. I'm too tired. I keep thinking 'twould be so easy to slip under the waves and find peace . . ."

Morgan felt a chill grip him at her words. He drew the blankets up around her shoulders. "You're tired, is all. Sleep now, and I'll have Mrs. Carey check on you first thing in the morning."

He rose to leave, picking up the taper holder from the table beside the bed. The flickering light cast strange shadows across her face and highlighted the gloominess of the stone chamber. He felt a compelling urge to stay. At the same time, he also knew 'twas out of the question.

"Sleep well, *Faeilean*," he murmured, lulling her to sleep with his gentle Welsh burr. "Know I'll let no harm come to you, while you're in my care."

Three

Kate slept deeply and awoke late. Since her arrival at the homestead where Morgan and Winnie lived and worked, she felt consolation for the first time, instead of fear. Though her eyes were still wrapped, she heard well enough to ascertain that the dreary rain had stopped at last. When Winnie tiptoed into her room a short time later, Kate's first request was to have the windows thrown open wide.

"Mercy!" Winnie exclaimed with real surprise. "Whatever for?"

"Why, to smell the fields after the rain, of course." Kate was surprised when a memory of rich, loamy soil came to mind. She aimed a winning smile in the housekeeper's general direction. "Please, Winnie?"

"Well . . ." Not approving, but anxious to please, the older woman bustled across the room. "Just for a moment, dear. We don't want you catching a chill."

"Thank you," Kate whispered. The moment the hinges creaked open, she slipped from the bed and fumbled her way towards the source of the cool, moist air pouring into the chamber. She felt each smooth, individual wooden joint beneath her bare feet and hesitated when she realized she must be on an upper floor. First levels customarily had sod floors. She didn't know how she knew such a fact, but she did. Falcon's Lair must be larger than she had imagined. She gripped the window ledge in both hands and leaned out, feeling her hair whip back in a sudden gust of wind.

"Oh! 'Tis breezy out. How fresh it smells!" She drew a deep, reverent breath into her lungs. Then she also caught the tangy scent of the sea. Close. 'Twas close. Too close. Her hands tightened on the ledge, and she made a faint, choking sound. Winnie hastened to pull her away and shut the windows.

"Poor poppet! You're shivering. Come back to bed."

"I'd rather not." Kate swallowed the rising hysteria the salt-brine smell had unexpectedly brought to her mind and tried to concentrate on other things.

"If you don't mind, Winnie, I'd rather get dressed and move about a bit. With your kind help, of course. My legs need some exercise. It seems they aren't used to lying about."

Winnie shrewdly studied Kate as she took the younger woman by the arm to guide her across the room. She almost made a remark about the girl's brown skin—like a serf's—then thought the better of it. 'Twas obvious Kate was a young woman of low birth, though attractive enough. Quite likely she was a dairy maid or a peasant's daughter, judging by her knowledge of the land and her unaffected airs. The only thing still puzzling Winnie was the girl's speech. Kate spoke no Welsh. Her English was cultured and bordered on insubordination when she spoke to Lord Trelane as an equal. Winnie was amazed he'd let the girl get away with it. Mayhap the Master pitied Kate. Aye, Lord Trelane was gentle in nature and with his hands, as Winnie often witnessed when he handled the newborn lambs. Morgan knew animals didn't fear or pity him. Because Kate couldn't see him, he apparently felt comfortable with her, too. It could not last, of course. Winnie felt saddened and relieved at the same time.

"Here's the settle, Katie dear. Now you sit tight while I go find the outfit I pressed this morning."

A delighted smile parted Kate's lips. "Why, Winnie. You were prepared."

"Aye," the housekeeper replied with a touch of pride. " 'Tis my place to anticipate whatever guests might need or want." She settled Kate with firm hands onto the cushioned bench.

"There. Now stay put. I'll bring another girl, Gwynneth, to fix your hair. We can't leave it all tumbled down and wild."

"Why not?" A male voice said lazily at Kate's right side. "I rather prefer it thus myself."

Winnie saw Kate's face light up at the Master's voice. She was radiant as she turned toward Lord Trelane. Winnie didn't miss the danger signal and was quick to step between them.

"Go on with you, now," she fussed. "This is a lady's chamber, no place for a man to be. Send Gwynneth up, will you, on your way out. I'll bring Katie down myself when she's fit for company."

Morgan's chuckle rolled low and rich throughout the chamber. "I intend inviting our guest downstairs to share my morning repast, Mrs. Carey. And I need a yea or nay, for Cook's benefit."

"Yea!" Kate burst out before Winnie had opportunity to protest. With a triumphant wink at his housekeeper, Morgan turned and left.

"Goodness," Winnie murmured a bit breathlessly. "I've never seen him look so happy."

"Isn't he usually?" Kate asked. She knew the answer before her caretaker spoke again. There was some hidden, deep sadness within Morgan Trelane, something she sensed rather than saw.

"Nay. Himself can be moody as the Irish Sea sometimes. 'Tis no wonder—" Sensing she'd overstepped her bounds, Winnie fell silent. The tense silence was broken by the arrival of another party, the maidservant Winnie had summoned to dress Kate's hair.

Gwynneth also brought a russet gown and kirtle for their guest. Winnie had debated over what Kate might wear. The torn breeches and blouse she was found in were out of the question, as was anything finer than servant's raiment. Besides, Winnie reassured herself, Kate couldn't even see the outfit. She suffered a pang of conscience anyway when Kate winced as the coarse, scratchy under-tunic was drawn down over her head.

Compliantly, however, she allowed Winnie to hook the bodice and adjust the whalebone stays about her waist. A stiff, plain wired collar, called a rebato, rose almost to Kate's ears. Worsted hose and leather shoes completed the outfit. Winnie stepped back and pressed her lips together, wondering why the sight of Kate in such thrifty attire didn't seem quite right.

"Ah," she nodded, mostly to herself. "Finish her hair, Gwynneth. I'll return shortly."

Kate was prepared to feel the deep, soothing strokes of bristles upon her hair again. The moment Winnie disappeared, however, the brushing became vigorous, almost rough. She raised a protective hand to her prickling scalp, hoping to provide a hint of some sort, but Gwynneth didn't relent. Was it deliberate? Surely not.

Kate had her answer when Gwynneth plucked several hairs from her head.

"Ouch!"

"Gray hairs, miss," the maid servant said with a faint, unmistakable undertone of malice. "I'm sure you'll be wanting me to get rid of them, now."

Shocked, Kate was spared a reply when Winnie burst back into the room. Winnie clucked with approval to see her patient's ebony hair crackling with blue highlights.

"The perfect touch," Winnie said, setting a dainty white lace cap upon Kate's ebony head. She clapped her hands with delight, not noticing, as Kate did, that Gwynneth remained mutinously silent and did not echo her approval.

When Kate's hand rose to finger the cap, Winnie explained, " 'Tis called a shadow. Most fitting for an unwed maid still wearing her hair loose."

"Mayhap I'm married," Kate suggested, though her mind was disturbingly blank in regard to any details about her former life.

"Methinks not." Winnie didn't add the why of her opinion. She knew no man would stand for his wife's wearing men's clothing. She added, "You were not wearing any jewelry, dear."

"Perhaps I was robbed before I washed up at Morgan's feet."

Gwynneth made a soft sound. It sounded suspiciously like a snigger. The maid was silenced by Winnie's disapproving cluck.

"Perhaps," Winnie echoed noncommittally. "Now I'm sure you'll be wanting to break your fast. Let me guide you downstairs."

Kate nodded. She rose and took Winnie's arm, walking carefully beside the older woman as they navigated the stone stairs. She still sensed Gwynneth's piercing stare on her back as they descended to the first floor. She wondered what cause she had given the maid to dislike her so. The strange incident was forgotten the moment she heard Morgan's voice.

"There you are. I was wondering what took so long." Kate sensed Morgan studying her; she also ascertained something was not quite right. Indeed, his tone sharpened. "Mrs. Carey, I wish to speak to you after the meal. I'll take care of Kate till then."

Morgan transferred Kate's hand to his own arm. She felt the fine lawn of his shirt under her fingertips. The material was soft, yet the definition of his arm beneath was muscular. She took a deep breath, wondering why she felt light-headed.

"I'll go slow. Lean against me if you wish."

If you wish. The words echoed in her mind and took on a different meaning. She restrained herself from doing what he suggested. Morgan's presence was comforting, yet disconcerting at times. His lips brushed close to her ear as he murmured, "I don't know your tastes, so I ordered some of everything."

"Except broth, I hope," Kate responded with a nervous little laugh.

"Oh, most definitely broth. I should enjoy any excuse to touch those rosy lips of yours again, albeit with a spoon."

The suggestive bit of banter caught Kate off guard. She felt a corresponding tightness in her throat. Her riposte was quick and playful. "Fie, sir, methinks y'are becoming a bit too familiar."

Morgan observed Kate's high color, the rapid beating pulse on her slender neck. He didn't know why he felt inclined to tease her in the first place. He saw how she responded. She was attracted to him. To a man she couldn't see and didn't even know. So, too, had a few women in his past risked such further knowledge, only to be shocked into screaming fits once they saw his marred face in the full light. He must harbor no illusions as to this acquaintance. It must, by necessity, end soon.

"Here's your seat."

Morgan's voice was suddenly cool and impersonal. Kate felt a sinking sensation in the pit of her stomach as his impersonal hands guided her onto the chair. Had she angered or disappointed him somehow? She felt obliged to make amends.

"Please, where are you going?" she asked, hearing his footsteps recede into the distance.

"To the other end of the table, of course. Otherwise

there won't be room for all of the dishes." Morgan made it sound a lighthearted jest. She knew his heart wasn't in it. She sensed his disapproval again and wondered what she'd done to displease him. Had she been too coy, too bold? Was he annoyed by her unsophisticated banter? 'Twas obvious enough, she was no courtly beauty. She felt awkward and ugly, almost on the verge of tears.

Her distress was set aside when a mouthwatering smell wafted down the table. Despite her upset, she found she was ravenous.

Morgan broke apart one of the hot, steaming scones and slathered it with creamy butter and preserves. Just as he was prepared to sink his teeth into the fresh-baked bread, he caught sight of Kate sitting at the other end of the table, hands folded in her lap, patiently awaiting his help. He could hardly ignore the hint when she licked her lips.

"Damnation," he muttered, realizing she wasn't yet able to feed herself without a disaster of one sort or other. He rose and carried his chair and plate of scones back to the other end of the room. There he sat and extended a scone towards the stubborn, set lips of his uninvited guest.

"Open your mouth," he ordered her. "I intend for you to sample one of Cook's world-famous scones."

"You don't have to feed me," Kate protested, her cheeks burning when she heard the resignation in his voice. She vowed she would not be treated like a child anymore, nor fed like an injured animal. But even as she did so, her stomach rumbled desperately.

To her mortification, Morgan laughed. "I'm afraid you've little choice, madam, unless you wish to have currant jam dripping down your bodice," he said. The instant her mouth opened with surprise, he thrust the scone halfway home. Kate choked and sputtered. The flaky pastry crumbled and melted in her mouth. Morgan chuckled at her incredulous expression and watched her down the remaining half with an endearing greed.

" 'Tis manna from heaven!" Kate declared, licking a dab of red jam from the corner of her lips. Morgan shared in her joyous discovery until he made a shocking one of his own. Sweet Jesu. He was aroused by every movement she made. He sat back in his chair, distancing himself from the bewitching smile and sweetly curved lips he knew were complimented by a bright pair of inquisitive, emerald-green eyes—eyes he knew would open wide, then clamp shut with horror once Kate got a real glimpse of him.

"Cook will be pleased to hear of your approval," he said brusquely, scraping back the chair as he rose. "I'll send someone in to help you with the rest of the meal. I just remembered I am needed in the shearing pens."

"Oh." Kate tried to conceal her disappointment and confusion over his abrupt departure. "Shall I see you later?"

"I doubt it. I'm busy this time of year. By all accounts, my work will run late. If there's anything you want or need, just let Mrs. Carey know. She's been instructed to fulfill your every reasonable whim."

Instructed by whom? Kate wondered. The master of the house? Morgan had never mentioned the man who held sway over them all, the same lord who played unwitting host to her now, one who might be rightfully outraged to learn a stranger was sheltered beneath his roof for so long. She feared for Morgan and the other servants, yet she selfishly wished to stay here forever. Here, at least, she felt safe, warm, and protected. Who knew what dreadful secrets the sea held in store for her? Kate shuddered to think of crossing those dark waters again, even in search of family abroad. Morgan might be convinced she was Irish by birth, but she prayed he was wrong. There was no excuse for her to linger if her kin were found.

How reasonable was it to want Morgan to stay with her now?
she wondered. She knew in her heart she was to blame
for his sudden change in mood. She sought to make
amends for all the trouble she'd caused.

"Morgan?" Her hand shot out blindly. She was lucky
enough to capture his arm before he escaped the room.

"Thank you. You've been too kind," she whispered.

" 'Tis nothing, *Faeilean*. Just a passing hobby of mine,
caring for little lost birds until they can fly again." He
gently pried her fingers from his arm. He held her hand
for the briefest of moments in his before releasing it. As
her hand dropped down to her side, abandoned, he left.

Morgan walked the water's edge at low tide, while
seagulls screamed and dived above him. "Skree, skree . . ."
Their haunting cries alternately scolded and mourned. He
almost felt as if he was being warned—against what, he
didn't know. Caring for Kate? Mayhap his emotions were
even clear to wild animals now. Clear to everyone but himself.

Morgan watched the gulls riding the currents on their
frosty white wings and wished he might be so carefree.
Duty was his sole destiny: Falcon's Lair and finding Kate's
family. To the latter end, he studied the various debris
scattered here and there along the rocky shore. Most of
the stuff was battered beyond recognition. Indeed, 'twas
a right wonder Kate hadn't been, too. By some miracle,
she'd been spared, except for a few cuts and bruises.

He raised his gaze to the clear blue horizon, scanning
the deceptively peaceful sea for any further clues. 'Twas
the first clear day he'd had to ride out in search of more
answers. There were too damme few to satisfy him here.
Surely the young woman he called Kate would eventually
remember her past.

Was it possible she lied about the memory loss for some

reason? Morgan shook his head at the thought. Kate had nothing to gain by pretending she'd been washed ashore on the Devil Baron's land. At best, 'twould irretrievably damage her reputation; at worst, she'd be viewed as yet another of his unearthly familiars.

Morgan chuckled, realizing that Kate, with her night-black hair and uncanny green eyes, might fit the towns-folk's notion of a sorceress or witch, albeit a beautiful one. *What manner of crazy tale will crop up next?* he idly wondered. He considered asking Mrs. Carey to keep an ear primed for the latest rumor in town.

Something dragged at his feet. Morgan glanced down, surprised to see a wet clump of material washed up around his riding boots. He picked it up and unfolded the soaked cloth to reveal a torn but recognizable standard of sorts. The red background had washed out to a pale pink, making the center emblem all the more pronounced: a black bird clutching a burning oak branch in its talons.

His grip tightened on the wet cloth as he remembered the amulet, and Kate's thoughtful whisper: *"Raven."* He knew there was some connection between the standard and the unusual amulet she was wearing when he found her. Morgan studied the fierce if bedraggled flag a moment more, then wrung it out and walked across the sand to tuck it in his mount's saddlebag. He realized 'twas an important clue. With this pennant, he might be able to trace the lost ship and his Kate's family. 'Twas likely her passage home.

His Kate's? Morgan recognized the covetous thought and, at once, tried to banish it. He had no claim to her, none at all. Yet, he thought, 'twould be easy to toss the flag back in the sea and tell Kate he had found nothing. He was startled by his own devious musings. Would he do anything to keep her here for a week, a day, even an hour longer? Aye, he decided, he would. For the first time in his life, Morgan Trelane didn't care to be honest.

Four

Kate ran her fingers down the length of the velvet gown. "Are you sure?" she asked Winnie again, turning a bewildered gaze in the housekeeper's direction.

"Aye. Himself was adamant about it. He doesn't want to see you dressed as a servant anymore." Winnie spoke the words with faint disapproval. Though she was fond of Kate, she didn't approve of encouraging airs in those of the lower classes. Even more upsetting was the fact that the gown had once belonged to Lady Trelane, Morgan's mother.

The instructions had been simple. The means had not. Morgan didn't want Mrs. Carey going into town to buy any female attire. He realized 'twould only encourage wild rumors and speculation among the villagers; neither did he want to see the girl wearing peasant garb. The quandary wasn't an easy one. Winnie had done her best.

Kate's "new" gown of deep green velvet was elegant, if simple. Spanish influence might be seen in the cut and style; at least Lady Elena had been tasteful enough not to choose gowns lavished with lace and embroidery.

Kate didn't know the history of this gown or the others donated to her cause. Winnie had merely told her that Morgan had arranged for a finer wardrobe. It appeared the girl was a little too stunned to question her good fortune.

"The fit is perfect," Kate said, stroking the gown's rich

material as she turned about. "I wish I could see it, as well. You said 'tis green?"

"Aye, a wee shade darker than your eyes. Speaking of eyes, dear, the wrap should stay on a few more days, at least until I'm sure the damage is healing well."

Kate sighed. She did so look forward to seeing the homestead, especially Morgan. "Very well. I'll try to be patient, Winnie."

"Have you remembered anything else?"

"Nothing, I'm afraid. I'm such a burden right now. I feel terrible about it. I hope I come from a wealthy family so I can repay your master properly."

Winnie was spared a reply by the vesper bells from the village. "La, Katie, we're just in time."

"For what?"

"The evening meal, of course. Take my arm and I'll lead you downstairs."

"Will Morgan be there?"

Winnie clucked at the familiarity. "I doubt it. He's working late in the lambing sheds. I daresay he'll wish to ask you some more questions later."

Kate fell silent, sensing the sudden change in atmosphere and Winnie's air of disapproval. The woman had always been kind to her, yet in the past few days Winnie's manner seemed cooler and more distant. What had caused the change? First Morgan, now the housekeeper. All of a sudden, she felt lost and alone.

This time, Kate knew, the meal would be solitary. At least she had managed to feed herself, if somewhat awkwardly. She smelled the pungent aroma of barberry candles long before she was seated and left at the massive table to fend for herself. The wood was smooth and cool beneath her fingertips; she fancied 'twas mahogany. By pretending she saw her surroundings, she effectively distracted herself for hours. Certainly there was nothing else to do, except think about Morgan, and 'twas beginning to be too painful.

She fumbled awhile with the utensils, then managed to spread a cloth over her lap. Suddenly she burst into tears of frustration, surprising herself.

"What's wrong, *Faeilean?*"

At the gentle query, Kate's head rose with a jolt. She realized Morgan was close. He must have been seated next to her all this time. Her cheeks burned as she quickly regained her composure.

"I didn't know anyone was here."

"I just arrived." He reached out and coaxed a tear from her cheek to his finger. "You're beautiful, you know," he said softly. "Too beautiful to cry."

Kate swallowed a painful surge of emotion. It threatened to push another ragged sob from her lips. "I can't be very beautiful with this hideous cloth tied around my head."

"Then I'll amend it to 'simply beautiful,' Morgan said, his tone teasing. "Are you ready to eat now?"

"I'm not hungry," Kate lied. She couldn't bear the thought of another humiliating episode, wherein Morgan was forced to hand-feed her like an injured lamb. Just as she spoke, her stomach gurgled. She felt another blush burn her cheeks and heard Morgan chuckle.

"Now, I won't have any nonsense, *Faeilean,*" he scolded, as he nudged a spoon against her lips. "Eat."

She ate. 'Twas delicious and filling; she soon heard her whalebone stays creaking in protest. Despite her upset, she was ravenous, and Morgan's approval of her hearty appetite made it all the easier to eat every last crumb. Finally, she shook her head and begged for mercy. Laughing, he gently wiped her mouth with a linen napkin. Kate sat back with a sigh, replete.

"Better," Morgan approved. "Mayhap you'll be able to concentrate upon what I have to tell you now."

She sat up straight. "You've found something."

"Aye." Morgan sounded reluctant for some reason to reveal his discovery. Nevertheless, he proceeded to describe the flag he had found, along with several other boards from smashed crates. He said the latter bore the Eastland Company's mark. "I'll venture to guess we can discover your identity within a fortnight now. 'Tis quite possible you were a passenger upon an English vessel."

"Are you certain?" Kate wondered. "You said I spoke in Gaelic when you found me. The English and Irish are always at odds."

"Yet your English sounds nativeborn," he pointed out. " 'Tis obvious, at least to me, you've been to England before; perhaps your family lives there. A mystery, to be sure; one which must needs be solved. With your permission, I wish to send out several queries about a recent shipwreck or any missing vessels in these waters. We shall soon discover if you have any relatives anxiously awaiting news."

"Parents, you mean?"

"Or a husband."

She turned towards him. "What makes you think so?"

"I can't imagine a woman so lovely would not be wed, or at least betrothed."

"Winnie said I wore no jewelry," Kate said, not sure why she felt obliged to point out the fact.

"Aye, you wore men's trews, as well. Mayhap your husband is more accommodating than I would be about such attire."

There was as much tease as threat in his tone, Kate discerned. She decided to play along for a moment: "Pray tell, what would you do, sirrah, if I were your wife in truth and I chose to wear men's garb?"

"Do you truly wish to know?" Morgan asked, his voice lowering an octave as he leaned close to her. His hand moved to cover hers, and she felt both a languid warmth and a strange, feverish excitement rising to engulf her.

"First of all," he murmured, "any lady wife of mine would suffer dire consequences for wearing such mannish attire. 'Twould be a grave crime against nature, especially if she were as comely as you. Should she disobey me, anyhow, *Faeilean,* she should forfeit a penalty."

A smile curved her lips at his mock threat. "In sooth, would you truly? Pray tell, Morgan, what would it be?"

" 'Twould be better if I showed you."

Kate drew in her breath when his lips grazed her own. She leaned towards Morgan, chasing his mouth with her own, her bold pursuit meeting with success. She felt his arm steal around her shoulders to steady her. After a moment's hesitation, he resumed the kiss, this time tracing her willing lips with the tip of his finger before he claimed her mouth again. With a sigh, Kate leaned into Morgan, her hand braced against the cool leather of his jerkin. She inhaled the musky male scent of him, a combination of leather and tobacco and wet wool. 'Twas oddly exciting to her heightened senses.

"Ah," he murmured at last, reluctant to draw the intoxicating kiss to a close. "You almost make me forget my honor, *Faeilean.*" He set her back from him.

Kate sensed Morgan physically and emotionally withdrawing from her. This time she was determined not to let it happen again.

"Morgan." She spoke his name with a clear affection she sensed startled him. "I owe you my life, thus my thanks as well. Yet there is some deeper bond between us now, and I ask you—nay, I beg of you, not to deny it any longer."

His silence frightened her. She felt a hand alight upon her head, tousling her hair like a child's. When Morgan spoke again, his voice was sad and low.

"There are reasons, *Faeilean,* why it cannot be."

"Why?" Her wounded whisper echoed throughout the

room. "Is't because . . . oh, Sweet Jesu, are you married?"

"Nay."

"Mayhap you're already betrothed yourself."

"No," Morgan repeated, an edge of anger lacing his deep tone. She heard his chair thrust back and sensed him towering over her. "I beseech you, Kate, to let it alone. Some things are better not discussed."

"You kissed me. You wanted to. I know you did."

She knew she sounded childish, yet emotion pushed all reason from her mind. She must know why Morgan denied their feelings, their future.

"Are you truly such an innocent, Kate? Any red-blooded knave will take what he can from a willing lady."

Morgan saw his deliberate jibe hurt her. She ceased all questions, though; 'twas his intent. He was sickened by the necessity of his own cruelty, for he was nothing, if not a gentle man at heart. She must harbor no misplaced affection for him. He was torn and relieved when Kate nodded, as if accepting his statement.

Then she rose from the chair beside him and addressed him formally.

"By your leave, sirrah, I wish to depart immediately."

"Just where do you plan to go, *Faeilean*?"

"Please stop calling me that. It sounds like an endearment, when it clearly is not." She bit her lip and forged on. "I think it wisest if I seek refuge elsewhere. There must be a nearby abbey or convent—"

"Ridiculous. You are in no condition to be traveling, and your family is yet to be found."

"Nonetheless, 'tis not my intention to impose upon this household any longer. I shall leave right now." With curt, angry gestures, Kate gathered up the cumbersome velvet skirts. She paused as he heaved a great sigh.

"How do you propose to find the nearest retreat, Kate?

Will you blunder about in the darkness, hoping to bump into the abbey bell?"

" 'Tis not amusing, Morgan."

"Neither is your behavior. Cease this nonsense at once, or I'll take you upstairs to your room. You are tired and distraught."

Distraught! When she was half in love with the cad and he knew it! Furiously, Kate jerked away from his touch when he moved to take her arm.

This was more the sort of reaction Morgan was used to. His eyes narrowed; he secured his fingers around her wrist. "There will be no hysterics in this household, Mistress Kate. You are going upstairs to rest now. 'Tis final."

"Curse you, sirrah!"

Sweet Jesu, she was magnificent in her rage, Morgan realized. She looked a far cry from the meek, frightened creature he had rescued from the sea. He almost shivered at the intensity in her expression; for some reason he envisioned a line of proud warrior queens in Kate's past. Each of them wore a pagan amulet; none of them needed or wanted a man. Morgan blinked, the vision vanished; instead he found himself faced with Kate, an ordinary if angry female.

"No arguments, *Faeilean.*"

Kate gasped with outrage when he lifted her into his arms. Her skirts fell topsy-turvy around her head as Morgan slung her casually over his shoulder, pinning her legs against his chest. His brisk stride carried her across the room, down the hall and toward the stairs. With each step, Kate beat a furious tattoo upon his back with her fists.

"Put me down, you blackguard! I'll not be handled this way."

Her outraged cries and threats went unheeded. Morgan didn't pause until he met with Mrs. Carey coming down the stairs.

"Lud-a-mercy!" Winnie exclaimed, pressing a freckled hand to her ample bosom. "What's all this?"

"Our guest was protesting her extended stay, Mrs. Carey," Morgan answered cheerfully, though not without some effort. His unwilling baggage now pounded mercilessly upon his ribs. " 'Tis clear our Katie doesn't know what's good for her. We had a bit of a tiff about it. I won."

He grinned good-naturedly. Winnie had to chuckle at his boyish air.

"By the rood, what would your father say if he saw you now? Carrying a young lady upstairs, slung over your shoulder like a sack of grain."

"Probably 'congratulations.' " Morgan's dry laughter rumbled through Kate as well. "Pray turn down her covers, Mrs. Carey. I vow our guest is nigh ready to retire. I'll entreat you to remain with Kate and deal with all those blasted hooks and stays."

"As you wish, milord."

The pounding on Morgan's back ceased.

"Lord?"

A surprised squeak issued from beneath all the layers of material.

"You . . . you're a peer?" Kate sputtered, pushing aside the velvet curtain tumbled about her head. "I don't believe it."

"Merely a baron, my dear," Morgan coolly replied. "Our good queen sees fit upon occasion to grace some of her rustic relations with titles, in order to keep the Welsh provincials in line."

"But you never told me . . . I never dreamed . . ."

Winnie pitied Kate's present position— not her undignified posture over Lord Trelane's shoulder so much as the shock in her face. 'Twas awkward enough lying for the Master these past days, and Winnie was relieved the ruse was over. Yet now the unpleasant truth was laid out for all. There was little consolation, even knowing 'twas for the best.

"Put the girl back in her room, if you would be so kind, milord," she said. "I shall see to her further care."

Morgan nodded and grimly resumed his march. He deposited Kate on her bed in her room and turned to leave.

"Morgan . . . Lord Trelane . . ."

Kate didn't even know if he was still there or not. Her head still reeled from the shock of her unpleasant discovery. She gathered her courage and spoke into the silent void.

"Indeed, and I do understand now. What would a fine lord want with the likes of me? You might have told me the truth in the beginning, milord. I need not have troubled you with my presence for so long."

"Damme, *Faeilean*, 'twasn't the reason."

She turned her head away, rejecting any answers or explanations. She sensed Morgan chafing with frustration. A moment later, he departed.

After he left, Kate stared into a dark void. 'Twas devoid of light or hope as was her life. Aye, this explained everything now. Explained it only too well.

Five

"I am leaving, Winnie. I don't intend to brook any further argument about it."

Winnie was lacing a dark green brocade gown for Kate. She did so as slowly as possible, in order to give the Master ample time to return from the fields. What would Lord Trelane say when he learned the girl had wandered off alone, blind, into the wilderness? Winnie already knew. He would be furious with both of them, but she alone would remain to take the brunt of his anger.

"Are you sure 'tis wise, Katie? These hills are full of brigands. A blind traveler doesn't stand a chance. Especially a maiden without an escort."

"Just direct me toward the nearest abbey. If I must, I shall crawl along the roadside until some kind wayfarer takes pity enough to guide me the rest of the way. What I *won't* do is suffer any further charity from Mor—Lord Trelane."

Winnie sighed. There was nothing to be done for it. Kate had her dander up; like most of the Gaelic, she could be pigheaded beyond reason.

"As for this gown," Kate continued, "I intend to assure Lord Trelane is recompensed for its loss. Just as soon as I find my family, I shall see he is compensated for every last coin spent on my behalf."

"What if you don't find your kin?" Winnie asked.

Kate paled and lifted her chin. "Then I must secure

some sort of work, of course, and send milord payment as soon as possible. I have only my word to offer, if he can accept the vow of a lowly Irishwoman."

Winnie did not take the bait. She gave a sigh of surrender. " 'Tis raining again, dearie. You'll need a warm cloak, as well."

"Is there one here? I shall, of course, pay for it as well."

"Aye, I'll fetch it." Resigned, Winnie went to retrieve the cloak. It had belonged to Lady Elena, too. No other woman, save for maid servants, had lived at Falcon's Lair since Morgan's mother died. Winnie fetched the cloak from the wardrobe and stroked the soft, fine black wool cape with its French hood. Cloaks, at least, did not go out of fashion as quickly as gowns. She crossed the room and draped it about Kate's rigid shoulders.

Kate sniffed with faint surprise. "It smells of damask rose."

"It belonged to Lord Trelane's mother. 'Twas her favorite scent."

"His mother? He never mentioned her. Where is she now?"

"Lud, she died, miss. Long ago."

As Winnie hoped, Kate asked no more questions.

"If you'll be so kind as to help me downstairs one last time, Winnie, I will be on my way."

"Best to let me fasten the cloak for you, dear. 'Tis chilly outside."

It didn't occur to Kate to be suspicious about Winnie's complacent assistance, not even when she was bid a calm farewell and left outside in the drizzling rain. Winnie had kindly turned her in the right direction before she left, yet the moment Kate swiveled about to wave good-bye, she was disoriented. She felt dampness from the soggy earth already seeping up through her thin leather soles. Rain drizzled down her neck. She tugged the hood of the cape up over her hair.

Despite the chill and miserable weather, it felt good to be thumbing her nose at Trelane's hospitality. Her break for independence restored a little of her dignity as she took a deep breath and set off with determination—and blundered into a bramble bush. The thorny branches pricked her hands and tore the cloak as she struggled to get free.

From the doorstep of Falcon's Lair, Winnie observed Kate's progress, if it could be termed thus. She shook her head sadly and watched as Kate plucked the last of the thorns from her palms and set off again. This time, Kate reached the rocky path leading down to the sea. Her smooth soles slipped in the thick mud. A second later, she tumbled halfway down the hill. Morgan rode over from the wainwright's cottage just in time to glimpse Kate rolling head over heels down the slope.

"What the devil!" he exclaimed, directing a sharp glance of reprimand at Mrs. Carey before he dug his heels into the gray mare he was riding.

When she ceased tumbling, Kate sat up and spat out wet grass and leaves. A moment later she heard the dull thud of approaching horse's hooves.

"Are you hurt?" Morgan called out, as he dismounted and hurried to her side.

"Nay." Kate lied. Her left ankle throbbed, her palms were scraped raw from the desperate attempt to break her fall. She was drenched to the skin and her teeth began to chatter from the cold. She felt Morgan grasp her arm, but she shrugged off his silent offer of assistance. "I can see to things myself."

She spoke curtly as she came to her feet. Morgan had no way of knowing she was furious with herself, rather than him. Her humiliation complete, Kate shook the thick mud from her hands and realized there was no recourse but to return to the keep. She had hoped to escape before Morgan's return. No wonder Winnie seemed unconcerned about letting her leave.

Morgan persisted. "You look unsteady. Here, I'll help you." He took her elbow with one hand, slid his other arm around her waist. Kate did not deny the support was welcome as they trudged up the steep incline.

"Now," Morgan demanded, "just what the devil is going on here? You were to remain inside till you were recovered. Why wasn't Mrs. Carey with you?"

" 'Twasn't her fault," Kate said. "I ordered her to let me leave the household. She was wise enough not to argue . . . well, not overmuch."

Morgan made an exasperated sound. At the top of the hill he did not release her immediately. Instead they stood pressed together, buffeted by the wind from the sea. A few moments later the rain stopped. A mist drifted in and curled about them in the fashion of a cloak. Kate felt its damp kiss upon her face.

"We need to talk, *Faeilean.*"

"There's nothing more to be said, milord. I'm leaving. 'Tis my final word. Even you cannot force me to stay."

"Mayhap I can persuade you instead."

Morgan's words rumbled like gentle thunder across the Welsh hills. Kate felt a tingle of anticipation when he tilted her face up to his.

"You're not wearing the wrap about your eyes," he said. He sounded uneasy. She knew how much Morgan had worried about her eyesight. She felt an unexpected warmth course throughout her body. Despite her anger at being deceived, she found his concern for her touching.

"Winnie said it might come off today. I insisted upon it."

"Can you see anything yet?"

She shook her head. "Just shadows and vague shapes. Winnie assures me my sight will return, however. Along with my memory, I trust."

He was silent a moment. "How long does Mrs. Carey think it will take?"

"The memory, or my eyesight? Both might be days yet, or weeks." Kate shrugged more bravely than she felt. "Or . . . mayhap not at all. There is some chance my vision will not be restored. My eyes were sorely burned, Winnie admitted. There might have been some damage from smoke or flying sparks, as well as salt water."

Kate heard Morgan swallow. How repulsed he must be by her sightless eyes, blindly staring up at him! She averted her gaze and sought for a safer topic.

"I hear the sea hissing at us. One might suppose it an angry cat."

"Yea, we're close to the cliff's edge. You might have had a misstep and met with disaster." Morgan's arm tightened about her waist. "I vow you're an even match for the sea, *Faeilean*. You hiss quite well yourself, when provoked."

Kate chuckled a little. "I do seem to be rather strong-willed, don't I?"

"Rather," he dryly agreed.

"Did I really resemble a drowned seagull washed up with the tide?"

Morgan thought a moment. "Nay. More a wet kitten, ready to sharpen her claws on the first man she saw."

"Oh! A helpless kitten, milord?" Kate's voice held a challenge, and jeweled green eyes swung back to him with unerring accuracy. Morgan gazed down into her beautiful eyes with a mixture of trepidation and hope. Was it possible the shadows she saw were enough to expose him? He steeled himself for a scream. Her lips parted in a soft chuckle instead.

"Cats have a great deal of independence, you know."

"As well as nine lives, according to legend. Perhaps I should release you to see if you totter off the cliff, after all."

The threat was halfhearted and Kate knew it. She laughed again, more freely this time.

"I didn't manage to land on my feet the first time, so you'd best keep a good grip on me now."

"You're not used to it, 'tis all. Had you been blind from birth, you should have got along quite well."

"I daresay you're right, milord."

"Pray don't call me 'milord' anymore. 'Tis a dry and irksome title used by old men. I have a Christian name, one you used willingly enough before last night."

"Morgan." She repeated his name in a reverent whisper. He felt a corresponding ache in his breast. An ache which was becoming all too familiar.

" 'Tis an unusual name for a man."

"It means 'white sea' in the old Cymric language. My father wanted me to have a strong name."

"I favor it also." Kate strained in vain for a glimpse of her savior. Despite her lingering hurt and anger, she longed to see Morgan. He had given her back her life, in more ways than one. How desperately she wanted to know him, touch his face again. She had already memorized the contours of his features and knew him to be handsome. Why wasn't he wed? He was no stripling in short pants.

She decided to ask him in a roundabout way. "Do you live alone, Morgan? Winnie said your mother is gone, and you mentioned your father once, yet I've not heard him spoken of around the household."

"He died five years ago. Aye, I live alone."

"I'm sorry. How painful it must have been for you."

Sensing Morgan's mood had darkened for some reason, she added hastily, "At least you know who your family was. I've yet to remember mine. They must be frantic with worry."

"I've sent several of my staff out to question the locals about any recent shipwrecks. We should hear word soon.

I've also sent a missive to the Earl of Cardiff, requesting his assistance in contacting the Eastland Company. Surely if a ship is missing, they have some record of it."

Kate nodded. She knew she was foolish to even consider striking out on her own, blind and helpless as she was. Her cursed pride made her appear the fool, yet Morgan was kind enough not to remark upon it. She realized he had gone to great efforts on her behalf. She found she could not resent him for his earlier deceit, anymore than she might despise him for helping her now. 'Twas in his nature to be generous and forgiving. Winnie and the other servants all spoke of Morgan with great respect; she owed him as much herself.

"Will you come back with me, *Faeilean*?"

She nodded at his question and slipped her arm through his. 'Twas not so much surrender as a practical decision, Kate reasoned. He was looking out for her again; if there was anyone she trusted, 'twas Morgan. He had vowed to find her family for her. She knew he would. She wondered why she didn't feel as enthusiastic as she should.

They started to walk back to Falcon's Lair, Morgan leading both her and his mount. Suddenly he stopped and stiffened. Kate heard a bevy of young voices on the road ahead of them. Children. They were laughing and jesting with each other, no doubt deliberately veering through all the mud puddles on their way home. They sounded happy, heading in her and Morgan's direction.

As the children neared, Kate felt Morgan's body tense beside her. "What is it?" she asked him. "What's wrong?"

Then she heard one of the little girls scream. Soon the rest of the children joined in. Their feet splashed noisily through a puddle, as they dashed across the couple's path and disappeared into a nearby copse, shrieking all the way. They sounded terrified.

Morgan grimaced. The timing for such an incident

could not have been worse. One stout lad, older than the rest, decided to linger, in an obvious attempt to provoke him. The boy boldly eyed Morgan, then crossed himself just to be safe. The lad bent, snatched something from the ground, and hurled it at the adults, and ran.

Kate flinched when the stone glanced off her skirts. She recoiled and clutched at Morgan's arm. "What was that?"

"One of the urchins just threw a rock at us," he said.

"Why?" She was shocked and confused. "They sounded so happy until they saw us here, then . . ."

"Children can be unpredictable little beasts sometimes." Morgan cut her short. "Especially those of peasant stock. I've no end of trouble keeping them out of my fields."

Kate frowned and looked confused. Morgan realized his harsh tone didn't belong to the man she knew. He was always tender with her.

"Am I all covered with mud?" she asked.

"No. Why?"

"They screamed as if they'd seen the Devil himself crawl from a bog." Kate shook her head and tried to laugh it off. "I fear there's no other explanation. My muddy appearance must have frightened them, for some reason."

"Nonsense," Morgan said, hurrying her along the path back to the keep. "They're merely base little wretches without any manners. Now, let's get you inside. 'Tis starting to rain again."

Henry Lawrence frowned as he dismounted from the enclosed coach bearing his royal coat of arms. The Earl of Cardiff gave a dismissing wave to his driver. As the vehicle pulled ahead to the stables, Lawrence studied the ancient stone keep rising before him. He had been to Falcon's Lair many times before Rhys Trelane's death.

The two men had been of the same era, and were great friends in their youth. Lawrence had visited less often since Rhys was gone. Young Trelane was not known for his hospitality.

" 'Tis understandable, though not excusable," Lawrence groused under his breath, as he hobbled across the yard. Trelane might favor the life of a recluse, but a baron had social duties, just the same.

Still a tall, imposing figure with a head full of beautiful white hair, Lawrence knew he commanded great respect in both his peers and lessers. His only misfortune was that time had not been kind to his legs. He leaned more heavily on his ivory-handled staff than usual. Nasty spring weather always made his old bones ache.

As always, however, the earl was impeccably dressed, his tawny velvet breeches and matching doublet slashed and pinked, in tune with the latest court fashions. Even here in godforsaken Wales, Lawrence was determined to preserve a shred of his English dignity. And others' as well, if need be. Such was the reason he was here.

Before he was forced to pound upon the great iron-chased doors, the entrance opened to expose a surprised face.

"Milord Lawrence," Winnie murmured, curtsying. Her tone was properly deferential. Lawrence studied the housekeeper as she rose. Winnie's ginger-colored hair, a source of fascination to the earl when he was much younger, was neatly tucked up under a broad lace cap. A few stray tendrils softened her round face, now liberally streaked with silver. Her complexion was smooth and unblemished as ever. Lawrence knew it must have been at least seven years since he had seen her last.

"By the rood, 'tis Wynne Carey. Nothing changes 'round here," he said by way of a compliment. "Ne'er the keep, nor the lovely ladies within."

Winnie blushed girlishly. "Won't you come in, milord? Lord Trelane is returning from the fields soon."

"Aye, lambing season, is it not?" Lawrence remarked, stepping past Winnie as she closed the double doors behind him. He studied the place, pleased to note young Trelane had not changed the decor overmuch. There were still several suits of armor in the great hall, polished to a high shine and standing along the right wall. On the left, beautiful old tapestries of rich claret and forest green graced the cold stone walls; Morgan's paternal grandmother, Matilda, had woven them. Lawrence remembered her fondly, a spirited beauty with great blue eyes. A true lady. She, at least, had hosted plenty of revelries at Falcon's Lair in her day.

Winnie took the earl's cloak and cap from him, and ushered him into the library.

"You'll be more comfortable waiting here, milord," she suggested, moving to the sideboard to pour their guest a goblet of hot, mulled cider. "This will take the chill from your bones. 'Tis uncommon cold out today."

"Aye, I believe another storm will soon be upon us," Lawrence agreed, as he accepted the drink and set his walking staff aside. Reclining in a red damask chair and stretching out his arthritic legs, he nursed the spiced cider and studied the room while Winnie chattered inanely about any number of things.

Trelane men had always been a bookish lot, Lawrence mused, eying the leather-bound volumes stacked from floor to ceiling. There was no doubt of their masculinity, however. The dark wood and leather library was dotted with hunting trophies and various art works depicting the hunts and hawking outings Trelane males so enthusiastically enjoyed. Shortly the library doors opened and Morgan appeared. His attire was more conservative than the earl's: black breeches and a crisp white cambric shirt embroidered with black-work at the neck and wrists. He greeted Lawrence warmly.

"Milord Lawrence. You do us all a distinct honor. No, Henry, don't get up. You've come many a league today. I see Mrs. Carey has already seen to your creature comforts."

As Morgan spoke, he felt the Earl of Cardiff's hawk-sharp gaze studying him. He crossed the room to clasp hands with the older man. He wondered if Lawrence was repulsed by his birthmark. It had correspondingly grown over the years along with Morgan; if Henry was taken aback, however, he was gracious enough not to say anything.

"Morgan, my boy, I can scarcely believe it. The last time I saw you, I trow you were still in short pants. You look the spitting image of your father when he was younger."

Morgan smiled, though both he and Lawrence knew quite well whom he favored. Rhys Trelane had been fair in coloring and half a head shorter, as well. Morgan resembled his Spanish ancestors: tall and swarthy with intense dark eyes.

" 'Tis good of you to come," was all he said. "What brings you all the way here in such foul weather?"

Winnie had slipped from the room and closed the double doors again, so the earl did not hesitate to speak his mind.

"Your message, of course. I must confess, I'm damme curious about this girl you found. You said she was washed up on the shore?"

"Aye." Morgan nodded. "She was in bad shape, of course, though fortunately not seriously injured. She's recovering at present."

"I like it not," Lawrence stated. At Morgan's quizzical look, he elaborated. "D'you know there are still Spanish ships lurking in these waters? Aye, the bloody papists still plot Elizabeth Tudor's downfall. The loss of Mary Stuart did not slow their ambitions one bit, my boy. Now, there's James the Scot to contend with. I wouldn't put it past the Catholics to send one of their spies ashore here, where she might have a safe haven and act as their eyes and ears."

Morgan was shocked by the notion. "Milord, I must protest such an assumption. The young woman in question is not Spanish but Irish."

"Almost as bad," Lawrence muttered.

Morgan ignored the comment, in consideration of the earl's age. "Moreover, she was grievously hurt. Her eyes are damaged and her memory gone."

"Most convenient, wouldn't you agree, for a spy seeking to infiltrate Her Majesty's realm?"

Morgan shook his head and made an exasperated noise as he moved to refill the earl's goblet. He also filled one for himself. He knew he was going to need it. He hadn't imagined a simple request for assistance in finding Kate's family might lead to this. He told Lawrence firmly:

"I insist you trust me in this matter, milord. I sent the missive to you because I hoped you might help me locate the woman's kin. Your connections in London are more powerful than mine, and I assume you still deal with the Eastland Company yourself upon occasion."

"Aye, I do. A finer trade service is yet to be found. As for the girl, Morgan, I pray you take heed of my warning. If not for your sake, then for hers. Even if her tale is true, she risks a great deal by remaining here at Falcon's Lair any longer than necessary. 'Tis well known you live alone, and if word gets out, tongues will wag."

"Let them," Morgan declared, pausing to take a long, deep draught of the spiced cider. He set aside the goblet and fixed his steady gaze on Lawrence again. "I no longer care what people think of me. As you well know, Henry, they have maligned my name for years."

"Wrongly so, from what I gather," Lawrence said on a kindly note. " 'Tis not what worries me, Morgan. Think of the girl. If she truly be some shipwrecked wretch, her family will demand satisfaction of their honor. If they be local folk or, heaven forbid, gentry, they will already know of your . . . ah, reputation."

"Satan's Son," Morgan said, with a bitter laugh. "I pray they might be more creative. But I see your point, milord."

"Exactly so." Lawrence obviously assumed he had won his case, and heaved a sigh of relief. "I might speak with the Mother Superior at Aberystwyth Abbey, suggest she shelter your guest until further information is found. Despite their pious airs, I've learned the papists ain't adverse to a little bribe now and again."

Offended by the remark, Morgan shook his head. "Thank you, Henry, but I must decline," he said politely. "I have decided Kate will remain here until she is sufficiently recovered to travel. At such time, I will see her removed to London, where I will begin further inquiries into her true identity. In the while, I trust you will keep this matter in strictest confidence."

"Of course. I beg you to reconsider your position, my boy. The life of our queen might be at stake."

"Be that as it may, I will not see Kate questioned by any save myself. Her health is still precarious; such far-fetched accusations could bring on complications."

"Kate? She remembers her name, then?"

Morgan hesitated. " 'Tis what we call her for lack of a proper Christian one." He saw the earl's suspicions were still strong, and immediately devised a plan. "You'll stay the night, of course. 'Tis too long a trip to Cardiff in this dastardly weather. With your permission, I'll bring Kate down to share our evening meal. I want you to meet her yourself, Henry."

Lawrence was surprised, but he agreed. He was curious

about this woman Trelane harbored in his household. He rose with Morgan's assistance, and the two men walked together to the door.

"I'll have Mrs. Carey show you to the guest chamber in the east wing," Morgan said. "Dinner is at six this evening. Will you require a manservant?"

"Nay, I brought my faithful Tibbs with me, though he suffers as badly from gout now as I. Ah, the years are not kind to old men, Morgan. I envy your youth."

And I your face, Morgan thought in turn. He bade the earl a temporary farewell. After Lawrence left, Morgan stood at the window and watched the boiling sea below. 'Twas indeed ironic, he mused. The same sea that had snatched away his mother over two decades ago, in turn gave him Kate to care for.

Six

"Y' are a vision," Winnie proclaimed as she drew the elaborately embroidered saffron gown over Kate's head. Belting it with a bejeweled girdle, she murmured her satisfaction and stepped back.

"Milord Lawrence appreciates courtly fashion, he does. A pity we haven't time to dress your hair, as well."

" 'Tis all right," Kate said quickly, hoping Winnie didn't suggest Gwynneth be invited back to brutalize her poor hair again.

Winnie was already busy in the jewelry box. "Methinks one strand of pearls for a simple yet elegant statement. What say you?"

"I trust your judgment," Kate replied and sensed the older woman beaming at the praise. A moment later, a long rope of pearls settled around her neck, reaching to her waist. She fingered their cool, satiny finish. "Who does this necklace belong to?"

There was the briefest of hesitations. "Lady Trelane. 'Twas her betrothal gift from Lord Trelane's father, I believe."

"What was her Christian name?"

Winnie decided to settle for a half-truth. "Faith, I only knew her as the baron's wife, dear. I was so young when I came to Falcon's Lair."

"Was she comely?" Kate tried to imagine how Morgan's

mother looked, seeking to feel closer to him by encompassing his family, as well.

"Aye. Dark she was, like some Moorish princess. She had a fiery temper, too, and a will as strong as iron."

'Twas hard to imagine such a woman dying young. "How did she and Morgan's father meet, Winnie?"

"I'm sure I wouldn't know, dear. Oh, 'tis already half past. The men will be waiting for us downstairs."

Winnie distracted her charge by leading Kate out of her chamber, down to the great hall. Kate tried to quell her own misgivings by planting a smile upon her lips. She didn't understand why the Earl of Cardiff should wish to meet her, but if Morgan desired her company at the table, she would comply.

She heard two chairs scrape back as the men rose in her presence. Winnie murmured a last reassuring word and left her.

Morgan moved to guide Kate to her seat. "You dim the sun rising over the sea," he complimented her, his gaze lingering on her dark beauty foiled by the golden velvet gown. He was certain Henry Lawrence would not fail to be charmed by Kate.

"Mistress Kate," he said aloud, "may I present the Earl of Cardiff, Henry Lawrence." He turned her in the older man's direction.

"Milord," she said, and started to attempt a curtsy.

"No need, m'dear," Henry Lawrence said, sizing her up and surprised by what he saw. Now he understood why young Trelane was smitten. The wench was lovely, even if her sightless stare was a bit unnerving. Her eyes seemed to gaze right into one's soul. Green they were, a pair of perfectly matched emeralds with a bit of blue flame flickering in the core. He was intrigued.

Morgan assisted Kate with her chair. The first course was brought out. Kate hardly ate, feeling embarrassed by the fact Morgan must sit beside her to help with the uten-

sils, and feeling humiliated by a certainty the earl was
staring at her all the while.

She took a few bites and shook her head when Morgan
offered her a roasted wing of capon. "Please forgive me.
I'm already quite full."

"Why, you hardly ate a thing, m'dear," Lord Lawrence
observed from a short distance away. "Don't you find
Welsh fare to your liking?"

Morgan glanced at the earl, sensing some hidden motive. Kate replied with her customary honesty.

"Nay, milord. The dinner is excellent. I fear I am just
not hungry this evening."

"Her recovery must needs be gradual," Morgan put in
for Lawrence's benefit. "The entire episode was a shock."

"Indeed," Lawrence murmured. "I understand you remember nothing of how you arrived here, Mistress Kate."

Kate hesitated before she answered. "I remember fire,
and rising water," she said at last, faltering at the memory
of her recurring nightmare. "Nothing else. I'm not certain I wish to, either."

"Surely you wish to remember your family," Lawrence
pressed her. He was surprised and a little discomfited
when her intense green eyes flashed in his direction.

"On the contrary, milord. They may have died in the
shipwreck. Then I shall be forced to accept the fact that
I am alone in the world."

Lawrence seemed subdued by Kate's spirited retort,
Morgan noted with satisfaction. The earl cleared his
throat and the meal was finished in virtual silence.

"I trust your fears are absolved," Morgan remarked after Kate had retired for the evening. The two men were
enjoying their spirits and a game of chess in the library.

"I admit I feel somewhat foolish to have imagined a
mere slip of a girl as an enemy of England. Yet there is

something about her story . . . it bothers me." Lawrence paused to take a puff on his cigar, and considered the position of his ivory castle on the parquet table. He moved his bishop instead.

Morgan captured the other man's knight with his ebony queen. "What concerns you specifically, Henry?"

"Her loss of memory. She seems to have knowledge of everything but who she is, where she came from. Why would she forget the most important parts?"

"Perhaps the shipwreck was too traumatic," Morgan suggested. "She must have seen others dying as the ship sank. If, as I suspect, she was traveling with her family, then she watched them drown as well." He didn't mention the fact Kate was found wearing men's clothing, a puzzling and inexplicable fact. 'Twould not serve to allay the earl's misgivings in any way.

Lawrence studied the chessboard a moment more, then sat back with a sigh. "You have me there, my boy. Your father would be proud."

Morgan picked up the pieces and rearranged them in their starting positions. "Would you care for another game?"

"Methinks not." The older man stifled a yawn. " 'Tis growing late and I need to set out early on the morrow. Would you be offended if I retired now?"

"Of course not, Henry." Morgan rose and stretched out his legs. "I confess I am weary myself. Those newborn lambs command a lot of attention."

"Your dedication has always paid off, Morgan. Your wool is the finest in these parts. I insist upon nothing else in my household."

"You are too kind." Lawrence's compliment brought a rare smile to Morgan's face. Had he not been titled at birth, Morgan knew he would have chosen husbandry. Animals were uncritical and undemanding, as his fellow humans were not. He enjoyed caring for the weak and helpless. His smile faded as he thought of Kate upstairs. What a joy she had been to him, how he would miss her when she left. Soon she would be strong again. Strong enough to fly free, like one of his falcons. Soon she would be gone.

"The moment I have any word about your unexpected visitor, I will contact you," Lawrence said, before he retired upstairs. "In the while, please reconsider my suggestion. I believe the girl would be better off in charitable, if need be papist, hands."

Morgan returned an even smile. "What am I if not charitable, Henry? She has nothing to fear from me."

Nothing except my misbegotten affections, he silently added, pausing to take one last stiff shot of golden brandy before he went up to bed.

"Whist, Katie dear, wake up."

Kate felt someone shaking her shoulder. She muttered into the pillows.

"Himself wants you downstairs first thing," Winnie whispered.

Kate stirred and stretched in her bed. She was so tired she still didn't open her eyes. "What time is it?"

"Just past dawn. Himself wishes to know if you feel up to riding."

"Riding?" Kate yawned, certain she hadn't heard aright. "In this beastly weather?"

" 'Tis a rare, lovely spring morn, clear and sunny as a dream. The master thought you might enjoy a bit of fresh air."

Riding with Morgan! Kate's eyes flew open. She was awake. She sat up in bed and self-consciously smoothed her tangled hair. "What can I wear, Winnie?"

"Here's a lovely violet wool trimmed with black braid."

There was also a matching Spanish lace mantilla, but Winnie didn't offer it. "I'll call Gwynneth for your hair."

"Nay, don't. I mean, please, can't you just brush it out for me? There's no need to go to any trouble."

"Nonsense," Winnie pertly replied. "I shan't have you looking anything but splendid today. I can't weave silk ribbons in your tresses like Gwynneth."

Kate braced herself for another assault upon her head, but with Winnie present, the girl didn't step out of line. Soon she wondered if she'd only imagined the previous incident, for Gwynneth was as gentle as a lamb this time. She threaded violet ribbons and silk Parma violets throughout the elegant chignon she sculpted from Kate's thick, dark locks.

Kate's formal hairstyle complimented the chosen attire. The woolen gown sleekly hugged her curves. Its huge slashed sleeves revealed purple silk pane inserts. The skirts were daintily embroidered with violets. Winnie described it to Kate with rising excitement, sounding proud of her charge.

"There, Katie. With your hair out of the way, this light wool cloak, and those sturdy boots, you'll do fine. Now, we'd best hurry. Himself doesn't care to be kept waiting." The housekeeper bustled off.

"Nay," Gwynneth agreed, her tone low and suggestive, for Kate's benefit. "He surely doesn't."

Kate hadn't imagined the animosity, after all. She pretended she hadn't heard the maid's comment. She moved to follow Winnie. Suddenly she tripped and almost sprawled across the hard floor.

"Careful, miss," Gwynneth said with barely concealed malice. "There's another piece of furniture there."

Furniture, indeed! Kate knew she had stumbled across something else—a human foot. Nevertheless, she righted herself with dignity and straightened her skirts.

" 'Tis kind of you to be so watchful for me, Gwynneth,"

she pointedly remarked before Winnie returned to take her arm.

"Oh, dear, I'm so sorry. I keep forgetting you can't see," the older woman apologized.

"Never mind, Winnie. I wasn't hurt."

"Praise the saints. Take my hand, dearie, and I'll take you the rest of the way."

"I'm sorry I'm such a burden," Kate murmured.

"Nonsense. If 'twas any difficulty for me, I'd have let you know it long before this. Here's the railing, now, on the other side."

Kate carefully navigated the stairs, supported by Winnie on one side and a smooth banister on the other. A short while later, she raised her face to the warmth of the sun, inhaled the earthy scent of nearby horses.

"Here she is, milord."

Kate heard Winnie's skirts rustle as she executed a curtsey. The woman departed, and, a moment later, Morgan's greeting warmed her to the core.

"*Faeilean.* You look exceptionally fetching today." He took her hand and she felt a lingering kiss upon it. "I trust you slept well."

"Quite well, thank you. Is the earl with you?"

"No, he left long before sunup. I'm delighted you agreed to join me on a morning ride. 'Tis my usual custom to go a'hawking before the mists rise."

"Falconry? Hunting with birds, is it not?" She turned with interest in his direction. "I've always wondered how it worked. Alas, I fear I shall not be able to appreciate the sport as I wish." She ruefully indicated her eyes.

"Perhaps the sight of a kill would distress you," he suggested.

Kate thought a moment about it. "Nay. I feel I've been hunting before. Knowing you, however, I suspect this excursion is not merely for sport."

"The meat is given to those less fortunate in my demesne," Morgan admitted. The sound of horses' hooves drawing close caused her head to turn.

"Here's Lloyd, now, with our mounts. The place I wish to go hunting, Madoc's Craig, is inaccessible by coach. With your permission, I'll lead your mare behind my steed. She is the gentlest of the lot, the most surefooted as well."

Kate offered him a serene smile. "I trust you completely, milord."

"Morgan," he reminded her.

"Morgan," she echoed. They had reached an understanding again. There was a brief silence. Kate sensed him studying her intently. She welcomed the distraction of a third presence.

"Ailis," Morgan exclaimed. "What brings you out of your domestic domain?"

He whispered aside to Kate, "Ailis has been in charge of Falcon Lair kitchens for nigh the past century. She rarely wanders from her lair. 'Tis but the second time in as many years, I vow."

She suppressed a giggle. The other woman spoke. Ailis's thick Welsh accent was tart and dry.

"Heavens, milord, I was fit to be tied, I was, when I saw ye fixing to 'ead off wi'out so much as a pasty," Cook declared. "Why, what if something should go awry? There's nothing like the comfort of good food on the road."

"Now, Ailis," Morgan said with fond exasperation, "we're headed out for a morning ride, not a fortnight's journey."

Cook sniffed. "Duw, I won't have it said I don't keep ye well fed, milord." There was a rustling sound as she handed something to her master. Kate heard Morgan's good-natured chuckle as he passed it on to Lloyd Carey so it might be secured to one of the saddles.

"Thank you for the basket, Mrs. Taggart," Morgan said,

by way of dismissal. Then, seeing Cook was not about to budge until introductions were made all 'round, he presented Kate.

"Croeso I Cymru, Mistress Kate. Welcome to Wales." The woman's greeting in the old Cymric tongue was friendly, but inquisitive. Kate sensed a pair of eyes taking shrewd stock of her. She knew 'twas important to earn Cook's approval.

"What a thoughtful gesture, Mrs. Taggart," she said warmly. "I should dearly love to sample more of your delicious cooking. It has been a genuine comfort to me from the moment I arrived."

Ailis warmed to the compliment. She sensed it was sincere. "Thank ye, milady. If ye have any favorite dishes, I'd be right pleased to make them for ye."

Kate thanked her again, and Ailis seemed satisfied, for she then departed. After Cook left, Morgan apologized for his retainer's curiosity.

"Oh, I don't mind. They're all such lovely people here. I almost feel as though I've come home."

Morgan did not reply, though she sensed he was pleased. When Kate felt his hands lift her to the mare's back, she thought they were a tad tighter about her waist than propriety decreed, and a bit possessive, too. She settled in the saddle and arranged her skirts.

"You've ridden before," Morgan observed, seeing in Kate's relaxed posture and good bearing, the natural confidence of one raised with horses.

"Have I?" she mused. "Yes, I'm certain you're right. I trow it feels familiar to me." She leaned forward to stroke the mare's neck. "What is the horse's name?"

"Patches, I believe."

"What color is she?"

Morgan studied the mare for a moment and released a chuckle. "I believe her name accounts for most of the colors."

A sweet peal of laughter rang off the stone walls surrounding the outer ward. Morgan doubted the place had heard its equal in many centuries. Kate's laughter warmed his blood. He smiled a little, his spirits lifting.

"Then I may assume she is kept for her good nature, rather than her beauty?" Kate inquired.

"Assume what you wish but, rest assured, Patches is not so sore a nag that you would be ashamed to be seen upon her," he replied. "Lloyd selected her for you because she is of a mild disposition, and well complements my stallion."

Kate tilted her head towards the second pair of hooves impatiently raking the cobbled drive. "He sounds high-spirited."

"He is. Patches here shall keep Idris content, long enough for you and I to relax and enjoy our morning ride. They are mates, you see."

Kate heard the creak of saddle leather as Morgan swung up on the stallion. His deep, steady voice soothed the animal. When Patches lapsed into a slow walk, Kate cupped her hands around her own high pommel for extra security.

Even though she was still blind, Kate could tell 'twas a beautiful morning. Winter's last kiss flushed her cheeks, teasing several curls loose from her chignon. She raised her face to the delicious warmth of the sun. The variations in light and dark were becoming more distinct, as was her excitement. She dared hope she would see again, and soon. The first person she intended to look at was Morgan. She would not be content until the man of her dreams had a face, as well as a name.

They rode in companionable silence until Morgan announced their destination: a high-mountain meadow wreathed with mist, framed by the bosom of Madoc's Craig. He described the great, slate-colored mountain rising before them, a lonely behemoth upon the valley floor.

To reach the mountain, they were forced to ride along a narrow cliff-side precipice. Morgan was confident of the trip. He had made it many times.

Morgan described the meadow and the wild Welsh countryside to Kate with all the enthusiasm and natural talent of a bard. Thanks to his colorful description, Kate easily imagined the harsh gray cliffs rising above a frothing blue sea and Cader Idris towering in the distance like a white volcano. Spring saffron, lavender, and the pungent scent of wild fennel lining the path up the mountain added to her mental picture of paradise. Only the image of Morgan remained indistinct, a blurred vision of heaven she knew she must be content to wait for.

Morgan was lost in thought, as well. Frequent glances over his shoulder reassured him of Kate's safety, yet also had an underlying motive. He never tired of drinking in her natural beauty; the half smile playing about her lips seemed almost provocative. Kate was enjoying herself, he saw. She seemed fearless today, utterly trusting in him. The realization swept a wave of emotion over him.

Mayhap he was falling in love? Morgan quelled the mad notion at once. He assured himself he was merely desperate to snatch up the first crumbs of kindness any woman tossed him. He felt a tic of irritation tug at his cheek and wrenched his hungry gaze from Kate. From then on, he gazed steadfastly ahead.

"Down you come, *Faeilean.*"

Hands on Morgan's shoulders to steady herself, Kate leaned into him as he lowered her to the ground. He did not immediately release his grip on her waist. He steadied her against his chest, and she felt the butter-soft velvet of his doublet beneath her palms. Then the mare jostled them and restored reality, and Morgan set her down.

"I'll lead you over to the rocks. I'm sure you'd prefer to sit, whilst I ready the bird."

Kate had forgotten all about the hawking. She felt breathless from the moment she was in Morgan's arms. "Aye," she agreed, wishing she might amend the word when his hand released her waist. He took her hand instead and guided her to a large boulder where she might perch out of the way. She reached out and felt warmed stone beneath her fingers. It felt delicious to sit under the blessed warmth of the sun; it seemed she had been so cold for so long. Despite the pleasure of the outing, she discovered she missed Morgan's company when he left to ready his falcon.

Kate heard him secure the horses nearby. Then a faint, harsh scream raised gooseflesh on her arms.

"I call her 'Ironbreaker,' " Morgan said. Kate realized he referred to his bird. "She broke free of the manacles her former owner kept her in. Not once, but twice. The second time, I found her on my property, suffering from abrasions and a broken wing. When the owner turned up to claim her, I sent the brute packing. She's a devil, this bird. I wager it makes her a proper Trelane."

"Nay." Kate protested. She heard the gyrfalcon scrabbling for a hold on his leather glove, and imagined its proud, fierce glare swiveling in her direction when she spoke. Mayhap the bird was blinded by a hood, unable to see her, yet she sensed its presence strongly.

"You're no devil," she added, for Morgan's sake. Though he was silent, she knew he heard what she said. "No devil would care for a complete stranger as you have me."

Still, Morgan did not reply. Instead he turned to concentrate upon the day's hunting. He did not trust himself to respond to Kate's observation. There was no true generosity in his heart, he knew—merely selfishness. The same selfishness kept him from searching too urgently for Kate's family or her true identity. He wanted her here, with him. Heaven curse him for his actions, but he could not bear to let her go. Not yet.

He spotted his quarry: a brace of red grouse in a nearby copse. He signaled Ironbreaker with a high-pitched whistle and tore the hood from her head. The magnificent predator let out a shrill cry as she rose from his hand and unfurled her golden-buff wings. True as an arrow, the gyrfalcon soared toward the sun, higher and higher in a dizzying spiral, until she gazed down upon her hapless prey.

Morgan watched with mixed emotions. Usually the hunt exhilarated him, entertained his mind long enough for him to avoid any more painful forages into his memory. This time, he was distracted. His gaze slid from the bird to Kate seated nearby, her skirts spread out over the mossy rock in a violet pool. She held her face to the sky as if she watched the hunt in progress. A smile danced upon her lips. Damme those lips. They haunted him day and night. As he already well knew, they were red as snow berries and twice as sweet. . . .

High above them, Ironbreaker let out a triumphant scream. Morgan saw Kate shiver at the sound. He did not know her spasm of fear issued not from the sound itself, but rather from the sudden memory it evoked.

A man's agonized face flashed before Kate's mind. She saw his hands thrashing about as he tread water, his mouth gaping open in a terrible plea. *Help me, colleen* . . .

She rose from the boulder, trembling violently.

"Faeilean?" she heard Morgan ask with concern. Yet his voice came to her as if from far away, fading fast into the background. Memories rushed down on her like the screaming bird above them, tumbling her about in a surf of invisible agony. She gasped for air as her hands paddled frantically against the rising water in her mind. Rain! 'Twas raining, a vicious downpour from angry black skies. Her weary arms churned the icy waves, as wooden boards

and loose debris from the ship smashed against her from all sides. She saw a head bob to the surface beside her, heard a man's faint cry as his hands flailed in her direction. *Help me . . .*

Morgan saw Kate's hands rise to her own throat, as if she fought for each breath of air. She made strangled, choking sounds. He ran towards her. She managed a faint scream as he grabbed her and held her in his arms. A terrible wail issued from her throat.

"Rory!"

Her cry shook him to the core. 'Twas full of despair—a terror so great, he almost shuddered at the intensity of it.

"Kate, what is it?"

She fought off Morgan's restraining hands. She did not hear him at all. Her mind was elsewhere, caught up in a spinning vortex of icy water and burning fire.

In her tortured mind's eye, she fought against the surging waves of sea water separating her from another man.

"Help me! I dinna know how to swim, Kat . . ."

"Rory," she cried again. The sea water was cold, so frightfully cold. Gradually her desperate battle against the brutal waves ebbed to cramping pains instead.

"Nay," she screamed, over and over. She reached in vain towards the drowning man, watching helplessly and horror-stricken as the waves closed one last time over that beloved auburn head. Rory's flailing hands slipped beneath the churning seafoam—forever.

Morgan supported her as Kate crumpled to her knees. Deep, wrenching sobs wracked her body. He could do little more than hold her tightly as he joined her there, kneeling on the grass.

Who was Rory? Morgan wondered again, when she quieted and nestled like a quivering fawn against him. Her brother? Father? *Husband?* The last possibility sent a jolt of pain through him. 'Twould make her a widow, at any rate. Fair game. Morgan was chagrined and ashamed by his own thoughts.

"Kate, what do you remember?" he demanded when he determined she was calm enough to respond. "Tell me what you saw."

The reminder sent another shudder through her. She raised her tear-streaked face to his, green eyes glittering like peridot.

"I remember," she whispered, and was silent long enough for him to become frightened, "I remember watching him drown."

Morgan swallowed hard. *Dear Jesu.* Yet he had to know. "Who, Kate?"

"Rory. 'Tis all I know. His name, his face. Sweet Jesu, his face." She shut her eyes and he watched tears seep beneath her lashes. "I remember he called me 'Kat.' Not Kate . . . Kat. 'Tis similar to the name you've given me, for lack of any other."

Morgan did not answer her. She forged on, choking on her tears.

" 'Twas horrible, Morgan. Rory begged me to help him. He couldn't swim well, you see, but I couldn't . . . couldn't hold him up. . . ." Her words rose to a keen of pure agony, a sound to rend the heart of the heartless. "Ahh, Jesu, why did I fail him?"

"Ssh, *Faeilean,* it does no good to blame yourself," Morgan murmured as he stroked her head. Her shaking subsided a bit at the sound of his voice. He always had the power to calm her thus. Trelane magic, they might have called it, centuries ago; now 'twas nothing less than a curse. Morgan's voice thickened as he continued speaking to her in a soothing vein.

"The sea is a beautiful, yet fickle, mistress, so man is always at her mercy. Even today, when she seems benign and peaceful, there is always the chance she will turn on him and render both he and his measly ship afloat."

"Yea, I know it. There is something more to this, I fear . . . something evil," Kat added. She clutched the front of his doublet as if he might save her from drowning, as well. Gently, Morgan pried her hands free and held them in his grasp.

"Listen to me. You are starting to remember the accident. I vow, it will come back to you, whether you want it to or not. You will be frightened, you may even be beyond terror at some point. Yet you must always come to me. I want you to promise me . . . Kate, Kat, my precious *cariad*. Come to me."

"Aye," she whispered, relieved. "Yea, Morgan, I will."

Seven

Kat's lips parted, ever so slightly. She tilted her head back in an obvious invitation to a kiss. With aching tenderness, Morgan touched his mouth to hers. He felt her sag with utter trust and relief against him. Her breasts pressed against his doublet, violet wool and forest-green velvet the only barriers between them.

Sweet. So sweet. Morgan's mind whirled with so many emotions, agony among them. Jesu, she was ripe for loving. He claimed her mouth with rising urgency, lowering them both into a grassy pool speckled with wildflowers. Her hands molded his face as they kissed. Morgan forgot the bane of his face, forgot all but the piercing waves of pleasure slamming over his body.

When he raised his lips from hers, her eyes were slitted in cat-like fashion against the bright light.

"Oh, my love," she whispered. There was awe as well as great joy in her voice. "I never imagined—"

"Nor I," Morgan replied, gazing with hunger upon Kat's serene face, wanting to memorize forever how she looked at this moment. 'Twas all he would ever have. His hand moved along her shoulder, slid down to her hip, and nestled comfortably in the curves nature had provided.

Kat wondered what he was thinking. Was Morgan as surprised as she to discover the depth, the intensity of their love? The simplicity, the absolute wonder of it. She wanted to shout with happiness, swoon with joy. They had no end of time to explore the wonder of it all.

"Morgan," she murmured. "Kiss me again."

'Twas both a demand and a plea. He decided if a single day must last him a lifetime, he might as well make the most of this one.

"With pleasure, *cariad.*" She was no longer just his lost seagull; she was his beloved, as well. His mouth slanted down upon hers, and passion swiftly rose again, so powerfully that he was helpless against its onslaught.

Morgan's fingers trembled as he unhooked Kat's bodice. A sheer lawn camisole hardly concealed her breasts from his gaze. If ever woman was perfection, she was. He ducked his head to capture a rosy nipple through the material and worried it with his teeth. Kat gasped, arched up against him with the newly found pleasure. Her fingers threaded through his hair as she urged him onward with hungry little cries.

"Aye!" Her tone was urgent, pleading. "Love me, Morgan."

He had every intention of doing so. From shattering grief to pure ecstasy, they both might fly as swift and true as Ironbreaker, now. Morgan eased down the lacy straps of the camisole, freeing her breasts to his admiring gaze. They were lovely, flawless, as was the rest of her. He painted them with his tongue. With his teeth, he drew upon the nipples until they were hard as rubies and twice as red and throbbed as insistently as his own maleness.

Kat shifted restlessly against him, drawing him up to her lips again. "Oh, Morgan," she murmured. Her half-closed eyes never seemed more seductive nor intense than they were at this moment. "I must tell you something. I lo—"

"Ssh, *cariad.*" Morgan cut off her confession with a swift, emphatic kiss. "Not now. I'll not see you tumbled quick as a country wench in a haystack. Come, let me help you right your clothing. I'll set out the repast Ailis made for us. I find salt air does increase the appetite, after all."

Surprised, Kat thought Morgan's abrupt departure from lovemaking must be due to propriety rather than conscience. She imagined he would have some explaining to do, indeed, if one of his serfs stumbled across the mighty baron rolling in his own fields. She giggled at the thought.

"Aye," she said reluctantly. "Let's sample the food, milord. Whether the salt air increased my appetite or not, I confess I find myself ravenous."

She accepted Morgan's steadying hand as she rose. By necessity, his assistance was also needed to rehook her bodice. Properly restored now, all but for her crushed chignon, Kat waited while Morgan fetched the luncheon basket. She heard him whistle three times. His call elicited a distant, thin cry and Ironbreaker's return. She repressed a shiver at the memories the sound evoked. Why a mere bird should upset her so, triggering such a strange and painful recollection, Kat might never know. She should be overjoyed to have a glimpse of her past, no matter how tortured. The pieces were beginning to fall in place, yet she somehow mourned the loss of innocence.

Morgan barely glanced at the bloody grouse Ironbreaker brought back. He tossed it into a saddlebag, anxious to return to Kat. He hooded the gyrfalcon and secured her on Idris's saddle before he returned to Kat's side.

There in the meadow, beneath snow-capped Madoc's Craig, the two of them feasted on Welsh mountain lamb roasted in honey; fried laverbread made from boiled, chopped seaweed and oatmeal; and a hard, sharp cheese. Ailis had provided a bottle of sweet white wine with two silver goblets. For once, Kat didn't feel humiliated as Morgan fed her. She even nipped playfully at his fingers several times. She captured his index finger between her lips and sucked upon it for a moment. He tasted of the wine he had spilled on his hands when he opened the bottle. He groaned at the sensuous action, but freed his finger at first opportunity.

"Greedy wench," he teased her, and she detected a tremor in his voice. "If you're so hungry, mayhap we should return to Falcon's Lair so I can ensconce you in my larder right quick."

Kat laughed. "My hunger might be appeased in an easier manner, milord."

"More expedient, perhaps, though not easier."

Gazing into her sparkling green eyes, Morgan drew a fortifying breath of air. 'Twas getting harder and harder to distance his emotions. He forced his gaze away from Kat's flushed face. He knew she would not deny him complete conquest, if he so desired. It only made him feel worse.

Sensing his downturn of mood, her smile faded. "Have I offended you somehow, Morgan?"

"Nay, of course not."

"What, then? Everything seemed fine until—"

A whinny captured their attention. Kat heard Morgan leap to his feet. She also heard the nearby, panicked bugle of the stallion, and a sense of foreboding washed over her.

"What is it?"

"Get down, Kat. Get down and stay down." Morgan thrust her unceremoniously to the grass. She lay rigid but obedient, knowing his gift of sight revealed dangers she could not appreciate. *Someone was nearby. Hurting the horses?*

"Morgan?" A spiraling fear clutched her. Kat moaned, half in pain, half in fear.

Oh, Morgan, pray be careful, she thought. Beads of sweat

broke out on her brow. She heard an angry shout, and judged it to be Morgan's. Then came the terrifying sound of a violent struggle nearby. She thought she heard a body fall. *Nay!* her mind screamed. She froze for a brief instant, engulfed in dark waves of horror and dread.

"Morgan!" She tried to scream, yet her voice emerged a mere croak, whisked away by the brisk wind on the mountain. She began to crawl on all fours, hand over hand, her senses honed keen by the bitter taste of fear. She heard hoofbeats galloping away into the distance. They faded, yet her resolve did not.

"Morgan," she called out again, this time in a stronger voice. "Sweet Jesu, answer me."

There was no reply save the rustling of the grass and the whicker of a horse—Patches. A keener sense of direction surfaced, and Kat headed toward the spot where she guessed the mare was hobbled. She paused when the horse stirred again. She might easily be trampled, and there was no way for her to ride the mare for help. Her fists clenched in frustration. Where in heaven's name was Morgan?

She was afraid she knew. She heard a faint groan issue from the direction of the cliff. Gathering courage into one solid knot in her mind, she started to crawl again. Her long skirts hampered her and snagged in various places along the way. Tears of frustration rose to choke her. Brambles scratched her hands, her face. She struggled along, gaining only the prick of thorns for her efforts.

The sea. 'Twas close now. Kat paused, sniffing the salt tang with apprehension. It threatened to bring a deeper fear to the surface again. The ship, the fire, the merciless sea. No! She forcibly blocked out the memory of Rory's dying cries, the vision of angry waves closing over his head. 'Twas the past. There was much more at stake here and now, her future: Morgan. He needed her. Inch by inch, Kat crawled closer to the cliff's edge.

She found a boot first and followed it up the leg. She groped her way up the fallen body, then hesitated when she realized it might be someone other than Morgan. Finally, her fingers crossed the familiar velvet of his doublet. She leaned down and sniffed, just to be sure. Morgan's scent was distinctive. Wool, horseflesh, wild mint. Aye, 'twas him. She felt relieved, then suffered a pang of fear again. His doublet was wet. Blood?

"Morgan," she whispered.

He groaned and stirred slightly. He was not dead. Kat's hopes were dashed when she realized she had no way of summoning those at Falcon's Lair for help. She and Morgan were trapped high in the meadow beneath Madoc's Craig, alone. Or perhaps they were not alone at all; mayhap someone watched them, even now.

Kat shivered. She felt an icy wind rush down off the mountain, yanking at her hair and skirts—winter's last kiss, or spring's subtle taunt. 'Twas foolish to risk moving Morgan herself, without the benefit of sight. Her tumbling thoughts were interrupted by yet another realization: Beneath her braced hand, earth crumbled and fell away.

Sweet Jesu! They teetered right on the cliff's edge. She reeled backward with fear and caught herself at the last second. Any disturbance, however slight, might cause the entire shelf beneath them to give way. Kat swallowed and waited to feel the ground before shifting again. 'Twas eerily silent, save for the furious roar of the wind, plucking at her skirts. Not even birds sang in the trees.

Which way? Kat pondered the matter. Bit by bit, she crawled backwards on her hands and knees, down to Morgan's feet. She wrapped her hands around his ankles and tugged. But she was blind and he was too heavy for her to drag more than a few inches. A sob of frustration broke from her throat. A second later, she heard another rock crack loose from the cliff and drop to smash against the boulders far below.

Patches snorted as if disgusted, observing Kat's antics on the cliff. The curious mare had wandered closer. A sudden idea was spawned in Kat's mind. Home! Loose horses usually went home. They made a beeline for the stables, where they knew warmth and food awaited them. When a riderless horse appeared at Falcon's Lair, someone was bound to come investigate.

A surge of hope rose in Kat. She continued to back up until she was clear of the dangerous cliff and closer to the mare.

How to capture Patches without getting kicked or killed in the endeavor? Kat rose, licked her dry lips, and started out, arms outstretched as wide as they would go. She crooned to elicit the mare's interest. She heard Patches snuffle, dismissing her presence, and resume grazing. Once Kat was reasonably certain of the animal's location, she bent and tore up handfuls of the lush grass near the cliff's edge.

"Here, colleen. A rare treat for you now."

Proffering the grass in front of her, Kat moved forward. She stumbled, righted herself, and continued walking. She almost wept with relief when she felt the mare bump her arm and begin to lip at her offering.

"Good girl," she said, sniffing back useless tears. "Run home and get help. If you will, I promise you, you can have all the grain you want."

Kat ran her hands down her mount's front legs, locating the hobbles Morgan had secured there. One was already broken. Her fingers undid the other knot with difficulty. She was aware of the danger, her face so near the deadly hooves. Fortunately Patches was, as Morgan had promised, an agreeable sort of beast. The mare chomped placidly upon the grass. Once free, however, Patches made no immediate move to leave.

Time was of the essence. Kat regretted the necessity of her actions, yet there was not a moment to be lost. She estimated where the horse's rump lay and lashed out with the flat of her palm. The stinging slap sent poor Patches thundering off, as she'd hoped. Would the animal simply circle back to resume grazing in the rich meadow?

Kat held her breath and waited for the sound of returning hoofbeats. She almost wept with relief when they didn't come. Maybe there was a chance, after all. She dropped to her knees again and began the tedious crawl back to Morgan's side. She was with him, come what may. If he died, the cliff might serve such a convenient purpose for her, as well.

Lloyd Carey was the first one to spot the mare trotting back towards Falcon's Lair. The stable master always kept an eye out for the Master's horseflesh. He recognized Patches at once. When he sized up the dragging reins and empty saddle, he set off at a run.

Patches's ears pricked forward, as she caught wind of her handler's scent. Lloyd was a kindly master; she came willingly to his whistle. After he secured her in the stable with buckets of warm mash and water, Lloyd set out on a fresh mount with a brace of men at his side.

His wife had suggested where Lord Trelane might have gone. Luckily, Winnie was right. The men from Falcon's Lair rode into a scene from a nightmare. Rigor mortis had already set into Trelane's black stallion. Ironbreaker had soared free, her jesses broken in the scuffle. The Master himself was stretched out unmoving on the crumbling lip of a cliff.

Then Lloyd noticed the young lady. At first he thought

she was dead, too. She lay unmoving beside Trelane, her arm wrapped about the Master's waist. As Lloyd approached, he saw her eyes open, and her body tensed at the sound of his footsteps.

" 'Tis Lloyd Carey," he announced from a few feet away. "What in the name of Our Blessed Mother Mary has happened here?"

Kat almost wept with gratitude and told him as much as she knew. Her concern for Morgan was first and foremost. She waited, with baited breath, while Lloyd knelt and examined his master.

" 'S'blood," Lloyd exclaimed with dismay, as he studied the gaping wound in Trelane's chest. "He's been stabbed, miss. Brigands, were they now?"

Kat shook her head, frustrated. "I don't know. I only heard the horse scream, then Morgan shout. Mayhap they were trying to steal the horses and he stopped them."

Lloyd grunted at her useless recollection. 'Twas not the girl's fault she could not see. She obviously didn't know the Master's horse had been stabbed, too, and now lay dead. He didn't see any purpose in telling her. Instead he reached out and gently grasped her arm.

"Come along, Katie, away with you. One of my men will take you back now."

"Morgan—" she began to argue.

"I'll see to milord, never you mind. 'Tis a sore wound, to be sure, but not mortal. I've dressed worse before."

Kat sagged with relief when Lloyd Carey took calm control of the situation. His voice was gravelly, yet not unkind. She allowed herself to be led away by one of his men. Though still in shock, she would never forget the return ride to Falcon's Lair, the nightmare of being impersonally handed up and down from a horse by invisible hands, removed from any knowledge of Morgan's welfare.

Even Winnie's familiar, soothing croon and warm embrace did not banish the fear in Kat's heart. Winnie confirmed Morgan's safe return to Falcon's Lair a short while later, yet told Kat little more than the fact that he still lived.

"His lordship needs his rest, he does," Winnie repeated after Kat's third request to go to Morgan's side. "As do you, Katie dear."

"Call me 'Kat,' please. At last I've started to recall my past."

"Kat, then. 'Tis a sorry day, to be sure." Winnie clucked her tongue.

"Morgan's dying, isn't he? That's why you won't let me go to him."

"Now, why would you think such a thing?" Winnie sounded shocked and hurt. " 'Tis for the best if the both of you get some peace and quiet."

Kat was not convinced. She threw off the quilts Winnie had wrapped her in before the fire and stood up.

"I am going to him," she announced. "Kindly show me the way, or by all the saints, I vow I shall scream until you do."

"Oh, dear," Winnie murmured. She sighed with surrender, then moved to take Kat's hand.

"Come along, then. I see no point in arguing."

"Most sensible of you," Kat agreed. She accompanied the woman down the hall to Morgan's bedchamber. Winnie entered without knocking.

"How is he?" Winnie asked a third party present.

Kat was shocked and a little jealous to hear the maid Gwynneth reply.

"He'll live," the girl said. Kat sensed Gwynneth's gaze scouring her from head to toe. "Utter foolishness, if you ask me. Riding out alone . . ."

" 'Twas a lovely day," Winnie interrupted in a mild tone. "One can't blame himself for wanting a brief respite from the lambing. How is the wound? Let me see."

Kat chafed with silent frustration while Winnie examined Morgan's injury and murmured her approval of its care.

"We'll change the dressing in the morn, Gwynneth. Mix up a paste of marigold and comfrey for me tonight. 'Tis a right angry wound, yet seems to be healing already."

"Has he wakened yet?" Kat asked.

"Aye," Gwynneth answered. "I gave him some sleeping herbs so he might rest again. He shouldn't be disturbed." There was a warning in her flat tone.

Weary of the girl's constant challenges, Kat decided to meet this one without reserve. "I'll sit with him now, Gwynneth. There's no need for you to stay."

There was a stricken, challenging silence. In the end Winnie asked Gwynneth to leave with her and help Cook with supper. Not daring to dispute her superior, Gwynneth moved to depart. The last look she threw at Kat before she left was nothing short of hate-filled. Kat didn't have to see it. She felt it clear down to her bones.

At the sound of the door closing, Morgan stirred. As he roused to full consciousness, he felt cool fingers move across his brow.

"You're safe now, my love," Kat whispered, relishing for a moment the reversal of their roles, the sensation of his smooth skin under her fingertips. She rather liked the role of caretaker. 'Twas preferable to that of the invalid.

"Faeilean?" he murmured drowsily, to her delight.

"Aye. Don't try to rise." Kat felt his muscular shoulders bunch and strain beneath her hands, and she eased him back against the bolsters. "You've been hurt, Morgan. A chest wound, though fortunately it struck no vital organs."

"I was stabbed," he reflected with some surprise. She

imagined his eyes were open now, if a trifle sleepy from the herbs. Then he remembered all. "Idris! Damme them!"

"Them?"

Morgan laughed, a bitter sound. "Aye, Kat, there were more than one. I've noticed cowards always travel in packs, like bloody wolves."

"I don't understand."

"They killed my horse, *Faeilean*. They murdered Idris right before my eyes."

Kat gasped in horror and outrage. "Dear Jesu, why?"

She felt his shoulders shrug beneath her hands. "Because I'm a peer. Because I'm their master and they resent it." *Because of my cursed face,* Morgan added silently.

"Why attack you, too?"

"An opportune moment, I daresay. They had me alone. There was a good chance I'd die before help arrived. No, perhaps all was not planned. I'd wager, we were followed there. I believe 'twas a warning of sorts."

"Of sorts, indeed! What manner of men would abuse their lord so? Oh, Morgan, I've heard nothing but good about you since I arrived at Falcon's Lair. I refuse to believe you are cruel or unfair to those in your care. These men must be sorely misled."

"Misled or not, they take their grudge quite seriously." He released a weak laugh, and tensed with pain. "Jesu, what I wouldn't give for a draught of my own fine brandy right now."

"How can you be so cavalier?" Kat cried. "Your fine stallion was murdered and you were attacked and almost died, but for the grace of God. I shall not entertain such thoughts any longer, Morgan Trelane." To the surprise of both of them, she burst into sudden sobs.

"Ahhh, *cariad.* Don't." Morgan's hand stroked her bent head. "I'm not worth the tears. Hush now, and come up here beside me."

Still sniffling, Kat lay alongside him in the bed, on top of the covers rather than beneath, yet close enough for Morgan to awkwardly drape his arm about her shoulders.

"There. That's better. Already I feel a new man."

She gave a grudging chuckle and gently poked his arm. "You're not out of the woods yet, sirrah."

"Morgan," he reminded her, punctuating his Christian name with a kiss upon her forehead. "Stay here with me, get some rest. For some reason I suspect you've had precious little of it until now."

"I couldn't sleep, not knowing if you were suffering or wanted me by your side," she confessed. "I decided I had to be with you, no matter what Winnie said."

"The cliff," Morgan remarked. "You were there, too."

"D'you remember what happened?"

"I heard you weeping. I tried to speak, tell you to get away. The ledge might have given way at any moment."

"It didn't. Nothing, Morgan—*nothing* would have induced me to leave you."

Kat's fierce resolve touched something in Morgan's soul, something buried so deep, he had thought it did not exist. He knew it for what it was, then: Love. A tentative thread of hope took hold in his heart.

"*Cariad,*" he murmured, shifting onto his side and ignoring the stab of pain which shot to his toes. "My little, lost beloved." He concentrated upon her lips instead, a lush source of comfort Kat seemed inclined to offer him again.

Those green eyes were shuttered to him now, yet Morgan sensed the love shining in them. "I started to tell you in the meadow, Morgan—I love you. Do with it what you will; neither of us can wish the truth away."

"Nor do I wish to," he confessed, before his mouth closed over hers.

From the doorway where the hinge was cracked, Gwynneth watched the tender love scene unfold through narrowed eyes. The pulse in her temple beat in rhythm with the clenched fist upon her thigh.

"Agatha Owen, a word with you."

The elderly woman tending the peat fire straightened and pressed a gnarled hand to her crooked back. "Gwynneth, child." Her face lit with pleasure; this girl was her granddaughter, albeit a bastard. "You have not come to visit me in a great while. Tell me, what news of Falcon's Lair and the Master?"

"I have no time for gossip, old woman." Gwynneth's words were insolent, her tone impatient. "I know you read the signs, you warned those at the keep. The woman came, just as you said."

"Did she, now?" Agatha's voice trembled. Realizing Gwynneth had no true interest in her welfare, she turned to tend the fire again.

"You said she would come from the sea. A daughter of the raven, fair of face and form. One who would make Trelane forget himself."

There was no reply, save the crackling and popping of the fire in the little cottage grate.

"Are you listening, old woman? God's teeth, you aren't going deaf, I hope."

"Nor blind," Agatha murmured, more to herself than to her visitor.

"Then you know even more than you have told the others. *She* is blind. For all her beauty, she is helpless and blind as one of his newborn lambs, just as he is helpless and blind to her intentions." Gwynneth's disgust was obvious. *So, too, is her raging jealousy,* Agatha thought. In this much, Gwynneth resembled her mother, Cairis. Agatha's only daughter had spawned this wicked child a year before her death. 'Twas almost as if Cairis herself had been reborn in the challenging gaze and insolent manner of the girl. Unfortunately, Gwynneth also inherited some of her mother's talents. Pray, not Cairis's ability to rouse dark spirits, yet enough natural skill in the old ways to make trouble for those who crossed her.

"How can I get rid of her?" Gwynneth demanded.

Agatha shuddered, and glanced from the fire into the equally flaming eyes of her granddaughter. "You cannot destroy the Morrigan, nor her chosen ones. 'Twould be foolish to even try."

Gwynneth snorted with disdain. "She is nothing, a blind little nobody. He fancies he loves her, but he does not know what love is."

"Not yet, perhaps," Agatha vaguely conceded.

"Then you have seen the future. Your talent is not gone, as you claimed." Triumphantly, Gwynneth pounced on this promising note. "She is not meant to have him."

"Neither are you, child. Far greater things are at work here. You must bide the wishes of the Lord and Lady."

"They will not help me. I will not wait." With this flat announcement, Gwynneth spun on her heel and departed from the cottage.

"Do not, child, for the sake of your immortal soul." Agatha called after the girl, her voice strong despite her age. She knew Gwynneth heard her, but her granddaughter did not return. She shuddered. Not even the fire warmed her old bones. Fate was at work here, in all its deadly guises.

Henry Lawrence heard about Morgan's injury by accident. The earl had not gone directly home as planned. Upon leaving Falcon's Lair, he made a roundabout course through Birmingham, where he visited a number of his cronies and shared in the latest Tudor gossip.

Always a staunch supporter of the queen, Lawrence was disturbed to hear about the latest development in Trelane's household during his fortnight away. Even in rural Wales, news of such shocking incidents spread rapidly, and Lawrence could not quell his earlier suspicions. They returned to the fore, insistent as ever. In his mind, there was no coincidence between Morgan almost being killed, and the odd circumstances of the young woman washed up on the beach. None at all. He believed there to be a papist plot underway and was determined to see it brought up short.

What if the wench charmed Trelane into marrying her on his deathbed? Lawrence hadn't heard any details about the stabbing, but he was certain the girl had co-conspirators hiding somewhere and was waiting for the opportunity to weasel her way into the Tudor court. A baron's wife, even a lowly Welsh one, had right, by title, to petition the queen.

Suppose the jade was clever enough to get a ring on her finger and prettily beg Elizabeth Tudor for an audience. Lawrence knew his queen was just; Bess would not refuse to see a widow, especially one so recently bereaved. Assassination would therefore be easy. Given Spain's irrational behavior of late, 'twas not unlikely. What better way to usurp the English throne?

It gave Lawrence stomach pains to consider the many possibilities. He was further concerned, recalling young Trelane's heritage. Though 'twas kept mum, the fact that Morgan was half-Spanish must not be overlooked now. Perhaps Trelane, too, was somehow involved. It could not be denied, the man was a recluse given to strange behavior and suspicious company.

However he looked at it, Lawrence saw his duty was clear. It included alerting the royal council, and if need be, Queen Elizabeth herself. He ordered Tibbs to pack his trunks. When asked by his cronies, he said he was headed by way of London to give his annual regards to Dear Bess.

Eight

"Morgan, you must listen to reason. 'Tis too early for you to be walking about. If I must have Lloyd Carey tie you down in bed, so be it."

Morgan listened with a faint smile to the threats Kat hurled down at him. He wasn't about to be hobbled in bed for another two weeks. He was a man who craved fresh air and exercise; a fortnight of mollycoddling from his various caretakers was quite enough.

"Mrs. Carey assures us the wound has sealed shut," he said when Kat finished her lecture. "There's no excuse for me to lie abed when there's so much work to be done."

Kat controlled her temper with effort. Though she made out only a blurred visage of Morgan, she knew him to be amused by her mothering instincts. "I don't care. You're not getting up. 'Tis final, sirrah." She yanked the covers up over him with a flourish and froze in place when he captured her hand.

"Sit and stay awhile, *cariad.*"

Morgan's deep voice held a plea. She stood there in indecision. This fortnight had been pure agony for her, because she loved him so. Morgan almost made love to her several times, yet for reasons unbeknownst to her, he always stopped. She assumed 'twas because of her blindness, or her lowly status. Neither reason was soothing to her fragile ego.

"I'll stay, on one condition," she said. "You'll remain abed the rest of the week without arguing."

"There's my Kat." She heard amusement in his voice. "Do whatever you can to win the day. Sit, then, and I'll read some more to you."

When she started to pull up a chair, Morgan corrected her. "Here."

He patted the ample space in the bed beside him. Her brow furrowed, but she obediently sat down to listen to a passage from *The Winter's Tale:*

> *When daffodils begin to peer,*
> *With heigh! the doxy over the dale*
> *Why, then comes in the sweet o' the year;*
> *For the red blood reigns in the winter's pale.*

Kat shivered at the mention of blood. Sensing her distress, Morgan chose some merry ditties and short limericks instead, eliciting a grudging smile from her lips. Then he read her more serious prose, including an ancient love ballad. As the romantic words flowed into the room, Kate's color rose.

"I must get some air," she murmured, and started to rise.

"You'll never find the window." Morgan's hand grasped her forearm. "Stay and hear the rest. It means a great deal to me."

Kat was hurt, and a little angered, by the request. She knew her heart was breaking. Morgan must know she loved him. Hearing him read words of love and promise aloud only made her ache all the more. Apparently, she meant nothing more to him than another lost, injured animal. Why didn't she accept her fate?

"As you wish, milord," she replied, pointedly reminding them both of their difference in status. She heard the book slam shut.

"I'll endure no more of this churlish behavior," Morgan said, sounding grim. "We must talk, Kat."

"If you wish."

"Aye, milady, I do." She felt his fingers lift her chin, forcing her to face him. "Tell me about your anger."

"I'm not angry."

"Yea, you are. I see it flashing in your sea-green eyes, Kat, as a summer squall appears on the horizon. What have I done to displease you?"

"Nothing," she said, attempting to rise. Morgan restrained her again, and brought her back down beside him.

"Then why are you trying to escape me?"

"I'm not," she muttered. "I'm trying to leave so you can get some rest."

"Y'are a poor liar, Kat, and a worse martyr. Nay, there is something powerful troubling you, and I vow I shall not rest till you tell me what it is."

"All right," she burst out, her pride pricked by his remorseless stance. "I shall tell you, then. Nigh a fortnight ago, I foolishly confessed my love for you, Morgan Trelane. Since then naught has been the same between us."

His momentary silence was not reassuring. "What do you mean, Kat? I thought nothing amiss."

"Aye, I trow you did not." She unleashed her rising agitation. "I speak of our future together. Something you have yet to mention."

"I attempted to explain to you once, *Faeilean,* why it cannot be." Morgan's words were calm, carefully spoken. His poise infuriated her for some reason.

"You explained *nothing*. All I know is that you are a baron, while I am quite likely a nobody. If it cheapens our love in your eyes, as it seems to, then I do us both further harm by remaining here."

"Kat, little Kat, I would not hurt you for the world." Morgan's voice was both hoarse and firm, coaxing and

kind. It only made her suffer more. "Please try to understand, 'tis for your own good I take this stance. You would
be grievously disappointed . . ." He stopped, and she felt
his hand tighten about her arm. "There can be no future
for us," he stated at last.

"Why not?"

"There are reasons. Trust me in this."

"We are speaking of two lives!" she cried. "Our lives,
no less, and . . . and love."

"Aye. How well I know it."

Morgan sounded sad. Kat wondered what the real
source of his misery was. "Please be honest with me, Morgan," she pleaded. "Tell me why we cannot wed. Is it
because you are a lord, and I am but a lowborn peasant?"

"No, Kat. 'Twould never stop me. I care not one fig
what others may think about our respective stations in
life. There are other reasons."

"I see. Then I would know them, too. I can think of
none sufficient to keep us apart." She drew a deep breath
and heard the trepidation in her own tone. "Tell me true.
Are you betrothed or married?"

"Nay."

Morgan would have gladly offered up his life than see
such an expression of mingled hurt and suspicion upon
her face again.

"For heaven's sake, why?" Kat whispered. Tears streamed
unchecked down her cheeks; she visibly struggled to compose herself. "I thought we were well-suited. I thought 'twas
mutual, these feelings between us."

"Aye," Morgan confirmed. He saw Kat's lips begin to
tremble. Ever so gently he framed her precious face between his hands, and wiped the wetness away from her
cheeks with the pads of his thumbs.

"What one hopes and dreams for is not always possible,
Faeilean. I wish there to be no misunderstandings between
us."

"Be assured there are none, milord." Kat withdrew and rose, brushing aside his concern and his touch. "I will take my leave now. You may rest, or not, as you will."

She turned and blundered into a chair. Morgan started to rise and offer assistance, but she squared her shoulders and proudly drew herself up.

"Nay, milord," Kat said when she heard him swing his legs over the side of the bed. "Do not come near me. Since my blindness revolts you so, I shall not impose upon your good nature again."

"Sweet Jesu, 'tis not that—"

"Please, no more lies." Kat was pleased to discover her voice did not shake, though her heart was shattered inside. She left the room before he might respond.

Morgan remained where he was, berating himself for letting Kat assume the worst, yet also relieved that it saved her heart in the end. Had she continued loving him, she would have been truly devastated if she ever regained her sight.

Suppose she doesn't? a tiny voice in his head argued. *Then you have just surrendered the only woman you ever wanted for a wife. Bloody fool!* he almost heard the ghostly voice of his father exclaim in the silence of the room. *You are letting your one chance for happiness walk out the door.*

In the week that followed Kat did not go to Morgan. She occupied herself instead with thoughts of where she would go and what she might do. The frightening, bleak prospect of her future loomed ahead of her, a black abyss. What might a blind girl hope to find in the way of work or mercy?

Nothing, Kat realized. Perhaps the nearby abbey would shelter her, but they would reasonably expect some sort of recompense, and she was useless when it came to chores such as tending animals or cooking.

Kat spent several nights weeping, and her eyes burned anew from the salty tears. When Winnie checked them later, the housekeeper lectured her.

"How d'you ever hope to heal if you won't follow my advice?" Winnie scolded. "Now, I'll put the medicine in once more. If you cry again I'll wash my hands of you."

The gruff threat wasn't serious. Kat was in such a state of mind she didn't think to smile.

"You wouldn't be remiss, Winnie," she replied instead, recalling Morgan's rejection. Perhaps he only desired a brief dalliance, knowing Kat would not be thus inclined unless she was promised something more. A baron would not seek a marital entanglement with a female of the lower class.

Kat considered the possibility. Aye, it made sense. Morgan had used her. As cleverly as he played a game of chess, he had moved Kat into position and started his careful siege. Well, two could play the game!

"Winnie," she said that evening before the other woman left. "I wish to look especially fetching tonight."

Winnie was dismayed but did not let her chagrin enter her voice. "Aye, dear. I'd recommend the plum velvet."

"Please be so kind as to have it pressed and brought up. I won't require Gwynneth's services, however. My hair shall be worn loose."

"As you wish. D'you favor a bath first?"

"Aye. A soak in hot water sounds heavenly right now. Would it be too much trouble?"

"I'll have a pair of lads bring up the tub. If you like, I'll even help you wash your hair."

"Thank you, Winnie."

Several hours later, Kat carefully carried Morgan's supper tray into his chamber, her head held high. She heard his exclamation of surprise and pleasure before he rose and crossed the room to meet her.

"There's too much furniture strewn about, I fear. Let me take the tray from you."

She nodded, waiting until he set it aside and returned to face her.

"I'm delighted to see you again, *Faeilean*. Yet I would know why are you here?"

"Why are you out of bed?" she countered.

"I went out to the fields today." At her sharp intake of breath, Morgan added, "I didn't ride, I promise. I'm still a bit too sore. A brisk walk did wonders for my legs. I just returned to my chamber before you arrived."

"You will injure yourself," Kat warned him.

"I think not. My body has survived worse, and, as you know, 'tis sheer luck whether one weathers a particular storm or not." Morgan studied Kat. Her high color warned him of her tempestuous mood. He wondered why she returned to him after the angry words exchanged a week ago. Nevertheless, his hungry eyes drank in the sight of her with the proud figure he loved so well. He swallowed hard when he realized his lower body had certainly not sustained any permanent damage.

"Faeilean," he said at last. "I wish to apologize for the walls standing between us now."

" 'Tis not necessary, milord."

"I find it so. Do not turn away from me, little seagull. I want you to hear me out. Yea, I was wrong to mislead you about my intentions. Yet I am just a man, and men are given to be wrong at times." *Jesu forgive me for this final lie,* Morgan thought, despising himself even as he spoke.

"I behaved most dishonorably toward you, Kat. I beg your forgiveness."

He saw her lips tremble; her lashes lowered over her brilliant green eyes. "There is nothing to forgive."

"Say I am forgiven, then."

She did not speak. He let out a sigh.

" 'Tis as I feared. You have every right to be angry with me. Can we not part as friends?"

Friends? Kat recoiled from the notion. Why, she would lay down her life, her soul to be with Morgan! She started to turn away from him. His hand caught her sleeve.

"Oh, nay, little Kat. Not like this. Never like this."

Step by step, Morgan drew her back to him. She trembled when his hands moved to cup her face, and his callused thumbs brushed the tears from her cheeks in a familiar, loving gesture. A second later his lips brushed hers, light as gossamer, exquisitely gentle, but with an unmistakable passion.

Her mouth opened as a flower to the rain, and their tongues touched. With a groan, Morgan pulled her flush against him. Kat felt the lean angles of his body even through her thick velvet gown and arched up against him, hungering for something even she did not understand. *Morgan!* her heart cried. *I must be with you. Oh Love, do not turn me away again. . . .*

He seemed to sense Kat's agony as keenly as his own. "Jesu forgive me," he muttered, to her and to the heavens, and resumed the passionate kiss, trailing his lips down the fragile column of her throat, till he found the precious pulse beating there. Fresh tears sparkled on Kat's face; he raised his head again to kiss them away, one by one.

"Morgan," she whispered, as her hands raised to mold his face. She smoothed back a stray lock of hair from his brow. "This time, do not stop."

"I can't this time," he echoed raggedly. "Beg off now, *cariad,* if you are wise."

Kat shook her head, gasping when his hand traced the curve of her breast. She did not protest when he began to unhook her bodice, nor when cool air kissed her exposed skin. Her nipples hardened at his touch and throbbed in the fashion of tiny heartbeats when he raked his thumbnail across the ruby peaks.

"I will wind thee in my arms . . . so doth the woodbine the sweet honeysuckle gently entwine," he recited softly, and drew a pointed nipple into his mouth. Kat cried out as he suckled her. She felt as if a burning silver cord ran from her breasts to her belly. Her head fell back in ecstasy, her unbound hair brushed the floor.

Morgan gathered Kat up in his arms. Moving slowly with respect for his recent injury, he carried her to his bed. He lowered Kat there, as if she were a priceless treasure, and cradled her against his heart until the last possible second. He removed her clothing, piece by piece, until she lay before him, her sole coverlet a swathe of luxurious hair.

Morgan mused a moment upon Kat's flawless beauty. Her skin glistened, like the finest ivory, by firelight. She looked at him searchingly, green eyes so intent that he was almost certain her sight had been magically restored. He shuddered at the thought and half turned away.

"Morgan." Her whisper drew him back like a moth to a flame. The fire would destroy him in the end, he knew, but he was powerless against its hypnotic effect.

She made a soft noise of frustration. "I want to see you too, Morgan. 'Tis not fair."

"Ssh," he soothed, joining her on the bed. "If you look closely, you can see me in your heart."

Kat realized he was right. She clung to her image of Morgan with fierce intensity. She visualized his magnificent body as he lowered himself beside her, saw each lean angle and muscular curve defined by firelight. He gleamed in her mind's eye like the bronze statue of a god. She closed her eyes and surrendered to an erotic feast of the senses.

Morgan nuzzled her neck. Kat outlined every contour and angle of his body, defining the bones of his face. When he flinched, she did not notice. Her fingers rested

on the birthmark once; there was only innocence in her
touch.

"Love me," she requested simply.

As if he would not. Morgan sighed and buried his head
between the luscious swell of her breasts, content as he
had never been before and conversely feeling twice as
damned. So damned, he almost wept. He tasted the sweet
saltiness of her skin and realized even hell had its consolation.

Kat drew him up for a fierce kiss as they joined as one.
The dew of her readiness greeted Morgan as he settled
himself between her thighs. He forgot his conscience, his
flawed face, all but the woman in his arms.

"There will be pain," he apologized.

"Then I shall weather it with you, my love." Kat suddenly arched into him so he drove true and deep.

He released a wondering cry as he sank deep into her
willing warmth. She met him without a flinch, trusting
and without reserve. Only a soft keening sound marked
the intensity of their joining. At once, they began to move
in rhythm, exquisite sensations carrying them both beyond the confines of the room, of their sheltered lives.
For one single, wondrous moment, Morgan felt his invisible fetters drop off. He was but a man, linked in an
ancient dance with the woman he loved.

"*Cariad.* Look at me, beloved." Morgan rained feather-
light kisses on Kat's fluttering eyelids. She answered his
fierce request. When their mutual crisis came, her jeweled
eyes flew open, hazy with passion, drugged with the po-
tent wine of love.

Intoxicated by her taste and scent and feel, Morgan
shuddered with emotion. "You're the most precious
woman on earth."

"Your woman," Kat whispered, and smiled when his
lips descended to confirm the fact. For the remainder of
the night, they rejoiced in their secret love, sharing pas-

sion and the essence of their souls again, in the manner of a timeless boon between man and woman.

Kat smiled sleepily, and snuggled deeper into the warm eider of her own bed. Her bed? She opened her eyes wide and was shocked to see the faint but distinct outline of a white bolster near her head. Her tousled head rose with a jolt.

"Morgan?"

The whisper echoed in the chilly stone chamber, empty now, save for herself. She was back in her own bed. The space beside her was empty. She had no need to feel it for herself. Sweet Mother and Mary. *She saw it.*

"Morgan!" Kat shouted his name, as she sat bolt upright in bed. She was startled to discover she was no longer nude. She wore a long white nightrail embroidered with Michaelmas daisies. *Daisies.* Kate stared with wonder at the tiny flowers intricately woven into the cambric. She began to weep as she called for Morgan again.

A moment later the chamber door opened. A blurry but recognizable figure hurried into her room.

"Saints, child, what is it? 'Tis barely dawn and here you're shrieking like a banshee."

"Winnie," Kat cried. She scrambled from the bed and startled the other woman as she dashed barefoot across the floor. She flung her arms about the stout housekeeper. "Oh, Winnie, Winnie, I can see!"

"Truly, now?" Winnie seemed astounded, perhaps a bit dubious as well. She held Kat at arm's length, studied her patient's tear-filled eyes. When Kat's gaze met and followed her own without mishap, she began to cry, too. "Praise be to all the saints and the mighty Lord himself! I cannot believe it."

"My eyes are still weak, but I can see now. I can see you at last . . . your red hair . . . your kind, wonderful, dear face. Oh, Winnie, you're every bit as beautiful as I imagined."

Touched, the other woman clasped Kat to her plump, motherly bosom. "There now, dearie, mustn't greet. What did I tell you before? 'Tis a happy day indeed. It calls for a celebration, not tears." Winnie's order was issued even through her own tears. Kat laughed and hugged the woman.

"Aye, you're right. The first to know of my recovery after you shall be Morgan. Where is he?"

Winnie withdrew and pursed her lips. "Ah, Katie, I'm sorry. Milord and his men rode out first thing this morning. There was a wee bit of trouble late last night in the village. Some looting and burning—probably the work of those devils who attacked the Master."

Kat's hands rose to her mouth. "Oh, no."

"Don't fret, dearie. He'll be safe this time. Milord's not alone. He'll be back long before nightfall."

Though disappointed Morgan was not here, and worried about his welfare, Kat reasoned Winnie was probably right. She was too delighted with her recovered sight to stay sober for long. Kat spun around in a circle, and got her first good look at her room where she had stayed in for over a month.

The four-poster bed was carved of heavy mahogany and gleamed in the morning light which slanted through lead-paned windows. The bed's wine-colored velvet canopy was roped back with golden tassels, and matching damask chairs flanked either side of the hearth. There was also a marble-topped table, and a green velvet settle. A portrait hung above the fireplace. The more Kat blinked, the clearer her vision became. She stared at the beautiful young woman in the painting. The lady was garbed in an elegant black velvet gown and simple ivory lace mantilla. Such stark colors only served to foil her dramatic beauty. Her dark eyes looked haunted and sad.

"Who's this?" she asked Winnie.

" 'Tis Elena Trelane, the Master's mother."

"You said you did not know her Christian name, Winnie."

The housekeeper fidgeted a bit. "Faith, I suppose it came back to me now."

"She was very young." Kat crossed the crimson Turkish carpet and studied Lady Trelane from various angles. "Was she Spanish?"

"Aye."

"Then Morgan—Lord Trelane—is half-Spanish."

"Aye."

Kat glanced at Winnie. "He's dark like his mother, isn't he? Why does he never speak of her?"

Winnie pressed her lips together. "I'm sure I wouldn't know."

"Was this her room?"

Winnie only nodded, as if not trusting herself to speak.

Kat passed beneath the portrait and strolled the length of the bedchamber to one of the four windows, where she looked out over the shimmering sea. For a moment, she simply watched the waves crashing against the cliff. She shivered and turned away. Memories of the sea, and what it had cost her, were still too painful.

"I wish to get dressed and see the rest of Falcon's Lair."

"Of course, dear." Winnie seemed to welcome the change of topic. "I'll have something suitable brought in. Wait here."

Kat had no intention of going anywhere just yet. She sank down into one of the chairs, drawn once more to gaze at Lady Trelane's portrait. There she hoped to find some answers to the hundreds of questions flooding her mind.

Winnie didn't notice Gwynneth's hands whiten on the embroidery the maid held. The housekeeper continued her dramatic tale, impressing the castle staff with what had occurred that morning.

"Had I not witnessed it myself, I should never have believed it. They say wondrous miracles do indeed occur during Lenten." Winnie nodded self-righteously, pleased to be the bearer of such good news. "Let it be a lesson to us all, I say, to keep our faith."

"Aye," the others echoed, nodding at her sage words. Only Gwynneth stayed silent, waiting until Winnie bustled upstairs with an armful of clothes for Kat. She tossed her handiwork aside.

"Nay," she muttered fiercely, her fingernails scoring the armrests of the stool she perched upon. " 'Twill not be!"

"Gwynneth?" One of the other girls overheard her and leaned forward on her own stool to peer around the butter churn. "What did you say?"

"Nothing, Eirlys," Gwynneth sweetly replied. *Stupid half-wit,* she thought as she rose. "I just remembered I must gather some herbs for Mrs. Carey. I promised to help her with the apothecary today."

Nobody attempted to waylay Gwynneth as she slipped through the kitchens and hurried outside, holding up her woolen skirts as she ran. Cheeks flushed with determination, she entered the little thatched cottage she shared with three other girls. Proceeding to her secret hideaway, she withdrew something from beneath the straw pallet and thrust it into the pocket of her kirtle.

With a wary glance about to assure she wasn't seen, Gwynneth left the cottage and headed into the nearby copse. A distant rumble of thunder hurried her along. Above her head, a canopy of oaks swayed and creaked in the rising breeze. She was not deterred. She was a creature born of wind and storm. A faint smile curved her lips when she broke from the woods and glimpsed her destination.

Gwynneth tucked her kirtle up around her waist and climbed the huge boulders up the lee side of Madoc's Craig. She paused a few times to catch her breath. 'Twas slow going. Finally, she hefted herself onto the lip of a cave partially hidden by underbrush. Panting for a moment, she glanced down upon the stone keep rising in the distance, then glanced further out to sea to the black thunderheads moving inland.

There was an ancient stone altar just inside the cave. Gwynneth freed her skirts and turned her attention to the altar. From her pocket, she produced a simple cloth doll. Several strands of dark hair dressed its head; its green eyes had been carefully embroidered to the last detail. It wore a scrap of plum velvet for a gown. The sharp, mingled scents of henbane, nightshade, and mandrake assailed Gwynneth's nostrils as she placed the poppet upon the altar between two melted candle stumps.

A saucer of sea salt also lay upon the altar. Dipping her fingers into the salt, Gwynneth sprinkled it over the doll from head to toe, chanting in Cymric as she went:

"I christen this Poppet Kat . . . it be her in every way. As she lives, so lives this Poppet. Aught that I do to it, I do to her."

Gwynneth trembled with anticipation as she concluded the forbidden ritual. Old Agatha was a fool to fear any repercussions from the Morrigan. Owen magic was stronger than any legends. She drew a familiar violet hair ribbon from her pocket. She tied it around the doll's neck.

A smile twisted Gwynneth's lips as she raised the poppet to dangle by its makeshift noose. It spun in circles and even did a macabre little dance before her eyes, just as a bolt of lightning crackled overheard, and the sky shattered with a clap of unearthly thunder like a million shards of glass.

Nine

Kat wrapped the woolen cloak more closely about herself, shielding her eyes from icy rain while she paced the parapet along the north tower. From her vantage atop Falcon's Lair, she might peer between the crenellated stones and gaze upon the distant fires of the village.

Almost twelve hours had passed since Morgan rode out with his men to subdue trouble in the village. Although Winnie didn't seem concerned, Kat was getting worried. She sought the dusky horizon for any sign of Morgan or the wagon Lloyd Carey said the men had taken. The rain increased as darkness fell, and soon Kat was forced to retreat indoors. There she paced another hour and perused the books in Morgan's library during the brunt of the magnificent thunderstorm. Finally the storm faded over mist-topped Madoc's Craig, though a steady drizzle persisted. *Was Wales always so dreary?* Kat wondered. She realized she hadn't cared how many storms passed over them each day. Morgan had always been there to brighten her day, even when the weather itself was beastly.

Kat went to the window in Morgan's library for what seemed the hundredth time. She scanned the darkness again. This time she saw several lights break off in the direction of the village and head towards Falcon's Lair. The rapid, bobbing up-and-down motion of the lights indicated they were torches carried upon horseback. With rising hope, Kat turned and hurried past the crackling hearth to find Winnie.

Even in Morgan's absence, a fire was kept going in his favorite room, and the library was warm and inviting. She paused to run loving fingers over a dusty, leather-bound volume of *Richard II* propped on the last shelf, then shook herself free of fancies and left the distracting books behind.

She caught a glimpse of her own passing reflection in a pier glass in the hall. Her hair was neatly braided, tucked beneath a white lace shadow. The gown she wore was a crimson red velvet with metal thread leaf embroidery on the sleeves and hems. Its train swished across the floor behind Kat as she entered the hall and called for Winnie.

Winnie appeared carrying a taper holder and shielding the flickering flame with one hand. She noted Kat's damp skirts and clucked. "Will you be tempting a fever, now?"

"I saw lights headed this way," Kat said breathlessly. "Perhaps 'tis the men returning, at last."

The news pleased Winnie. "I'll rouse Ailis to set out a late repast. Like as not, all shall be invited to sup with the Master in this weather, as reward for a job well-done." She added kindly, "Let me send Gwynneth to fetch a dry gown for you."

Kat declined. "I fear his lordship has seen me in worse repair before. I'll take no chances on missing him this time. I want to share the good news myself. Please, Winnie, will you ask Cook to offer a stout mead this evening? I trow, the men will be chilled to the bone."

Winnie nodded and hurried off to the kitchens. The meager light left with her. Unlike the library, the great hall was cold and damp. The huge hearth was dark. Kat remained in virtual darkness until she fumbled her way to a table and found several tapers. She lit three candles. Taking a taper for herself, she turned to follow Winnie.

The shadow of a large figure, lurking before her, brought a quick cry to her lips. Then the wavering candlelight revealed a suit of armor for what it was.

Foolish chit, Kat scolded herself, gathering up the folds of her gown with one hand in order to protect the hem. *'Tis just an old keep, and your fancies are getting the best of you.* She was too anxious to share news of her recovery with Morgan. The slightest thing rattled her nerves. She had started for the kitchen when Winnie reappeared, shrugging on her own cloak and hood and carrying a large satchel.

"Pray, you aren't going out in this rain to meet the party of men?" Kat inquired with some confusion.

"Nay, dearie. I just spoke with Cook. There's a girl giving birth out at the miller's tonight. The wee one is turned the wrong way and, without my help, they both might die." Winnie shook her head. "There's no help for it now. I've got to go. I'll trust you to let the Master know of my whereabouts when he arrives."

"Of course I will. Do you need any help?"

Winnie shook her head. "I've all I need in my satchel here, including some good, stout rope, if I've a need to tie Molly down." She didn't appear to notice Kat's shudder at the matter-of-fact comment. "I doubt I'll be back before dawn. Can you oversee matters alone?"

Kat nodded. She was determined not to let Winnie down.

"Bless you," Winnie said, with obvious relief. A moment later, the housekeeper was gone. Her exit admitted a brief sheet of rain with the opening and closing of the door.

Kat debated what she should do next. She decided she'd best check with Cook and see if Ailis needed any help serving a meal to so many hungry men. Before she left the hall, there came a muffled pounding at the door. Assuming Winnie had forgotten something, Kat set down her candle and opened the door. She was immediately brushed aside by a small troop of men clad in rain-soaked uniforms. Their dripping leader was a tall soldier with a square jaw and a scraggly brown beard. His glance dismissed the dimly-lit hall and found Kat instead. His eyes roamed her up and down. His gaze lingered on her breasts.

"Well, what's this now?" He winked at Kat and said aside to his men, "I see Trelane's got his pick of the ripe wenches hereabouts."

Outraged by his crude manner, Kat raised her hand. She intended to slap the sneer right off the soldier's leering face. Then she noted the merciless glint in his eye and reconsidered. Instinct warned her not to reveal her true identity to these men. Instead she curtsied meekly and let them assume what they would.

"Are you seeking shelter from the storm, good sirs?" she inquired in what she prayed was a suitably servile tone.

"Nay. We seek a blind woman his lordship is inclined to shelter from Her Majesty's justice," their leader replied. He didn't seem to notice Kat's eyes widening. He was staring instead at the impressive suits of armor lining the hall.

"God's nightshirt," he irreverently swore. "Came these from the Crusades?"

"I know not, sir," Kat answered, dropping her gaze when he glanced her way again. She was the blind woman they sought. But why? Kat knew she was in grave danger, though she dared not imagine why. When all the soldiers moved forward to examine the ancient armor, she seized her chance.

"I'll summon milord," she murmured with another curtsy. She realized they did not know Morgan was away. They made no move to pursue her. She retreated until she was safely hidden in the shadows of the great hall, then turned and fled toward the kitchens. She burst into Cook's domain with a ready cry on her lips.

"Ailis! You must help me."

The kitchens were empty and silent, save for the merry crackling of a fire in the great hearth. With mounting despair, Kat ventured into the kitchens and pantry, calling for Ailis or any of the other servants. Where had they all gone? She remembered Winnie mentioning the staff might attend evening vespers in the village. With a choked cry, Kat fled the kitchens in search of a better hiding place. She chose the servant's passage. She doubted the men in the hall were patient sorts, and she suspected they would come looking for her soon.

She carefully navigated several sets of narrow, spiraling steps. It seemed they went on forever, clear to the upper reaches of the keep. Thankfully, the way was lit, a few sconces tracing the walls. There were any number of nooks and crannies where she might hide until Morgan or the others returned, but which was the best? The taste of fear turned sour in Kat's mouth long before the stairs ended. She discovered the door at the top was locked, mayhap bolted from the other side. Kat tugged on it a few futile moments, then sank down on the steps, huddled in her voluminous gown.

Soon she heard a man curse and footsteps pacing below in the hall. She pressed a hand to her trembling lips to still any inadvertent outcry. She waited, rigid with terror, hoping the soldiers would eventually give up and go away. She wondered who they were and why they sought her out. She recalled their uniforms were green and white, albeit the white was liberally stained with mud and ale—Tudor colors. Sweet Jesu! Did Elizabeth Tudor herself believe Kat was an enemy of the realm? Or did the queen already know Kat's identity in truth and sent her men to mete out due justice?

Kat still did not know who she was. She realized that

in her past she might have been a felon: anyone from a humble thief to a cunning murderess. Perhaps others knew her real identity. Mayhap they had come now to serve her with her sentence. If so, only one man might save her now.

Morgan! she silently cried. *Help me!* Kat listened in vain for the sound of an approaching wagon. Instead there came the ominous, pounding echo of footsteps up the stone stairs. She shrank down as if to make herself invisible. A sensation of something wet against her skin made her shudder and glance up. She saw a chink in the stone above her. Rain began to drip down in a steady stream, soaking through her gown. In her present terror, Kat cared not, until she was reduced to violent shivers. When a soldier appeared at the base of the stairs, she glanced at her sodden crimson skirts and saw they had darkened to the color of blood.

Morgan heaved the wooden bucket over the smoking rubble and doused the glowing sparks with a satisfying sizzle. He tossed down the bucket and turned to face the line of men, wiping his soot-streaked brow with the back of his hand.

" 'Tis all we can do for now," he announced, painfully aware of the young woman standing just a few feet away, weeping. She owned the burned cottage. A stair-step of children clung to her skirts, the oldest not more than eight. Bile rose in Morgan's throat as he surveyed the senseless wreckage once again.

Someone had torched Iona Sayer's home after she and her family had retired for the night. The widow and her children barely escaped; all of their meager belongings were destroyed by the fire. Morgan was certain the malicious act was aimed as much at him as the Sayer family. When Iona's husband had died last winter, Morgan deeded her the cottage and enough land to keep her self-sufficient so she might feed her brood.

Morgan's simple act of mercy had not gone unnoticed; it had also been misconstrued. He approached the Widow Sayer now, unable to blame her when she averted her face.

"I promise I will do all I can to catch the villains who did this," he said in a low voice. "I must ask you once again: did you see or hear anything?"

Iona shook her head too quickly. Morgan couldn't blame the woman for being frightened, but he was frustrated by the misplaced loyalty among these proud people.

"You and all your children would have perished, if not for Evan Howell," Morgan stated, gesturing at a youth who stood nearby, soot streaked upon his beardless face. Thirteen-year-old Evan had seen smoke rising from the Sayer cottage and rushed in to save the family, without a thought for his own life. Yet Evan, too, was mutinously silent about who had set the blaze.

Iona nodded and swallowed. "Thank ye for tryin' to save me home, milord," she whispered, risking a nervous glance at Morgan as she hugged the wailing baby to her breast. Just as quickly, she averted her gaze again.

"I'll see another cottage is built for you," Morgan promised the widow.

"Nay! I—I mean, thank ye kindly, milord. Oh, I've been thinkin' of leavin' anyway, to join me kin up in Cardigan." Iona babbled the excuse as she scraped back strands of ash-stained hair from her face. She juggled the baby to her other arm. The babe let out a thin, hungry cry. Iona must have sensed Morgan's rising frustration, for she wouldn't meet his eye.

"As you wish," Morgan said shortly. "I trust there is someone you can stay with until morn? It does not appear the rain has any intentions of stopping soon."

Iona nodded. An older woman, who had been closely

observing their exchange of words, moved forward. Her expression was belligerent.

"I be Iona's cousin by marriage," the woman stoutly declared. "Since Vaughn's death, I been keepin' an eye out for Iona an' the wee ones. They'll be stayin' with me now."

This one didn't shrink from meeting Morgan's gaze. He didn't mistake the mixture of thinly veiled contempt and hatred. The emotions shone, dagger-fashion, in her eyes.

"Then I guess we can depart, men." Morgan turned and wearily addressed the handful who had accompanied him from Falcon's Lair. "There's not much else we can do here."

When he turned and walked back to the wagon, Morgan heard several hisses aimed in his direction. 'Twas no use singling out the culprits. Most of the villagers milled about in the rain and muck, gawking at the burned cottage and their overlord. Morgan kept walking, rigid with anger. But he was too tired and dispirited to try and reason with these folk. The same men and women casting him dark looks now were the ones he anonymously sent food and clothing to during the hard winter months. Morgan knew them for the proud, independent people they were; he wondered what they would do if they learned he had been their secret benefactor. He knew of none who had refused his aid. They most probably assumed it came from the nearby abbey. Why they would accept charity from the Church, and not him, was maddening indeed.

Iona Sayer was one of the few who directly experienced Morgan's generosity. He saw what it had cost the widow and her family. He swore he would not waste his efforts again.

Someone stepped forward from the shadows, just as

Morgan prepared to leave with his men. 'Twas Evan Howell, nervously twisting his sooty hands before him.

"Milord," the towheaded lad stammered, glancing about furtively. "I know who set the fire."

Morgan glanced at the boy as he stacked the wagon bed with empty buckets.

"Speak up, then."

Evan worried his lower lip between his teeth. He obviously feared the confession to come. But the truth finally won out, spewed out as poison from a festering wound.

" 'Twas Renfrew, milord," Evan blurted.

"My own steward?" Morgan was incredulous for a second. It did not last long. He recalled the man's repeated insubordination and base thievery over the years.

"Aye, milord." Evan hung his head and scraped at the dirt with a bare toe. "He wanted to rut with the Widow Sayer, only she'd have none of him, milord. He called Iona . . . ah . . . a kept woman in front of everyone."

"God's teeth," Morgan swore. "Why?"

Evan blushed bright red. " 'Cause you gave her the cottage and land scotfree, after her husband's death."

"Ridiculous," Morgan snapped.

Mistaking the baron's ire for anger aimed at him, Evan added:

"I know 'twas only kindness on your part, milord, but some of the others thought different-like."

Morgan frowned. "Is there more, Evan?"

Evan gulped. He was almost stricken dumb in Morgan's presence. He could hardly speak, much less spout any sort of impressive rhetoric before the baron. With great effort Evan continued, his prominent Adam's apple bobbing up and down in his throat.

"Renfrew warned all of us that to work for you was to work for Lord Satan himself. He promised to keep the villagers safe from you, milord, if they gave him a third portion of their profits."

Morgan looked appalled and Evan quickly added, "I ne'er believed it for a minute, milord. I remember you was nothing but kind to me and my mum a'fore she died. You gave us food and shelter. You even came to the house when Mum was dying. Brought the priest with you, clear from Tregaron. I know those books I have came from you."

With some effort Morgan followed the lad's rambling conversation. "Books, Evan?"

"Aye, y'know the ones. 'Bout the knights and fair maidens in the olden days." Evan blushed again. "You talked to me for a long time about books then. 'Twas you who wanted me to read, weren't it?"

"Wasn't it," Morgan corrected the boy. He smiled a little and ruffled Evan's pale hair. To his credit, Evan didn't flinch.

"I ne'er learned to read, milord, but I still have the books. I used to look at the pictures all the time. I would fain make up stories about them," Evan shyly admitted. "I suppose you want them back now."

"I confess I'd forgotten all about the books, Evan. Keep them. I am glad they bring you pleasure." Morgan paused and added, "I know your mother died several years ago. Have you any other kin here in the village?"

"Nay, milord. I sleep in the smithy's stable. Master Drewsey pays me a penny a week to help with the horses."

"Would you like to live at Falcon's Lair and learn to read those books of yours?"

Evan's eyes rounded. "God's toenail, would I! I . . . I mean, aye, milord, if you'll have me."

This time Morgan's smile broadened. " 'Tis settled, then. Run get your things and load them in the wagon here. I'm sure Master Carey can use an extra hand with the horses."

* * *

Outside the village, on the winding road back to Falcon's Lair, Morgan and his men met up with Mrs. Carey trudging home from her midnight midwifery.

Winnie's skirts were splattered with mud and blood. She looked as bone-weary as Morgan felt. He offered her a hand up into the wagon bed.

"Trouble?" he inquired succinctly, as Lloyd slapped the reins and urged the horses onward.

"Aye, milord." Winnie wearily pushed back her wet hood. The rain had stopped and clouds drifted apart to reveal a star-spangled, glittering night sky crowned with a stark, full moon. Glancing heavenward, Winnie heaved a great sigh. " 'Twas too late to save the both of them. The poor babe was born dead."

"The mother?"

" 'Twas a close call, milord, but Molly will live to have others. She's young. Altogether a sorry business, to be sure."

Morgan realized Winnie had been absent from Falcon's Lair most of the evening.

"How did you find Mistress Kat today?" he asked her.

"Duw, she seemed in fine spirits." Winnie glanced at the Master's moonlit profile. She detected more than a polite query in his tone. She sensed something significant had happened between Kat and his lordship, but kept any speculation to herself. "She said she intended to wait up for your return."

Morgan shook his head. "I've been at the village all day and half the night. No sooner did we settle the matter of the missing grain and resulting riot, when another fire was lit just after we left. Luckily Evan was able to save the family and catch up with us on the road." He gestured at the towheaded lad sitting beside Lloyd on the driver's seat. Overhearing Morgan's words of praise, Evan straightened a bit.

"We went back and were finally able to douse the flames, but the cottage was lost."

"I thought I smelled smoke," Winnie said.

" 'Tis quiet now. At least for the time being." Morgan realized he sounded bitter, but he was tired. He was weary of trying to change the villagers' opinion of him and frustrated by their ludicrous and dangerous superstitions.

Morgan thought of Kat instead and his heart lightened. He looked forward to seeing her at Falcon's Lair. It had been damme difficult to get up that morning and leave her. He had lingered over Kat's sleeping figure, drinking in the precious vision in his bed. She looked ethereal in her slumber, Shakespeare's Titania curled up in her fairy garden, her long hair strewn about like glistening strands of silk. Morgan called upon all his reserves not to awaken Kat with urgent lovemaking. Instead, he carried her back to her own room, slipped her into a nightrail, then beneath the covers. She never stirred.

Morgan wondered what Kat's first thoughts were upon waking. He knew what his own had been. His heart was so filled from love last night that even his secret had ceased to matter. He decided to tell Kat the truth, and if she still accepted him and his suit, they would wed. A half-smile played about Morgan's lips as he imagined the exchange of vows. Kat must be garbed like a princess, in a regal gown of white silk and seed pearls, with a train half a mile long. After the marriage the Trelane heirlooms would be hers to wear. He recalled a group of matched emeralds set in gold filigree; they matched her eyes.

"Milord," Winnie exclaimed, shattering his pleasant musings. "Faith, in my weariness I almost forgot! Our Katie has her sight back."

"What?" Morgan whipped his head around to stare at the woman. "Are you certain?"

"Aye." Winnie's sausage curls bobbed emphatically.

"Your wee birdie awoke this morn, able to see. 'Tis a bit misty yet, she says, but no mistake about it, she can see. Praise the saints for that."

"Indeed," Morgan murmured, discomfited by a churning sensation in the pit of his stomach. What difference did it make now if Kat saw him, or not? He chided himself for his dark thoughts. She loved him. Kat implied as much even before last night; he must trust, 'twas enough.

Just when Morgan was no longer in a hurry to reach Falcon's Lair, the castle appeared, rising before them in the moonlight, a craggy altar to ancient gods. 'Twas almost entirely dark inside the keep; only a few flickering lights attested to any human occupation. Lloyd drew up the team in front of the stables, and his passengers clambered down wearily.

"Go along with Master Carey," Morgan instructed Evan. He had already told Lloyd of his decision to keep the boy. Lloyd had nodded, sized the youth up, and seemed pleased. As Evan promptly moved to unhitch the horses from the wagon, Lloyd looked on with a smile.

Morgan also dismissed Winnie for the night. She joined her husband. Soon the trio would retire to their cottage. Lloyd had already promised Evan a warm bed at their hearth.

Morgan realized his work was done for the night. He bade them all good sleep, then crossed the inner ward to the keep, taut with apprehension. He slowly mounted the row of stone steps. He was anxious to see Kat, yet wary of her reaction. His courage was fading fast. He must get it over with.

Morgan was surprised when a maid servant greeted him at the door with a taper in her hand. He assumed all the staff to be long abed. 'Twas only a few hours until dawn.

"Is aught amiss?" he asked the girl, entering the great hall. Several candles burned there, but he hardly noticed the graceful curtsey she executed for his benefit.

"Oh, milord, we didn't expect you so soon," she babbled, and trailed Morgan across the hall. Her voice was husky, as if she had just woke from sleep. "I heard tale that there were terrible happenings in the village tonight."

"Aye, there were. 'Tis settled now," Morgan absently assured her, as he strode to the stairs and waited in vain for Kat to appear. He had selfishly assumed she had waited up for him. She obviously hadn't. He heard the maid close and bar the heavy door in its casing.

Morgan could not restrain his impatience. He turned to the maid servant. "I suppose Mistress Kat is abed?"

For a second, the girl stared dumbly at him. Silence shrieked at Morgan; instantly, he knew something was wrong.

The maid seemed bewildered by his question. "Did you not know of her plans to leave today, milord?"

"Leave?" Morgan echoed. He looked stunned.

"Aye, I assumed you knew."

Gwynneth secretly delighted in the stricken expression on Morgan's face. She would comfort him, once the memory of Kat faded. 'Twould fade much sooner, if he just opened his eyes to her instead.

"What happened?" Morgan demanded. His voice shook.

"A man came, and they went away together."

"A man? What man?" Morgan went from being shocked to furious in a matter of seconds. He strode forward and seized Gwynneth by the shoulders, shaking her like a sack of grain. "Was he some kin of hers? Her father, mayhap?"

Gwynneth bit her lip, striving for an artless look, as if struggling to remember. "Methinks not. They seemed quite familiar with one another, milord. Why, they kissed and hugged with great abandon right here in the hall.

To be sure, it seemed a bit bold to my eyes, but then I didn't know Mistress Kat very well."

Morgan abruptly released her. His face was pale but the crescent on his cheek had darkened to deep crimson. 'Twas all the more sinister by the flickering candlelight in the hall.

Even Gwynneth might have feared him at that moment, did she not love him so much. Morgan turned away from her, with a haunted look in his eyes. Dazed, he headed up the stairs. He paused only once and asked over his shoulder, "Did she leave a message?"

"Nay. Wait, there was one thing." Gwynneth enjoyed her rare spurt of creativity. "Mistress Kat thanked us for taking her in when she was a poor blind wretch, milord, but said now she can see again, she'll be moving on."

Gwynneth saw Morgan flinch at her little cruelty.

"Good night . . . Gwynneth," he said at last, suddenly remembering her name. His voice was hollow, laced with pain. He continued up the stairs. Each thud of his boots echoed fainter than the last.

Gwynneth stared after him, twisting a greasy strand of brown hair between her fingers. Poor Morgan had taken the news harder than she had expected. Perhaps he truly carried some sort of misbegotten affection for the black-haired bitch.

With a shrug, Gwynneth decided she had only done what was necessary. Betraying Kat's hiding place to the Tudor soldiers had been an act of loyalty to the English queen. Besides, the wench must have done something truly terrible to warrant her being hunted down by the royal guard.

Her momentary pang of conscience gone, Gwynneth turned and headed through the kitchens. She paused beside the great fire in the hearth and extracted the poppet from her pocket. She tossed it carelessly into the flames and hurried out the door.

Ten

Kat stumbled and fell face-first in the mud. The impact knocked the breath from her, bringing a fresh round of jeers and catcalls from the watching men. A leather thong tied her wrists together; the lead was attached to the pommel of the captain's saddle. When his horse started forward again, there came a vicious jerk. It almost dislocated her wrists.

Kat cried out in agony. Yet she could not get up. After what seemed endless miles, her sodden skirts were twisted round her legs from being dragged, and her hands were numb from trying to grip the lead and lessen the tension. She lay in a heap on the road, unable to move despite the pain.

"Get up, wench!" The captain tugged impatiently on the tether securing his captive. He saw she either could not, or would not, obey him. He was furious.

"I'll teach you to delay the queen's guard." He vaulted down from his horse and marched back to where Kat lay unmoving in the road. Grabbing a handful of her muddy hair, he jerked back her head. She moaned. Her eyes remained closed. He noticed his captive's face—badly scraped and cut from her fall—was rosy and shiny with sweat.

"S'blood!" Captain Howard swore. "The mort's burning up with fever." He released his grip. Kat collapsed where he left her. He looked at his men. "We'd best stop and see to her. Milord ordered that no harm was to come to the wench."

"Then why d'you string her along like a fish, Cap'n?" Lieutenant Cobblestone sniggered—He was nicknamed "Cobble" by the others for his pockmarked skin.

Howard straightened and glared at his second lieutenant. "I'll not answer to dunderheads for what I do. I found the girl, didn't I? Even though she tried to lie her way out of it, 'twas clear enough she's the one milord seeks."

Cobble chuckled again and rubbed at his groin. "Can't says I blame 'im either, Cap'n," he said, eying Kat's splayed form. "She's a tasty bit o' fluff. I even likes 'em skinny like et. I'd enjoy a turn at this one meself, I would."

"Don't be a fool," Howard snapped. "The wench has a damme fever. We'll be lucky if she makes it alive to London. There's a purse of gold nobles for each of us if she does."

His men began to argue about who would care for Kat while Howard untied her wrists and dragged her to the side of the road. "We'll camp here for the rest of the night," the captain announced, carelessly tossing a motheaten blanket over the ill woman. "We'll take turns with the watch, and looking after the mort."

"I ain't touchin' nobody with fever," Cobble declared. "What'f 'tis the white throat or the pox?"

"Ye've had every ailment there is and survived 'em all, Cobble," another soldier laughed. "Nothing could make that mug o' yers any uglier or shrivel yer cony any smaller. Shut up and take yer turn."

"Aye, Lieutenant, you'll have first watch. Fetch the wench some water."

Cobble scowled at Captain Howard, then warily eyed the unmoving figure beneath the blanket. He reasoned he could at least cop a feel of the jade while she was passed out. She was quite a piece of work. That gown alone probably equaled a year's worth of his pay. 'Twas ruined now, else he'd ask the captain if he might have it when they reached London. *Lor', what magic Nell Hatchet wouldn't do fer a bit o' toggery like et!* Cobble felt himself harden at the thought. Most of the morts he futtered were prostitutes; this one seemed nigh a princess by comparison. Grabbing a leather bag from his saddle, he crossed to a nearby stream and filled it with water. He returned to the roadside and crouched beside the woman. He thrust the spout against her lips.

She choked and sputtered to consciousness. Cold water splashed upon her face and streamed down her neck. She shook her head in an attempt to evade the relentless trickle.

With a lewd chuckle, Cobble thoroughly doused her bodice next. Seeing her nipples inadvertently harden through the velvet, he licked his lips and moved the bag even lower.

The bag was snatched abruptly from his hand.

"Enough," another voice ground out. A boot kicked Cobble away from the prisoner. The other man bent to yank the blanket up over her drenched bodice.

"Gallant Frenchie, eh?" Cobble jeered. Lucien Navarre regarded him with a challenging, ice-blue stare. Cobble had tangled with Navarre before. Even a tasty mort wasn't worth a battered face. He muttered beneath his breath as he slunk into the shadows.

Lucien was disappointed when Cobble retreated without a fight. The man was an imbecile, and he would have taken great satisfaction in bashing the lieutenant's thick skull against a rock.

"I'll take first watch, sir," he offered to Captain Howard, thrusting the torch he carried into the earth. Lucien hunkered down beside the young woman. Howard glanced over at him, grunted his assent, and moved off into the darkness, obviously in search of a spot to relieve himself and toss down his bedroll.

After the other men had settled for the night, Lucien studied the captive again. Only half of her face presently showed; her other cheek remained pressed against the hard ground. He felt a mixture of distress and secret outrage at her plight. It went against his grain to treat a woman so. Lucien had been raised by his parents to treat the gentler sex with chivalry, and seeing his fellow soldiers abuse a helpless woman gave him strong misgivings about serving in the English regiment.

Of course, it was an honor and great distinction, and Lucien was proud enough when he first joined the ranks. When he made the rank of sergeant, Elizabeth Tudor had even seen fit to reward him during a formal ceremony at Court, personally pinning her colors to his uniform and gracing him with a kind word about his parents.

Lucien shook his head as he gazed upon the prisoner. He dared not help this woman escape, but he might make her trial a little easier. He carefully slid his left arm under her head, tilting her face upward. He winced at the scrapes and bruises revealed by the light of the torch. In the sunlight, he knew there would be many more.

Lucien started and almost dropped her when her feverish gaze suddenly opened on him.

"Hot," she murmured, gazing at him with bright green eyes. She licked her dry lips. "Thirsty."

Lucien picked up the water bag Cobble had dropped. He supported her while he dribbled a thin stream between her lips. She looked grateful and, after a few swallows, lay quiet in his arms. Lucien lowered her back to the ground and tucked the blanket higher about her neck. He sat back and watched over her the rest of the night. Whenever she roused, he offered water and a few words of comfort. He spoke softly in French so the others might not hear or understand. When dawn arrived, he

helped her up and managed to convince Captain Howard
not to bind her hands again.

The mysterious fever left Kat on the third day. By then,
she and Sergeant Navarre had lapsed into a routine of
sorts. He protected her from the other men, and she in
turn cooperated with him. 'Twas no longer necessary for
her to walk. She was no longer prodded along by Captain
Howard. She and Sergeant Navarre rode double upon his
bay gelding. Her initial terror abated somewhat upon dis-
covering she had an ally of sorts in Navarre. Although he
was not foolish enough to sacrifice his own career in an
attempt to help her escape, he was man enough to treat
her as a lady, even under such adverse circumstances.

As soon as Navarre took Kat under his wing, Cobble
ceased trying to hurt or harass her. Even in the delirium
of her fever, she recalled the lieutenant crudely groping
at her breasts. Cobble's pockmarked face still leered in
her direction now and again, but he dared not approach
or accost her. His superior never left her side.

Surprisingly, Captain Howard had not argued when
Navarre insisted Kat ride with him. Mayhap the captain
realized they would make better time, and it also relieved
him of the burden of her care. The sergeant had assumed
a command of sorts where she was concerned.

She gazed around at the scenery while they rode.
Quaint cottages with thatched roofs gradually gave way
to country manor houses fashioned from brick or stone;
humble wooden churches to Gloucester's great cathedral;
Hereford's apple blossoms to the white chalk hills of
Berkshire.

They were almost to London, Kat realized. Navarre had
informed her that England's greatest city was their destination. She wrapped her arms tighter about the sergeant's waist as his bay horse commenced a trot up a

steep incline in the Cotswold Hills. Soon the narrow, rutted lanes gave way to a road sufficiently wide for coaches to pass one another. They started to pass a number of folk riding wagons or trudging on foot to the city. Most glanced curiously, some pityingly, upon Kat as the contingent of guards thundered by. She felt a sick sensation in the pit of her stomach, grasping the full measure of her plight. For some reason she was under arrest. She had been too afraid of the answer to ask Navarre why.

When they stopped to water the horses at the Thames, she decided to risk the reply. Sergeant Navarre was safely distanced from the other men, checking his mount for lameness. Kat wandered casually over in his direction.

"D'you know why I have been arrested?" she asked him outright, deciding to be blunt in the interest of time. He had been pleased to discover she spoke French—and they were to converse in that tongue ever since. Most common soldiers, Captain Howard included, had not the benefit of such learning, and thus their conversations were private. They took care, however, not to make Howard or the others suspicious by conversing too intently or at great length.

Navarre glanced at Kat, and for a moment she was disconcerted by the startling sky-blue color of his eyes. He was a strikingly handsome man, golden-haired, with elegant manners. She did not recall the sergeant at Falcon's Lair with the others when she was taken prisoner. Mayhap he had other duties then—tending the horses or such.

"*Non*, mademoiselle," Navarre replied at last, in his pleasant accent. "I do not know. We were told to locate a blind woman who requested asylum from Lord Trelane."

"I am not blind," Kat pointed out.

"*Oui*, but a servant told Captain Howard who you were, and where you were hiding. She swore you had just regained your sight. You also fit the description given the captain."

"Who is looking for me?" Kat asked.

Navarre shook his head. "I am sorry, but I know nothing more." He unfastened the saddle bag on his steed, handing Kat the food left from his own small ration. "I saved some cheese and a crust of bread for you. Eat it quickly, before the others notice. You'd best get a drink, too, if you want one before we leave."

Kat nodded and retreated to a sheltered, grassy spot beneath a willow tree. She greedily devoured Navarre's offering. The bread was dry, the cheese rimmed with mold, but she was too hungry to care. Likewise, every muscle and bone in her body screamed with fatigue and pain, and her musings were laced with misery. *Morgan will come for me*, she thought again, as she did each day. This time her conviction faltered. It had been almost a week. *Surely when Morgan heard what happened, he was outraged. He will spare no effort to find me.*

That night, Kat wondered why she tried so hard to convince herself of Morgan's love. When Navarre made her a bed beneath the starry sky and rolled out his own blankets a few feet away, she stared through tearfilled eyes up at the beautiful sky. Despite her misery, she still prayed Morgan would come. Perhaps he studied the same stars this night, judging his direction and distance in order to reach her. Mayhap he was waiting for a more opportune time to waylay the travelers. He was outnumbered, after all. Under cover of darkness, doubtless 'twould be safer.

During her captivity, Kat remained rigid and nearly sleepless each night, listening for any approaching sounds which might herald a rescue attempt. When the glimmer of a new dawn appeared on each horizon, her hopes faded a little more. On the last morning before arriving in London, when Morgan still had not come, she turned her face into the blankets and silently wept.

* * *

Sergeant Navarre drew his lathered bay to a halt on a stone bridge spanning a wide, gray-brown river.

"London, mademoiselle," he announced, urging Kat to see for herself. He tried to sound cheerful, as if they were merely sightseeing, not headed for a grim reception somewhere in the city. "Have you been here before?"

"I cannot remember," Kat replied, certain she would not have forgotten such a noisy, dirty place. Her nose begged to be pinched when a peculiar stink wafted in their direction. She glanced at the river and swallowed hard at the sight of several bloated animals drifting lazily downstream.

Navarre sensed her dismay. "Give me Paris any day," he agreed and nudged his horse after the others. They were soon caught up in the flow and press of hundreds of peddlers and tinkers headed into London. Soon the shrill cries of vendors assaulted their ears:

" 'ere comes the fishman! Bring out your dishpan, Porgies at five pence a pound!"

"Raaaaaaspberrrrrries! Blaaaaaackberrrrrries!"

"Roses for yer lady, violets for yer Ma; daisies for yer buttonhole an' fresh shad for yer craw!"

Most folk were honest peasants or tradesmen selling their various wares, Navarre informed Kat, but there was also a customary sprinkle of cutpurses or thieves among the crowd, hoping to catch some poor traveler unawares.

Kat saw the sergeant's hand drop to the rapier strapped at his waist. By all appearances Navarre rode casually into the fracas, but she felt the tension in his body and knew his blue eyes flicked from side to side, keen as Ironbreaker's.

Captain Howard led the procession; she and Navarre brought up the rear. The contingent wound its way down narrow, cobbled lanes and streets crowded with people.

Kat felt faint from lack of fresh air. She clutched Navarre's waist with a fierce resolve in order to keep from swooning. The nightmarish journey was drawing to a close, but she was even more terrified of what awaited her at the end.

As they neared the Strand, she felt Navarre's hand close over her own. "Courage, Katherine," he whispered and squeezed her hand briefly before he let it go. Kat wasn't sure what startled her more: his simple act of kindness or the fact that he knew her Christian name, if indeed her name it was.

They reached the Strand. A procession of regal homes lined the river's edge. Captain Howard halted the procession before an elegant, H-shaped brick mansion. Dismounting, Howard paused to smooth his crumpled and stained uniform. He donned a gaily feathered hat before proceeding up the walk.

Kat determined that the captain intended to impress someone. She leaned forward and whispered in Lucien's ear, "Who lives here?"

Navarre shook his head. His silky, golden hair brushed against Kat's cheek. She drew back a little.

"I have never been here before, Mademoiselle Katherine. It is obviously a fine residence and no doubt belongs to someone of note."

Kat's curiosity overcame her fear. She watched as Captain Howard was admitted into the mansion and chafed with frustration when the great door closed behind him, betraying nothing of its owner. She and Navarre and the rest of the soldiers were forced to wait. The other men chose to dismount and stretch their legs after the long ride.

After what seemed an eternity, Howard reappeared. The captain wore a strange look upon his face. He stroked his pointed beard absently as he hurried towards them. His eyes narrowed when he met Kat's gaze.

"Get down, wench," he ordered her. "This is the place."

Sergeant Navarre swung down from the saddle first and gallantly offered his hand to Kat. She was painfully aware of her disheveled appearance when Navarre lifted her down, and her tattered, soiled skirts unfurled around her ankles. Nevertheless, she held her chin high. She saw Captain Howard scowl when Navarre steadied her.

"Take care, madam," Navarre said in English, responding to his superior's frown with a dismissing glance. "There is still ice on the street. It must have been a cold night here."

"Thank you, sergeant," Kat replied, meeting Navarre's gaze for a moment so he would understand her gratitude went deeper than she might express. He nodded, a faint smile forming on his lips. Then he retreated.

"Come along," Captain Howard said impatiently.

Kat followed the officer with trepidation. The closer they got to the mansion, the weaker her knees became. She feared what lay behind those deceptively benign carved doors. Howard closed in behind her as she mounted the steps to the elegant residence. Escape was impossible. Kat waited, nerves taut, while the captain yanked the bell pull again.

The door opened a crack, revealing an eye. As if he had never seen Captain Howard before, a manservant disdainfully inquired, "Who may I say is calling, sir?"

"Captain Howard, you oaf. I was here not less than a minute ago!"

The captain's thunderous reply did not impress the haughty servant in the slightest. "A moment, please."

The butler shuffled away to consult someone else, while Captain Howard tapped his boot on the stone stair. Kat squelched the absurd impulse to laugh, realizing there was nothing truly humorous about the situation. A moment became minutes, and Captain Howard's neck

turned red. Kat watched with interest as his face started
to mottle, as well.

"What are you staring at, wench?" Howard snapped,
raising his hand as if to strike her. Kat stepped backwards
to avoid his blow and nearly fell down the stairs. She
caught the hand railing and spared herself a painful tumble just as the great doors opened again.

"This way, sir," the manservant said. His tone and expression seemed more grudging than respectful.

Howard grabbed Kat's arm and pushed her roughly
through the entrance. His grip did not slacken until he
hauled her down the length of a richly decorated hall.
Then he thrust her into a parlor decorated in the Tudor
fashion.

Stumbling into the elegant room, Kat regained her balance and turned to glare at the captain as she chafed her
bruised forearm. She assumed Howard would remain to
guard her, but he was obviously anxious to effect a quick
escape himself.

"Here she is, milord," he announced. "Good riddance,
I say."

Kat realized there was a third person in the room. Surprised, she whirled about as Captain Howard stormed out
of the parlor. She met the calm gaze of an elderly man
with a crown of beautiful white hair. He was ensconced
in a leather chair with a tartan throw cozily arranged over
his lap.

"Welcome to Lawrence Hall, m'dear," he said, and a
jolt of recognition and shock coursed through Kat at the
sound of his voice—'Twas the Earl of Cardiff, Henry
Lawrence.

"Cry mercy, milord, 'tis you," she exclaimed with relief,
suppressing the urge to burst into hysterical tears. Her
knees gave way at last, and she sank in an exhausted heap
to the Turkish carpet. She extended a hand towards him.

"You can't imagine what has happened to me, Lord Lawrence. Yet you must know, for you rescued me."

He continued to regard Kat levelly as she spoke.

"I was taken prisoner by Captain Howard and his men for no good reason, milord. After many agonizing nights upon the road, I gave up hope of ever seeing a familiar face again."

Lawrence stared at her. He appeared more amused than confused by her rambling speech. Kat experienced her first prick of unease. The earl cleared his throat and, giving somewhat of a dry laugh, said:

"M'dear, I must congratulate you. You are an exceptional actress. I thought your blind act at Falcon's Lair most convincing, yet I doubt this little dramatic scene can be outdone. Surely you have performed for King Philip's court?"

"I know not what you mean," Kat stammered, rising quickly to her feet. Humiliation smothered her relief. She felt heat swamp her cheeks, and realized he only took such sign as evidence of her guilt.

"Lord Lawrence," she began again. Her voice shook a bit, but she plunged on. "There has been a grievous misunderstanding. Before my faith, I vow I was kidnapped from Falcon's Lair and brought here against my will."

"I trow I can warrant that much myself," Lawrence countered, a thin smile appearing at last on his lips. " 'Twas I who ordered the deed done. While I apologize for the captain's lack of manners, 'twould be unseemly for him to treat a common criminal like a queen, would it not?"

"Criminal?" Kat stared at the earl in disbelief and mounting horror. "Oh, you cannot think—"

Lawrence snorted, silencing her protest. "Save your breath, m'dear. There are others who will question you at far greater length. 'Tis my duty to the Crown to expose you for what you are; the Crown's to decide upon a proper course of punishment."

Kat's stricken gaze never left his. "There has been a terrible mistake, milord," she whispered. "Morgan would never permit such a thing to happen."

"Morgan, is't now? 'S'blood, y'are a cheeky wench. I warned Trelane; he would not listen to me. Mayhap that Spanish pup has also had a hand in this little conspiracy, eh?"

"Nay," Kat cried, understanding too late her attempt to absolve Morgan only increased her own guilt in the earl's eyes. "Nay," she repeated more quietly, fists clenched at her sides. "He knows no more of this madness than I, milord. I beg you, summon him here to London. He will quickly clear up this matter."

"Impossible," Lawrence snapped, dismissing her plea. " 'Twill make little difference, in your position. Obviously Trelane does not miss you overmuch; he did not mount any sort of heroic rescue, did he?"

The brutal reminder thrust a stab of pain through Kat. "What do you intend to do with me?"

The earl nodded as if 't'were the first sensible question she had asked.

"First I wish to see you cleaned up and made marginally presentable. Tomorrow I shall escort you elsewhere for questioning."

Kat did not favor the dour threat in his tone. "Questioning, milord? Of what sort?"

He gave her a hard look. "I did not say torture, did I? Nay, mistress, you will find me a fair man so long as you are honest with me. In turn, I vow you will be dealt with just as honestly. If you tell me everything about this papist plot y'are involved in, I may even ask for clemency in your case. If not—" he shrugged, indicating his low value on her life, "—then I shall not be responsible for the consequences. D'you understand me, mistress?"

"Aye," Kat whispered, averting her gaze from his merciless stare.

"Good. I suggest you go along with Ellie and see about restoring your appearance somewhat." Kat glanced over and saw the earl gesture to a shriveled, gray-haired servant who had mysteriously appeared beside his chair. "Mind you, Ellie's stone-cold deaf, so you needn't waste efforts trying to wheedle her sympathy or aid in escaping justice."

Kat nodded and stifled a temptation to challenge the earl into producing his evidence. She realized 'twas futile to continue to protest her innocence. Obviously, Lawrence had already branded her an enemy of England. Mayhap once she had a moment to compose herself, she might be able to think of some way to reason with him. She tried not to let her fear show, but the effort sapped the last of her strength and much of her dignity. Nevertheless she walked past the earl's glowering countenance with her head held high.

Someone was shaking Kat's shoulder.

"Winnie?" she murmured, opening her eyes. Her smile faded when she encountered the scowl of an old woman leaning over the bed: Ellie. Kat quickly rose and donned the threadbare dressing gown she had been given the night before. Without a word, the servant thrust a wooden cup of water and a stale crust of bread at her. Kat accepted both, then glanced over her surroundings. In her misery, she had not paid much attention to the room the previous day. Except for the dismal food, Lawrence's makeshift prison might qualify as pleasant. The bedchamber was decorated in muted shades of blue and rose—obviously a lady's room. How odd that it should serve as a jail. There was even a gold-framed pier glass and a plush Turkish carpet. The canopied bed was soft and wide. Kat had slept dead to the world until morning light.

After a nibble of bread, she set aside the crust and water and watched Ellie shuffle across the room and silently lay out a gown and kirtle. Ellie departed again without a word. The only sound to be heard was the loud rattle of a bolt and chain as the servant secured the door from the hall.

Kat unbraided her hair as she walked over to inspect the clothing Ellie had left. The servant had lugged up pails of hot water the evening before so Kat might bathe. She soaked and scrubbed for almost two hours until she was satisfied she was rid of most of the filth. There was no help for her skin, though. Kat paused to examine the myriad of cuts and bruises on her face and hands in the pier glass. She looked a sight, like a maid beaten by her master for insubordination.

She turned her attention to the gown and kirtle. Fashioned from coarse brown homespun, the cloth was clean and neatly mended, but fit for a tiring woman. The petticoats and undergarments were not much better. Yellowed with age, they had the texture of sand. Kat shuddered at the thought of drawing such harsh material over her raw, tender skin.

As she brushed out her hair, Kat reminded herself "criminals" could not be choosy. Hence, the bread and water to break her fast. She might as well get today over with, she mused with a sigh, donning the clothes and a pair of worn leather shoes Ellie had left behind. She then devoured the remainder of the dry bread and drank the brackish water, finishing just as the door opened again.

Ellie motioned her to follow. Kat handed the servant the empty cup in passing, and Ellie nodded her approval. They went down a curving staircase in silence. Kat had the opportunity to examine Lawrence Hall more closely than she had the night before. Portraits graced the walls in every direction—the earl's noble ancestors, she presumed. A variety of swords and ancient weapons, ranging from maces to battle axes, also lined the stairwell. Kat supposed they belonged to Lawrence; if so, he obviously valued them. Unfortunately, all of the weapons had been placed too high for her to reach.

Kat realized her thoughts must be revealed on her face. Too late, she tore her gaze from the display of arms and found Lawrence himself keenly observing her from the base of the stairs.

"Wise of me to place my prized collection out of reach of mischievous children, don't you agree?" he said by way of greeting.

"Most wise, milord," Kat coolly agreed, joining the earl as Ellie once again melted into the shadows. Kat forced herself to accept Lawrence's proffered arm as he turned to the door. He was elegantly garbed in dark blue velvet. His brocade doublet and trunk hose bore a gold and silver thread design. His matching stockings sported embroidered clocks.

"We are going out, Hemgart," Lawrence informed a more modestly attired servant standing sentinel by the doors. The butler merely nodded. Kat sensed Hemgart staring at her and stared at him in turn. He quickly averted his gaze.

"My coach awaits you, mistress." Lawrence indicated the direction with his ivory-handled cane. He did not seem to fear Kat might bolt. To her surprise, there were no other servants waiting outside to assure the earl's safety. For a moment she toyed with the idea of toppling the old man down the steep steps and sprinting off down the street. She suspected 'twould be futile; Lawrence confirmed as much a short time later.

"I confess, I am impressed. You passed the test, m'dear," Lawrence said, once they were in his coach and their journey underway. "Had you tried to assault my person within or without Lawrence Hall, I instructed my staff that you were to be cut down where you stood. You obviously value your neck, mistress."

"I know not what you mean, sir," Kat stiffly replied.

"Come now," he chided her, "we both know you might have easily overpowered this old man. Perhaps even gone free for a time, until the price on your pretty head was sufficient to stir interest among your own kind. In my experience, criminals are a faithless lot who will betray one another without a great strain of conscience."

"Then 'tis most fortunate for you I do have a conscience," Kat snapped back, struggling to keep her temper in check. "Despite your repeated accusations, milord, I am not the criminal you claim."

"Such remains to be seen, mistress. Ah, here we are." Lawrence leaned forward to rap his cane on the wall of the coach, signaling his driver to stop.

Kat glanced out the window and saw a mighty stone structure rising ominously into the haze over the city.

"What place is this?" she demanded. Her mouth went dry and her heart pounded at the sight of the dismal fortress.

From the other seat, Lawrence regarded her coldly. "I trow y'know it well enough by now, mistress," he replied. " 'Tis Newgate Prison, the only proper residence for base-born criminals such as yourself."

Eleven

"Nay!"

Kat's cry was drowned out by other sounds—screams and wretched moans issued from a passing cart designed with high, barred sides. 'Twas crammed full of unfortunates also destined for Newgate.

She felt a stinging blow to her cheek and cradled the burning flesh in her palm. She glowered at the earl through shock-filled eyes.

"I'll tolerate no hysterics, mistress," Lawrence said, waving his cane at her in a threatening fashion. "I vowed you would be dealt with honestly, and this is the only sort of honesty your kind understands. Lest you think to escape even now, rest assured my driver stands just outside the door to waylay you, if need be."

Outraged, Kat stared at the earl. But she was more infuriated by her own naivety. She had taken Lawrence at his word. He implied she would be treated fairly if she cooperated. She had done nothing to incur his wrath. She should have shoved the old man down the mansion steps when she'd had a chance!

Kat expected no fair trial. Henry Lawrence was going to abandon her to rot in Newgate, a fitting end to an endless nightmare.

Instead of uselessly railing at the man who had deceived her, Kat steeled herself for what was to come. Lawrence looked surprised by her composure and muttered grudgingly, "You've backbone, m'dear, I'll grant you that."

The door to the coach swung open, admitting the sights and smells of even more human misery. As Kat stepped down from the coach, she was greeted by a pail of waste flung down from a window above. The excretion missed the ditch by a country mile, splattering her skirts instead. She choked at the smell and clapped a hand over her nose and mouth.

"Dammed unpleasant business," Lawrence said mildly, descending from the coach beside her. "We must accept the just dues of our crimes, however."

"My sole 'crime,' milord, was trusting you," Kat replied, her voice muffled by her hand. She vowed never to be so culpable again.

Lawrence did not immediately reply. Instead he fastidiously tugged on a pair of white gloves—a sight so incongruous in a prison yard that for a moment, Kat just stared at him in shocked fascination.

"I confess I am somewhat discomfited by this place," he said at last. " 'Tis not my usual daily fare."

"By your composure, milord, I vowed you did this quite regularly," Kat retorted, removing her hand from her mouth so he might hear her clearly this time.

"Nonsense." Lawrence appeared genuinely offended. "I simply do this for queen and country's sake. A pity, m'dear, that Sir Walsingham no longer presides as secretary of state. There was no deceiving the good man; I know he would have been interested in your case."

"Why?"

He waved aside her ignorance. "Come now, mistress. You and I both know Walsingham's reputation. He managed to extract confessions from even the canniest of criminals. 'Tis regrettable he is gone. Walsingham's expertise with the rack will not soon be forgotten." Kat shivered as the earl's musings continued:

"It cannot be denied, Walsingham had a true calling for the *peine forte et dure*. With the careful placement of a single stone, he oft persuaded guilty papists to a different confession before they died."

Lawrence sighed, as if he missed the greater glory of days gone by. "Now, of course, criminals are merely hanged as a matter of course."

"Milord, please listen—"

But Lawrence was not listening. He glanced back at the coach, where his driver was shouting and waving in order to attract the earl's attention.

"Milord! 'Tis 'er Majesty!"

Kat turned to look, too, when the noise in the streets increased in a sudden din of confusion and discord. Everyone shouted and pointed in the same direction. She and Lawrence both strained to see what induced the frenzied outburst. Proceeding down Newgate towards the prison came a gilded carriage, drawn by four milky white horses and guarded by a brace of Tudor soldiers.

"The Virgin Queen! 'Tis ol' Bessie 'erself!" someone cried.

"Quick, lads, move the cart." One of the prison guards shouted the order at his fellow jailers. The cart full of wailing wretches was swiftly pushed out of view behind a low stone wall in the prison ward.

Kat stood rigidly at Lawrence's side, unaware that the earl had already made a leg for the passing queen. Her nerves quivered with a variety of emotions: fear and outrage, even unwilling fascination. She neglected to make her obeisance when the royal coach began to pass. She was too caught up in her own predicament to concern herself with etiquette.

One of the queen's guards mistook Kat's mien for rebellion. He hurried in her direction, aiming his pikestaff for her knees. Before he dashed her to the earth, however, the coach stopped so abruptly it rocked back on its wheels.

Kat glimpsed several pale ovals framed by the open windows of the royal coach—women's faces. A moment later she heard a scream.

"Sweet Jesu! Kat!"

The cry was followed by the descent of a figure from the coach. The young woman almost tripped over her train of black taffeta, as she dashed across the prison yard. The hood of her black cloak fell back, unfurling a cloud of burnished copper curls. She cried hysterically all the way. Her sobbing speech was incomprehensible until she reached Kat and the earl. There was silence in the prison yard as everyone stared wide-eyed at the unfolding drama.

"Dearest Kat." Gasping for breath, the young woman moved as if to fling herself into Kat's arms. "Heaven's mercy, we thought you were dead."

Kat swiftly stepped back from the stranger. She saw a flash of hurt in the redhead's gray-green eyes.

"I know you not," she said, forcing aside a faint sense of recognition. It stirred in the fogged depths of her mind, frightening her even more than the woman's intensity.

"Indeed, young lady, you must be mistaken," Lawrence interposed, addressing the well-dressed maiden more kindly than he ever did Kat. "This woman is a baseborn criminal, and I have brought her to Newgate in order that she may confess her many crimes against the realm."

"Nay," the redhead protested. She sounded indignant and gave her bright curls a fierce shake. "There is some terrible mistake, milord. Her name is Katherine Alanna Tanner, and she is my sister, presumed lost at sea."

At the shocking declaration, a stunned silence fell over Henry Lawrence. Meanwhile, Kat met the desperate gaze of the woman claiming to be her sister. There was such intense pain and hope in those gray-green eyes, Kat was forced to look away. She felt guilty for not being able to confirm the fantastic tale.

Kat could offer neither reassurance nor denial of the other woman's claim, though she knew Lawrence bristled at the notion she had any relatives at all, much less one so wellbred and obviously favored by the queen.

A rustling of taffeta could be heard across the yard, along with a murmur of voices. Kat turned with the others and saw the queen herself descending from the coach. Flushed with embarrassment, Kat remembered her manners and quickly knelt. The woman claiming to be her kin observed Kat from the corner of her eye, as she, too, made her obeisance to the approaching monarch.

"Damme." Lawrence swore under his breath. He had not yet risen from his earlier leg and felt his joints aching from his hips to his toes. Still, he gritted his teeth and held his position as Elizabeth Tudor approached. The queen moved briskly indeed for one dragging several yards of bejeweled velvet. Two young girls chasing her train fell over themselves trying to keep pace. A moment later, she arrived.

"You may rise." The regal voice matched the sharp, dark eyes and pointed face framed by a fan-shaped ivory ruff. As the earl and his prisoner came to their feet, Elizabeth turned and addressed the lady clad in mourning. "Mistress Tanner," she said a trifle sternly, "I trust there is suitable cause for this scene?"

"Aye, I believe so, Your Majesty."

"You believe so?" The queen's lips twitched, and Kat realized her crusty heart held a soft spot for the pretty redhead. "Because of your bereaved state, I am prepared to listen, m'dear, but make it swift. I feel far from patient today."

"Aye, Your Majesty." The redhead raised a teary gaze

to her liege and stated, "I have cause to believe this woman is my sister."

She gestured at Kat, who saw the queen's keen regard shift to her.

"Y'are certain, child?"

Mistress Tanner nodded. "I have no doubts, Your Grace."

Elizabeth did not speak again but merely nodded and returned her questioning gaze to the redhead. Taking a deep breath, Mistress Tanner continued her tale:

"Nigh two months ago, my parents received word one of our ships was lost at sea. They sent notice to me at Whitehall, Your Majesty may recall." When Elizabeth nodded again, Mistress Tanner appeared heartened.

"The ship that sank was the *Fìach Teine*. 'Tis Gaelic for 'Fire Raven.' 'Twas captained by my sister Katherine, who we all dubbed "Kat" with great affection."

Mistress Tanner turned and looked directly at Kat. "All hands were reported lost. I just returned from Ireland and the mass wake which was held for my beloved sister and her crew."

Kat stared at the redhead. She saw convincing tears flow unchecked from the woman's eyes at the telling of the incredible story. She tried to remember something as Mistress Tanner spoke; other than a brief flash of the red-headed man drowning, her mind was disturbingly blank. No answers or excuses came to her lips. She summoned no emotion, save pity for this poor creature, whose mind was obviously unhinged due to grief. Apparently Elizabeth deduced the same thing.

"Dear Mary," the queen said kindly, "I barely remember Katherine myself, as she was hardly prone to appear at Court, yet I do recall her a willful sort, given to wearing men's garb and oft behaving in untoward ways. Katherine favored your mother's people, the O'Neills. Would she have managed such a graceful obeisance as this lady? Methinks not. As much as you loved your twin, m'dear, you must admit Katherine had not a drop of manners in her body. She was all Irish and twice as stubborn as those folk are wont to be."

Twin! Kat heard little more of what Elizabeth said. Her stunned gaze flew back to the woman the queen had called "Mary."

"Please, Your Majesty. I know not why Kat does not remember me, but I know of others who can verify her identity. Uncle Kit, for one."

"Very well, child," Elizabeth soothed the maid, reaching out to pat Mistress Tanner's fair cheek with visible affection. "Inquiries shall be made, if you wish." She turned and regarded the earl with some surprise. "Milord Lawrence. I did not recognize you at first. Are you given to frequent Newgate nowadays?"

Lawrence flushed and bowed. "Well met, Your Majesty. 'Tis I who seek to deliver this woman into the custody of the Crown. I have proof she is part of a conspiracy with Spain at the core and brought her here in order to effect a more speedy confession."

Elizabeth raised an eyebrow. "Indeed," she murmured, flicking a glance at the grim stone tower nearby. "Pray, tell where you found the woman."

"Wales, Your Grace. She was in the custody there of a minor Welsh noble of Spanish descent."

"Ah." Elizabeth nodded thoughtfully, then turned to scrutinize Kat again. "Have you memory of aught we have spoken of, mistress?"

"Nay," Kat admitted. "Such speculation only serves to distress me further, Your Majesty. I remember nothing before Wales, though at times I do dream of fire and the sea." She shivered and met her monarch's piercing gaze for the first time. " 'S'truth, Your Majesty, I know not at all who I am, though I can and will vow I am not part of any conspiracy against the Crown."

Elizabeth pursed her lips, musing upon the matter.

Lawrence hastily interjected, "Proof, Your Grace, lies in one's actions. This clever wench pretended to be blind when she was in Wales. As Your Majesty may now note, she appears to see perfectly well."

" 'Twas God's mercy restored my sight, naught else," Kat angrily exclaimed. "Those at Falcon's Lair can confirm my tale."

"Certainly they shall be given ample opportunity to do so," Elizabeth stated, apparently not taking offense at Kat's outburst. "Methinks the matter bears further investigation. What say you, Lord Lawrence?"

"Aye, Your Majesty," he reluctantly agreed.

"Very well. 'Tis settled for now, or at least until we receive a missive back from Falcon's Lair." Elizabeth looked to Mistress Tanner. "Would it please you to bring this woman back to the palace?"

"Oh, aye, Your Majesty. Thank you," Mistress Tanner cried, seizing the queen's hand and reverently kissing it. She turned to regard Kat somewhat apprehensively.

"I know you don't remember me yet, Kat. I vow to be patient until you do. Will you come with me now?"

Kat hesitated. Then she nodded, accepting the hand the redhead held out to her. When the other woman's fingers laced with hers, she felt a brief, tingling sensation, like the charge in the air before a storm. *Twins.* How could it be? The two of them looked nothing alike. But when she joined Mistress Tanner and the queen's retinue, Kat's heart felt lighter than it had in many a day.

"I still cannot believe it," Kat said, trailing a finger over the edge of a carnelian-topped table. She occupied her sister's apartment at Whitehall. Upon the table was a miniature of two young women, painted a year or so ago. One of them was definitely her; there was no mistake.

Kat glanced at the stranger in the mirror for what seemed the hundredth time.

" 'Tis but a fantastic dream," she whispered.

"Believe it you must, dear Kat," her sister said, suddenly overcome by emotion. She approached with her arms outstretched. When Kat accepted the embrace with obvious hesitation, Mistress Tanner was crestfallen but effected a brave smile.

"How thin y'are, Kat. You've been through too much in the past weeks. We must put some meat back on your bones. Now, I insist you rest whilst I summon Jane to see about some suitable clothing."

Kat glanced down at her sorry attire and nodded. There was no question, her outfit must be a source of embarrassment to her sister. Certainly, she didn't blame the other ladies when they had politely suggested Kat ride in an open carriage behind the queen's coach, so as not to offend their monarch with the stench of her soiled skirts.

After Mistress Tanner departed to find her tiring woman, Kat looked curiously around the small apartment. There were only two rooms: one for receiving and the other a bedchamber. Her sister said they would share both. It should prove quite interesting. The bedchamber was half the size of the one she had occupied at Falcon's Lair, and the redhead had already appropriated every visible inch.

A narrow double bed took up the majority of space in the bedchamber. There was a vanity table with a variety of cosmetics and crystal flagons in evidence and a wardrobe with five drawers. The receiving room contained a small table and the pier glass. A pair of worn velvet chairs flanked the tiny hearth. Other than that, the apartment was quite mean.

Kat had expected much more of a great palace like Whitehall. Could it be their queen was clutch-fisted? She almost laughed aloud; Elizabeth Tudor's gem-encrusted gowns were anything but plain. Mayhap such frugality only applied to others, Kat thought with a wry smile.

By the time Mistress Tanner returned with her maid servant, she was full of questions again.

"Her Majesty called you 'Mary.' Is't your given name?"

The redhead looked startled for a moment, until she apparently recalled Kat's loss of memory.

"Nay. My Christian name is Erin Meredith Tanner. My middle name first belonged to our paternal grandmother. In her day, Grandmother was a favorite of the queen and was called Merry, as in good cheer, for her sweet disposition. I am said to resemble her. My godmother, the queen, nicknamed me thus when I was born and it stuck. Even our family calls me Merry now."

Kat could see why. Merry's bubbling enthusiasm was infectious.

"What do you do here at Whitehall Palace?" she asked.

"I am Mistress of the Music," Merry replied. When Kat chuckled, she added loftily, " 'Tis a duty of great importance. Her Grace enjoys playing the virginals from time to time, and I am responsible for keeping her music in order."

With some difficulty, Kat restrained her amusement. "Whatever do you do with the rest of your time?"

"Oh, the same things all young ladies enjoy. Embroidery, gossip, listening to music, and dancing whenever I can."

"Not the same things as all young ladies I fear. Such frivolous notions sound positively dull to me."

Merry appeared scandalized by Kat's comment. "These are considered only proper for a maid at Court. Methinks I should not be surprised by your scorn, though. You always laughed at me for indulging in such pastimes."

"Did I?" Kat asked with surprise. If she was indeed Katherine Tanner, she realized she was much the same even after the tragedy at sea. She apparently had little patience for such trite amusements.

"I envied you, y'know," Merry reflected. "You were always so outspoken, so brave, so daring. You crossed the seas like a sailor born to it, whilst I still quake at the sight of water. You called me a ninny back then. I must admit, I still am. When father gave you your own ship, I was wildly jealous, even though I couldn't bear to walk a deck myself."

Merry sighed and shook her head. "Oh, Kat, how I wish Father and Mother knew you were alive. I will send a message to our kin in Ireland, but 'twill be no use trying to reach our parents. They have just sailed again for the Indies, taking the eldest boys with them. The three younger remain with Grandfather O'Neill in Ireland. We have five little brothers, all told."

"Our parents sail together?" Kat was surprised.

"Aye, both he and she captain their own vessels. Theirs is an unconventional marriage," Merry said with a faint air of disapproval. "Father being English and Mother Irish made it difficult in the beginning, I understand. Fortunately, Elizabeth Tudor is a just queen."

O'Neill. Of course. But why the image of a black raven leaped into her mind was beyond Kat's grasp. She frowned. Then she remembered the amulet she was wearing when Morgan found her. He had also mentioned a tattered flag he'd found with the image of a bird bearing an oak branch. The raven again? The amulet was still at Falcon's Lair, and the standard, too—assuming Morgan had not discarded or destroyed either one or both.

She pushed aside thoughts of Morgan. She still ached for him, especially at night, but the pain was too fresh to examine as yet. She sought to distract herself. With growing curiosity, she asked Merry, "What of the O'Neills? Do they all live in Ireland?"

"Yea, Kat. Uncle Dan and all his boys—how can you

forget your favorite cousin Derry?—live up near Bally-
castle. You used to spend summers with them on the
farm. Aunt Glynnis said you were a handful."

"Didn't you go along to visit them, Merry?"

"Nay." Merry shook her head. "I asked our parents if
I had to, and they said I didn't. I'm not like you, Kat. I
don't enjoy dirt, wind, or water. Ireland has too much of
all three to suit me." She gave a delicate shudder. "Of
course, Grandfather O'Neill lives with Uncle Brendan
and Aunt Glynnis on the farm now. He deeded Raven
Hall to you when Mother and Father built their own
house. You always were his favorite," Merry added, a trifle
wistfully.

"Brann O'Neill," Kat said, not even realizing what she
had uttered until Merry seized both her hands with excitement and obvious triumph.

"Aye! You're starting to remember now, aren't you?"

"Not really," Kat said. "A few things are starting to
surface, though—mostly flashes of people's faces, bits and
pieces of names."

Still grasping her sister's hands in her own, Merry proceeded to pull Kat to the narrow window overlooking the
Thames.

"I know how to make you remember," Merry vowed,
dropping one of Kat's hands in order to point out a row
of grand houses on a distant rise. "See the white mansion
on the farthest end? The one with the columns?" When
Kat nodded, Merry said, " 'Tis called Ambergate. It belongs to Uncle Kit, our father's elder brother. 'Tis where
I spend much of my free time when I'm not at Court."

Kat looked at Merry confused. "Why?" she asked.
"Why don't you live in Ireland, with the rest of the family?"

A slow flush rose on the redhead's porcelain cheeks.

"Father and Mother said I might come to England,"
Merry answered, a bit defensively, keeping her gaze fixed

on the elegant mansion. "They knew how much it meant to me to come to Court and serve our queen. Besides, I wanted to spend more time with Maggie."

"Maggie?"

"Uncle Kit's youngest daughter, one of our English cousins." Merry chattered on, quickly and carelessly. "She's a dear sister to me, y'see, for we have so much in common—"

Merry clapped a hand over her mouth, her gray-green eyes widening with dismay. Kat nodded with sudden understanding.

"Whilst you and I don't," she concluded. "I understand things better now. Though we shared our mother's womb, we're completely different, you and I. You hated living in Ireland, didn't you?"

" 'Tisn't half so grand or fun as being at Court," Merry confided, with visible relief. Kat's gesture of understanding prompted her to confide her true feelings.

"Marry, 'tis quite boring in Ireland, Kat. For one thing, there are no suitable men, and I'd remain a virgin maid forever before I'd wed an ugly, old farmer or fisherman."

Kat released a peal of laughter at Merry's remark, then sobered a bit when she realized a deeper truth hidden beneath her sister's declaration; Merry was ashamed of the O'Neills, ashamed of the fact she herself was part Irish, and her twin acted more a Celtic warrior-queen than a proper maiden.

"Here are your gowns." Merry turned to address a brown-haired servant who entered the apartment with a mound of glistening material in her arms. "Be careful with those, Jane. They are too costly to replace."

"Aye, mistress," Jane panted, as she carried the voluminous pile to the bed. There she laid out two outfits almost reverently, smoothing the shining folds back with great care, as Merry looked to Kat.

"Which d'you fancy wearing for your debut? I shall have Jane set aside the other for now."

Both gowns were beautiful, displaying huge paned sleeves and elegantly embroidered skirts. One was a shimmering blue-green silk with watchet satin sleeves and cloth-of-silver insets; the other, a rich velvet in a shade of blue bordering on purple, with cloth-of-gold petticoats trimmed with sarcenet.

Kat sensed the servant girl surreptitiously studying her as she replied. "I know nothing of courtly fashion, I fear. You choose for me, Merry."

Pursing her lips, as if such a decision was of monumental importance, Merry said thoughtfully, "Methinks the violet for your presentation. We'll save the other for the midsummer masque. You can borrow my pearls on both occasions. I'm sorry I haven't any finer jewels to lend, but y'know a Maid of Honor is forbidden to wear anything of greater worth until she's wed."

Kat didn't know, but she nodded anyway and allowed Jane to help her disrobe. Feeling self-conscious, she quickly slipped into a silk chamber robe Jane held for her, then tied the sash herself.

"I'll have a bath sent up for you," Merry said. By the tone of her sister's voice, Kat could tell she was expected to act awed and grateful. Merry continued:

" 'Tis rather difficult to procure such niceties, but Uncle Kit taught me that a few well-placed coins can work miracles at Court."

"Thank you, Merry."

Merry smiled in return, though Kat sensed she was disappointed by the lack of ebullience in her thanks.

" 'Twill not be so difficult once you get used to it, dear Kat. I will teach you all the rules of Court, and you and I shall get along splendidly. What fun we two shall have till Mother and Father return! What a tale we shall have to tell them, too."

While Jane departed again to see about Kat's bath, Merry began to set out the various cosmetics and perfumes she intended to experiment with today. Watching for a moment, Kat remembered with aching clarity the scent of wild lavender Winnie had used to wash her hair at Falcon's Lair. A sense of loss gripped her like a dark hand—Would she ever see Morgan again? Surely by now, he should have sent word, an inquiry, something. He had seemed so determined to help her find her family; why would he care so little for her fate now?—Or had it never occurred to him to wonder what had happened to her? Such agonizing questions plagued Kat day and night, but she found no answers. Day by day, Morgan came ever closer to becoming a part of her past. She was in a different world now. Kat knew she should direct her attention to surviving at Court, but her memories were relentless. So, too, was the realization that she would love Morgan Trelane until her dying day.

Less than a fortnight later, Kat received a partial answer to her questions about Morgan. A missive from Falcon's Lair reached the queen. It was delayed by the Court's move to Nonsuch Palace in Surrey, where Elizabeth Tudor retired for a summer hunt. Morgan confirmed Kat's story of the shipwreck with a single terse passage. The curt paragraph revealed nothing of his true thoughts or what had happened between them.

Merry cheerfully relayed the contents of the letter, never suspecting Lord Trelane's words might wound Kat. For weeks, Merry had planned for the day when Kat could be properly presented at Court, and now that her sister's identity was established, she was delighted at the assurance of success.

"At last we are able to formally introduce you at Court,

dear. So you needn't mope about these rooms any
longer."

" 'Tis some relief, I grant," Kat replied with a touch
of asperity. "I was beginning to think I was your best-kept
secret, sister, short of being stowed beneath the bed."

Merry shook her head. "Please try to understand the
queen's caution, Kat. Till the truth of your tale was
proven, 'twas wisest to placate critics like Lawrence. He
did seem to take a fearful dislike to you. Now all appears
resolved, and we can finish planning your debut."

Kat had already decided she would leave such details
to Merry, a master intriguer. Her thoughts were of Morgan and the letter. She was devastated far more by his
cutting reply than she cared to admit. Yet she found it
impossible to despise him. Instead, more questions came
to mind. Why had Morgan not inquired as to her fate,
even her health? Why had he chosen those hateful
phrases, so clipped and cold? They conveyed a notion of
complete and utter contempt for Kat and her plight. She
realized she would never know what prompted his scorn.
She dared not write Morgan and ask such questions herself; there was too much risk that a message would be
intercepted by the queen's spies or betrayed by a messenger and summarily misinterpreted. Far more likely, Morgan would never reply. Did he think so little of her, then?
Had his declaration of love been a fleeting lark, a means
by which he might amuse himself with a blind woman
too foolish to see past her own heart?

Such dark musings occupied Kat's mind one evening,
as she watched Merry excitedly preparing for her Court
presentation. Days of exhausting etiquette lessons and
nights of rigorous coaching in courtly manners had apparently rendered Kat acceptable, at last. She wondered
why she felt inclined to rebel. She would not hurt Merry
for all the world, but she was weary of the superficial and

oft foolish conduct required of those who would grace the Tudor Court.

Before Kat had dressed in her formal attire, Merry drew a flat case of Moroccan leather from her bureau. She opened it and revealed a long strand of creamy white pearls and matching earbobs.

"Father gave them to me on our sixteenth birthday," Merry said to Kat, lifting the necklace out. She ran it lovingly through her fingers, then pressed it into Kat's palm. "He knew how I longed for my own jewelry. 'Twill be the perfect touch for your gown this evening."

"What happened to my own pearls?" Kat wondered.

Merry laughed. "You never begged for any jewelry; you wanted your own ship, and nothing else 't'would do. Father and Mother arranged for it somehow, the boys saw 'twas decorated with all manner of finery, and the moment you saw the ship, you christened her the *Fiach Teine*."

"Fire Raven," Kat whispered, an ache rising in her breast when a thread of memory teased at her. She closed her eyes and fancied she felt the gentle rise and fall of a deck beneath her feet. A breeze teased at her hair, filling the sails and her lungs with crisp brine air. She touched her neck, expecting to feel something cool and round—a metal disk. The amulet—'Twas gone. Kat's eyes flew open, and the image shattered into a thousand shards of memory, whisked away by an invisible wind. She almost remembered. Almost . . . Yet something prevented the full revelation, something she dared not dwell upon. She shivered, even though she was covered by her velvet gown and layers of petticoats. Merry did not seem to notice.

"La, I'll admit to being jealous, Kat. The arrival of your mighty present quite upstaged the play I had planned for everyone the same evening at Raven Hall. Rowan and Devlin were relieved to have any excuse to escape their roles—the naughty villains—and Kerill—well, he was a hopeless Sir Lancelot anyway. Of course, baby Blase and Sebastian were too young to appreciate my efforts at all."

Kat shook her head, still unable to picture her five younger brothers. She tried to hand back the necklace her sister had given her. " 'Tis obvious you love these pearls well, Merry, and I do not wish to usurp them from you."

Merry smiled conspiratorially. "Keep them, dear. As I said, pearls are the only permissible jewelry for a maid to wear before the queen. However, after your presentation, I shall not be required to attend Her Majesty any longer, as she is having a late meeting with her advisors. With any luck, it should last well into the wee hours of the morn.

"So I intend to wear something else with my gown this night, Kat. Something a bit more elegant, perhaps even a trifle daring."

With a twinkle in her gray-green eyes, Merry withdrew another, slightly smaller, velvet case from the drawer. This one opened to reveal a beautiful necklace of rose-gold, with a single, teardrop-shaped blue gem dangling from its center.

Kat granted 'twas a pretty bauble but didn't understand why it was considered daring. Merry glanced at her expectantly, so she merely said, "Interesting."

"*Interesting?*" Merry exclaimed, disappointed to have her prize reduced by such a word to paltry insignificance. "Marry, sister, don't you recognize a priceless sapphire when you see one? With all your grand voyages, I thought you were the expert on precious gems. More importantly, 'tis from a secret admirer who begged me in romantic verse to wear it this night, so he can seek me out amidst the others."

Kat gazed with amazement at her precocious sister. "D'you mean to encourage a stranger to a tryst?"

Merry colored. "Nay, of course not." She sounded indignant. She shut the case and slid it back into the drawer, just as a rap came at the chamber door.

"But it cannot hurt to encourage more gifts, can it?" she hissed at Kat beneath her breath. Another rap came at the door.

"Enter!" Merry called, and the door opened to admit Jane and a pair of male servants lugging a heavy oak tub. A maidservant followed, bearing pitchers of steaming water. Jane poured the water into the tub under her mistress's watchful eye. After dismissing all save her tiring woman, Merry added the crowning touch: a generous dollop of some sweetly scented oil. The cloying scent caused Kat to wrinkle her nose.

"What is it?" she suspiciously demanded.

"Attar of roses, dear. A lady cannot be properly presented at Court without everything on her person which is the very height of fashion," Merry explained. She corked the bottle and set it aside. Then she folded her arms and looked at Kat. "Into the water with you now."

Suppressing a grin at the maternal tone Merry used, Kat obediently shed her robe and sank into the tub. It was almost too hot at first. As it cooled to a perfect degree, however, Kat sighed with satisfaction and began to bathe at her leisure. Jane shortly returned with two more pitchers and helped Kat wash her hair and rinse it out. While Merry supervised Kat's toilette, she gossiped about the latest courtly affairs and speculated on what she herself would wear this night.

"Sky-blue silk, I think, the better to set off my magnificent new jewel," Merry mused. "Or, mayhap, dark blue velvet, to make me seem more mysterious. What do you think, Kat? *Kat?*"

Merry leaned forward from the velvet footstool where she perched beside the tub. She peered down at her sister with exasperation.

"By the rood," she exclaimed. "Kat's fallen fast asleep."

" 'T'would seem so," Jane agreed, amused. "If ye don't mind my saying, mistress, she's an odd one, this sister of yers. Ye claim yer twins?"

Merry nodded absently. "Nineteen this spring past."

Jane crossed herself while Mistress Merry wasn't looking. Her mum always said twins were unlucky, and Jane vowed this dark-haired wench was a stark contrast to her sunny-natured mistress. Indeed, it seemed too strange that *she* had appeared just when Mistress Merry reached the height of her popularity at Court. Why, what if the green-eyed jade tried to steal Mistress Merry's admirers from her? Granted, Kat was beauty enough to do it. Jane frowned at the unsuspecting woman in the tub.

Mistress Merry was no beauty, to be sure. 'Twas whispered at Court that her coloring was too vivid to be fashionable, her mouth a trifle too generous for perfection. Mistress Merry's sweet laughter, however, was a pure delight, her sense of humor well known and appreciated by courtiers. Her gray-green eyes always sparkled with mirth, and her personality alone drew men to her side, as bees to honey.

Yet what a mouse Mistress Merry is beside this sister of hers, Jane thought. All the sweetness in the world couldn't counter a pair of sultry, emerald-green eyes, nor a waterfall of hair like black silk. Jane shivered, looking for any excuse to leave the apartment. There was some odd sort of shadow hovering about Mistress Kat which she didn't trust. Jane's mum had told her daughter she possessed the Sight. If 'twas true, Jane feared Mistress Merry had a date with disaster, just as surely as her twin sister did.

Twelve

The man in the garden stiffened when he heard the night watch call out the hour. A moment later he relaxed, the lips beneath his trim black mustache thinning into a satisfied line. Just past compline; already it was dark. Any moment now, he expected to see a figure hurrying along the dimly lit garden path, breathless and bemused as she sought out her secret admirer.

Adrien Lovelle experienced a brief qualm. The first time it had been difficult. Destroying such a spirited woman seemed wrong. Kat Tanner had fascinated him. She still did, even in death.

Now he must strike again and further fulfill his and his sister's burning need for revenge. Remembering the greater outrage dealt his beloved Gillian, he shrugged aside any last-minute considerations for mercy where Merry Tanner was concerned. Instead he relived the bitter circumstances that led him here.

Fools! All the English are fools, Adrien thought. They assumed "Count Saville" was a charming representative of Henri IV's Court; none suspected, in truth, what prompted Adrien to follow the Tudor Court in its annual procession.

Vengeance—Revenge—The words contrasted with the gentle stillness of the night. Adrien mouthed them, lingering over each syllable in French. He had never appreciated their beauty so keenly before.

Sometimes Adrien wondered at his own obsessive need

to right a wrong nearly a score of years old. Whenever his resolve faltered, he took out a miniature of an angel-faced woman. She smiled serenely at him from the past. Something inside him burned whenever he gazed into those pale blue eyes.

Had Slade Tanner felt any hesitation when he force fed Gillian red salvarsan? Obviously not. Had the English-man mused over the dosage at all, or had he dumped the entire amount in a goblet of sweet wine and handed it to poor Gillian with a devilish, knowing smile?

Adrien felt perspiration break out on his brow. Memo-ries, anger, flooded back in a surge of dark emotions. He was but twelve when his sister returned to France and told him the story of how Tanner ruined her beauty. Slade had deliberately exposed her to the pox. He sought her death so he might marry an Irish wench of lowly birth.

Young Adrien cut his teeth on tales of Slade Tanner's treachery. When he became a grown man, he realized what he must do.

'Twas not enough to kill Slade Tanner nor his precious bitch of a wife, Bryony. Gillian had kept careful track of the Englishman's accomplishments over the years and noted Slade's success with rising agitation. Discreet in-quiries revealed the extent of the man's personal fortune, paid with the price of Gillian's beauty. Tanner was a wealthy man now, almost untouchable. The Tanner Trad-ing Company was renowned for its honesty, staked upon its owners' reputations. Slade shared everything—success and fair fortune—with his Irish wife. They even sailed together, trading in far away lands, such as Barbados and the Indies. Both Courts—English and French alike—were intrigued by the notion of the couple; their obvious popu-larity enraged Gillian. It took years of waiting, watching, and a few carefully placed spies in Tanner's multinational crew to finally reveal the couple's one fatal weakness. It had been obvious all along. Gillian crowed with delight when she seized upon the answer.

Neither loss of fame nor fortune would serve to destroy Slade and Bryony Tanner—The death of their children, one by one, was the only way to shatter their hearts, their lives. The first triumph came when they heard news of the death of their eldest daughter, Katherine. 'Twould be advanced when they were devastated by the demise of the second.

The five Tanner boys were young yet, Gillian had said; there was still ample time to plan. Besides, the two eldest sailed with their parents. 'Twas too difficult to get them alone. The three youngest Tanner boys remained in Ireland, guarded by that fierce old pirate, Brann O'Neill. Their grandfather never let them out of his sight.

Adrien hand slipped inside his doublet and withdrew a jeweled dirk. The precious rubies in the hilt glittered by moonlight. He stroked the blade thoughtfully, musing upon what he must do. 'Twas such a pity to stain fine Damascus steel with blood. 'Twould be quick and nearly painless, which he regretted. Certainly, Slade Tanner had not shown his sister any such mercy. Gilly almost died an agonizing death a fortnight after surviving the pox. With the help of her loyal maid servant, Elinor, Gillian had tried to prove Slade was a murderer. To this end, she cleverly substituted the body of a village wench who died from the pox. Maid and mistress dressed the deceased in Gillian's finery and partially burned the body to make identification impossible. The dead girl resembled Gillian closely enough to satisfy the sheriff. Hence, Slade Tanner was arrested.

It seemed small recompense for the loss of Gillian's famed beauty, had Slade succumbed to Tower Green. He had not. Thanks to an old hag's meddling, Gillian told Adrien, her death was ruled a suicide instead. 'Twas a double outrage. First she lost her renowned beauty, then was relegated to the status of an anonymous corpse buried in unhallowed ground. Even Elizabeth Tudor withdrew her favor in the end and refused to attend the funeral of her former lady-in-waiting.

Gillian had shared the rest of the Tanner family's lies with her little brother. Slade told numerous falsehoods at his trial, chief among them that Gilly was a whore unworthy of remembrance—To this day, a faithless woman was still dubbed a "gillyflower" at Court—Their surname, Lovelle, was rendered a disgrace in England. Elizabeth Tudor forbade any branch of the family, English or French, to visit her Court.

Assumed dead and thus forced to flee England, Gillian returned to the land of her birth, where she found young Adrien quite malleable. He was willing to be coached in the ways of love and revenge. Family honor suggested it; his conscience demanded it. *Oui*, the Tanners would pay.

Adrien tightened his grip on the dirk. Justice must serve a different master now, he thought. When Slade learned of the fate of his second born, he would wither away a little more through grief. 'Twas as close to a living death as any man might suffer.

Adrien ran his tongue over his teeth. Much like the proverbial wolf, he lay in wait for his unsuspecting prey. Anticipation of another kill raced through his blood, as the moon streaked across the night sky.

"Sweet Mother and Mary!" Kat gasped, pausing in the gardens outside Nonsuch to press a hand to her aching side. "I never danced so much in my life. I cannot breathe."

"Nonsense," Merry laughed and took Kat by the other hand, tugging her sister along the moonlit garden path. "You simply need a bit of air. I'll grant the galliard can be tiring at times, but 'tis such fun."

Kat shook her head goodnaturedly and followed Merry further from the palace into the coolness of the late spring evening.

"I vow, my stays will burst one of these days," Kat grumbled. She glanced down and saw her bosom still heaved dangerously above the décolletage of her violet gown. 'Twas no use trying to tug the lace any higher. She had already tried, much to Merry's chagrin and amusement.

With such a precarious bodice, Kat tried to minimize her activity during her Presentation. Her curtsies were a bit shallower than usual, and she favored no dance where there was much hopping about. Yet all the courtiers were anxious to meet her. It seemed every popinjay present had demanded the honor of a dance. Kat could not deny she was flattered, but their lecherous eyes and roving hands left her feeling defensive and rather indignant. She quickly discovered she was not one for flirting and coy bantering, like her court-bred sister.

Despite Kat's conservatism, Merry had declared her a success. 'Twas due to Kat's exotic looks, Merry claimed, and didn't seem to mind at all. She hurried Kat along now, glancing right and left with a hopeful gleam in her eye.

"I know he's here somewhere," Merry said. Kat suddenly understood her sister's preoccupation. The gift of a sapphire had captured her greedy feminine heart and piqued her curiosity. Merry was determined to follow her mystery suitor's instructions to the letter.

"Mayhap I should return to the hall," Kat suggested.

Merry shook her head. "Stay, sister. I want you here to witness everything so I know I'm not dreaming. Mayhap he and I can steal a quick kiss or two in the shadows, with you acting as lookout before the queen joins the Court, or one of her tiresome spies wanders out into the garden."

"Merry!"

"Goodness, I forget, you're such an innocent some-times." Merry sounded exasperated. "Rest assured, dear, I shan't presume to advance any further in my admirer's affections. I am still a maid in every respect. It does no harm, however, to encourage generous men a bit. What possible danger can come from a quick cuddle?"

Plenty, Kat thought darkly, remembering Morgan and his smooth seduction. It seemed so long ago, now. She had foolishly given him her heart, her body, and now she had nothing to show for it. She wished she could talk with another woman about what had happened to her. Mayhap Merry?

With a glance at her flighty sister, Kat decided not to risk spilling out her heart. Merry, for all her canniness about Court, seemed terribly young.

They waited almost an hour for Merry's secret admirer to appear. Disappointment was reflected upon Merry's face. She stamped her dancing slipper on the grassy knoll they stood upon.

"Marry, 'twas all a rare hoax! One of the other girls must have played a joke on me. Ooh, I'll even place a wager as to which bawd 'twas: Anne, perhaps, or Elizabeth Howard. Beth always was a catty one. 'Tis likely not even a real sapphire. Paste!"

Merry snorted with disgust and fingered her necklace. The large jewel dangled between her breasts, reflecting the hue of her sky-blue silk. Angry as Merry was, 'twas clear to Kat she was reluctant to part with the jewelry as yet.

Kat smiled, knowing the dusk concealed her mirth. "It doesn't seem apt that a man might wait here in plain view of the Court. Wooing one of Bess's maidens must be done discreetly, I trow."

Merry drew in her breath. "Of course. What a ninny I am! My hidden knight must remain hidden. So where do I begin to find him, Kat? His message said the gardens, yet there are leagues of garden to be had."

The redhead sighed, gazing hopelessly around at the myriad of flowers and bushes stretching off into the velvety dark. The nearest maze was illuminated by the shining lights from Nonsuch itself. Within the palace, the revelries still continued, faint music and laughter echoing in the distance, making an eerie refrain in the night.

"Where is the least likely place a couple might be discovered?" Kat asked.

Merry thought a moment and snapped her fingers. "The boxwood maze. How simple, yet how perfect, like the single red and single white rose he sent me last night. Surely 'twas a clue, sister."

Kat recited softly:

> *One blushing shame, another white despair:*
> *A third, nor red nor white, had stol'n of both . . .*

Merry glanced at her, startled. "Where did you learn Shakespearean sonnets?"

"In Wales." Morgan once read those same lines to her; Kat had never forgotten them. Pain touched her at the memory, but Merry seemed immune to her distress.

"Yea. A Tudor rose, both red and white, said to be planted by great King Hal himself in the center of the maze. How apt." Merry drew in her breath with anticipation. "He must be waiting for me there even now. Mayhap he watched me dancing earlier, his eyes for me alone. We can only hope he has not given up and left."

"Aye," Kat agreed, a bit dryly. Despite her cynicism, she admitted Merry's enthusiasm was catching. She agreed they must proceed to the maze. "There we shall quit ways," she told Merry. "I mustn't be part of any such intrigue, for in truth, I'm not sure I approve of it."

"La, Kat, how can you say such a thing?" Kat glimpsed

Merry's pout. "You've had more than your fair share of adventure already. Granted, 'twas not with men, but 'tis much the same. A bit of danger is always exciting, is't not?"

"Real or imagined?" Kat parried. Merry didn't answer, pausing instead to free her skirts from a thorny bush.

"The silk has been torn. God's toenail!" Though she fancied herself a lady, Merry could outswear a sailor, when warranted. Kat burst out laughing.

Merry glowered at her by moonlight. " 'Tis no cause for mirth, Kat. What if he is put off by my torn gown?"

"I'll wager he'll not even notice, he'll be so busy rending it further," Kat said.

Merry sniffed at her sister's remark. A second later, she forgot her ire in the excitement of the moment. "Here's the maze. Take my hand. Oh, 'tis terribly dark here, is't not? 'Tis so romantic." Merry shivered with anticipation.

Kat experienced a genuine pang of fear. She didn't know why the great maze frightened her tonight. She had explored here before during the day, whilst the Court was out hunting. Enchanted by the clever design, she had wandered the maze for hours. But it seemed almost sinister at night, lit by a thin sliver of moon.

"Have you finished the entire maze before?" she asked Merry.

"Aye, but only in daylight. This may prove quite a challenge." Nevertheless, Merry gathered up her cumbersome skirts and squeezed into the narrow corridor.

With a sigh, Kat followed suit, staying as close as she might to Merry without entangling their skirts. Boxwood hedges rose just above their heads—a vast, impenetrable wall. Kat fought back a rush of fear. After the first turn, the maze branched off in several directions—a pitch-dark labyrinth. Merry paused for a moment, then chose the left path.

"Men are always contrary," she said by way of explanation. Despite her unease, Kat had to smile at this airy observation.

For several minutes, they blundered along in the darkness. Merry yelped when she lost a slipper, and when she bent to retrieve it, her hair snagged on a branch.

"Next time I'll demand earbobs and a bracelet to match," she huffed. Apparently, determination was a Tanner trait, for Merry straightened herself once more and set off again.

Within a halfhour—even after several wrong turns— they luckily reached the center of the maze. There the Tudor rose bloomed in elegant solitude, a parti-colored descendant of the Red Rose of Lancaster and the White Rose of York.

Merry suddenly screamed, startling Kat. A dark shadow loomed before them on the maze path.

"*Bon soir,* Mademoiselle Tanner." A male voice spoke, almost menacing in its quiet vein. As if he had not scared Merry out of her skin, the man raised her hand to his lips. Kat saw the shadowy profile place a gallant kiss upon her sister's hand. "I was not at all certain you would come."

"Count Saville." Merry apparently had to think a moment to remember his name, yet she seemed pleased. She curtsied, her skirts whispering over the grass. "La, sir, what a fright you gave us. Didn't he, dear?"

"Indeed," Kat echoed, trying to deny the intense terror the man's smooth Gallic voice instilled in her. Why? Lucien Navarre was French, but he did not frighten her in the least.

"Who is the sweet dove flying beside you tonight, *ma chère?*"

Merry giggled a little at his endearment. "This is my sister, Count Saville." Kat noticed the shadow stiffen. Merry prattled on blithely. "Her name is Katherine, but we call her Kat because of her green eyes. Kat, dearest, this is Count Saville. He is visiting Court this season."

There was a brief moment of silence. Kat assumed she had imagined the tension till her own hand was lifted and summarily brushed by a pair of cool, invisible lips. She shivered at the contact.

"Vraiment! I never guessed you to be sisters. Even by moonlight, I can tell your hair is the hue of a blackbird's wing, Mademoiselle Katherine, while Mademoiselle Meredith's is the color of spiced apple wine."

Merry drank in the count's clever speech. Kat smiled warily and withdrew her hand. Discreetly wiping it on her skirts, she said, "I fear I must leave now. I imagine you two have a great deal to discuss in private."

"Aye," Merry said. "First, though, you must tell Count Saville about your grand adventure, Kat."

Sensing Kat's unwillingness to cooperate, Merry continued chattering:

"Our Kat is accounted to be most popular at Court, sir. She experienced the most exciting event and is being called upon to tell the tale over and over again. She was shipwrecked, y'see, and nearly drowned off the coast of Wales. We almost lost her, but for the grace of God."

"Indeed?" Kat sensed the man's gaze shifting to assess her. By twilight she hardly made out his features, yet the feeling of panic persisted. She could not wait to escape his company.

"I am most interested to hear how you escaped such a dire fate, Mademoiselle Tanner."

"Oh, you may call her Kat, as we all do," Merry insisted. "We must all be great friends this season, *n'est-ce-pas?"*

Merry began to practice her atrocious French on the count. She thanked him for the necklace, then continued to flirt with him in increasingly bold, bad French. In the meantime, Kat grew more uneasy. She looked for any opportunity to escape the couple. She started to inch backwards through the maze while they talked. With a sinking heart she felt the count's attentions shift back to her. He had the advantage of the moon behind his shoulder, and saw her attempt at retreat.

"I must accompany you and your charming sister back to the palace, Mademoiselle Tanner." He spoke to Merry, while eyeing Kat. " 'Twould be remiss of me to allow two maidens to wander in this darkness. There may be rogues lurking about."

"We will be fine, sirrah," Kat replied.

Merry delicately shivered. "I, for one, would appreciate the escort, Count Saville."

"Then I insist." He gallantly extended his arm to Merry, and, with a coy giggle, she placed her hand upon his sleeve. "Y'know, you may only walk us to the hall. I fear, our good queen is protective of her ladies' reputations."

"*Bien sûr.* Before we part ways, I must beg another favor. Do call me by my Christian name, Adrien." He gushed another meaningless French compliment under his breath to Merry. Kat heard her sister loose a breathless sigh.

"Naturally I do not wish to encourage rumors," Saville continued, still addressing Merry, "and I have the greatest respect for your reputation, mademoiselle. Therefore we shall part ways before we enter the palace. 'Tis enough for now that you have graciously accepted this small token of my affection."

Merry fingered the sapphire. "La, I confess I could not resist. Jewelry is my one true weakness, as dear Kat here can confirm."

Count Saville turned his predatory smile on Kat. "And you, Mademoiselle Katherine? What is your weakness?"

Something in his words chilled Kat to the bone. Something deep within her sprang to her defense.

"I have no known weaknesses, sirrah," she answered,

meeting his burning black eyes with a steady gaze. "Certainly I cannot be bought or sold with trifles."

The insult seemed to escape Saville. He merely inclined his head and placed his other hand possessively over Merry's on his arm, effectively pinning her sister there. Kat realized he issued subtle warning in his own way. Merry stood between them now. He would not hesitate to hurt her, should Kat prove a threat to his hidden agenda.

"You needn't be nervous. You look lovely," Merry assured Kat. The open coach they rode in proceeded at a fast clip through amber-studded gates surrounding the white mansion on the hill.

"I know Uncle Kit will be delighted to see you, Kat. It has been years since you visited England, and he's never traveled to Ireland himself."

"Tell me more about our uncle and his family," Kat requested. Mayhap idle conversation would lessen her nervousness. Meanwhile, she leaned forward, eyes shaded by her hand so she might drink in the sight of the manicured green lawn and leagues of neatly clipped rose bushes surrounding the quaint family estate known as Ambergate.

"You'll find out yourself," Merry said. "Uncle Kit is kind and funny. He used to be one of the queen's favorites until he got too old to dance attendance upon Elizabeth, and gout set in—or so he claims. Faith, I'm not so sure he wasn't looking for any excuse to spend more time with his beloved Isobel." Merry smiled, then added, "You'll also meet Isobel, Uncle Kit's second wife. I'm sure you don't remember stories of his late wife, Elspeth. She died before we two were born. Elspeth was the natural mother of Uncle Kit's three girls. I hear tell she was a horrid woman. Later Kit and Isobel went on to have three more boys of their own. They've a big, boisterous family now."

Kat had second thoughts about meeting the English side of the family. What would they think of her? Would they be hurt or insulted when she couldn't remember them? 'Twas too late to retreat, however. The great door to the mansion had already opened, and a man came down the steps, waving at the approaching carriage.

Merry half-rose from her seat. "Uncle Kit!" she cried, bouncing up and down on the springy seat. Her red hair flew in halo fashion around her heart-shaped face. "Here she is. Look, our little lost Kat!"

The auburn-haired man quickened his pace. 'Twas obvious to Kat he was in some sort of pain and favored his right leg. But he displayed nothing, save the warmest of smiles, as he moved to greet his visitors. Sir Christopher Tanner was stockily built, his crest of bright hair now laced with silver. Merry was right; kindness was written all over his face. When the carriage swayed to a halt, Kat didn't hesitate. She stepped down into his open arms, touched when they closed around her.

"Thank heavens you're safe," Uncle Kit declared, his hands alighting on Kat's shoulders after the warm embrace. He drew back apace to look at her. "I can hardly believe it. You've grown up, Imp."

"Imp?" Kat echoed, puzzled. Merry and their uncle exchanged quick glances, then laughed in unison.

"I never thought you'd forget your nickname here, Imp. It has been many years, I fear. Far too many." Their uncle curled a hand around Kat's shoulder as he led her up the steps. "I pray you two will stay the weekend."

"Aye," Merry replied as she hurried after them, the train of her carnation-colored silk gown trailing behind. "Her Grace has given me leave for three whole days. She knew how I longed to bring Kat here to show off our English roots."

"Good. 'Tis settled, then." Uncle Kit escorted them into the mansion's foyer, then turned and faced them with a broad smile. "You've picked a fine time to visit, girls. Isobel is presently in town, but Anne and Maggie are both home."

Merry clapped her hands in delight. "Oh, I can't wait to see my dear cousins again. How are they?"

"You can judge for yourself. Meantime, I shall see to some refreshment. You've had a long drive from Nonsuch in uncommon heat." While their uncle departed to instruct his house staff, Kat looked to Merry with a confused expression.

"Isn't there another daughter?" she asked.

Merry nodded and answered her in a low voice. "Yea, the middle girl, Grace. She is not oft spoken of. She ran away and joined a convent two years ago, in direct defiance of the queen."

"Why?"

"Elizabeth Tudor had arranged a good match for Grace. The ungrateful chit said she didn't wish to marry, not now or ever, unless 'twas with her true Lord, Jesus." Merry shook her head. "Apparently a servant girl gave secret instruction to Cousin Grace over the years. She was surely the catalyst behind Grace's decision. I suppose Uncle Kit never forgave himself for hiring the papist jade. At least I shouldn't, if I were he."

"Uncle Kit has had an unhappy life in the past," Kat observed. She didn't know why she said such a thing, for there was certainly no visible suffering in Sir Christopher's green eyes now. Yet Merry confirmed her statement with a nod.

"Aye. Between his shrew of a first wife, Elspeth, and Grace's treason, the dear man has not had an easy time of it, I trow." Merry lowered her voice further so as not to risk being overheard. "Uncle Kit also lost his first son, Christian. Father mentioned that the babe was stillborn.

It happened a long time before we were born. I hear tell there's a wee grave tucked away among the wildflowers at Dovehaven. Someday I shall look for it."

"Dovehaven?"

"The little estate in Kent set aside for my dower portion. Remember, Kat, you have your ship—or at least you did. I'm sure Father will replace it, so you won't be penniless when you decide to marry."

"I doubt I ever shall," Kat replied, thinking of Morgan, the only man she had loved. Merry, too, fell abruptly silent for some reason. Perhaps she sensed the topic was uncomfortable.

Both glanced up with relief when a rapid clatter of boots broke the silence. Two half-grown lads dashed down the mahogany staircase towards them.

The boys thundered down the stairs, their hair disheveled, their clothing askew. One was fair, the other dark. Both sported identical grins. They appeared to be a mischievous pair, indeed.

Spying Kat and Merry in the hall, the two skidded to a stop on the Turkish carpet and exchanged panicked looks.

"Gervase! Terence!" shrieked an outraged female voice from upstairs. "You come back here at once and clean up this frightful mess."

Moments later, a flustered young woman appeared on the upper landing, with the obvious intent of chastising the lads further. Noticing the guests below, she gave a soft cry and rushed down the stairs instead.

"Cousin Merry. Is't really you?"

The two lads seized the opportunity to escape. Dashing past Kat and Merry, they disappeared through a door leading to the kitchens. Kat glimpsed them running past a window round the back of the house. Neither of the redheads appeared to notice or care.

"Maggie!" Merry exclaimed, with equal delight. She

rushed forward to greet the other young woman. The pair of them looked remarkably alike, for cousins. Maggie Tanner's auburn hair was several shades lighter than Merry's, but her face was so similar as to be startling. *These two might be the twins, not Merry and I,* Kat mused as she studied the other two standing side by side.

"Oh, Maggie, 'tis so good to see you again. You'll never believe who I have here with me. D'you remember your own cousin, Katherine?"

"Dearest Kat!" Maggie hugged the startled Kat in the same impulsive manner Merry always did. "I cannot believe it! We had word you and . . . that there had been . . . some sort of a terrible accident. Oh, dear." Maggie pressed a hand to her lips and looked helplessly to Merry.

" 'Twas a grievous rumor," Merry put in quickly. "As you can see, our Kat is very much alive. The queen is in progress to Hampton Court. So I brought Kat here for the weekend to visit you all. Uncle Kit said Anne is home, too. How is she?"

"Mayhap, you'll see her later," Maggie said wryly. "She is presently resting. Anne rests only when she is not busy being an absolute terror. She's breeding again, y'see, and poor James sent her here for the weekend in order to get a bit of relief for himself and the girls."

Merry chuckled. "I know she vowed not to have another babe so soon after the first three."

"Aye, but James wants a boy, as all men do. Despite Anne's determination not to become *enceinte* again so soon, I fear her husband won the duel. I reminded the little goose that once is enough. Methinks she's learned the truth of it, by now."

How worldly Maggie Tanner seemed for her young age! Kat thought, amazed. She mused a moment upon what her cousin had said. Once is enough . . . once is enough . . . unconsciously, Kat's hand moved to touch her velvet stomacher. She shuddered. Was it possible she carried Morgan's child beneath her heart? Surely not. Yet her insides knotted anyway when a maid servant approached them with a tray of sweetmeats and goblets of watered wine.

Kat shook her head at the proffered refreshments and welcomed the distraction of her uncle's return.

"Are you weary, girls?" he inquired. "Y'are welcome to retire early, if you wish. 'Twill not hurt our feelings one bit, will it, Maggie? The country air always tires me out at first, too."

Merry shook her head, nibbling at a sweetmeat. "I couldn't sleep a wink, Uncle Kit," she declared. Obviously remembering Kat then, she added kindly, "Perhaps you are tired, dear."

Three gazes shifted to Kat. Truth to tell, she *was* weary, having stayed up so late the previous evening and rising to travel at dawn's first light. Often, courtly revelries themselves continued till dawn. Kat realized she would disappoint them all by retiring so early, though.

"I would much prefer seeing Ambergate than taking a nap," she replied. "Merry has told me much about your beautiful house, Uncle Kit."

He smiled when she used his nickname. Kat saw that Ambergate was her uncle's pride and joy when he led them on the tour. The mansion ranked only a small step beneath his precious daughters, as was obvious when Uncle Kit took Maggie's arm and placed it upon his with an affectionate pat.

"Come along, m'dears. I'll show you all the latest renovations. Mayhap someday this estate shall belong to your son's son, Maggie, and if my prayers come true, our family will be just as close in future as now."

Trailing a pace or two behind, Kat cast her sister a puzzled look. Merry obligingly explained in a whisper.

"Thus far, Anne has produced only girls. Of course Grace shall not bear any children now, whilst she is on a ridiculous mission to become a nun. Maggie is betrothed to a baron, one she has not met, but who is doubtless virile enough to see to the task God and Uncle Kit intend for him."

"Merry!" Kat protested, with a shocked giggle.

Merry shrugged. "If Maggie does her proper duty by the family and has sons, Ambergate will most assuredly be hers. Kit's boys by Isobel have other prospects. The eldest, Nathan, is away at Oxford. He intends to work for our Uncle Phillip when he finishes his studies. Gervase and Terence are too young yet to manage any properties, but Uncle Kit has seen to their futures and purchased other lands nearby.

"Cousin Maggie is the lucky one. How pleasant to live out one's days here in the country, yet still be close enough to Court for frequent amusement."

"The house is beautiful," Kat agreed, pausing to admire the gallery where their uncle had led them. Portraits of Tanners down through the ages—most of them sporting distinctive red hair—lined both walls in either direction. Kat studied them one by one until she came upon a painting whose subject looked startlingly familiar.

"Merry, I didn't know you'd already had your portrait done."

Merry laughed. Uncle Kit and Maggie returned to look at the portrait. The painting Kat had indicated depicted a lovely, auburn-haired young lady garbed in Court regalia, her gray-green eyes twinkling as she gazed loftily upon a smitten admirer kneeling at her feet.

"This is the original Meredith Tanner," their uncle explained. "Your paternal grandmother on the Tanner side. A strong resemblance, isn't there?"

" 'Tis unbelievable," Kat gasped, turning to stare a moment at her sister, then back at the portrait. "Why, it gives one shivers. Even their expressions are the same."

Merry chuckled again. "La, I'll admit it even gave me

a start the first time I saw it, too. 'Twas like peering into a looking glass. Now you see why the queen calls me Merry, instead of Erin. I have always been dubbed thus by Her Majesty and must remain so.''

Kat tore her curious gaze away from the portrait. She felt her superstitious Irish blood rebel against the strange coincidence of identical women living in different times. It didn't seem natural. 'Twas almost frightening. As Merry hurried ahead to catch up with her favorite cousin, Kat hesitated beside her uncle.

"How did Grandmother Tanner die?" she asked Kit quietly so the chattering redheads wouldn't overhear.

He didn't seem to sense her unease and answered matter-of-factly enough, " 'Twas an unfortunate accident. Though Meredith was married and the mother of four sons, she was still ardently pursued by several swains at Court. Father was powerless to put a stop to it, I fear, and since the queen demanded Merry's presence at every Court function, Mother had no choice but to go.''

"What happened?" Kat persisted.

Her uncle hesitated, his eyes shadowed. "Two of Mother's love struck courtiers got into a violent quarrel over the favor of a dance with her. Words shortly turned to weapons in the yard. Mother tried to stop them, I was told, but to no avail. In all the confusion, she hurled herself between the men just as they lunged for each other.'' Uncle Kit shook his head, obviously reliving his role as a terrified young boy who had seen his beautiful mother's broken, bleeding body brought back to Ambergate.

"Of course, Bess Tudor was appalled and sent both of the guilty fellows promptly to the block. Yet even our mighty queen could not restore a mother to her sons.''

Kat vigorously rubbed her arms up and down to banish a sudden chill in the gallery. "I've not heard such a tale before. I'm sure I wouldn't have forgotten it.''

"Your father, Slade, was the youngest of us boys. He

was only four or so when it happened. I'm sure he doesn't
remember it himself. There was no reason for him to
repeat such a sad tale to his own offspring. In fact, I
confess I'm a bit guilty myself of distorting the truth at
times. I'd rather remember Mother enjoying her old age
here at Ambergate, as she deserved. I'll wager, Slade's
stories about your grandmother are more my invention
than reality.''

Kat didn't reply. She couldn't. While Uncle Kit had
told her of the unfortunate tragedy, she thought not of
her grandmother. Instead she remembered Merry's innocent laughter as she flirted with a mysterious man calling
himself Count Saville.

Thirteen

'Twas a blessing, Winnie realized, whenever Lord Trelane left Falcon's Lair for a time. Never had she dreamed to rue the day when the Master was home, yet in the last three months, she found herself hoping he would be delayed somewhere whenever he rode away to attend to his demesne.

Ever since Mistress Kat had departed, the Master had been in a mood blacker than the hell the good Father painted for sinners. He was short and curt with all the staff nowadays—even the Careys—and downright merciless with those who truly earned his wrath. The former steward, Renfrew, who had terrorized the villagers and burned the Widow Sayer's cottage, was recently located in Tregaron, where he was discovered gleefully drinking down the last of the Lord Trelane's pilfered coins. Renfrew was seized, publicly whipped in the city street, and driven from Wales without so much as a shirt on his back or a crust for his supper. Those who lived in the village were forbidden to aid the man or shelter him in any way, on pain of death.

Lord Trelane bought another stallion to replace Idris; unlike the noble black he had once ridden through the hills, this ugly roan was so evil-tempered that even Winnie's husband, Lloyd, was unable to handle the beast. Bit by bit, the Master had cleansed Falcon's Lair of each and every trace of Kat, from the gowns she had worn to the faithful Patches, whom he sold on a whim to a gypsy tinker wanting a nag to pull his cart.

The Devil Baron, in truth, 'tis what himself is now, Winnie thought with a shudder. Nothing more, nothing less. At first she had no idea the Master's rebellion went so far as to succumb to the nightly ease Gwynneth offered him. Winnie only noticed the serving girl getting too full of herself. When she sought to bring Gwynneth up short one day, she was shocked by the results.

"Mind your place, nosy old cow," Gwynneth retorted in a tone of pure insolence. "The Master's got no complaint with me, you can be sure. He'll not take kindly to your nasty remarks. You and the others best take heed; you will all be sent packing before me."

At last Winnie understood. Old and slow she might be; blind she was not. She did not understand the Master's choice, though. He was hurting, 'twas obvious to everyone. Yet Winnie knew there were better ways to fill the void Kat had left in his heart than with common trash like Gwynneth Owen.

Winnie did not bear the maid servant's insolence much longer. One day she dared speak her piece to Morgan himself, risking his wrath.

"What you need is a wife, milord," she said. By this time, she had had quite enough of his ill temper and Gwynneth's blatant disrespect. "You need a lady wife of proper breeding; one who'll give you a league of sons to fill Falcon's Lair's empty cradle."

She spoke out of place and out of turn. To her surprise Morgan looked thoughtful, seriously considering her advice.

"I believe you are right, Mrs. Carey," he said at last, albeit somewhat ominously. "I shall make some inquiries."

To Winnie's considerable shock, he had. Lord Trelane had simply nonchalantly informed her and the rest of the staff that he would be gone to London for a time. The unspoken inference was that he sought a wife.

As she watched the Master ride away on a fine summer day, with Jimson acting escort, Winnie shook her head. She prayed the Master would return in better spirits, preferably with a bride as sweet-natured as he was sour. She wiped her hands on the apron protecting her skirts, sighed, and returned to the keep. She was confronted at the door by Gwynneth. The girl's furious, tear-splotched face told a tale of its own. Judging by Gwynneth's violent reaction, Winnie knew 'twas true the Master had decided to take a wife.

"You gave him the idea, you old witch!" Gwynneth shrieked, raising her callused hand as if to strike Winnie. Winnie was tired of the girl's hysterics. Grabbing Gwynneth's wrist with her strongest hand, she wrenched the girl's arm down and held it fast at her side.

"I'd best be avoiding any talk of witchcraft, if I was you, wench," Winnie retorted. "I hear tell of your love potions and binding spells, missy, and wonder if there's not far more brewing up on Madoc's Craig than thunderstorms."

Gwynneth paled. Her mouth turned down in an ugly sneer. "I've more power than you'll ever dream of having, you old cow," she hissed, yanking her arm free and fleeing from the keep.

Winnie let the girl go. Her gaze narrowed after Gwynneth. *Something must be done about that one,* she mused, before the Master returned with his new bride.

Morgan made good time en route to London. His new stallion, as yet unnamed, had a wild streak and carried him south at a reckless pace. His man, Jimson, was hard-pressed to keep up but didn't dare grumble. Trelane's temper was infamous nowadays for good reason; none of

the servants wanted to cross the man known as the Devil
Baron even in his younger years.

'Twas true enough, Morgan intended to fetch an English bride. What Winnie and the others didn't know was
that the contract had already been drawn up and signed
over a month ago. Winnie's suggestion had made Morgan
realize what he was missing. Damme, he was a man, and
a man had a right to heirs and some small portion of
happiness. To this end, he needed a woman, a girl of
good stock and decent upbringing, who would give him
strong sons to carry on the family name.

Once, not long ago, he had shied from the thought of
forcing any woman to take his name and bear his children. Now he no longer cared. A properly raised maid
wouldn't question her fate; arranged marriages were the
norm throughout the Tudor realm. A biddable wife was
all he sought and, according to his London source, he
was betrothed to a Mistress Margaret who should prove
suitable enough.

Morgan scarcely glanced at the miniature he received
after negotiations were settled. He had little interest in
how the wench looked. She might well be as ugly as himself—indeed, it might be preferable—and then Morgan
should not feel inclined to apologize for his own appearance.

When he and his manservant stopped to sup at an inn
on the way to London, Morgan found curiosity getting
the better of him, at last. He dug through the saddlebags
to find the sheaf of correspondence from London, accompanied by a small, painted portrait of his intended.
He had not requested the miniature. By tradition, the
girl's family supplied it along with the contract.

Morgan found the papers and the miniature. After a
hasty supper of boiled lamb and cabbage in the inn, he
retreated upstairs to his private room, lighting a second
candle in his room to better reveal the miniature's detail.

Even as he studied his fiancée's ordinary and agreeable
features and idly noted the flaming red hair, Morgan
compared Mistress Margaret to another woman he had
yet to forgive, or forget.

Kat. *Damme her brilliant green eyes and night-dark hair.* Morgan also cursed the memory of her upturned face. Lips
sweet and soft as rose petals, parting delectably under his
own. Glorious tresses of ebony silk. With a disgusted noise,
he tossed the miniature aside. How could he do honor by
Mistress Margaret and her family, when he wasn't able to
rend that traitorous bitch from his thoughts?

Heirs were what he needed. A brace of strong sons by
this English girl to assure that the Trelane name would
not die out. Then mayhap . . . God willing, someday he
might forget.

After a brief sojourn at Hampton Court, the queen's
retinue retired to Whitehall for the remainder of the summer. The novelty of traveling with the Court had quickly
worn thin for Kat, as did the endless parade of coxcombs
seeking her favor. She seized any opportunity for privacy
and soon discovered her favorite place was the garden.

One fine August day, she occupied a stone bench
alone, alternately contemplating the charms of the Shakespearean garden and the irony of her life. Royal sword
lilies and handsome yellow broom contrasted the wild
sweetbrier and humble Michaelmas daisies and clove-
scented gillyflowers. Bees droned around her, adding a
lazy touch to the pastoral scene. She had slipped away
from her duties in anticipation of a moment of rare peace
from the usual hustle and bustle. Her time at Court had
been fraught with difficulty—much of her own making,
she knew. Kat doubted she would ever fit into her sister's
worldly frame. Merry might find scheming and flirting as
natural as breathing; indeed, she seemed to enjoy it. Kat

was already weary of the trite and shallow life she lived beneath the shadow of the throne.

She discovered she was no more cut out for curtseying and gossiping than Merry was for striding a deck. As ludicrous as 'twas to imagine her sister commanding a crew at sea, 'twas no less laughable whenever Kat tried to lisp as Merry had taught her or effect a simpering air whenever a man glanced her way. It went against her grain. Kat soon rebelled against the notion altogether.

Since her arrival, she and Merry argued constantly over Kat's refusal to adopt the role of a helpless female or to execute a proper curtsey. After her presentation at Nonsuch, Merry had rebuked Kat for donning men's garb in order to ride with the hunt. She still cringed whenever Kat was called to attend the queen in chambers; fortunately 'twas not often. Kat suspected Elizabeth Tudor recognized her true nature and was content to let her alone, as long as Kat did not corrupt Merry or her other ladies-in-waiting. 'Twould be hard to corrupt such a gaggle of goose brains, Kat reasoned, unless one tried to inject some common sense into their empty little heads. She loved her sister with all her heart, but Merry exasperated her quicker than anyone she knew—even Morgan.

A shadow fell over her in the garden, blocking the light by which she admired the blossoms. Kat glanced up with trepidation, startled from her reflection. 'Twas not Count Saville, as she had feared.

"Sergeant Navarre," she exclaimed with genuine pleasure and surprise, her gaze drinking in the familiar features of the soldier who protected her during the long journey to London. It seemed so long ago, yet Kat had never forgotten his generous deed, nor would she ever be able to repay him in kind.

"*Captain* Navarre," the golden-haired man modestly replied in his accented voice. He offered her a formal bow and doffed his feathered green hat, tucking it beneath one arm. "I confess, I have been promoted since we last met. I am delighted to make your acquaintance again, Mademoiselle Katherine."

"Doubtless shocked, as well," Kat replied with a smile, patting the empty space beside her on the stone bench. Both spoke French without a second thought. "Please do join me."

"Why should I be shocked?" Navarre asked, looking bemused as he sat beside her.

"You must have believed me a criminal, at least, a traitor to the Crown, at worst."

Navarre shook his head. His golden hair was longer now, drawn back into a queue with a black velvet ribbon. Kat admitted he looked dashingly handsome in his green and white Tudor uniform. A wide golden sash accented his lean waist.

"*Non,* never a criminal," he softly replied. "A lady fallen upon unfortunate circumstances, perhaps."

"You are kind."

He offered Kat a broad smile of white teeth flashing against his tanned skin. "I confess, I was relieved to learn the truth came out through Her Majesty's persistent inquiries."

"Then you knew my fate?"

"I fear gossip is as commonplace here at Court as rain in the English spring, Katherine. Even so, I admit I noted your arrival at Whitehall with more than a passing interest."

Kat's heartbeat quickened when she saw the open admiration in his sky-blue eyes. "Captain Navarre—" she began.

"Lucien, *s'il' vous plaît,*" he corrected her. "I must also confess I have admired you from a distance these past months, as you graced our Court. Though I am doubtless not the only man enchanted by your beauty and your wit, I finally decided to presume upon even something so small as our past acquaintance in order to gain your attention."

Kat plucked nervously at the plaits of her murrey-colored silk gown. Though she was delighted to see him again, Navarre's intensity made her uneasy. Part of her feared he was laughing at her—if only a little—for she was hardly a favorite at Court.

" 'Twas not necessary to presume upon anything, Lucien," Kat replied at last. "I fear, however, I am accounted more a viper than a true wit. I'truth, 'tis hard to hold my tongue whenever that gaggle of courtly geese starts yammering."

Lucien laughed at her wry remark. "I find your honesty refreshing."

"As I am ever grateful for your kind assistance whilst I was suffering dire circumstances. I welcome the chance to thank you again."

Lucien extended his index finger and raised Kat's chin so he might gaze into her eyes.

"Would I be amiss in asking you to show your appreciation by accompanying me to the queen's masque a fortnight hence?—Unless you have already found a partner."

Kat shook her head. Merry had tried to badger her into going with every suitable courtier from here to Yorkshire. But she had gradually withdrawn from all social activities, except those where the queen herself specifically requested her presence.

Aye, Kat knew she would never be suited to the same sort of tiresome life her sister was. She longed for something else, something more, something beyond her grasp, as ever. She succumbed to a sudden, ridiculous urge.

"Yea, I accept your escort, Lucien. I have only one trifling favor to request in turn."

Lucien raised a golden eyebrow, clearly anticipating a feminine wheedle for jewelry or such.

"I want you to practice fencing with me."

"C'est tout?" He stared at her a second and tried to laugh off her request. "Surely you jest, mademoiselle."

"I do not, sirrah." Kat raised her chin a notch, stung by his laughter and the incredulous look in his eyes. "You need not fear that I shall prove a poor pupil. I am a trifle rusty, aye, yet not wholly unfamiliar with a sword."

Lucien licked his lips and glanced about, as if he expected a party of jesters to materialize from the shrubbery. When he realized she was serious, he shook his golden head.

"It seems incredible, but somehow I believe it. You are unlike any woman I have ever met, Katherine."

She smiled, assuming he meant it as a compliment. Unwillingly, her mind flooded with longing for Morgan, even as she gazed at the hopeful, handsome Lucien.

"Will you be my fencing partner?" she asked him.

"Oui. Against my better judgment. Where may we practice?"

"Right here, each daybreak. The courtyard is large enough to serve, I think."

He nodded, glancing about the enclosure. "It is a trifle small, yet there seems enough room to move. May I assume it is important that others do not learn of our little assignation?"

Kat reached out and mischievously patted his knee. *"Certainement,"* she whispered, delighting him with her sudden playfulness. Perhaps each hour she spent in Bess Tudor's realm had not gone to waste. Kat had forced herself to learn a few coy mannerisms in order to eavesdrop upon the vague and troubling phrases Saville murmured in her sister's ear.

She had been unable to dissuade Merry from seeking out Saville's company during the Court's progress, however, and a great rift had grown between the sisters. Kat was still wary of the French count and suspected his motives were based upon anything but honor.

As she chatted desultorily a few moments more with Captain Navarre, she realized she had a perfect opportunity to get some answers.

Before Lucien departed, Kat asked him if he had heard of Saville. He looked puzzled for a moment, then shrugged.

"*Oui*, I know a little of him. It is rumored the count is a wealthy courtier visiting from the Bourbon Court, yet I found it odd I had not heard of him, as I grew up in Paris."

Kat jumped up from the stone bench and began to pace the garden path. Lucien rose, too, regarding her sudden agitation with dismay and obvious concern. She turned to face him and demanded, "Is't possible Saville is an imposter?"

Lucien looked surprised by her intensity. "Anything is possible, I suppose."

"Is there some way you could find out? Make discreet inquiries through your family in Paris, perhaps?" Kat returned and placed her hand upon the captain's doublet, appealing to him with all the feminine charm she could muster. " 'Tis most urgent, I trow. I would not ask this of you, were it not."

Lucien nodded. "I believe I can help. I will find out all I can. Perhaps by the night of the masque, I shall have some answers for you."

"*Merci*," Kat exclaimed, rising on tiptoe to impulsively peck his cheek. Just as quickly, she withdrew, before Lucien's arm could close around her waist.

Lucien sighed when he realized he would not receive more passionate thanks. "*Au revoir*," he said, giving her a good-natured grin in his disappointment. He donned his feathered hat.

By the time Navarre left, Kat already looked forward

to her fencing lessons and the night of the masque. If Saville was indeed an impostor, 'twould be the perfect opportunity to expose him. She knew Merry would accept nothing less than irrefutable proof that the man courting her had sinister motives. Better yet, Kat would be prepared for any danger Saville presented. She must not count upon Morgan or Captain Navarre to save her now. She had learned the hard way to trust in herself alone.

What Kat was not yet able to deduce was the possible motive Saville might have for hurting her sister. But the uneasy feelings persisted whenever he was around, sometimes leading her to the point of blind panic whenever she heard those smooth French nothings trip off his tongue.

The odious popinjay was seducing Merry, but to what end? Why, of all times, must Merry herself be so gullible concerning Saville and obtuse about taking a sister's advice? Kat shook her head in despair. She had the ominous feeling events were starting to spiral beyond her control; she also feared what awaited Merry in the end might be destruction of terrifying proportions.

Merry sighed as she unpinned the jeweled brooch securing her cloak. She tossed the cloak over a chair. For once, she was too tired to be annoyed by Kat's critical gaze. She knew her sister sought for traces of Adrien's love bites on her throat and breast.

She collapsed beside Kat on the bed they shared, dramatically flinging an arm over her eyes. "Never again!" Merry vowed. "Never again shall I dash off to Ambergate, only to spend the entire weekend trying to console our featherbrained cousin."

Kat was surprised but relieved by this announcement. She assumed Merry had secretly met with Saville, not visiting their relatives. "What happened?"

" 'Twas Maggie again. She's inconsolable over the match Uncle Kit made for her."

Kat had heard tell their cousin was betrothed again, but she hadn't paid much attention. It happened to girls by the hundredfold, many before they were Maggie's age.

Merry refreshed her memory further. "Recall that I told you Maggie's first betrothed, William Scone, died from a lung fever shortly before you arrived? Of course Uncle Kit had to search for a suitable replacement. Maggie should be grateful her father didn't condemn her to the life of an old maid, like Cousin Grace. She won't be." Merry sighed again, as if quite put out by the ungrateful attitude of their cousin.

"Maggie's heard some wild rumor that her new betrothed is deformed, and nothing will do to comfort her now. She's convinced the man must be a stark mad, raving beast, at least to hear her talk."

"Is he?" Kat idly asked, not much interested.

"I doubt it. Someone is just playing a cruel jest on our cousin. I can't imagine Uncle Kit giving away his favorite daughter to some monster." Merry shrugged. "Anyway, the man's a baron. 'Tis what really counts. She'll have a title; there will be lands for any sons they have. I don't know why the little chit is being so stubborn and disagreeable about the matter."

"What would you do?"

"What do you mean, Kat?"

"What would you do if you were in Maggie's place? Would you go meek as a lamb to the slaughter?"

Merry sat up on the bed and stared at her sister, in mixed outrage and shock. "Marriage is not like that at all, Kat. 'Tis a holy estate, a sacred union between man and woman before God."

"Be that as it may, shouldn't the two people involved at least be agreeable to the deed?"

Her sister's mouth turned down in a matronly frown.

Merry looked annoyed. " 'Tis not a woman's place to question the wishes of God and her parents."

"Ah, I see. So if our father betrothed you to one of those ugly old farmers or fishermen you complained of back in Ireland, you'd be obedient and wed him?"

"Ohhh!" Merry squealed, turning red. "Unfair, Kat. There isn't any comparison. For one thing, Maggie's betrothed isn't a lowly Irish peasant, he's a highborn baron. Secondly, Father would never be so cruel or thoughtless as to barter me off to a man I didn't approve."

Kat triumphantly pounced. "Oh?"

Merry sputtered for a second. "You . . . you're impossible! I don't know why you argue with everything I say, Kat. Simply for spite, I suspect." She gave her auburn curls an angry toss.

"I'm not arguing, Merry, but merely pointing out a few things you may not have considered."

"Oh, if you're so *very* clever then, why didn't you stay in Ireland and be a proper wife to your own husband?"

The moment the words burst from Merry's lips, she clapped a hand over her mouth, her eyes wide with horror and dismay.

Silence strangled the air between them. Kat stared back at her twin.

"What did you say?" she whispered, fearful of pursuing Merry's slip, yet determined to ferret out the truth.

"I . . . oh, Kat . . ." Merry groped for words, paling with distress. She reached for Kat, as if to offer a hug. Kat warily withdrew from the gesture.

"Explain yourself," she demanded, shaking with the intensity of the emotions tearing through her. She sensed she was close to making another discovery of some sort, this one far more terrible than all the others combined. She steeled herself for the worst.

"Kat!" Merry was sobbing now, though not enough to render her incoherent. "Don't force this, please. 'Twas agreed by the family you need never know. 'Twould only hinder your recovery—"

"As't shall hinder your life, sister, if you do not immediately tell me what you speak of," Kat snarled. In a burst of temper, she felt something break free inside. A hot, boiling rush of memories poured over her—molten lead in her heart.

"Rory! You're speaking of Rory!"

"Nay!"

"God's blood, so that's who the redheaded man was! *Rory was my husband, wasn't he?*"

Her accusation echoed in the room like a clap of thunder. Furious, Kat hurled herself at Merry, their painful collision cushioned somewhat by the bolsters. Over and over the two rolled, off the bed and onto the hard floor, while Merry struggled and kicked in self-defense.

"Tell me," Kat cried, straddling Merry and throttling her as she might a man, finding fleeting satisfaction in the other's cries for mercy. All of a sudden, something choked off the rage, a deadly calm. By then she was but inches from her twin's face, staring into the terrified graygreen eyes of her sobbing sister.

"Had I my *scian* now, bitch, I'd thrust it through your lying little ribs," Kat hissed, as she shook Merry by the shoulders. Her sister wept. Nothing touched Kat now— neither regret nor pity—as she stared at Merry's tearstained cheeks. Comprehension finally dawned.

"Sweet Jesu," Kat whispered, "you lied to me. All of you, all along! Not a word about marriage, until today. I always wondered why you avoided the subject. Not a word about Rory till I brought him up. I shared my strange memories with you many times and felt a fool for it. You always shrugged them off."

"What good does it do now?" Merry wailed. "Rory is dead; naught can bring him back. I—we all thought if you did not remember the tragedy, you would not grieve so. Nothing would be served by it."

"Least of all your interests, sister." Kat made no attempt to soften the deadly sarcasm in her tone.

"I cannot deny, I did not want a weeping widow hanging about me at Court," Merry whispered, shamefaced. "But I cried enough for the both of us when I heard Rory was lost at sea. We all adored him, Kat. He was kind and funny and wonderful."

Rory. A kind and funny and wonderful man she did not remember. Spasms of guilt and anger coursed through Kat. She suddenly rolled off of her sister, rose, and paced the room in a fury of agitation.

"How?" she demanded. "How and when did Rory and I come to meet and marry?"

Merry sat up, smoothing her crushed skirts and wiping her tears. "We've both known Rory Shanahan and his family since we were eight or so," she shakily began. "La, I confess I fell in love with him at first sight. He had nothing to do with me. 'Twas always you, Kat. You and the sea. You two had that in common from the beginning."

"Marriage, though? Sweet Mother and Mary, I cannot fathom it. Why? When?"

Merry pursed her lips and chose her words carefully. "I will be honest, Kat. Methinks 'twas a business arrangement, in the beginning. You wanted to build a trading empire as father and mother had, yet sought no charity from them. Rory had the means, not the ship. When you received the *Fiach Teine*, I gather this union seemed natural to you both. You were terribly fond of Rory, I believe. 'Twas no passionate love story, but he was good to you, and you had two happy years together, before . . ."

"Before he died. Drowned like a rat, while I looked on and did nothing." Kat's laughter was harsh and self-deprecatory. "I did not even have the decency to mourn him a single day. I cannot have loved him very much, then."

"Dear Kat, you cannot blame yourself. The shock must have wiped away your memories, to save your mind. Take some comfort in the fact Rory perished at your side, at sea, as he would have wished. 'Tis for the sake of your own sanity you do not remember the past."

"Nay," Kat whispered, denying Merry's words. " 'Tis not enough. Sweet Jesu, how can I forget a man like Rory, much less any husband of mine? What kind of woman fails to mourn a beloved mate?"

"One who grieves deeply, I fear." Merry rose from the floor, as she tentatively approached and touched her sister's arm. Kat shuddered, yet did not reject the peace offering.

"Why did we never have any children? Or have I forgotten them, too?"

Merry shook her head. " 'Twas God's will, you told me once. You and Rory were hopeful, but the babes never came."

" 'Tis just as well, I suppose. I should doubtless make as appalling a mother as I did a wife."

"Oh, Kat—"

"You must not scold, Merry. I must come to terms with this in my own time and way."

Merry was silent a moment. "Aye, I trow it. Mayhap what you need is a hiatus from Court."

"Aye, perhaps I do," Kat said, walking to the window.

"I'm sorry, Kat. I didn't mean to hurt you."

"Of course you didn't." Kat turned back to face her sister, forgiveness and repentance filling her heart. "I know I've caused nothing but trouble for you since I've arrived. Neither of us are happy with the present arrangement. There's no reason I can't go live with Grandfather O'Neill or Uncle Brendan, till Mother and Father return."

"Please don't go," Merry cried, startling Kat with her vehemence. "You can't mean to leave now. I promise I will try to be more agreeable in the days to come. 'Tis just that—" Merry took a deep breath, meeting Kat's curious gaze with a guilty flush on her cheeks, "I've been so *jealous* of you," she finished quietly.

"Jealous? Of me?" Kat stared at her sister in disbelief.

"Aye. From the day Rory looked at you instead, I've seethed with envy. You're lovely, Kat—you truly are, y'know—and don't think I haven't noticed the way the courtiers look at you. Why, even stuffy Lord Huntingdon changed his tune once he got a glimpse of you. He wrote an ode to your emerald eyes."

"Being serenaded by an elderly fop is not necessarily a compliment, Merry."

Merry smiled wanly. Tears sparkled in her gray-green eyes. "I overheard Essex say I'll never be the beauty you are."

Kat shook her head, rejecting her sister's words. "Robert Devereux may be the darling of the queen, but he is naught more than a foolish coxcomb." She had never been impressed with Essex, despite his fine figure and elegant little speeches at Court. She suspected him a fortune-hunter whose greed oft outshone his wisdom. Someday he might pay a dear price for such ambition.

"Adrien asks about you all the time, too," Merry continued, provoking a shiver of unease in Kat. "I'll admit I've wished at times you'd never come to London. But never did I wish you ill, Kat. Please believe me."

"I do." Kat nodded, holding out her hands to her sister. Hesitantly, Merry accepted them. Kat gave Merry's a reassuring squeeze. "Let's call a truce now, Merry. No more harsh words or feelings. I want our last days together to be happy ones."

"Last days?" Merry cried, dismayed.

"Aye. I've decided to return to Ireland. 'Twas not something I decided overnight. I've been thinking about it for some time. After the queen's masque, I intend to go home. In truth, 'tis where I belong. 'Tis the land of my birth; I pray, the same place holds the key to my memory—memories of Rory Shanahan, of the life I had before I lost everything."

"You're not leaving because of me?"

"Nay." Kat smiled and kissed Merry's cheek. "Let's just say our destinies lie in different directions. We must both be content with that."

Fourteen

"Mandritti."

At Lucien's command, Kat brought the rapier down in a sweeping gesture from the right. He was quick to counter, and the echo of mated steel rang off the stone buildings. Without a pause, he continued the measured drill:

"Roversi."

With a sudden flourish, Kat switched the sword to her other hand and delivered a left cut from a backhanded position. Lucien looked startled by her speed and strength, but recovered in time to deflect the strike. Kat fancied a few ladies might wander into the garden to track the source of the clashing sounds; if so, they would find nothing amiss in the sight of Captain Navarre and a young lad engaged in swordplay. Not without reason did Kat don a page's uniform for her lessons—velvet breeks and a canvas shirt, a doublet and trunk hose. Beneath the shirt, her breasts were bound both for practical and obvious reasons. Her hair was braided and tucked beneath the flat velvet cap of an apprentice.

"Prime. Seconde. Tierce. Quarte." Lucien barked the guards at her in rapid sequence, observing and timing Kat's reactions. Several times, he stepped forward to readjust her position. On *Quarte,* he turned her hand nails-up, pushing the point slightly farther, up and out.

"Better," he said. He handed her a short, slim dagger.

"Try it with the dagger in your left hand for defense. Now, begin again."

A dozen times, they rehearsed each classic move, including thrusts and parries and guards, till Kat gasped for breath and moved too slowly to suit Lucien. He grabbed her right wrist and steadied the gleaming steel above her head.

"You are not pacing yourself," he chided her. " 'Twill be your downfall in the end. You are smaller and weaker than a male. 'Tis a matter of fact, not a manner of insult."

Kat nodded, wiping her brow with her sleeve, after he released her wrist. Aye, she knew her limitations. Even the thin rapier seemed to weigh a hundred stone now; she could barely lift it after their exhausting drills. She had learned to fence with a heavier weapon, a small sword with a true basket hilt in the fashion of Scottish claymores. Lucien insisted she learn the Italian method, using a lighter weapon with a *schiavone* swept-hilt. The design was less constricting to the wrist and offered a whole new range of motions. It also meant she had to master every move again and learn to balance the weapon, besides. After two weeks, she still felt as clumsy and slow as a country farmer attempting a courtly lavolta.

Lucien ignored the distress in her eyes. "Again."

"Faith, I cannot." Kat saw that her hand shook where it gripped the hilt, and she fought back a sudden urge to weep. Sweet Jesu, she would never master swordsmanship. Mayhap she was better suited to idle feminine gossip and courtly intrigue than she knew.

"You are improving. Certainly you are closer to success than you suspect." Extending the flat of his own blade, Lucien nudged her chin up. "Do not be a fool and surrender now."

"What chance have I against a master?" Kat burst out.

"None, if you do not continue learning. Take heart, *ma petite*. I have something new to teach you today."

"How to gracefully accept defeat?"

Lucien frowned at her levity. "I must have your sworn oath that what I teach you today does not go beyond this courtyard, Katherine. You must never attempt it unless your life is in absolute peril, and, even then, I will deny having taught it to you. Do you agree?"

Curious, despite her exhaustion, Kat nodded. "I vow it."

"*Bien.* Have you heard of Saviolo?"

"The Italian fencing master? Of course." Even Shakespeare had not missed opportunity to remark upon Vincenzo Saviolo, albeit in satire. Kat recited:

"*More than prince of cats . . . the very butcher of a silk button . . .*"

Lucien nodded and looked grim. "His book is all the rage, here and abroad. It is fashionable now to ape Saviolo and other fencing masters. But a true master never divulges his secrets in written form."

Kat remained silent, sensing Lucien would proceed at his own pace. After a moment, he continued.

"A few of my own men know that I once studied under Saviolo on the Continent. In fact, I was among one of only three students Saviolo accepted later in life. Perhaps he shared the greatest secret of all with the entire trio; I doubt it. I believe he took a particular fancy to my close-mouthed nature."

Wondering why Lucien shared this with her at all, Kat waited for an explanation.

"Saviolo taught me the *botta secreta.*"

Kat drew in her breath, despite her panting, and stared at Lucien in disbelief. "Tricks, you mean? Like the thrust?"

She knew the fencing thrust, usually advanced on a pass, had only been recently acknowledged as an acceptable movement. Some of the old school—noblemen in particular—still refused to accept the thrust as dignified or fair play.

Lucien nodded, still seeming preoccupied. "There are a number of thrusts described in Saviolo's book. *Stoccata, imbroccata, punta riversa.* These, then, are not genuine secrets. I speak of another movement entirely; one of the *botte secrete* the master never divulged in print. *Lunge flèche,* a running attack which culminates in a carry of the forward foot to its fullest extent. It is one of the swiftest and deadliest movements a fighter can execute."

"Designed for defense?"

"Designed to *kill.*" Lucien's sober blue gaze bored into hers. "Make no mistake, *ma petite,* it is a risky and dramatic endeavor. It is the very last resort for a cornered man—or woman. One misstep or miscalculation, and you will plunge onto your foe's sword. Once the attack is launched, it cannot be withdrawn."

Kat listened with respect. "Why share this with me?" she asked.

"Because I never again want to see you at the mercy of animals like Lieutenant Cobble," he replied. "I despised myself then for not doing more, and this is one way I know to make it up to you."

Touched by Lucien's words, Kat reached out and patted his arm. *"Merci."*

"You will continue to practice?"

"Aye, Master Lucien, I will."

'Twould be the event of the Season. There was no doubt in Kat's mind, as she entered the great hall on Lucien's arm, immediately swept away by the grandeur of Tudor England and Elizabeth Tudor. For the two were inseparable, she had learned. At this moment, mayhap for centuries to come, mighty Elizabeth *was* England.

Her Majesty presided this evening upon her throne. The raised dais permitted her to view the colorful crowd thronging Whitehall's gallery. Since Elizabeth had decreed the royal masque, great care had gone into her own costume for this magical event.

Elizabeth Tudor was garbed in cloth-of-gold from head to toe, her voluminous skirts fanned out so that tiny diamonds, arranged in a sunburst pattern, were visible even from the farthest bench in the gallery. Long ropes of pearls and golden filigree adorned the queen's neck; a white ruff, embroidered with metal thread, reflected the lights around the room.

Displaying her infamous sense of humor, Elizabeth wore a mask tonight, as did everyone else in her Court. Hers was of finely beaten gold, shaped to resemble the face of Apollo.

Kat drew in her breath at the queen's magnificent display. Quite purposefully, Elizabeth had chosen to represent the Sun—the god Apollo. 'Twould serve as a sharp reminder to those who tried to control Bess, or marry her off to some paltry prince from another land, Kat thought.

Standing beside Elizabeth's throne was the Earl of Essex, her latest favorite. Robert Devereux bent to whisper some bit of nonsense in his monarch's ear, and Kat saw the aging queen blush like a girl. A knave with rich auburn locks and keen black eyes, Devereux needed no costume to foil his good looks. Young Essex wore an outfit of purled tawny satin, the sleeves slashed with gold panes and a velvet doublet stitched with fat jewels. His matching jerkin hung heavy with a dozen rich gold chains—no doubt, another sign of favor from their besotted liege.

The rest of the Court was presently distracted by the festive madrigal singers performing one of Thomas Morley's famous songs, "Now is the Month of Maying."

As the lilting voices rose in perfect harmony, Kat saw Elizabeth Tudor nod her austere approval. Kat also noted one of the queen's bejeweled slippers tapping in time with the rhythm, revealing their monarch's renowned

love of music—'twas one thing Elizabeth had inherited
from her sire, Henry VIII, besides his infamous temper.

Tonight the entire Court seemed a palette of exotic
swirling hues. Lucien and Kat blended into the crowd
with ease. They had planned their costumes together. Kat
decided they had accomplished a fair success, as evidenced by the surprised looks cast their way.

Playing upon the unique differences in each of their
colorings, Kat had suggested the idea. Lucien agreed with
her notion. All of this had been done in advance of the
masque, without any knowledge of the queen's costume.
Yet now Kat saw they complemented Elizabeth's theme,
as well.

Clad in sky-blue velvet to match his eyes and foil his
golden hair, Lucien represented "Heaven." His white, silk
half-mask barely concealed his handsome features. Kat
had predicted his costume would be a success. She overheard several jealous courtiers making snide remarks. But
the good ladies of the Court seemed most appreciative
of Lucien's dazzling appearance this night.

Kat had found use for a gown of green silk. 'Twas one
of Merry's discards and dark enough to serve as a mourning gown, though she could not honestly mourn a man
she did not remember. Altered by a clever sempster into
a costume, the cloth-of-silver train descended in shimmering waves, several yards behind her, adorned with an oc-
casional precious pearl. She depicted "Sea," and, to
emphasize the likeness, Kat wore her dark hair loose and
unadorned as a mermaid's tresses. Her mask was crafted
of the same silk as her gown; like Lucien's, it but partially
obscured her face.

Kat smiled at the reaction her unusual costume provoked. She did not doubt Bess's Court was a bit shocked
by the titillating glimpse of ivory flesh she had thus far
kept concealed. Her tan had finally faded after months
indoors; Merry had assured Kat 'twas all to the good. She

had never felt so headily female before. Dozens of male eyes widened at her approach.

"You are a success, *Chère* Madame Katherine," Lucien murmured in her ear as they squeezed through the throng. His grasp tightened somewhat possessively around her arm. "I am not certain I approve, however."

Kat chuckled. "You have no reason to be jealous, Lucien. There is no competition for my affections."

"Ah, would it were true," he sighed.

"Remember, I am a widow, hence too worldly for you. Besides, you are too poor yet to seek a bride. You must wait until you are promoted again in the queen's guard, and then a bevy of proper young maids shall flock to your side."

Lucien laughed at her mock advice. "Will you pick one for me, *Chère?*"

"If you promise to consider the wisdom of a dear friend." Kat smiled beatifically at him, then glanced about as the Court adjourned to the banqueting hall. Gazes were still riveted upon her and her escort—some envious, others admiring. She was certain the novelty of her costume would fade, once the Court got a glimpse of her sister. Merry had planned her costume for almost a year; only Kat and Jane were privy to the surprise. Thoughts of Merry caused Kat to pause and look about the hall in vain. 'Twas not like Merry to be so late in making an entrance. She was getting worried.

Lucien distracted her with a reminder of another sort.

"You wished to know something of Count Saville," he said low, under cover of the madrigalists' song. "I received word from Paris just this morn. Your instincts were right, *Ma Chère* Katherine." He paused. "There is no such person."

"I knew it," Kat exclaimed with triumph.

"Listen, *ma petite*. It does not mean he is not from another province, perhaps in the north."

"Nay." Kat shook her head. "Saville mentioned Paris and Fontainebleau many times. There is no doubt in my mind. The man is dangerous. I must warn Merry."

"Warn her of what?" Lucien inquired, with a practical, Gallic shrug. "He has done nothing untoward, has he?"

"I am trusting my instincts, Lucien. They have saved me before. Just as I once instinctively trusted you, my friend, I distrusted Saville on sight."

"Friend?" Lucien sighed, turning to face Kat so he gazed down into her eyes. "Is this all I will ever be to you, Katherine? A fencing instructor, *mon collègue?*"

Kat hesitated. There was no mistaking the intense look in Lucien's blue eyes, nor the undercurrent of sadness in his voice. She would do anything to keep from hurting him, but she could not promise a heart already lost to another.

"Time shall tell," she replied at last, so as not to wound him more. Lucien's expression brightened; he had obviously decided 'twas enough for now.

"I vow, I shall throw myself from London Bridge."

Maggie Tanner's passionate declaration made Merry sigh. She felt extremely cross. She had lost all patience with her cousin. She shook a finger in a motherly fashion at the rebellious Maggie.

"I'll not hear any more of this nonsense, coz. Were Aunt Isobel or Uncle Kit here, they'd quickly shake some sense into your silly head. You agreed to come to Whitehall tonight and enjoy the masque, now y'are ruining it for both of us."

" 'Twas before the letter arrived," Maggie sullenly responded. She sat in a dejected heap upon Merry's bed, the skirts of her costume drawn around her. "What manner of country oaf demands a midnight wedding without waiting for the banns to be read? Worse yet, a hasty exchange of vows at the smallest, drabbest church in the city. Y'know I made plans on a grand ceremony at St. Paul's. I shall be made a laughingstock!"

"Ridiculous. 'Tis little matter where you are married when your intended is a respected man," Merry replied, reasoning 'twas not a total lie. Rather, what she had heard at Court was that Maggie's betrothed was feared by his peers, yet she might assume respect followed fear.

Maggie was not to be consoled. "He must be a monster, as I've heard; mayhap he'll even change into one when the church bells sound."

"Nonsense," Merry said, for what seemed the hundredth time. Realizing Maggie was not listening to her, she wearily changed tactics. In a sweet, wheedling tone, she said:

"Think not of the man you wed, coz, but the great honor bestowed upon the lady wife of a baron, and the adorable babes you shall have one day."

Maggie sniffled. " 'Tis hardly any consolation to imagine my children might favor their sire."

Throwing up her hands, Merry thought for a moment. "Y'are not being fair to the man, Maggie. You have never met him nor even seen his likeness, and cruel gossip is rarely known to be true."

" 'Twas true enough, his mother took her own life when he was born," Maggie said with a shudder. "Even Papa did not deny the tale."

"Would good Christian folk blame an innocent babe? La, cousin, you've more common sense. Mayhap the superstitious Welsh delight in such myths; here at Court, we are more practical and never lend an ear to such mischievous yarns."

"Indeed? Then why is the gossip so rampant here at Whitehall? Why have I heard naught but terrible whispers about the deformity Lord Trelane wears in crownlike fash-

ion? And why, pray tell, if such rumors are untrue, did
my betrothed not send a miniature in kind?"

"Men are not so vain as women. 'Tis not in their nature,"
Merry reassured her cousin, with faltering conviction. She
pictured the prancing fops who often surrounded the
queen.

"Well, I'm not going," Maggie repeated firmly. "Milord
can come and drag me screaming to the altar, yet he shall
have not one whit of my own assistance in the deed."

Merry was resigned. She asked, "Can I at least trust
you not to hurl yourself from London Bridge if I go to
the masque without you?"

Maggie nodded. "I have neither the courage nor the
cruel nature to break Papa and Isobel's hearts. Nay, I
realize they did their best. If only my dear Will had not
died! By morning light, I shall likely be a married woman,
but Trelane will have to find me first."

What deviltry is Mistress Margaret up to? Morgan wondered when he received the news from Ambergate. A
lengthy apology from Sir Christopher Tanner did little to
improve his foul mood, nor did a fervent promise that
the errant maid would be properly chastened, when and
if she was found.

Morgan reluctantly agreed to attend a masque at Whitehall, with Sir Christopher's assurance he would be intro-
duced to his future wife there and allowed to escort
Margaret directly to the church afterwards. The demand
for such a hasty wedding clearly left the Tanner family at
a loss, but Morgan knew they dared not question his ec-
centricities for fear of losing such a great match, altogether.

Arriving at Whitehall, Morgan set his jaw with the effort
of getting through the social crush and whirl. He had
missed the formal dinner, and the dancing had already

begun—He cared not. He detested Court, though he had visited it when he was a young lad. His father sought to engage him as a page, a common practice among the lesser peerage. To this end Morgan, received weeks of etiquette lessons and stern instruction in a page's courtly duties. Once again, Rhys denied his son's shortcomings. Spurned by his elders and cruelly mocked by his peers, Morgan survived one miserable week at Court before he ran away. Due to the fact 'twas winter, Rhys was summoned from Wales to help locate his son. Morgan was discovered sleeping in the royal stables at Richmond. Horses were far better companions than his fellow pages, and warmer-natured besides. Rhys never forced his shivering son to return to Court. Instead they retreated to Falcon's Lair in silence.

Now Morgan found himself ensconced in the masque at Whitehall with no option of escape. He didn't fear being recognized or scorned by any of his peers, due to the fact of his virtual obscurity and present manner of dress. He had, of course, chosen his costume with care. His black velvet doublet and breeches were unprepossessing, as was the black velvet mask concealing most of his face. 'Twas nothing to draw particular attention to him, other than the fact of his considerable height in contrast to other men.

If anyone inquired what character or notion he portrayed, Morgan had already planned the dry and somewhat sardonic reply that he represented Lord Satan. *'Twould certainly rock a few courtiers back on their heels,* he thought with satisfaction.

Gazing around at the colorful throng, Morgan felt cool contempt for the entire proceeding, especially for the participants. Most of the ladies—he decided the term must be used loosely at best—were outlandishly garbed, powdered, and bejeweled like the tasteless tarts they were. The half-bare bosoms and stockings sporting naughty designs seemed to be the fashion of the day. Many tottered upon ridiculous pantofles, stilt-like cork heels with which it seemed they either intended to impress others, or to break their own necks in the attempt.

The men were scarcely an improvement. Without exception, they, too, wore huge, cartwheel neck ruffs and layers of costly baubles. Their outfits were pinked, paned, and slashed to the point of garishness.

Morgan had to swallow a laugh at the sight of one elderly fop bouncing up and down in poor imitation of performing a galliard dance, looking more like a barnyard rooster, pecking and hopping about, than the gallant swain he aspired to be. Incredibly, the fellow wore bright yellow satin breeches, a red leather jerkin, and a tuft-taffeta doublet of alternating orange and purple stripes. His stockings were a particularly bilious shade of green. Nay, mused Morgan, he favors not the cock rooster, but a parrot his former fellow pages had kept in a gilded cage.

Lord "Parrot"'s partner was a much younger woman, a would-be mermaid garbed in seawater silk. Unlike her aged companion, her goffered ruff was of modest size. When the dance shifted to a lavolta, she lifted her skirts a bit in order to execute a graceful leap. Morgan noted her stockings were plain. Either Lord Parrot was fortunate enough to have a practical wife, or he kept a modest mistress.

Morgan's gaze shifted to the open windows—the sole source of fresh air in a hall reeking of perfume and stale sweat. A thin slice of peach-velvet moon showed the hour was growing late. He had left word at his London residence that when the wayward Mistress Margaret was found, she must be immediately brought to him. They would depart for the church and head back to Wales the next morning. Morgan didn't intend to waste a moment more than necessary in this odious den of Tudor fops and trollops. By tomorrow, he planned to be a well and married man, hopefully with a son making an appearance in the new year, as well.

Morgan concealed a yawn behind his gloved hand. As he glanced towards the entrance, he saw a redheaded woman enter the crush. Her furtive stance, and the fact that she seemed to be looking for someone, caught his attention. Her vivid mane of hair was threaded with some sort of ridiculous female frippery he gathered was supposed to resemble leaves.

The woman's costume matched the loud hue of her hair, a frenzied mixture of red and orange. Her décolletage was alarmingly deep. Despite such a tasteless display, she proceeded through the crowd, gaining exclamations from the others present. Morgan assumed the women remarked upon her belated appearance and the daring nature of her costume. He didn't have to guess what the men said. The randy fellows swarmed about the redhead, ogling her breasts as they bowed over her little white hand. Morgan began to burn.

He didn't stop to reason further. He recalled the face from the miniature. Though this young woman wore a mask, the red hair was distinctive enough to make her identity obvious; Mistress Margaret Tanner had made her tardy, albeit dramatic appearance, and he intended to set her straight.

When someone seized Merry's arm, she didn't take immediate offense. Tudor swains were known to be bolder than they were wise. She knew none dared maul her in the presence of the queen. She tossed her head in a coquettish fashion and whirled to face her assailant.

"Fie, sir, have a care. Perchance you will crush my wrist," Merry simpered in her customary manner. The man's icy dark eyes froze further words in her throat. His gaze scoured her, head to toe, reflecting neither admiration nor base lust.

Merry shivered. There was no emotion at all in those coal-colored eyes behind the mask. No mercy, no passion, nothing save a hardened resolve which set her heart to pounding. S'blood, the rogue was uncommonly tall, too. He gripped her wrist tightly, without regard for her female frailty. Something in his manner frightened Merry to the core.

She squeaked in protest. His laughter was harsh and brief.

"Come, Mistress Tanner. You play the mouse now, yet a moment ago you were only too eager to launch yourself into the arms of any willing knave."

Outraged, Merry gasped. How dare he assail her morals? Who was this cad? Surely she would not forget a courtier so tall and grimly disposed, one with breeding every bit as boorish as his costume.

Merry straightened and adopted an arrogant attitude. She decided 'twas not easy for one of a naturally loving disposition.

"May I assume I offend you in some manner, sir?" she coldly inquired, imagining what her forthright Kat might say in similar circumstances.

"Aye. Other than the fact you have already proven yourself to be a scatter-brained and most irascible female, I do, indeed, take exception to your wanton behavior this night. 'Tis apparently not enough to prance around half-naked among such pitiful male specimens, but you must needs encourage them, too."

Merry scowled. The nerve of the boor! How dare he insult her thus? She would inform Bess of his audacity. Marry, where was Adrien when she needed him? Her dear count would make short work of this rude fellow, she vowed.

She tossed her head again, provoking the man's eyes

to narrow. "La, sir, what possible concern is it of yours whom I consort with? Much less choose to wear."

At her challenge, Merry saw the set of his jaw harden beneath his velvet mask. In a single rude yank he pulled her closer, dislodging several carefully placed leaves from her hair. She released a furious squeal. Her "Autumn" costume was ruined!

"Mistress Tanner, you will be biddable and come to the church as agreed, or by all the saints, I swear I'll not hesitate to bind and gag you."

Merry's thoughts were a tumble of confusion. Then realization dawned. Sweet Jesu, he thought she was Maggie! Her mind bloomed with sudden recognition, but she couldn't force her mouth to work as quickly. Heavens! 'Twas Lord Trelane. Her cousin's bridegroom was livid, too, as evidenced by the reddening of his neck and the brutal grip he maintained on her wrist.

Before she might inform Trelane of his grievous mistake, another man arrived on the scene.

"Is there a problem, monsieur?" Captain Navarre inquired in the silky voice he normally reserved for new recruits. Despite the softness of the query, Merry was aware of the danger lurking beneath Navarre's innocuous question.

Morgan did not release her, but merely shifted his cool gaze to the golden-haired man with the French accent. "There is no problem here which concerns you," he pointedly replied.

Another voice intervened, close on the heels of a distinctive scent of wild lavender. Morgan turned and discovered the mermaid from the dance stood behind them. She addressed him boldly as any man.

"Kindly unhand my sister at once, sirrah. Or I trow you shall live to regret it."

Fifteen

The stranger in black did not immediately reply. Kat saw her sister pale.

"Merry? Is aught amiss?" she demanded.

Kat glanced at the stranger again. A second later, she gasped and pressed a hand to her throat. Her eyes widened in disbelief.

"Morgan," she whispered. Yet how could it be? He was in distant Wales. No doubt remained when the man holding Merry's wrist released his prisoner and pivoted full around to stare at her instead. That soft Welsh burr sounded hauntingly familiar; now she knew why.

Recognition impacted Kat. She felt dizzy, shocked to the bone. Never for a moment had she doubted the image her mind had already formed of Morgan. How ironic she should be proven right. He was tall, exactly as she imagined, with a square-cut jaw not fully concealed by the mask he wore.

Morgan's hair, though deepest ebony, gleamed with mahogany highlights where the ends touched his shoulders, and a single wayward curl brushed the padded roll of his falling band. The reddish hue: 'twas testament to his Spanish ancestry, she thought. He was a fine figure of a man; the elegant if stark cut of his black velvet attire only emphasized his narrow waist and broad shoulders.

Morgan's eyes were the only part Kat had not imagined correctly. In her fantasies, they were warm and dark. Not this hard, glittering jet. His accusing gaze threatened to pierce her to the core.

Morgan stared in turn at the woman he had simultaneously loathed and loved over the past months. Kat. How many nights had he cursed her face, her name? Shouted her name in the midst of a raging thunderstorm, as if heaven's fury might purge her from his heart. He saw Kat move quite close to the handsome Frenchman who had first intervened on the behalf of the redhead, as if she sought his protection. This golden-haired knave, then, must be the lover Gwynneth had told him about. Something fierce and hot stabbed his heart, something too akin to jealousy for Morgan's comfort.

Silence reigned whilst Kat gathered her wits, and Merry rubbed her throbbing wrist back to life. The redhead gave a nervous little laugh and tried to clear the air.

"By the rood, I vow there has been a rather amusing mistake," Merry began, drawing the weight of three pairs of eyes upon her. Everyone looked desperately to her for answers. Merry proceeded with what little she knew. Turning to Morgan, she said, "I suspect you seek my Cousin Margaret, milord. In truth, I well understand your mistake and your misplaced anger, too, but 'tis still no excuse to mishandle a lady."

"Who the hell are you?" Morgan abruptly demanded, not feeling the least bit inclined to apologize for his rudeness. Kat's unexpected presence at the masque shocked and wounded him more than he cared to admit. The added discomfort of her gaze affixed to his face, the sight of her hand resting with obvious familiarity on the other man's arm, worsened his mood.

"My name is Meredith Tanner, milord. I am Mistress Margaret Tanner's first cousin. 'Tis said we closely resemble each other; now I know it must be true. You, of course, are Maggie's outraged betrothed."

Kat inwardly reeled from each slap of her sister's words.

She could not believe it. Morgan here, to claim a bride! At Court, of all places, in the presence of those whom he obviously disdained and despised. Here stood the man she loved, cool as night and twice as wicked, with every intention of taking another to wife. Worse yet, her own cousin. How much bitter light was cast upon her lot. Kat saw now, with aching clarity, the truth of what had really happened at Falcon's Lair; she was hurt and angry, yet curiously desperate to hear the how and why of things from Morgan himself.

"Aye," Morgan replied to Merry's statement, shifting his intense gaze from Kat back to her sister, "I am indeed Lord Trelane. And I doubt not there has been a grave mistake."

Lucien interrupted with a snort of disgust. "Some manner of mistake indeed, milord! You owe Mistress Merry an apology, one I fully intend to hear from your lips before you leave."

Morgan turned on the Frenchman, bitterly aware of the perfect features lurking beneath the half-mask the other wore. "I repeat, sir, this is no business of yours."

The Frenchman drew himself up, for all he was a hand shorter than Morgan. "I fear I must make it my business whenever the fair sex is insulted, milord."

"Please." Kat intervened, unable to bear the dangerous undercurrents between the two men. Knowledge of what had happened to her English grandmother—the original Merry Tanner—rang through her mind as she stepped between them. "This is neither the time nor place for outraged chivalry."

She stiffened when she felt Morgan's eyes score her body like a gyrfalcon marking its prey. She knew he was furious; she sensed fury emanating from each hard angle and plane of his rigid body. How dare he act so maligned? She had far more right to be the more outraged of the two of them.

"I believe 'twould be best if I sought to settle this matter with Lord Trelane in private."

Her announcement startled the others. Kat heard Merry's gasp and Lucien's sharp intake of breath. Where her hand rested on Lucien's arm, she felt him tense with protest. She said to them both in a low voice, "I know the baron. I can explain matters to him more easily."

"I like it not," Lucien growled under his breath, his sky-blue eyes never leaving Morgan's masked face.

Kat turned to her sister, instead. "Please, Merry. Mayhap I might help smooth things over for Maggie, as well." She begged Merry to accept Lucien as a temporary escort.

With a worried sigh, Merry agreed. She wanted to demand what was going on, the emotions swirling about the other couple were so intense, yet she was more anxious at the moment to escape and repair her costume before she was summoned by the queen. With a preoccupied air, Captain Navarre offered Merry his arm instead. The two of them disappeared into the crowd between songs.

"There is no word I wish to hear from your lips," Morgan said to Kat when the others left. "Doubtless 'twould be a lie."

His harsh statement stabbed at Kat's heart. She tilted her head back in order to glare at Morgan more effectively—he was so tall—but his mask disconcerted her. She found herself at a loss.

A painful silence erupted between them. Morgan made a soft, angry sound and began to leave.

"Wait, please." Kat blurted the entreaty, and reached out to still his retreat with a quick hand upon his sleeve.

Morgan stiffened as if her touch soiled him. But he made no further move to escape.

"We cannot talk here," Kat said, with a glance at the crowd hemming them in on all sides.

She saw a faint tic of a smile tug at Morgan's lips. She

was heartened by the sign until he sarcastically observed, " 'Twould appear we have little choice."

He nodded towards the musicians on a nearby dais, who, on cue, began strumming on a variety of instruments. Kat saw Elizabeth regally accept her pair of virginals from one of her ladies, and realized they dared not risk offending the temperamental monarch by slipping away now. A moment later Merry appeared at the queen's side and presented the royal sheet music with a curtsey. She remained to turn the pages, as well.

Morgan extended his hand to Kat, palm-down at an angle. "Escape is impossible now. We may as well have the benefit of one dance. 'Twill be the last time I ever visit Court."

Hesitantly, Kat placed her hand upon his, and they moved into place in the line of dancers. When the music started, she almost smiled. 'Twas a Basse Dance, a slow and stately procession designed to permit talking between partners, unlike the breathtaking galliard or the leaping lavolta. This particular song was known as "Die Katze," the Dance of the Cats.

Morgan apparently recognized it, too. "Curse your cat-eyes," he whispered when Kat glanced at him. Surely she imagined the raw mixture of anger and pain in his voice.

She and Morgan circled the room together in formal fashion, a handspan from the couples on either side. Fortunately, their low conversation was concealed by the dramatic music and the hum of chatter coming from the other dancers.

"I never imagined seeing you in London, milord," Kat began. She could think of nothing else to say to the man who still occupied her dreams. She steadied herself for his reply, vowing to remain calm and reasonable, come what may.

"Likewise I never anticipated finding you here. I confess 'twas a most disconcerting moment."

Kat felt warmth suffuse her cheeks and suspected it came not from the closed chamber, or the bodies pressing about them, but the simple presence of Morgan at her side. Disconcerting was not the word, she decided. Not when she dreamed of Morgan every night.

For some reason, Morgan did not seem surprised she could see him. Of course, Winnie must have told him of the miracle. What had Morgan's reaction been? Doubt? Delight? She desperately wished to know.

"Milord," she said, faltering again. She was unused to formalities where Morgan was concerned. After all, he had nursed her back to health for nigh two months and made love to her on a glorious night she would never forget. Cheeks scarlet, Kat rushed on. "I fear I never thanked you properly for your kind hospitality."

Morgan looked at her. She felt his gaze resting upon her with the weight of a hundred millstones.

"Must you continue playing these games, Kat?" he coldly inquired. "If Kat is your true name."

She forgot her vow to remain calm and reasonable. "Aye, it truly is. It so happens I have found out who I am, Lord Trelane, no thanks to you. Though I may come from a humble family by Tudor standards, 'tis not altogether a worthless one, and 'tis apparently fine enough for you to marry into."

Morgan paused in the dance processional to stare at her. "What is your full name?" he demanded.

"Katherine Alanna Shanahan." She hurled it in his face like an insult, pleased to see him stiffen.

"What relation is Mistress Margaret to you?"

"She is my first cousin on my father's side."

"Yet Mistress Margaret is a Tanner."

"Aye." Kat refused to satisfy Morgan's curiosity or confirm his suspicions. In truth, she was not ready to discuss Rory yet, and Morgan's behavior this night was most undeserving of reward.

"Then you and the other redheaded vixen—" he began.

"Are sisters." Kat nodded. "And twins." At his disbelieving look, she added coolly, "It sounds fantastic, milord. But 'tis true, I assure you. Though I have learned only a little more of how I came to be in Wales, I know that I captained my own ship on that fateful day."

Morgan didn't question this part of her story. Instead he asked her, "How did you come to remember your past?"

"I didn't. 'Twas bits and pieces Merry helped me to put together. For example, seeing the Tanner estate." Kat realized she sounded defensive, and was angry she had allowed her emotions to push aside her common sense. "Anyhow, I find it difficult to believe this interests you in the slightest, milord. After all, you never questioned my disappearance from Falcon's Lair."

"There was no need to question the obvious." The bitter tone in Morgan's voice surprised her. The hand beneath hers suddenly balled into a fist.

Before Kat might demand what he meant by such a remark, the dance ended. The line of dancers sank into deep curtsies or bows, as befitted their sex and rank. As she rose beside Morgan, Kat sought in vain for any clues swirling in his impenetrable onyx eyes. The mask concealed his emotions, frustrating her attempts to see the man behind the façade.

"Now is our chance to escape," she said, quickly and quietly, "whilst Her Majesty is looking the other way."

"Careful, Kat. Why, it almost sounds as if you plan a tryst," Morgan retorted. Despite his attitude, he did not protest when she drew him down a long corridor leading to the garden.

The evening air was cool and crisp, heady with the scents of night stock and clove gillyflower. Kat turned to

face Morgan in the moonlight, aware of every movement
he made. She knew now might be the only chance for
answers she would ever have. If he refused to hear her
out, any chance they had was forever lost.

"Please, Morgan," she began once more, raising her
gaze to meet his, no matter how painful or difficult she
found it to meet his impenetrable stare. "I must know
what happened. Why you did not come for me?"

Morgan's dark eyes narrowed through his mask. "D'you
truly expect me to pursue a woman who left with her lover
of her own free will?"

Kat gasped. "You thought such a thing of me?"

"There was little evidence to the contrary, my dear.
Gwynneth Owen bore witness to the fact you greeted your
lover at Falcon's Lair before her eyes. Several others confirmed the tale of several horses leaving the stables just
before I returned that night. Having suddenly and miracu-
lously gained your eyesight as well, 'tis understandable you
were eager to quit my company and return to your lover."

"And you . . . you believed it of me."

"I believe you are a clever opportunist, aye."

With a cry of frustration, Kat spun around and stared
in vain into the depths of the garden. Her fists clenched
at her sides. The pain was intense, shattering. Sweet
Mother and Mary, Morgan had believed such lies. He believed Gwynneth, over her.

"I took no lover in all my life," she whispered, "save
one, and 'twas you."

"As you say."

Morgan sounded wary, unconvinced. Without looking
at him, Kat continued her tale in a low, choked voice,
gazing instead upon leagues of moonlit summer blossoms.

"Nor have I known but two men at all, and the first
was lost to me long before my ship sank in the Irish Sea."
She was silent until she regained her composure. "I have

since learned I am widowed, Morgan. My husband, Rory, died along with our crew."

She heard Morgan's sharp intake of breath, then:

"Jesu, Kat. I'm sorry."

She sensed his regret was genuine but shook her head. "Nay, do not pity me. I will be honest with you. I do not truly remember Rory Shanahan and thus cannot do his memory justice. I believe he was a good, kind man, but I also sense there was no true love between us. Respect, perhaps, mayhap even passion, but not love."

Morgan was silent a second, digesting her words. "Then if a lover or your husband did not come to fetch you, how did you leave Wales?"

"You heard nothing, I suppose, of the Tudor guards who came to remove me bodily from Falcon's Lair?"

"Tell me." He sounded skeptical again.

"Very well, milord." Kat whirled back to confront Morgan, temper snapping like fire in a winter grate. She was tired of his insinuations. "For your benefit I will repeat what happened to me in clear, agonizing detail. I doubt I shall ever be able to forget the terror of that night.

"First of all, while I faithfully awaited your return from the village, I was betrayed by your sniveling maid servant, Gwynneth. She revealed my hiding place to the queen's men who came to rout the leader of a supposed papist plot. 'Twas not enough they abused and humiliated me with such ridiculous accusations. Oh, nay, milord—" she was shaking now, making it difficult to continue, "—then I must needs be hauled to London by that lot of crude, evil-minded soldiers. I was almost dying of fever en route. I would have died, but for Captain Navarre."

"Navarre? The Frenchman?"

Kat detected a jealous note in Morgan's query. "Aye, the captain you had the honor of meeting earlier at the masque. Lucien protected me from the others, saw I at least had food and water. He protects me still at Court. I will be eternally grateful to him."

Kat challenged Morgan with her defiant stare. She sensed his dismay and suspicion at the thought of another man caring for her. No matter how innocent the circumstances, Morgan would be hurt. In the end he must accept the existence of her first husband and Lucien's continuing role in her life. She continued her tale in a choked voice, the lashes rimming and her eyes spiked with tears.

"Lord Lawrence was behind the kidnapping plot. I was brought to Lawrence Hall, where I told him the truth. The earl did not believe me." Quietly, Kat explained the circumstances of her capture and arrest. She matter-of-factly told him about the close call with Newgate prison. Though Morgan did not interrupt, she sensed his pent-up frustration at the many unanswered questions.

" 'Tis incredible," he whispered, when she had finished, and she stood awaiting the sarcastic words. They never came.

"What a fool I was to assume the worst. Forgive me, Kat, but I never suspected foul play in your disappearance. Lawrence took it upon himself to bring you before the queen, I swear it. 'Tis understandable, though not forgivable, to suppose my own household was duplicitous, as well."

"I suspect Gwynneth took it upon herself," Kat remarked. "She disliked me from the outset."

"She had no cause. Why would Gwynneth lie to me?"

"She loves you, milord."

"Love?" Morgan seemed genuinely surprised. "When she knows—"

"Knows what?"

"Never mind. I do not wish to talk of Gwynneth now." Morgan reached out and coaxed Kat into the circle of his arms. Gently, somewhat hesitantly, he ran a hand down the unbound length of her hair.

"Someday, I vow, you shall say my Christian name again, little mermaid," Morgan said, "and you shall say it with affection, not anger. Though you have every right to hate me for what I did."

"I could never hate you," Kat whispered, her throat burning with unshed tears. "Though Jesu knows I tried."

He laughed a little then, and they both relaxed.

"We must talk more," Morgan said. His dark gaze sought hers with urgency, almost a plea of sorts. "Much more."

Kat nodded. "Aye." She remembered how she had prayed, dreamed, waited for the day when she would be able to see the man she loved. He was here, at last. "Morgan, your mask—"

"Ssh. Someone comes."

He drew her from the path into the shadows as the sound of feminine laughter reached their ears.

They froze as a couple passed within a handspan, their features obscured by darkness. But the voices were all too familiar to Kat.

"I do not know if I should allow such familiarities, Adrien," Merry giggled as she clung to another Frenchman's arm. "The queen will miss me soon, and within minutes my reputation shall be tattered as my costume."

"Ma chère, what harm can a stolen moment of secret pleasure bring?" As he spoke, Saville maneuvered Merry up against the trunk of a tree and pinned her on either side with his outstretched arms. Oblivious to the danger Kat already sensed, Merry continued to laugh, peeking at him between her splayed fingers like a little girl. Saville ignored her antics and spoke with an odd intensity.

"Sweet Meredith, this is the first time you and I have been well and truly alone. Your amazon of a sister seems always between us. I never dreamed the day would come you'd agree to meet me alone."

"Kat acts a mother-hen at times," Merry admitted, becoming serious again. Her voice held a cross note. " 'Tis most unlike her, I trow. Methinks she well knows your true intentions, sirrah."

Kat noted Saville's odd reaction to her sister's words. He stiffened, as if Merry's idle remark somehow constituted a threat. Moonlight shifted across his saturnine features, silvering his smile with shadows. Kat shivered when Merry continued speaking in a playful vein. The redhead tapped Saville on the arm with her folded fan.

"La, count, has the cat got your tongue this night?" Laughter trilled from Merry's lips at the bad pun. "I fear m'dear Kat is right, isn't she? You have something important to ask me."

Now. Kat saw Saville mouth the single word, and an icy trickle of fear gripped her. She noticed the man stared down into her sister's gray-green eyes, almost as if mesmerized. Saville's right hand slipped inside his doublet while the other snaked out and encircled Merry's tiny waist.

"Oui," he whispered ominously. "I do, indeed, have something to ask you, Mademoiselle Tanner."

Oblivious to the dangerous undercurrent in his voice, Merry continued gazing insipidly at Saville. Her eyes widened when the Frenchman commenced speaking in a tight voice.

"I wish to ask you about my sister. Certainly you must have heard the tale of Gillian Lovelle. She was once accounted the most beautiful woman in England, known as Aphrodite at Court. No doubt your father boasts of her sad fate quite openly at your family gatherings."

"Of what do you speak?" Merry asked Saville, puzzled. She looked concerned by the sudden wrath in his tone. He restrained her against the tree.

"Surely you know by now, Meredith. Or are you really so naive? Ah, I fear you are. Such a pity." Saville raised his hand, stroked Merry's cheek. Merry started to tremble.

Outraged, Kat stepped forward to intercede on Merry's behalf. Morgan restrained her, for some reason. Tense and fearful for her sister, she was forced to hear the further exchange.

"Stop it, Adrien. I—I don't like this game."

"Game?" Saville muttered, grabbing Merry and savagely shaking her by the shoulders. "You think this is a game, little girl? Slade Tanner destroyed my sister's life, and I have spent seventeen years of my life waiting for revenge."

Sixteen

As the scene unfolded before her eyes, Kat inadvertently released a faint cry. She felt Morgan grasp and squeeze her arm in restraint and warning. She looked at him with a silent plea. If only she had her sword! Morgan shook his head, assuring her with his steady gaze that he would protect both she and Merry, but 'twas critical for them to hear Adrien out.

In the intensity of the moment, Saville did not hear Kat's gasp.

"*Sacre bleu!*" he swore instead, when Merry's blank stare registered. "Little idiot. You still do not understand, do you? 'Twas I who seized and burned your sister Katherine's ship. Ah, do not look so stunned. You could never be as shocked as I, when I saw *Le Petite Chatte* here at Court, quite alive, every bit as defiant as she was when I confronted her on the high seas."

Adrien smiled at the memory, his gaze boiling with lust of a different sort. "Poor, stupid Meredith," he said almost conversationally as he toyed with a strand of Merry's bright hair. "I fear you will never be the firebrand your sister is. Nor half the beauty either—such a disappointment. How could you truly believe I desired you?" He laughed cruelly at the misery he saw sketched in Merry's pale face.

"Ah, I see you did, little one. Well, 'tis your one true

failing, *ma petite:* Never trust any man who says you are
beautiful."

Merry whimpered. Saville drew the unprotesting Merry
into his arms as if to embrace her. Kat knew her sister
was in shock, unable to fight or defend herself. She heard
Saville mutter:

"My true name is Adrien Lovelle. Say it, bitch! I want
to hear it on your lips before you die."

He punctuated his demand with another fierce shake.
Merry seemed a rag doll in his cruel grip, her head snapping back and forth. Her lips parted; all that escaped was
a pitiful sob. Infuriated, Lovelle hurled her back bodily
against the tree trunk and continued to rave.

"I will have my satisfaction, do you hear me? Tanner
may have ruined my sister's face, yet he cannot escape
justice forever. Though your queen sided with Tanner,
Elizabeth Tudor, too, will come to appreciate the length
and breadth of Lovelle justice."

With a calculating smile, Adrien mused aloud at the
thought of what forms his revenge might take.

"Perhaps I should just slash your cheeks, scar you as
my sweet Gillian was scarred. A living death is worse, to
one accounted fair. Yet you are hardly a beauty," he criti-
cally observed. *"Non,* 'tis not enough. Only death will suffice to right a wrong so grievous. I wonder what *Capitaine*
Tanner's reaction be when he hears of your demise, *ma
petite?* Ah, I really must go to Ireland and find out. Perhaps he will even be driven to madness—perhaps—"

As the disgusting diatribe poured forth from Lovelle,
Kat felt as if a great iron gate crashed opened in her
mind, spilling details and pictures so quickly she was unable to assimilate them all. She was drowning again, albeit
in a new way. Sensing the emotional flood coming fast
and fierce, Morgan seized and held her in his strong embrace, cradling her protectively against his chest. Kat

shook with silent sobs as the terrifying scene replayed itself.

Once again, the redheaded man's agonized expression flashed before her eyes. This time there was a name and history attached to the face, making it all the more agonizing.

Rory Shanahan: Her first mate, her young husband. Together, they had learned the ropes from the deck up, and if Rory's Irish temper exploded like a thunderstorm in moments of stress, it just as swiftly melted to sunny skies a moment later. Tolerant Rory, who let Kat tag after him when he was fourteen and she was still a little girl, more a mischievous irritant in those days than material befitting a future wife. Kat rode on his broad shoulders until she was old enough to swab a deck and shimmy up a mainmast as well as any boy.

Rory had grudgingly ruffled her hair as the O'Neills did, until Kat grew too old to be cosseted, and then he wooed her instead. Her five little brothers and all the other clan children all feared and admired Rory, who, at fifteen was already as big as a Celtic warrior of old and sported a wild banner of flaming-red hair besides.

Romantic Rory, who wed Kat on St. Agnes' Eve, because, at seven years old, she had glimpsed her future husband's face in the spring waters of Ennis Brock and was foolish enough to tell him so. Passionate Rory, who made love as tempestuously as the sea they sailed together, whose passions ran as deep as those waters. Later, the same sea he loved would lay claim to his life. Ah, blessed, vital, gentle Rory, who had shared everything with his bride, even wept like a babe beside his young wife when the disappointment of their barren union became clear.

Dear Rory! Kat had never loved him as he deserved to be loved, as she loved Morgan, heart and soul, yet she never desired his death, and he had not deserved such a cruel fate. Rory had met his end thanks to this spineless French coward. Kat recalled the soft hands belonging to the immaculately dressed, arrogant man who murdered her crew. Those same hands now moved to draw a thin, wicked blade from the doublet of a man called Adrien Lovelle.

"Beautiful it was, an offering to the gods," Lovelle reflected almost dreamily, as he described the burning of the *Fiach Teine* to Merry. "She was proud, your Irish bitch of a sister, proud and defiant to the end, raining Gaelic curses down upon my head. Jesu, she was stunning, even in her rage. I was mightily aroused. I had to mount the first woman I encountered after burning the ship. She just happened to be my sister." He laughed at Merry's visible disgust and horror. "Surely you do not begrudge me a little pleasure after such unpleasantry, *ma douce?*"

"You are insane," Merry cried, struggling in vain to free herself from his ferocious grasp.

"No more so than your noble English sire when he tried to poison Gillian," Adrien snarled. "I shall see justice done if it takes a hundred years. Fortunately your sister seems to have a weak memory now, but eventually Kat will remember me. Such a risk is unacceptable. So, you see, when you are found dead in the morning, Katherine will soon follow. Rest assured, little Meredith, you shall not be alone in the afterlife. You and your sister were born together and will die together, as well."

Merry gasped. Kat saw the sharp edge of the knife digging into the gap between her sister's stays. Merry surely realized by now she could not escape the madman, nor hope to overpower him, but she tried to stall him nonetheless.

"Adrien, there has been some terrible mistake. Oh, nay, wait," Merry begged, clinging to her assailant's shoulders.

Lovelle ignored her. "Kiss me," he demanded, and

crushed his hard mouth down on hers, intending to thrust the knife into Merry's rib cage as he did so. Then a crashing blow sent him reeling sideways. The knife flew from his grip, and Lovelle was dashed flat to the ground.

Kat rushed forward to shield Merry, while Morgan wrestled to restrain the other man on the grass. Morgan landed several solid blows before Lovelle gained his feet. With a burst of strength fostered by madness, Lovelle threw Morgan off and staggered back. He came back at Morgan once more, this time clutching the knife he had dropped.

Kat and Merry clung together as the two men grappled with one another in the moonlight. Lovelle managed to hit Morgan, dislodging his mask. It flew aside, unnoticed as they continued struggling together, and then went rolling across the lawn in a fearsome tangle of flying limbs. Morgan was the larger of the two, but Lovelle was driven by insanity. The two shadows blurred and became one. Kat cried out when she heard Morgan exclaim in pain. The shadows separated, and then the taller one rose, cradling his cheek. She glimpsed a dark trail, wet in the moonlight—blood.

The remaining shadow came at the two women. Kat saw Lovelle burst from the shrubbery. He paused to stare at her and Merry for a moment, his gaze both wild and fearful. He seemed to be debating the wisdom of rushing at them in a final bid for revenge. In a protective gesture, Kat thrust Merry behind her.

"Lovelle," she hissed, drawing her own dagger from the false pomander tied to her waist. Lucien had given her the little weapon in its clever disguise as a birthday present. 'Twas too small to afford much defense, but God willing she would lead Lovelle to the grave. She remembered Lucien's words from one lesson in particular:

"*Make no mistake, ma petite, it is a risky and dramatic en-*

deavor. It is the last resort for a cornered man—or woman. Once
the attack is launched, it cannot be withdrawn."

Kat's hand stopped shaking. Her intense love for Morgan and protective instinct where Merry was concerned
completely banished any fear of the madman. Though
she had no rapier to test Saviolo's *lunge flèche* properly,
she found she did not need a sword to assuage her
nerves. She was gripped by a curious, exhilarating calm.

Lovelle glanced at her dagger and gave a deprecatory
little chuckle.

"Come on, Lovelle. I'm here, waiting for you. Easy
prey. Kill me if you can. Take the risk to discover again
that cats truly have nine lives."

To Kat's satisfaction—and admitted surprise—Lovelle
crossed himself instead. She almost laughed with triumph. The coward was more superstitious than any
Welshman!

"You have not heard the last of me," Lovelle vowed in
a trembling voice, before he ran off into the protective
cover of the night. Kat heard a murmur of curious voices
in the distance. Having overheard the commotion in the
garden, a number of courtiers poured from Whitehall,
quickly forming a protective half-circle around the two
women.

Merry sagged against the tree, sobbing. Seeing her sister was all right and safe amidst the crowd, Kat tucked
away her dagger and hurried to Morgan's side. She
reached up to frame his face, while he covered the left
side with the palm of his hand.

"You are wounded. Let me see—"

"Nay!"

The unexpected harshness in his tone wounded her.
Morgan shook off her attentions, keeping his face and
his gaze averted from her. This darkness was a curse. Kat
only knew he was injured, not how badly. She glimpsed

fresh blood trickling through the fingers clenched upon
his left cheek.

"Morgan, you are hurt," Kat protested. "I must tend
to the wound. Lovelle's blade was dirty, it might well become infected—"

"I shall tend it myself. See to your sister."

Morgan's tone was hardly short of brutal. Taken aback,
Kat retreated, trying to understand this surge of violent
emotion. Morgan was obviously in pain and had snapped
at her like a wounded animal. 'Twas understandable. Still
she stood there, numb with shock, long after he turned
and stalked off in the shadows.

"Did you deliver the message first thing this morning?"

The page nodded, looking a little frightened by the
hollowness of Kat's voice. Summoning his courage, he
spoke up.

"Aye, for all the good it did, Madam. Lord Trelane left
his residence before dawn. There's no word when he
might return."

Kat stared at the lad, her knuckles turning white where
they gripped the door to her and Merry's apartment. "I
see," she said, her shoulders sagging with defeat. She gave
the boy a coin and closed the door, leaning against it to
stare into empty space.

What had happened last night in the royal gardens?
She had relived each moment over and over, observing
everything from various angles, as if directing one of
Shakespeare's plays in her mind. She moved the charac-
ters in her head, recreating their actions so she might
better understand Morgan's behavior. She was helpless to
find any explanation or excuse for his actions. After his
abrupt departure from the garden, she tried to find him
after Merry was safely removed to Ambergate. There was
no trace of him at Court, and when she finally located

him at Hartshorn, his London residence, he refused to answer her plea for an audience.

Kat's first fear was that Morgan had been more seriously wounded than she thought. But after waylaying Morgan's hired man at his stables, she was assured Lord Trelane was recovering nicely.

Pressing a hand to her throbbing temple, Kat tried to reason things out. Something had changed in Morgan before, during, or after the struggle with Lovelle. Had that vile Frenchman whispered some dastardly lie in Morgan's ear even as they fought? She doubted it. Even had Lovelle done so, Kat was certain Morgan would not believe anything the villain said, after witnessing the man trying to murder her sister. Had Morgan seen her wield the dagger, perchance mistaking its purpose and her actions? She continued to go over and over the previous night's events in her mind until she thought she would scream.

Exhausted from her sleepless night, she went to the window and gazed at the serene vision of Ambergate in the distance. The sight of the Tanner family mansion smoothed a comforting balm over Kat's troubled thoughts. She decided to retreat to the country for a few days of peace. There she might also question Merry and their cousin Maggie in her quest for answers.

"I would know of Lord Trelane."

Kat noticed Merry and Maggie exchanging quick glances when she asked them about Morgan. She didn't miss the unspoken tension at the mere mention of his name.

"Well?" she demanded, facing the two redheads in the relative privacy of Ambergate's conservatory. Uncle Kit, Aunt Isobel, and the boys were gone. Just as well, Kat thought. She intended to badger her sister and cousin until she had some acceptable answers.

Merry spoke up first. "Please, Kat, I'm too distraught by what happened last night to go over it again." She passed a hand over her brow with visible agitation. Her gray-green eyes held a plea for understanding. "I was nearly murdered, y'know."

"But for Lord Trelane's timely intervention," Kat reminded her sister. She turned to pace the Turkish carpet. "Both of you listen to me. I also owe Morgan my life. He was the man who saved me after Lovelle destroyed my ship. Morgan nursed me back to health at Falcon's Lair, without knowing who I was or what I had done in the past. As time passed, I fell in love with him." Her gaze found and locked with Merry's. She heard both women gasp.

"Aye, you heard me aright. I feel no need to defend my feelings for Morgan."

Cousin Maggie released a soft wail. "Alack, Kat—him of all men." She clapped a hand over her mouth, her eyes wide with dismay.

"I know 'tis wrong to covet another woman's intended. I regret any pain my honesty causes you, Maggie."

Maggie shook her head. "I care not for Trelane," she murmured. "Would I had the freedom to refuse his suit."

"What do you mean by that remark, coz?" Kat demanded.

Again the redheads exchanged furtive looks. Kat became more agitated by the moment. "Speak up, curse you!"

"Kat!" Merry protested.

"Oh, dear," Maggie wailed in unison.

"Sweet Jesu! Spare me your ladylike outrage!" Kat cried, waving her arms for emphasis. "Are you two such a pair of addlepated goose brains you must sit in judgment upon me? Look at yourself, Merry. Toying with a fake French count all season long, letting him sample you as he would." She swung on Maggie. "And you, cousin. I'faith, don't deny you've dabbled in love yourself, after the courtly tales I've heard of you and young Will Scone."

"Will was my betrothed!" Maggie exclaimed.

"Aye, as is Lord Trelane now." Kat regarded her cousin levelly. Maggie wouldn't, or couldn't, meet her accusing gaze.

Merry spoke up again. She sounded weary. "What do you want of us, Kat?"

"Merely the truth. I have a feeling you two know something I don't. It must concern Morgan. Therefore 'tis something critical. I've a right to know what that is."

After a brief, tense silence, Maggie spoke up.

"You've heard me call him a monster," she began.

At Kat's furious look, she added hastily, " 'Twas the sum, all told, of the tales others told me. Trelane's never been wed, y'see, and has kept to himself since birth. There's rumor of some strange deformity upon his person."

Morgan, deformed? Kat almost laughed. He had the most beautiful male body she was ever privy to feel. Even Rory, God rest his soul, could not compare. Besides, she had explored Morgan inch by inch when she was blind, and knew her hands had not betrayed her.

She regarded her cousin coldly. "Go on."

"Alas . . . there's the story of his mother, as well."

When Maggie trailed off, Merry chimed in reluctantly, "Aye, Kat. The story goes Lady Trelane committed suicide after her son was born. 'Tis said she could not face her husband after Morgan appeared."

"Cruel rumor hardly constitutes fact."

"Too many know the tale," Merry said. "There must be a kernel of truth somewhere."

"What is it, then?"

The other two shrugged in unison. Maggie finally ventured, "Mayhap the deformity."

Kat tried to reason things out. "There are other possibilities. Mayhap Morgan was the result of another man's throw. 'Tis common enough in any class. Lady Trelane would have felt ashamed if her son did not resemble his father."

" 'Tis rumored Trelane favors his true sire," Maggie whispered. "Lord Satan himself."

"What nonsense." Nevertheless Kat felt an unbidden chill at her cousin's words. Morgan's behavior last night had been so strange, she was at a loss to explain his actions to herself or anyone else. Something troubled him deeply, something she was half-determined, half-afraid to discover.

"You can see why I would not wed Trelane willingly," Maggie continued. "I can but pray he has given up this mad notion of marrying me."

Poor Maggie was proven wrong. A messenger arrived at Ambergate while Kat was there, bearing a missive for Sir Christopher. The message flatly demanded Mistress Margaret Elizabeth Tanner be present at St. Ethelburga's by the time the bells sounded the midnight hour. As Maggie read the note aloud and started to tremble and weep, Kat grew increasingly furious and hurt. So Morgan intended to proceed with the marriage to her cousin. Why? Kat knew he still harbored feelings for her, despite his actions. He had begun to confess his true feelings before the incident in the garden with Merry and Lovelle. There was not one whit of logic in this whole affair, and she was determined to know why.

Answers were forced to wait, however, until Kit and his family returned from town to deal with the matter of Maggie's sudden marriage. After reading the missive himself and digesting its tone, Kit Tanner grimly regarded his daughter.

"I fear there is nothing I can do, Maggie."

Maggie gave a sharp cry, turned, and ran across the room. There she hurled herself into her stepmother's arms and wept. Lady Tanner's embrace closed protectively around the younger woman. Physically, Lady Tanner was accounted plain, yet she possessed beautiful poise and such a serene countenance that everyone adored her on sight, including Kat.

Garbed in soft yellow satin this evening, Isobel was radiant as she appealed to her husband. "There must be something we can do, Kit. Delay the wedding, if nothing else. Mayhap the queen would even reconsider the match."

Kit considered his wife's words, then shook his head. "Bess is determined to settle Maggie for us, ever since Will Scone's untimely death. She believes any unmarried female of such advanced age lives in an unnatural state."

"Now, there is great logic coming from a Virgin Queen," Kat acidly remarked.

Her uncle did not rise to the bait, but Kat fancied the corners of his mouth twitched a bit. "I warrant, Bess approves of Trelane as much as any man. There is no help but to proceed with the wedding, despite Trelane's unconventional request."

"I trow, even Her Majesty would scold him for such insensitivity," Merry put in. "Why, there has not even been time enough to finish the bridal trousseau."

"You *would* think of gowns and gewgaws when our cousin's happiness is at stake," Kat snapped. When the others cast her startled looks, she realized how waspish she sounded. With good cause. She was jealous, green with envy, because Morgan intended to marry another—her own cousin.

Isobel still held the sobbing Maggie. Her large gray-blue eyes pleaded for her husband to intercede, however he might. "Is there nothing we can do, dear heart?"

Clutched in an agony of indecision, Kit studied his

weeping daughter for a moment. Then he looked at Kat, his gaze equally assessing. 'Twas obvious, the wheels were turning in his head.

"Mayhap," he mused at last, then motioned for his wife to see Maggie removed upstairs before she became hysterical.

Seventeen

Morgan stiffened as the cathedral bells began to clang—once, twice, thrice. The deafening peals echoed throughout the small nave, where he stood awaiting his bride. He set his jaw and tried not to think of the previous night; of Kat's honest hurt and confusion when he had refused her aid and her heart; of the agony and searing pain in his own breast when he denied her.

'Twas for the best, he reasoned. He would not shame the Tanner family or risk enraging the queen by refusing the match at this late date; this practical marriage would also free Kat to accept the care of Captain Navarre, whose angelic face was better suited to Kat than his own would ever be.

Kat claimed she had not loved her first husband, yet Morgan feared she was mistaken. He could not compete with Navarre nor a ghost; Rory would always haunt them both, he knew. He had made love to a woman whose fragile mind had denied her memory to prevent the pain of loss. Margaret Tanner did not need to hate him; he despised himself enough for them both.

Morgan impassively watched as the elderly priest approached the altar, ready to perform the ceremony linking man and wife for a lifetime. The cleric wore formal white robes and a tall mitered cap, but looked put-out at being called upon to perform the service at such an ungodly hour. He peered a moment at Trelane's tall, black-clad figure through rheumy eyes, then moved to light a few more candles in the nave.

"Nay." Morgan stilled the man with a quiet request. "I prefer the dark."

Thus might he remain safely shadowed throughout the long ceremony. Since he could not wear a mask in a house of God, Morgan preferred the shield of darkness. Sooner or later, Mistress Margaret would be bound to catch an unbidden glimpse of him—hopefully, after the marriage was already consummated, when she had no possible avenue of escape.

The bells finished pealing. All was silent. Morgan frowned when he realized his bride had not appeared, as ordered. Had she dared defy him again?

The groaning of the cathedral doors heralded the late arrival of a third party. Father Benedict moved to greet the newcomers. Morgan turned and saw Sir Christopher enter the tiny chapel, steadying a young woman on his arm. The rest of the Tanner family was noticeably absent. 'Twas fine by him.

His virgin bride was exquisitely gowned in pearl satin and cloth-of-gold, with a train nearly a yard long. Her face was obscured by the heavy gauze veil, but Morgan glimpsed several bright red locks dangling about her shoulders. He also saw that she trembled. Suddenly he despised himself for forcing the poor, innocent creature to heel. 'Twas too late to make amends now. He had made his choice.

Sir Christopher spoke softly to his daughter, chiding her, perhaps, for her obvious reluctance. Afterward, it seemed she straightened her shoulders as she approached the altar. Mayhap her sire had reminded her of her duty or the family honor. Either way, it had worked. Mistress Margaret reached his side and continued to gaze steadfastly ahead.

Apparently sensing nothing amiss, the priest started the

ceremony without preamble. Father Benedict rattled on and on about marital responsibilities and the prescribed duties of man and wife. Morgan grew restless and darted a quick glance at his bride.

Margaret had neither moved nor spoken during the interim. He wondered what she was thinking. He caught a glimpse of her white-gloved hands, nervously twisting together, and felt a disconcerting pang of pity. God's blood, 'twas not his problem if the chit did not favor her lot, he told himself. Likely she had been outrageously spoiled by her family and was brought up short by this unexpected turn of events. Once she held their first son in her arms, she would accept her fate. Still, Morgan would ensure that she was never left alone with the child, just in case the madness which had seized his own mother might somehow overcome this delicate English wench, as well.

Morgan's mind wandered farther afield. He suddenly realized the priest was waiting for his reply. "Aye," he said, and he saw his bride stiffen. He repeated his vows in Latin, following Father Benedict's lead.

When 'twas her turn, the new Lady Trelane barely managed a meek whisper. *What a spiritless creature she is*, Morgan thought. *Mistress Margaret will never throw the sons and daughters my Kat would have!*

Nor would Margaret ever capture his heart. He would be kind, he would be tolerant, but he would never love her. 'Twas Kat's bright green eyes he imagined when the time came for the nuptial kiss. He longed to lift the heavy veil and gaze into the eyes of the only woman he wanted. Yet he knew the eyes awaiting him beneath the veil were blue, not green.

To his chagrin, his lady wife recoiled and stepped back, refusing his gesture. Margaret's veil fell back in place as she tugged it free of his grip and hurried back to Sir

Christopher's side. He thought he heard soft weeping issue from beneath the veil.

Anger seized Morgan. *Kat never refused your kisses,* an inner voice mocked him. He stared after his retreating bride as she fled to the safety of her father's arms. She was weeping, damme her, like a woman condemned to the stake.

Morgan did not hear what Sir Christopher said to his daughter, as the priest droned meaningless congratulations at him, muffling the other man's words. Margaret was obviously pleading with her father about something. Morgan saw the other man shake his head firmly. At least Sir Christopher was an honorable fellow; he would stick by his word. By this time tomorrow, Lady Margaret Trelane would be Morgan's wife, in every sense of the word.

"Tell your mistress she has an hour to prepare herself. No more, no less."

Morgan spoke to the inscrutable tiring woman who had accompanied them to Hartshorn where they would stay the night before departing for Wales. Without a word, the woman nodded and moved to shut the heavy door in his face.

After Trelane's footsteps receded down the hall, the "servant" pulled off her brown wig and shook out a mane of bright auburn curls.

"La, I feared I could not keep a straight face," Merry Tanner cried, turning to face the other woman propped in the center of the huge eiderdown bed. " 'Tis been nigh a year since I played with the mummers at Richmond."

Kat smiled. "You're a wonderful actress, Merry. I don't think he suspected a thing." She glanced at the pile of baggage where her own red wig was stored away, and released a burble of laughter. Faith, she would never forget the crackling fury in the air when she refused Morgan's kiss! She wanted to accept his kiss, yet she daren't risk him recognizing her, even in the gloominess of the old chapel.

"I trow, you and Uncle Kit are both quite mad. You don't know what Trelane will do when he finds out the truth," Merry said. "How long can you hide it from him? He seems an angry, unforgiving sort of fellow."

"On the contrary, sister," Kat said, as she brushed out her long, dark hair, "Morgan is the kindest, gentlest man you could ever hope to meet."

"Aren't you afraid?"

"Of Morgan? Never." Kat shook her head and set down the ivory hairbrush in her lap. "Perhaps he will be a trifle vexed with me for the deceit we all practiced on him today. But I know Morgan's heart better than he does; he will eventually come 'round, I've no doubt."

Even as she spoke so confidently, Kat couldn't suppress a shiver of apprehension. Suppose Morgan was furious with her. What then? Had he truly desired the match with her cousin Maggie, or, as she suspected, merely hoped to banish the memories of their time together in Wales by rashly wedding another? Guilt did strange things to one's conscience, she knew.

The slim hour Morgan granted her passed more swiftly than she wished, and soon Merry was forced to don her disguise again and head for the door. Before she left, Merry hugged Kat and fervently declared, "I'll pray for you, dear."

"Don't you dare. Just think of me as happy, and you will know 'tis true."

Merry nodded, looking worried, and slipped out of the chamber—not a second too soon. A rap came at the door.

"Madam?" 'Twas Morgan's voice, curt and low. "Are you presentable?"

Kat glanced at the dark green silk nightrail she had

chosen for her wedding night and rushed to extinguish the candle on the table. "Aye," she called out in a low voice, diving back under the covers as the door cracked an inch.

Relieved to find the bedchamber dark, Morgan entered and barred the door behind him. He stared at the unmoving lump in the bed. A weak stream of moonlight gilded the room, and his eyes took a moment to adjust. He was tired and dispirited after the events in the church. He knew Margaret Tanner had never desired his suit. He sensed the tension permeating the room now.

Briskly he unfastened his doublet. "Madam, you have my word I shall be gentle with you. I have no wish to bring dissention into our household."

She didn't answer him.

"Of course, as all men, I am desirous of sons. Once you provide me with several heirs, there shall be no further need of . . . this." Morgan fell silent and groped for words. How did one define lovemaking to a virgin? He wryly realized he was not so experienced himself.

Again, there was only silence. Morgan found himself annoyed by his wife's unresponsiveness. He shrugged out of his shirt, dropped it where he stood, and stepped over to the bed.

"I find myself chilled. Kindly move over."

Suppressing a sudden urge to chuckle, Kat slid over. Morgan sat on the edge of the bed in order to remove his boots and breeches. She gazed at the strong curve of his spine, spangled with a soft veil of moonlight. She longed to reach out and caress him, trail her fingertips down his silken flesh. She restrained herself, withdrawing as Morgan turned around. She slid hastily beneath under the covers. He made an irritated noise as he sought for her hand. She slipped it beneath the covers, too, deftly avoiding his touch again.

"Very well, Madam. You have made your distress clear.

I shall not attempt to court you any further. Shall we be done with this, then?"

Kat had no heart to continue the masquerade; Morgan was agonized, no less than she. She would not prolong his suffering.

"Morgan," she said softly. Just his name, no more. He stiffened and shot to his feet, turning to stare down at the bed as if a viper had crawled into it.

"By the rood—" he began. As Morgan feared, a familiar pair of cat-green eyes materialized in the moonlight. He averted his face and shakily demanded, "What the hell are you doing in my marital bed, Kat?"

"I am here rightfully, milord—as your wife."

"Then there has been a mistake." Morgan spoke without emotion. Still his heart pounded wildly, and he could not deny the tiny flicker of hope. He brushed it aside, appalled at his own weakness. Kat Tanner—Shanahan— did not belong to him. She never had.

"We were wed at midnight this evening," she said.

"If I'm not mistaken, 'twas your cousin Margaret I wed at St. Ethelburga's," Morgan countered. "I saw her red hair quite clearly even beneath the veil she wore."

"You saw a wig, Morgan."

"What of the contract?" His voice shook. With anger or hurt, perhaps both. Kat plunged ahead, determined to set things straight.

"The light was poor in the chapel. You desired it so, I understand, and thus contributed to your own downfall. You then signed the contract without properly noting the names. I assure you, Morgan, my full Christian name is present on our marriage papers."

He was silent a moment. "What deceit do you practice upon me, Kat?"

"Deceit!" she cried, sitting bolt upright in the bed. "You *dare* speak to me of deceit when only last night you admitted your affections, then rashly turned and demanded to wed my cousin tonight? Will you continue to lie to me as well as to yourself? I know not the real reason you have refused to accept our love, but I will not sit still and watch you exchange it for a loveless union with my cousin."

Morgan raked a hand through his hair, but wouldn't confront her directly. He didn't seem to care that he was naked, or that she stared at him with mixed frustration and hope. He kept his face averted the entire time they spoke, and Kat began to fume. At least Morgan owed her the decency of looking her in the eye as he rent her heart again. She felt a sting of rejection lance through her soul.

"I have told you many times," he finally continued, "why it cannot work between us. When will you accept it?"

"Never. You never offered a reason I could accept."

" 'Tis foolish and shortsighted of you, Kat."

"Aye. Mayhap the reason I cannot accept your denial is the same reason you will not accept your mother's death," she parried.

Kat saw Morgan stiffen. Her words had thrust home. Maggie and her sister had not been mistaken. There was some kernel of truth to the cruel rumor.

"I know how Lady Trelane died," she said, when Morgan maintained a chill silence. "It matters not to me. Your mother was a human being, Morgan, with human failings. Elena made a foolish decision to end her life; nobody shall ever know why. 'Tis pointless to blame yourself for her death. You were but an innocent babe."

His abrupt, harsh laugh startled her. "In sooth, Kat, you offer answers so easily. Would I could accept them as you do. Alas, I cannot. To pretend otherwise would do us both a grave disservice."

"What are you telling me?"

"I am saying, madam, this charade of yours shall not work. On the morrow, I will have this marriage annulled."

Kat flinched. Did Morgan truly hate her so? Her heart told her otherwise. "Trust your instincts," her own mother had said to her many a time. "They will not fail you." She was startled when her mind suddenly supplied the forgotten bit of advice.

"I see," Kat said. She was quiet a moment, thinking hard. "You realize, of course, there will be questions— questions about our marriage and my unsuitability as a wife. D'you intend to accuse me of perfidy?"

Morgan cleared his throat. "Mayhap some other solution can be found. Since I was unknowingly duped into this marriage by you and Sir Christopher, 'tis not legal in the eyes of the Church anyway."

"Do not blame my uncle. Kit but sought to save his beloved daughter, to placate his wife, and to grant me my heart's desire, all in one fell swoop. He is frightfully soft when it comes to the women in his household."

"Nevertheless, 'twas wrong to deceive me," Morgan replied. His voice was hard again, his manner unforgiving.

"Nothing can be solved tonight," Kat said. Her voice softened, not with tenderness but rather defeat. "We are both tired. We need to get some rest."

Instead he moved to gather up his clothes. "I shall seek out another chamber."

"Oh, Morgan, desist!" she cried, pummeling her fists on the coverlet. "This is ridiculous. We are not strangers. We were lovers . . . or have you forgotten that, as well?"

"Nay," he said quietly. After a moment's hesitation, he rejoined her in the bed, slipping under the covers on the far edge of the bed. He lay back and slung an arm crosswise over his face.

Frustrated, Kat propped herself up on one elbow and tried to make out his expression. "What's wrong?" she asked, moving to touch his cheek in a gesture of comfort. Morgan flinched and rolled over on his side, away from her. She quelled the bitter pang of rejection and laid back beside him, staring at the lacy patterns of moonlight dancing upon the ceiling. Neither of them slept.

Before dawn broke, Morgan had already dressed and left the bedchamber. Kat was startled by his stealth; he moved as swiftly as Ironbreaker. She glimpsed his face and the fresh bandage fixed upon his left cheek. Lovelle must have wounded him more grievously than she had first assumed.

Swinging her legs over the side of the bed, she reluctantly faced a new day alone. She was Lady Katherine Trelane now, clearly against Morgan's wishes. What would he do? Her mood plummeted when she remembered Morgan's violent reaction to her deceit. She was certain he loved her; there must be something, beyond his mother's death, serving to keep them apart.

She rose and dressed in an elegant gown of straw-colored taffeta, with exquisite lace edging; 'twas one of Merry's courtly cast-offs and had been lengthened by a sempster to fit her taller frame. The petticoats were embroidered in gold thread, as were the gartered hose. As she moved to wash her hands in the pitcher on the stand, Kat's gaze fell upon the simple gold band Morgan had slid onto her finger last night. She would treasure it always, even if their marriage was annulled.

She dashed cold water on her face, gasping as it brought her fully awake. A moment later, she grabbed a cloak of black silk grosgrain and left the house. The Trelane London residence, Hartshorn, was a modest but stately mansion on the Strand. It had been closed for years and was dusty from neglect and its owner's disdain. Kat knew Morgan rarely came to London. His father had been the last Trelane to entertain, and that was in King Hal's time, judging by the period furniture and dated outfits she glimpsed in the wardrobe. A small handful of staff had maintained

Hartshorn over the years, but they seemed indifferent to its potential and to the new Lady Trelane, as well. Kat made a mental note to secure her sister's advice on hiring competent staff and restoring Hartshorn to some semblance of its old glory—if she were allowed to remain Lady Trelane for more than a day, she mused.

Morgan had long since departed, but his man in the stables protested his ignorance as to where his master had gone. Kat demanded he drive her to St. Ethelburga's in the rickety but serviceable coach. She did not doubt that Morgan was attempting to wrangle an annulment from the priest.

Morgan was not at the cathedral, however. He still intended approaching Father Benedict about an annulment; surely the unusual circumstances warranted one. First, he went to Ambergate, in search of answers. He demanded an audience with Sir Christopher Tanner. He was shown to a cozy parlor where Ambergate's owner preferred to receive his visitors. Sir Christopher appeared shortly. He did not seem surprised to see Morgan.

"Good morn, milord," Sir Christopher said, cheerily. "May I offer my belated congratulations on your marriage?"

"What you may offer, sir, is your heartfelt apology," Morgan thundered. He faced the other man without hesitation. The bandage hid the hideous mark from view, and, even had it not, Sir Christopher had doubtless already heard the tale of the Trelane family's curse.

The other man appeared unruffled by Morgan's rage. "If you wish an apology, you shall certainly have one, milord," he mildly replied. "Though I doubt my niece would take kindly to the notion she is to be regarded as a burden."

"Kat, it seems, has many untoward notions about me,"

Morgan retorted, "beginning with the assumption I wished to wed her."

Sir Christopher's auburn eyebrows rose. "Methinks Kat is wiser than you give her credit for, Trelane. At least wiser than your own heart."

Morgan reddened at the polite insult. " 'T'won't work, I tell you. This marriage must be dissolved. Immediately!"

"Why?"

"Why? Come on, man, you must have heard what they call me, whether at Court or in the remote reaches of Wales: The Devil Baron! My God, you nearly sacrificed your own daughter to such gossip. Do not insult my intelligence by feigning ignorance of such tales, now."

"Fair enough. I shall not. I heard whispers long before I agreed to your betrothal with my Maggie. I'truth, I had to wonder. I am not given to be a superstitious fool, however, and I knew your father quite well. He spoke of you with great pride and affection, and Rhys Trelane was a modest man. I knew you would not hurt my Maggie. Once she came to know you better herself, I believed she would come to ignore the rumors and perhaps even come to love you, in time."

Morgan was silent a moment, looking at the man. Sir Christopher had great poise and an ample dose of common sense. 'Twas hard not to hear the logic in his words. 'Twas also, Morgan discovered, difficult to stay angry with this fellow. He was refreshingly frank.

"However," Morgan continued, "you did not sacrifice your youngest daughter, but your niece. Why?"

"Because only an old fool who has been in love can recognize others destined for a similar estate. Like you, I lived in misery for many years, milord. 'Twas not until dear Isobel ripped the blinders from my eyes and freed me from the shackles of my own making was I finally able to live, and love. 'Tis never too late, Trelane."

" 'Tis for me," Morgan murmured in reply, and passed

a hand wearily over his eyes. He had not slept a wink last night with Kat lying beside him. He watched her body stretch luxuriously upon dawn's first kiss. It had been difficult, nay torturous, watching the watered green silk rippling over her sweet, full breasts, then concaving at her belly. His instincts cried to make her his again; his sense of dignity refused to let him resort to such base behavior. She was newly widowed, for heaven's sake. Their marriage was not only highly improper, but 'twas hardly short of indecent. Sir Christopher must know it as well, but the man's expression was benign, almost satisfied.

Another realization dawned. "Elizabeth Tudor will be furious," Morgan warned the other man. To his surprise, Sir Christopher chuckled.

"Aye, when is she not? Our righteous queen first suggested the match herself. Bess is inordinately fond of dabbling in others' affairs. She knew we sought another title for Maggie after young Scone's death; she also knew we dared not refuse any suggestion she made. A baron is quite a catch, milord—even a Welsh one."

Morgan gave a grudging smile. "I heard your brother wed a Welsh woman some years ago."

"He did, and it caused quite a scandal, too. George is your equal in rank. Lady Tanner is a busy little whirlwind and was quite delighted by the notion of your wedding our Kat. Dilys is even a distant cousin of yours, I believe."

Morgan shook his head. "Do all of you conspire against me?"

"Only for your own good. Now, as we are family, I must insist you call me Kit. Pray, share some port wine with me, Morgan. I vow, I can convince you of the wisdom in staying wedded to Kat, at least until the child is born."

Morgan stared at the redheaded man.

Kit noted Morgan's shocked expression and sighed. "I doubt my niece knows it herself yet. When we received word of your latest demand to marry Maggie, and Kat heard my agreement, she swooned. It did not take my wife long to figure out the true cause.

"I believe every man has a right to know his issue. If you would still set my niece aside, Trelane, at least give the babe a name. Kat has done you no wrong."

Morgan found he had to sit down. His knees would scarce support him.

"*Sweet Jesu,*" he whispered.

"Precisely. Now do you see the depth of my predicament? I do not ask you to pretend that nothing is amiss; just give our Kat a chance. She loves you, milord, without regard for your rumored deformity or anything else."

Morgan drew another shaky breath. "A babe? Are you sure?"

Kit regarded him with twinkling green eyes, too similar to Kat's for comfort. "Reasonably so. Mayhap you wonder why my niece has no issue from her first marriage. 'Twas assumed by all the family that Kat was barren. I wager, the fault lay with young Rory, not her—a scandalous theory on my part, I trow. Yet my brother Slade noted young Rory had lain with a dozen wenches in his wilder days, before settling down with Kat. None bore bastards."

Morgan was silent a moment. "Does she know?"

Kit shook his head. "Not yet. Isobel thought it prudent not to upset her any more than necessary. I concur with my wife's decision. Besides, there is no point enraging Bess further if 'tis not true."

"Let's assume 'tis so. When is the child due?"

"Christmas. Be advised, twins run on both sides of the family. You would do well to keep her abed after the fifth month."

"Of course," Morgan muttered, still dazed. "Of course." He rubbed at the bandage on his cheek, and, to his chagrin it came completely off. He winced as Kit's gaze encountered his secret.

"Set it aside, milord. There's no need for pretense any longer. Kat deserves the truth."

Morgan nodded. "Aye, I suppose you're right . . . Kit."

The other man smiled broadly, though whether at the use of his familiar name or at the success of his plot, Morgan did not care to guess.

Eighteen

Kat left St. Ethelburga's with mixed emotions. Morgan had not sought an annulment yet. Then where was he? She paused outside the little cathedral to gather her thoughts. She had annoyed the priest by demanding an audience at this early hour, especially after their hasty midnight service. Father Benedict was loath to assist Kat in finding her missing husband. A wife, he informed her righteously, did not question her lord and master's whereabouts or business. Kat stifled a burst of disrespectful laughter during the priest's not-so-subtle reprimand. Father Benedict obviously assumed Morgan had sought out another's bed on his own wedding night, and, as usual, the poor abandoned wife must needs shoulder the blame and burden of it!

Kat sighed. She didn't know what to do about her predicament. She wandered the slumbering streets of London for a time, digging into the pockets of her skirts for a few coins. She purchased a bag of hot chestnuts and a hunk of cheese to break her morning fast. One by one, the stalls came to life, each vendor declaring their fish the freshest, their fruit the sweetest. After she finished the nuts and cheese, Kat was seduced in turn by a basket of bright oranges and bought one from a little orange girl who spoke with a charming lisp and displayed a mass of honey-colored, corkscrew curls. The price was dear; the reward was heavenly. While Kat peeled the orange and let the sticky juices run down her chin, she perused other stalls and their offerings. It had been so long since she strolled a marketplace. A pang of something—a flash of memory—came to her. Hadn't she and Rory once shopped for bargains in Dublin?

A pair of young lovers, hand in hand, passed Kat on Bishopsgate; the girl was laughing, her fine dark hair blowing in the breeze. Her red-haired swain dangled a bit of ribbon and a bunch of daisies before her eyes until, mischievously, she snatched them from his fist and ran. He gave merry chase, shouting her name so that it echoed off the alley stones:

"Ahh, Kaitlin, sweet Kaitlin, wait!"

His thick Irish brogue sent a cold shiver through Kat. Suddenly, she found herself weeping and didn't know why.

Morgan arrived back at Hartshorn only to discover his wife missing. He felt a rising frustration as he questioned his apathetic servants. None knew where Kat had gone; only the stableman had bothered to note that she left several hours ago. Kat must have run away after he had rejected her.

Cursing himself for a fool, Morgan called for his roan to be saddled. He downed a quick mug of ale and a handful of biscuits before he went in search of her. He decided to head to Whitehall first. If Kat believed herself well and truly spurned, 'twas logical she would turn to her sister for consolation.

He took care to don his half mask again in public, though it proved a waste of effort. Merry Tanner was nowhere to be found. Her tiring woman, Jane, was diplomatically evasive about where his new sister-in-law might be. Morgan realized the servant assumed him to be one of the queen's spies. None of his wheedling arguments—

not even a whole crown—could serve to pierce the woman's reserve. She denied any knowledge of her mistress's whereabouts.

"You're a good girl, Jane," he said before he left, and, with a gesture of defeat, he pressed the crown into her palm before he left. "A loyal servant is worth ten of these. I shall see you are properly rewarded one day soon." Jane dropped him a dutiful curtsey, eyes wide with curiosity and some trepidation. Morgan realized his mask was disconcerting to others by daylight and suddenly hated it with a passion. Jesu, he was so weary of the charade.

Softening a little, Jane blurted, "Captain Navarre inquired earlier after Mistress Kat, sir. Mayhap he has found her by now."

Navarre. The name set his teeth on edge. Morgan realized the French captain was a logical choice. If Kat had not gone to her sister, perhaps she had turned to a trusted friend for advice or consolation. He tried not to think of the latter possibility, when he scratched at Navarre's door in the barracks. Morgan warned himself not to be surprised by whatever he found. He deserved the worst. A sleepy Navarre answered the door. The handsome captain did the wrong thing when he recognized Morgan: He smiled.

Morgan caught a glimpse of the bed over Navarre's shoulder. He saw a fan of dark hair across the pillows.

"You bastard." Reason went out the window, as Morgan's fist connected with Lucien's jaw. The naked Frenchman stumbled backwards into the room with the force of the blow.

"Mon Dieu!" The woman in the bed screamed, shrill as a fishwife, and pulled the covers over her head.

Morgan stepped into the room, over Lucien's faint protests, and went to the bed. He whipped the covers back; he froze, staring down at the bawd with Kat's dark hair but a coarser face. She whimpered beneath his cold assessment.

With an oath, Morgan tossed the blankets back over the wench's trembling form. He spun on his heel to leave, just as Navarre came around.

Gingerly touching his bruised jaw, Lucien shook his golden head free of stars. He stared up at Morgan. "I demand to know the meaning of this intrusion, monsieur."

Without answering the captain, Morgan demanded in turn, "Have you seen Kat?"

"I've a mind not to tell you anything, after what you've done here," Navarre replied. He came to his feet a little unsteadily, and met Morgan's gaze. Then he reached for a murrey silk dressing gown and drew it over his broad shoulders. He sighed as he belted the robe about his body. "Katherine has never come to me."

"Never?" Morgan heard himself demand, sounding suspiciously close to a jealous husband.

Lucien's blue eyes twinkled. "You are a possessive man, Trelane. I thought as much the night of the masque. *Non*, Katherine has never been my lover, though I will not deny I wished otherwise. She is a priceless pearl and you cast her foolishly aside."

Morgan's jaw tightened. "I did nothing of the sort."

"Then why are you looking for her here?"

"My wife is missing. I thought perhaps—"

"Your wife!" Lucien's exclamation was both of shock and envy. He chuckled. "So you thought the worst, eh, Trelane?" For some reason his piercing blue gaze suddenly softened on Morgan.

"Yea, she is my wife. I see you . . . admire Kat. And she speaks of you quite often."

Lucien knew what it cost the other man to admit his envy. "You are a fool," he said, shaking his head. "*Oui*, I admire your wife greatly. Especially her courage. But I knew Katherine loved another from the moment I declared my own intentions. She was too kind to hurt me, but I saw from the beginning I had no chance. We are great friends; alas, I still find rejection hard to accept. If she came to me now, I would not turn her away."

Morgan stiffened. The handsome captain was honest, too honest. He quelled the urge to strike the man again. Damme! He *was* jealous.

Yvette, the woman in the bed, had gathered her wits by then and spoke querulously in French. Lucien turned and curtly addressed her complaints. When he turned back to Trelane, he was gone.

"Where's Uncle Kit?" Kat demanded, the moment Merry stepped into Ambergate's parlor.

"Dear Kat. Where have you been? Everyone has been looking for you. Uncle Kit called at Hartshorn some time ago and was told you were out. He went in search of Lord Trelane instead. Isobel had just taken Maggie to the dressmakers, and not a moment too soon. We have all received a royal summons for this evening. You realize what this means?"

Kat sighed and reached down to massage her aching feet. "I'm too tired to worry about it. I walked about London most of the morning, Merry. I had some thinking to do."

"Goodness, it must have been rather heavy thinking. I cannot blame you for dreading the queen's reaction to the news of your wedding. I understand Bess is in a fearful froth. Uncle Kit intends to try and placate her, once he tracks down your wayward husband."

Kat shook her head. "The queen is the least of my concerns, Merry."

Her sister looked shocked. "It bodes ill to be cavalier where Bess is concerned. Come, dearest, sit down, and I'll send for a pot of hot, strong tea and some of Cook's delicious biscuits. We must discuss a strategy for this evening. Certainly, we must plan on a suitable costume. Mayhap you can wear my yellow damask? You are not fond of it, I know, and such a shade makes brunettes look sallow, but I've learned 'tis wise to feign ill health when one requires Her Grace's sympathies."

"Nay, Merry. I can't stay." Kat took a deep breath. "I've made up my mind; I'm leaving for Wales straightaway."

Merry's jaw dropped. "Wales? Are you mad?"

"Mayhap."

"Lord Trelane—"

"Morgan must do as he sees fit," Kat said wearily. "I've no more stomach for these charades."

"Your husband was here early this morn," Merry said. "He and Uncle Kit spoke at great length here in the parlor. Alack, I couldn't hear what they were saying, though 'twas not for lack of skill nor trying."

"No doubt 'twas about dissolution of our marriage. Morgan vowed he would seek an annulment. He was furious, Merry, absolutely furious that we all tricked him. It appears the queen shall have her champion in this cause, after all."

"Then why go to Wales, where you are not wanted? Stay here at Ambergate, where you are safe and loved."

Kat set her jaw, and, in that stubborn expression, Merry caught a glimpse of their mother, Bryony.

"Nay. I've a right to return to Falcon's Lair and stay there, until Morgan or the queen tell me otherwise. Besides, I never thanked the Careys for their hospitality, and I feel a strong need to walk the shores where the *Fiach Teine* sank. I must deal with the tragedy, once and for all."

Merry sighed. "You can't let it rest, can you?"

"Rory was my husband. The entire crew was like family to me. Mother and Father would understand."

"I wish they were here to dissuade you now."

"They would understand better than anyone, I think." Kat paused, blinking back tears at the memory of all the beloved faces she had grown up with and sorely missed now.

Over the past few months, the names and faces of her crewmen had slowly surfaced, one by one: Rogan Keane, first mate, a dear cousin; Ty Dempsey, their burly bosun; Corby MacQuaid, the lookout; Little Barry, the cabin boy, not quite twelve when he died; Higgins, a cranky but amazing cook, who served nigh two-score in her parents' fleet. Slade had lent Higgins to his daughter, with a wink and a grin. Kat ached when she imagined telling her parents how she had failed. She recalled both of them as proud, especially her mother. Kat was said to resemble Bryony Tanner in more than looks. While her mother still sailed the high seas without a qualm, Kat had suffered terror of water ever since the tragedy. She knew she must deal with it eventually. Returning to the site of Adrien Lovelle's treachery, and Rory's death, was the first step in the direction towards the healing of her heart.

Merry sensed her unwavering stance and sighed again. " 'Tis utter madness to defy the queen, Kat. You have already roused Bess's ire by snatching Maggie's intended and by wedding the baron under false pretenses."

"Maggie was glad to be quit of Trelane's suit, and as for Morgan, I thought he would come 'round to the notion. He is not, it seems, pleased to find me his wife today, yet the deed is done. Short of the annulment, he must deal with me. I will seek my answers in Wales, Merry."

Another sigh came from her sister. "How will you get there?"

"I pray Uncle Kit might lend me a mount."

Merry shook her head. "Don't be foolish. 'Tis too dangerous for a woman to travel such a distance alone. If you must go, you will take one of the coaches. And I shall go with you. If you must defy Bess, you shall not be alone."

Kat did not conceal her relief. "Would you risk so much for me?"

"What are sisters for?"

They crossed the Welsh border on a stormy, windswept day. Slowly and painstakingly, the elegant Tanner coach continued rumbling northward, Kat and Merry ensconced within its cozy velvet depths. Jem, the coachman, had been reluctant to spirit them off on such a lark.

" 'Don't favor this one bit," he repeated whenever they stopped to change horses or frequent an inn. He ominously shook his grizzled head. "There are rogues and brigands all about, miladies, and the Master would rightly have my hide should anythin' happen to either of ye."

"Uncle Kit will understand the necessity of the matter," Merry reassured the old driver at their last stop before the border. "I left him a letter in great detail, explaining our actions. Please, Jem, you know me to be a reasonable and mature young woman. Faith, I would not accompany my sister north were it not absolutely necessary."

Jem digested her words as Merry sat back against the cushions with an artless smile. Nay, Jem conceded, he couldn't claim Mistress Tanner was reckless. She'd been raised at Court, proper as you please, and seemed a mite more levelheaded than the other young ladies he'd attended over the years.

Merry Tanner also knew how to use her charms to the utmost when she needed to wheedle her way. Jem didn't realize this. He walked off to hitch the horses, still shaking his head but swayed by her convincing air.

When the coach set off again, Merry's smile changed from sweet to smug. "D'you see how 'tis done, Kat? Men are all the same, no matter their age or class."

But Kat wasn't listening to her sister. Her gaze hungrily scoured the countryside for her first glimpse of Falcon's Lair.

At Merry's insistence, she had donned an elegant crimson velvet traveling outfit with rose-colored satin sleeves, and her hair was dressed in a married woman's fashion. She was glad she had taken Merry's advice, when they arrived at the keep. Among the servants who watched her disembark from the fine coach, she noted a new, instant respect in their eyes.

Only Winnie forgot her place in all the confusion. "Dearest Katie!" she cried, running down the steps with her apron flapping in the breeze. Kat didn't have the heart to correct Winnie. She returned the housekeeper's embrace with equal ferocity and fondness.

Winnie wiped away her tears as she stepped back. "Why, Katie, look at you! A grand lady now." There was surprise and a little uncertainty in her voice. Her gaze shifted to the redhead standing a measure behind Kat.

"Mrs. Carey, may I present my sister, Mistress Meredith Tanner. She kindly agreed to escort me back to Falcon's Lair."

As the housekeeper bobbed a confused curtsey, Kat explained, "At last I found my kin, Winnie. They had assumed me lost in a shipwreck at sea. Thankfully, most of my memory returned whilst I was in London."

"Praise the saints," Winnie murmured. Her keen gaze affixed at once on Kat's fourth finger and remained riveted upon the gleaming gold band.

"I know 'twill come as quite a shock for you," Kat proceeded, "but Lord Trelane and I were wed in London."

"Oh. Congratulations . . . milady." Winnie bobbed another curtsey, this one a little stiffer than the last.

"Nothing has changed, Winnie. I might be Lady Trelane now, but I have not forgotten the kindness you showed me when I was but a stranger here." There was an awkward silence after she concluded her speech. Kat forced a cheerful note into her voice. "Please do say we can still be friends."

"Of course, milady."

"Kat, if you please."

Winnie nodded but made no further attempt to be familiar. "Is the Master with you?"

"I daresay he shall return shortly." As Kat and Merry exchanged glances, Winnie moved off to see to the readying of several rooms for their stay.

Merry moved up beside Kat. "You were too familiar with the woman, my dear. You will lose the servants' respect."

"I cannot act as if I don't know Winnie." Chagrined by the implication that she must forget the friendships she had made here, Kat frowned at her sister. "Good heavens, Merry. The woman saved my eyesight."

"Still, you mustn't encourage such familiarity. I daresay Mrs. Carey herself was shocked by your actions. You would do better to maintain a cordial, yet remote, relationship with all the staff."

Kat suddenly felt miserable. "I thought things would be wonderful when I became Lady Trelane. I had hoped I might make things easier for everyone here."

Merry fell silent, studying the huge gray stone keep rising ominously above them against a cloud-flecked sky. She didn't understand Kat's misbegotten affection for such an ancient old pile of rocks or such shockingly forward, countrified servants, but then, she had never understood Kat at all. She clearly had her work cut out for her. With a sigh, she motioned for Jem to follow them with the baggage to the entrance.

"I shall see you settled in, Kat. In a few days' time, I'll head back to London and reassure Uncle Kit of your safe arrival. Doubtless by then, Bess will be one of the screaming Furies, but she is known to have a soft spot for us redheaded Tanners. Between Uncle Kit and me, we can plead your cause."

"Oh, don't leave so soon, Merry! Please." Kat was frightened at the thought of being left to fend for herself. Those who had once been dear friends were mere retainers now, as evidenced by their respective bows and curtsies as she passed them in the hall. Even Ailis, the jovial old cook, wouldn't meet her eye. Like the rest, Ailis murmured a formal phrase, a stiff welcome that sounded anything but jovial.

Kat was shown to a bedchamber different from the one she had previously occupied. This one adjoined Morgan's and was both larger and colder, with its northern view. 'Twas dusty and neglected, as all of Hartshorn had been. Winnie quickly promised 'twould be put to rights.

Seeing how miserable Kat was in her unfamiliar role of authority, Merry took over. She informed the housekeeper of their needs, then dismissed the woman with leave to see to her assigned duties.

" 'Twill never do," Kat moaned, after her sister joined her and the door closed after Winnie. "They are right to resent my presence here as lady of the house. They all expected Morgan to return with a wife of noble upbringing."

"There is nothing humble about the Tanner name," Merry replied, a trifle sharply. "Uncle Kit has been knighted and has been a long-standing favorite of the queen. Our grandmother Meredith was one of Elizabeth Tudor's dearest confidantes, as I am one of her maids of honor. Our father served in Her Majesty's fleet for many years. Both our parents bear the queen's favor. 'Twould be most churlish for a motley handful of *taffy* staff to look down their noses at you."

Kat winced at the slur Merry used. "Aye, but they don't know anything of our history. For all I know, they think I'm an Irish upstart of a serf. At the least, they must suppose me a greedy opportunist who's taking advantage of their Master's generous nature."

Merry threw up her hands in frustration. "Y'are giving up before you have begun! All is not lost, Kat. But you must take back the little authority you have left before it disappears altogether. Now, listen to me:

"First of all, you must not hide away in your room. 'Twill only cause mischievous speculation on the part of the staff. They are expecting Lord Trelane to arrive and explain everything at any moment. You and I know Trelane will not save you, so by the time he does appear, you must have them firmly in hand."

"Aye," Kat sighed, "I suppose you're right."

"Of course I am. Now, we must needs see you made presentable. Are there any decent maid servants to be found?"

Kat thought of Gwynneth and shuddered. "Nay."

"Hardly unexpected. Then I'll help you myself. We must change you from that dusty traveling attire into something suitable. I assume dinner will be served at a civil hour?"

Kat replied in the affirmative, although she wasn't sure. 'Twas best not to argue with Merry when she adopted one of her lecturing tones.

"I brought along a red taffeta trimmed with pearls. Mayhap 'tis a tad short for you, but 'twill serve nicely in a pinch. We will find a sempster to alter the rest of the gowns for you. As for me, I hope Maggie won't miss her blue velvet too soon."

Kat chuckled. "Did you truly raid her wardrobe?"

"There was no time to buy a proper trousseau for you or indeed, for me to pack my things. You wouldn't let me send for our wardrobes from Whitehall, remember."

"I confess, I was too anxious to reach Falcon's Lair. I fear I have made a terrible mistake, Merry."

"Well, we are here now. We must make the best of it."

Nineteen

Merry Tanner was in her true element at Falcon's Lair, directing servants and supervising a great household. She was mortified by conditions inside the positively medieval keep and by the appalling lack of servants. But when she questioned Mrs. Carey as to the reasons, she learned the meaning of close-mouthed.

"Lord Trelane has no complaints," the freckle-faced housekeeper sniffed. " 'Twas he who hired all the staff you see here."

Merry frowned, planting her hands on her hips. "D'you mean to say he has no more retainers? Mayhap some have run away in his absence."

"Oh, nay, milady. This is all there is. We're content to serve all his needs."

" 'T'won't do, my good woman. Not at all," Merry exclaimed. "Falcon's Lair is huge, even as castles go. 'Twill require a great deal of hired help to run properly. I shall have Lady Trelane authorize employment of at least two more cooks, a brace of stable hands, and half a dozen maids."

Winnie blinked. "Begging your pardon, milady, but wherever will you find them?"

Merry looked aggrieved. "From town, of course," she replied. "Surely there is a settlement of some sort nearby?"

"Well, there's the village—"

"Excellent. You may begin looking there."

" 'Tis not quite a real village, more a settlement of sorts. . . ."

Merry shrugged. "Are there able-bodied men and women in this settlement?" At the housekeeper's reluctant nod, she airily proceeded. "Then what are you waiting for, Mrs. Carey? Ride out at once and secure the necessary staff to fill Lady Trelane's orders."

Winnie wanted to inform this little snip of a red-headed virago that any order, even this one, must come from Lady Katherine directly, and not her sister. She refrained from doing so. 'Twas no use arguing with a *Sassenach*. Bold as brass, this one was. She sighed and bustled off.

Merry stared after the woman and released a vexed sigh of her own. This whole business was beginning to weary her. Every time she turned around, it seemed there was more work to be done. More headaches. The servants—if they might be called such by any stretch of the imagination—were as blasé as any she had encountered. Truly, she was beginning to wonder if all the Welsh weren't a bit touched in the head.

Kat walked along the seashore, feeling the waves rush up and curl around her feet. Heedless of the cold water seeping through her fine hose and shoes, she headed south along the border of cliffs lining the Trelane land.

Gulls screamed and swirled against the sky, white wings riding the currents. Kat brushed back a tendril of loose hair from her face and stared out to sea. The benign water glimmered and mocked her with its secrets: Somewhere out there, the skeletons of the *Fiach Teine* and her crew rested together in a watery grave.

Kat moved to a boulder where she might perch and watch the waves rolling ashore. She didn't know what she looked for, nor what she hoped to find, but some measure of peace gradually stole over her, as she watched the sun sinking into the western sky.

The sea had been part of her once, a friend she might turn to in good times or bad. 'Twas the balm for her troubled soul. Kat smiled a little. Had she changed? The water no longer held the fascination it once had for her. She felt no desire whatsoever to resume her life upon these capricious waters or to command a new ship under her own name. She thought of all the things she had missed while she played at being a sailor: Wales; Falcon's Lair; Morgan; most of all, a place she could call her own, where she could plant deep and permanent roots; a man she could love wholly, without reserve. Bit by bit, she felt her obsession with the sea dwindle and release its choke hold on her heart, just as a strangling vine is severed from a rose so that the flower might fully bloom.

"Rory," she whispered, regretful, remembering the young man who had once sailed beside her. It seemed so long ago, now; another age, another life. A vision of Rory Shanahan's face, strong and clear, surfaced for the first time in months. For one aching, bittersweet moment, Kat looked into Rory's aqua-colored eyes again, smoothing the fiery mane of his glorious auburn hair.

"Kat, love," Rory called to her from his watery grave.

She rose on shaking legs and stared out to sea. *"Sweet Jesu."* Guilt and shame warred within her at the possibility that Rory somehow lived in spirit and knew what she had done. She had failed to save her husband, then turned faithless to his memory almost overnight. "I'm so sorry, Rory. Ahhh, Sweet Mother and Mary, what I wouldn't give to relive that day again," she shouted.

Only the ebb and surge of the waves answered her cry, and, when the echo from the cliffs faded, Kat wiped her streaming eyes, feeling both foolish and sad. She only imagined Rory was there. Her guilty conscience surely sought to make amends, however it might. But Rory was long gone, claimed by a sea as fickle-natured as his wife.

" 'Twas not your fault, Kat. 'Twas my time to go."

Kat started at the gentle murmur near her ear, then fancied she felt something brush her arm.

"Rory?" she cried, whirling about. She saw nothing. She was alone. Yet she was not.

"Aye, colleen." Kat noticed his voice no longer held heartache or terror or despair. The drowning man from her dreams was gone. To the contrary, Rory sounded content, at peace.

"Kat, love, I must go now. You've a life to live without me, a life with the wee one I could not give you."

Startled, Kat touched her stomach. Aye, she felt a faint swelling there. Dared she hope? She sensed the invisible presence withdrawing from her, and she gazed out at the implacable depths to which it returned.

Mayhap 'twas only the wind. Or the waves hissing as they rush ashore. Nay. She could not take the chance. Another broken cry issued from Kat's lips and echoed off the cliffs. "Rory! Don't go. I must needs explain—"

"Ahh, sweetheart. Love needs no explanation. Farewell, Kat, farewell. Wish me godspeed. . . ."

She did not mistake the moment of severance. Rory's last earthly link was broken, and Kat herself felt a physical jolt—part pain, part joy—as his spirit rose from the sea and vanished into the sun. Whatever vestige of Rory Shanahan haunted these waters was gone forever.

Gradually the wind dried the tears on Kat's cheeks. 'Twas turning twilight. She looked over the water one last time. The sea was almost golden now, mesmerizing in its beauty. Even the gulls had stopped shrieking and squabbling for food and now nestled along the cliffs with their heads tucked beneath their frosted wings.

Kat heard her mount whicker restlessly in the distance and realized 'twas time to head back. With a final glance, she turned from the sea. One strange, inexplicable moment after Rory had left, she experienced a desire to turn and walk calmly into those shimmering waters and let the cold waves close over her head and join her to her crew, as their good captain. . . .

Nay, Kat. She did not need to hear Rory's voice again to know the notion was foolish and forbidden. She had a new life now, Rory had reminded her—one with Morgan, and their child. Or did she? She shivered and pulled her cloak more snugly around her shoulders. Merry would be frantic if she didn't return promptly by the dinner hour.

It took Kat some time to find the faint trail snaking up between the boulders. She shielded her eyes against the rocks' reflection of the sun's dying glare. She traced the path upward with her gaze. By chance, she glimpsed the yawning mouth of a cave, high above on nearby Madoc's Craig. It piqued her curiosity. Kat debated the wisdom of trying to reach it before nightfall, then realized she might suffer a serious misstep or fall, and nobody would be able to find her.

Instead, she moved to fetch her gray mare. She could always ride out on the morrow and explore the cave at her leisure in the safety of daylight. She mounted her horse and turned it in the direction of Falcon's Lair.

After Kat left, a pale face materialized from the depths of the cave. Gwynneth Owen's lip curled under as she watched Kat ride away. Beneath her breath, she vowed the new Lady Trelane would never leave Wales alive.

When Kat reached Falcon's Lair, she was surprised to see a fine yet unfamiliar coach parked outside the great door. Praying 'twas not the Earl of Cardiff, Henry Lawrence, she slipped from the gray's back and handed the reins to Evan. Her stomach tightened with dread. She

sighed. "How fares poor Uncle Kit? Is he languishing in the Tower even as we speak?"

Bryony laughed, planting her hands on her hips. "Bess knows better than to rile an old adversary again. The O'Neills and Tanner families are irretrievably linked now. O'Neills defend their own. The only prison dear Kit shall ever visit will be Ambergate, where I vow he is quite content to spend all his days."

Frustrated at having been left out of the conversation, Merry interrupted, sounding peevish. "Did you speak to the queen about me?"

Slade shrugged. "Concerning what?"

"Father! Don't tease so. I pray you at least reassured Elizabeth Tudor of my constant devotion and unswerving loyalty."

"I fear, it slipped my mind," Slade replied with a twinkle, winking at Kat and his wife.

Merry stamped her foot, petulant as a little girl. "If I have lost my position at Court, I shall never forgive you!"

" 'Twas your choice to accompany your sister here, Merry," Bryony put in. "I was prouder of you than ever when I heard what you had done."

"Aye, Mother, but I'm not the born rebels you and Kat are," Merry wailed with distress. "My whole life is Court. Bess promised to make me a fine match someday."

"In this much, our good queen did not disappoint," Slade said. "If you are agreeable, Merry, you will wed Sir Jasper Wickham come spring."

"Of the Carlisle Wickhams?" Gone in an instant were Merry's tears; in their stead, a calculating gleam appeared. "I hear tale Sir Jasper is rich and comely. He will suit me quite well, I trow."

"Wickham is also accounted rough and crude and brutal," Bryony said dryly. "Though I suppose a border man must be."

Merry tossed her head. "My betrothed is hardly a bar-

baric Scot, Mother. You have been listening to too many O'Neill ballads. Elizabeth Tudor would approve no man for my husband who was not refined and accomplished in every way."

"Then you agree to Wickham's suit?" Slade asked.

"Aye, Father."

"Merry," Kat protested, "you have never laid eyes on the man."

"Just as you never saw Morgan Trelane and loved him anyhow," her sister retorted. There was nothing Kat might say in response. 'Twas true enough.

Kat saw a shadow cross her father's face, and all traces of mirth was forgotten.

"Kit told us a little of your frightening adventure," Slade said to her. "I would fain hear the tale again, from your own lips."

Kat wondered where to start. "D'you speak of Wales and Morgan Trelane?"

"I know how you came to be here and heard Lord Trelane was the one who nursed you back to health. Also, that you were later taken to London, a prisoner of Henry Lawrence."

"Mark my words, the odious old goat shall hear from me," Bryony interjected on an ominous note.

Kat shook her head. " 'Twas not Lawrence's fault, Mama. He but rightfully sought to protect the queen. The strange circumstances of my survival and resulting blindness would give any man pause. I believe Lord Lawrence is good at heart. A trifle overzealous, perhaps."

"You are generous, Kat," her mother said. "More generous than Lawrence intended to be with *you.*"

"I would not incur the resentment of Morgan's neighbors. I am Lady Trelane now, which behooves me to show a generous nature."

Bryony looked surprised. "I'truth, daughter, you have

grown up in a few short months. I am both pleased and
a little sad. You seem different, somehow."

"Aye, Mama. I am different," Kat conceded softly. "I
am in love."

"With Lord Trelane?"

"With Morgan, with Falcon's Lair, with all of wild, beautiful Cymru." Kat met her mother's searching gaze, and
added gently, "Ireland and Rory Shanahan are part of
my past now. So is the sea."

Something seemed to slump in Bryony's proud posture.
"Are you certain, Kat?"

"Aye, as I ever shall be. Do not mourn, Mama. I have
never been so happy as in these past few months with
Morgan. Rory and I shared a beloved hobby, nothing
more. Morgan and I connect on a far deeper level, mayhap one of the soul."

Bryony only nodded, too stricken for words.

"I regret the reminder, dearest," Slade said to his wife,
"but we came not to chide Kat. She was almost lost to us
forever and I, for one, am simply grateful she is alive."

"You're right." Looking abashed, Bryony stepped forward to hug Kat again. "Forgive me, colleen."

"There is nothing to forgive. I know how much the sea
means to you and Father. 'Tis your life. Once 'twas mine,
too. Until a terrible fire consumed my ship, my crew, and
almost my life. Like the legendary phoenix, I was miracu-
lously reborn from the ashes." As she spoke, Kat realized
the words rang true. She trembled with emotion, and
Bryony held her even tighter.

"Mayhap we should rechristen you "Fire Raven," instead of your lost ship," Bryony murmured. "With a certainty, the clan's mascot watched over you." She withdrew
and glanced at Kat's bare neck. "Was the amulet lost at
sea, too?"

"Nay. Morgan kept it here for me. I found it in my

room. I will send it back to Ireland with you and Papa
for safekeeping."

Bryony shook her head. "The amulet chooses its
owner. When your Uncle Brendan gave it to me, he said
a strange, powerful force compelled him to part with it
then. I felt the same thing when I handed the amulet to
you on your twelfth birthday. You will know, when the
time is right, to do the same, Kat. Until then, do not
abandon or reject the power. It surely saved your life."

For the first time in years, more than a handful of din-
ers occupied the great table at Falcon's Lair. The staff
had outdone themselves in order to impress Lady Trelane's family. Kat was pleased and touched by their efforts.

A gleaming silver service proffered a choice selection
of mountain lamb, roasted in honey, glazed Welsh rarebit,
and grouse. Ailis's famous laver bread, three varieties of
local cheeses, and a stout mead were offered, along with
watered wine. There was even a colorful assortment of
unusual-looking flowers arranged in silver vases. The Tanners had not arrived empty-handed, either. Slade intro-
duced his daughters to a rich liquor called rum. He and
Bryony brought dozens of great barrels of rum back from
their Caribbean voyage and enriched Kat's new household with several.

Bryony's contribution from their latest voyage was a
colorful array of exotic fruits and nuts. There were bright
green oval fruits called limes; curious-looking yellow ba-
nanas; round, hairy coconuts; and long, woody pods filled
with something called cacao beans. Receiving such a
windfall of strange new foods, Cook had done her best,
but Kat bit her lip and struggled against laughter when
one of the staff brought in a bubbling kettle filled with
an assortment of everything.

With a glance in the kettle, swimming with fruit rinds

and stems, Kat tactfully requested saucers of clotted cream and berries for dessert. The odoriferous kettle was set aside and the family enjoyed simpler fare.

Kat wished Morgan were there to preside as lord of his own table. She sensed her parents' unspoken questions and concerns about her second marriage and assumed they had heard rumors of Morgan's reclusive nature or, worse yet, his supposed disfigurement.

After dinner, Bryony accompanied Merry upstairs to begin planning her second daughter's wedding arrangements. Slade lingered at the table with Kat.

"I wanted to wait until your mother retired," he said. "I fear Bryony might be too upset by the next subject to remain calm."

Kat steeled herself for a bevy of accusations—questions about Morgan and his rumored deformity.

"I heard Merry was almost murdered at Whitehall by an old nemesis of mine."

Kat was surprised and almost relieved by the topic. "Did Uncle Kit tell you?"

Slade shook his head. "Kit knew little more than any other courtier. Nay, 'twas Trelane himself who told me."

"Morgan? Then you've met my husband already."

"Not in person. Our exchange took place by way of correspondence. After learning of your marriage, I called at Hartshorn but was told his lordship was out. I left my congratulations. Shortly thereafter, a message was sent to my ship, informing me of the terrible events at Whitehall. Your husband was quite concerned about you and your sister. He sought to warn me of the danger."

"Morgan and I were both witnesses," Kat admitted. She hesitated, remembering Adrien Lovelle's ugly accusations. She was too embarrassed to ask her father outright about his relationship with Adrien's sister, Gillian, yet Slade spared her the agony. He said:

"I was once betrothed to a woman of French descent,

one of Bess Tudor's ladies. 'Twas before I met your mother. Gillian Lovelle was likened to Aphrodite, with good reason: She was faithless as a snake, as heartless as she was beautiful." Slade leaned back in his chair, seeming subdued, and continued the tale:

"Gillian was not content with my prospects. I fear she sought richer, titled game. Bess pressed us both to marry, despite our mutual unhappiness. After I met your mother, all thoughts of Gilly disappeared. Except the uncharitable ones."

"Her brother claims you tried to murder her," Kat said.

Slade stiffened, and his green eyes flashed. "The pup was not there to witness the truth. Gilly contracted the pox. I was framed for Gilly's murder, 'tis true enough, and almost lost my head at Tower Green. Now I learn she is still alive, that I almost died for naught. Worse still, Gilly has apparently gone mad and seeks to revenge herself upon my innocent family. Would I could strangle the little bitch now! My one regret is that I did not do it when I had the chance."

Kat was alarmed by her father's outburst. 'Twas unlike him. He was such a calm, levelheaded man. She reached across the table and took his large tanned hand in her own.

"Oh, Papa, I believe you. Only a madwoman would act as she has. Take comfort in the fact that Gillian Lovelle has failed twice and cannot make the attempt so easily again. Morgan, Merry, and I all know who Adrien is now, whatever guises he may adopt to ford our defenses in future."

"Aye, but you have five little brothers," Slade growled. "Rowan and Devlin have been sent back to your grandfather in Ireland, for safety's sake. Bryony does not know of my concerns. I trow she would sail to France and execute Gilly herself if she knew what had happened. S'blood, I cannot risk her life. I love her too much."

Kat patted his hand. "The secret is safe with me. Merry, however, is inclined to chatter. You'd best take her aside, and speak to her before she tells Mama what happened at Court. Then I think it best you return to Ireland. The greater the distance, the better. There is safety in numbers."

Slade considered her words and nodded. "Aye, you're right, Kat. I hate to leave so soon without meeting your husband, but I fear each passing moment increases the danger. Will you welcome another visit from the whole clan, mayhap in the spring?"

If I am still here, Kat thought, but smiled to put Slade's concerns to rest. " 'Tis a lovely notion, Papa. By then you shall be a grandfather, y'know."

Slade's face lit with wonder and delight at her shy announcement, and he squeezed her hand so hard, Kat almost gasped.

" 'Tis the greatest boon you've ever given me, sweetling. When you and Rory could not—"

"Aye, I know," she quietly replied. " 'Twas a grievous disappointment to us all."

"Shall we find your mother and tell her now?" Slade eagerly rose from the chair, still holding her hand and beaming, ear to ear.

"You go ahead. 'Twould be fun for you to share the happy news first. I'll come up later. First I want to thank the staff for all their efforts tonight."

Slade nodded and left to impart the news to her mother. Kat knew Bryony would be equally excited and pleased at the prospect of becoming a grandmother—although Madam Tanner scarcely looked the part, without a single strand of gray hair!

Kat summoned Winnie with the little silver bell beside her plate. She noticed the housekeeper's look of trepidation when Winnie entered the dining hall.

"I wanted to thank you for organizing a fine repast,"

she said. "The table is gorgeous. The linen and silver are exquisite, the food divine. These flowers are an especially charming touch."

Winnie's gaze moved to the vases Kat indicated. She looked shocked. "I did not order flowers, milady."

"Nay? Nevertheless 'twas a sweet gesture from one of the staff." Kat saw Winnie pale. "What's wrong?"

" 'Tis Bloody Fingers, milady."

"What?"

Winnie bit her lip. "A deadly plant, milady, oft used by those who seek to harm others." She avoided Kat's eyes. " 'Tis also said to be favored by those who practice the dark arts."

"Witchcraft, you mean?" Kat shrugged off a pang of unease. "Mayhap the maid who picked them did not know. 'Tis a pretty enough arrangement."

Winnie said nothing, still visibly upset. Kat dismissed Winnie with a message to thank the rest of the staff for her. Then she plucked the flowers from the vases. She ventured up to Falcon Lair's battlements and tossed them from the bailey. They fluttered away on the evening breeze, their delicate petals torn to shreds by the wind. How could something so innocuous and beautiful be deadly?

From the favorable vantage point, Kat looked down the curving road leading to the village and southward—no sign of Morgan. Obviously he did not care to return to Falcon's Lair while she was there. She felt a faint flutter in her belly and touched her abdomen with wonder and a little sadness.

Please, Morgan, come home.

There was no answer but the keening of the wind.

Twenty

"This is it, milord. We can't go any further. The river's washed out the road clear up to Aberystwyth."

Morgan cursed under his breath and dismounted from the roan stallion. He looked past Jimson to see the truth in the man's words.

"We should not have taken the shortcut," he observed.

"Aye, we'll never make it with the horses through all that mud."

"Then I suppose we've no choice but to find a nearby inn."

"Or return to London, milord," Jimson suggested hopefully.

Morgan shook his head. "We'll press on once the weather clears. Take my mount, Jimson. I wish to explore a bit farther ahead."

Reluctantly, Jimson moved forward to take control of Morgan's stallion. The roan skittered and tossed his head at the unfamiliar hand on the reins. The animal was the ugliest beast Jimson had ever seen, mayhap a fitting mount for Satan's Son. He glanced anxiously after Trelane, praying the baron would hurry back and relieve him of his dangerous charge.

Morgan carefully crossed the remnants of a wooden bridge spanning a rain-bloated stream. Three days of sudden, heavy rains had all but washed out the back road north, and he saw, by the number of retreating tracks, that other travelers, beside himself and his manservant, had been waylaid. 'Twas still raining, though 'twas a quiet drizzle compared to the angry torrents which sluiced upon them earlier.

Morgan frowned, wondering if his wife had made it safely to Falcon's Lair. At first, he had been furious learning of Kat's secret departure. Even her uncle's reasoning had been unable to calm him down. Didn't the chit have a single drop of common sense in her veins? Mayhap one, Morgan conceded grudgingly, as Kat had at least taken a coach and her sister along. He scowled at the thought of Merry Tanner. What possible help would that scatterbrained redhead have been if the women had found themselves in dire circumstances?

Morgan's frown altered into a slight smile. He remembered, not without a trace of amusement, Kat's clever ploy at the altar. If she didn't love him, a tiny voice whispered inside, she wouldn't have gone to such lengths.

A moment later, Morgan felt uncertainty grip his heart. Perhaps she had only wed him out of pity. By now, Kat's cousin or sister had surely told her about his birthmark and the Trelane family history. He couldn't bear the notion of Kat feeling sorry for him. Better to be alone than to be subjected to cloying sympathy.

Morgan made an angry noise at the thought and stepped down off the bridge to survey the damage on the other side. A sliver of the previous road remained, but he knew they dared not trust the horses' weight on the bridge. They would have to swim their mounts across.

'Twas cold and rapidly getting dark. Morgan realized the remainder of their journey must wait till morn. He turned and crossed back over the bridge. He arrived just in time to save poor Jimson from getting kicked in the backside by the fractious roan.

* * *

Morgan sat alone in a shadowy corner of *The Hart and Hind*, nursing a nut-brown ale beside the crackling hearth. He attended to the lively discourse going on about the inn's common room, as a small band of traveling Scots discussed the price of political freedom.

"Och, I say we hae a care this time," a huge, heavily bearded man growled into his cups. "What with Her Majesty seeking persecution of the Highlanders at every turn, 'twould be well-advised to wait for better opportunity."

"Freedom doesn't wait for opportunity!" Another tankard slammed down for emphasis. The second voice was higher, younger, fueled as much from ale as any cause. "Would you sacrifice our motherland for the whims of an old maid, Hugo? Even the Vikings respected our fierce defenses. They braved few settlements along our wild shores. Why? Because—we—would—not—wear—the—yoke—of—servitude!"

Morgan glanced over at the party of Scots. A dark-haired youth poked the bearded giant's leather jerkin with each impassioned word he uttered. Morgan saw the larger fellow redden and expected to see the giant fell the impertinent lad with one sweep of his huge fist, but for some reason Hugo held his peace.

"Ye've always had a silver tongue, Lindsay," Hugo muttered. "I kin wield naught but a sword."

"Och, but what a sword it is!" the youth exclaimed, hopping up from the bench where he sat. He urged Hugo to draw the gleaming weapon from its rusty scabbard.

Proudly the bearded giant laid the claymore across the board plank table, where it might be duly admired by the other patrons.

"Look," young Lindsay cried, wrapping both his hands around the jeweled pommel. He heaved. He grunted. He strained. Sweat broke out on his brow. He was small for his age, mayhap all of fourteen years. Indeed he appeared almost waif-like, so 'twas little surprise when he did not lift the sword higher than a few feet.

"Fifteen shillings says no man in this room can heft the sword with one hand and circle it thrice about his head," Lindsay challenged the others present. He gasped with dramatic relief when he set the claymore down.

"Stand aside, boy. Let me try," said a fellow traveler, a burly blacksmith. He tossed the shillings at Lindsay as he passed, obviously assuming 'twas an easy task to lift the sword. The smithy rolled up his sleeves, exposing arms thick as oak saplings and swaggered forward to impress the crowd. His eyes widened with measurable surprise when he grasped the hilt of the great claymore with his right fist and hefted. It raised but a few feet above the table.

Lindsay struck a cocky pose. "Not so simple, eh?"

The smithy reddened and cursed, throwing all of his effort into the trial. At last he lifted the claymore, but his thick wrist shook so with the effort, he was unable to steady the sword, much less swing it about his head. Had he tried, Morgan was certain he would have lost his ears in the attempt.

The men watching exclaimed with disbelief. One by one, they stepped forward, eager to proffer their coin and try their hand at lifting mighty Hugo's sword. One by one, they tested their strength against the weight of the weapon, laughing drunkenly at the others who failed till they themselves were proven a weakling, in turn.

Watching from the corner, Lindsay grinned at the spectacle he had created, while surreptitiously counting the growing mound of silver in his palm. Morgan supposed the lad might be accounted handsome, was he not so damned sly. A shock of dark hair dangled over young Lindsay's brow. His eyes were a peculiar shade of violet-blue. He obviously had the canny instincts of a fox. Aware of being watched, Lindsay's gaze swept around the inn's

common room until they alighted on Morgan sitting
alone in the corner.

"Good sir," the lad called out, "will you not try your
hand at Hugo's sword? You look a sturdy sort."

Morgan deliberately turned his bare left cheek to the
light of the torches. To his credit, Lindsay didn't flinch.

"Fifteen shillings," the lad coaxed.

"I've no time for your Highland Games," Morgan replied, rising and tossing his black cloak around his shoulders. He reached into the kid purse tied to his waist and
pitched a few coins upon the plank table as he left.

Lindsay stepped directly in his path. The lad was a full
head shorter than Morgan, and his chest had scarce filled
out. His confident stance betrayed no awareness of the
fact Morgan was irritated.

"Well met, sir. Methinks you were privy to our earlier
discussion. I note by your speech and manner y'are of
Welsh descent, yourself. I'd would fain know, before you
leave, what think you of the notion of independent na-
tions?"

Morgan glimpsed a mischievous twinkle in the violet
eyes.

"What I think," he replied, with deliberate emphasis,
"is that you have imbibed too much drink, Master Lindsay."

"Och, 'tis a sorry day indeed when a Highlander canna
hold his ale," Lindsay moaned, slapping his forehead in
dramatic fashion and speaking in a thick, Scottish burr.
Morgan was not fooled. Only moments before, the lad's
English was as flawlessly executed as his sham with the
sword. He and Hugo the Giant had apparently cooked
up some bit of tomfoolery to relieve unsuspecting patrons
of their hard-earned coins.

Noting Lindsay's surreptitious glance in the direction
of his purse, Morgan took a perverse delight in lingering

and baiting the lad. He folded his arms and matched the boy's casual stance.

"Concerning politics, and being a Welshman myself, y'know I must be loyal to the Tudor line."

"Och, I see it. Else how would ye acquire such a grievous wound?" Lindsay peered closer at Morgan's face. "Sweet Jesu, mon, ye should hae that cut stitched. 'Tis a right angry sight. Did ye earn it in battle for yer Virgin Queen?"

"Nay. Rather, I should think, with Satan." Morgan gave a short laugh, obviously confusing the youth. "Speaking of battles, boy, I believe 'twould do you well to practice a more honorable art than picking pockets."

Lindsay's brow furrowed. His roving fingers swiftly withdraw from Morgan's cloak.

"Are you so greedy a nip a few crowns are worth your life?" Morgan inquired.

Despite being caught in the act, Lindsay summoned a brash grin. *S'blood*, Morgan thought with amazement, but Lindsay was a cheeky fellow, bold as a badger and cunning as a fox.

"I would but inquire after your tailor, sir," the lad innocently rejoined. "The cut of your cloak is uncommonly fine."

"So is the cut of my blade," Morgan retorted.

Feigning surprise, Lindsay blinked his violet-blue eyes—pretty eyes which, like as not, called upon him to defend his manhood now and again. Even the lad's lashes were too long and far better suited to a girl, Morgan decided. Though doubtless Lindsay's good looks and charming manners had freed him from many a scrape before.

"Further," Morgan added, gesturing to the doorway behind Lindsay, "were you not a baseborn thief, you would surely be accounted a blithering fool for spouting such treasonous slop before a contingent of the queen's guard."

Lindsay's jaw dropped. He didn't notice Morgan's de-

parture as he whirled to confront a set of unsmiling faces
looming in the doorway of the inn. They belonged to six
soldiers wearing the Tudor green and gold.

Morgan heard the fracas break out in the inn below
his rented room. While idly listening to the shouts and
curses and clashes of steel, he peeled off his leather jerkin
and doublet, set them aside, and tended his breeches and
boots. For the better part of an hour, the floor beneath
him vibrated with the screams and groans of over a dozen
men. He heard an enraged shout, resembling the bellow
of a baited bear, and gathered the mighty Hugo felt compelled to lift his claymore for the Cause.

With a wry head shake, Morgan finished undressing
and slipped beneath the threadbare covers onto a hard,
lumpy mattress. The shouts became less distinct as a chase
ensued, and the excited whinny of horses and hoofbeats
pounded off into the night. He wondered if young Lindsay had eluded his fate. He suspected the knave had escaped due justice before.

Morgan closed his eyes and thought of Kat instead. He
wondered if she were safe at Falcon's Lair and, if so, what
she was doing this very moment. Mayhap she slept, curled
into an endearing fetal position, even as his child so slumbered in her womb. *Sweet Jesu*. His babe. Morgan's eyes
flew open, his breathing quickened. The consequences
had not truly dawned on him until now. Children oft
resembled their parents in feature and form. What if the
damned devil's mark surfaced for another generation?
Another line of doomed Trelanes. 'Twas little wonder he
couldn't sleep.

The road was scarcely passable in the morning, but
Morgan and Jimson pressed on. Mud slopped about the

horses' fetlocks and made their progress cursedly slow. They passed any number of mired coaches and wagons, and Morgan was glad he'd left the rest of his men at Falcon's Lair rather than traveling with a full brace of escort. Else he should feel obligated to stop and assist each stranded traveler, and he was anxious to reach home.

While he rode, Morgan remembered his first and only audience with England's aged queen. When the summons had arrived a few days ago at Hartshorn, he debated refusing the royal order, risking the danger of imprisonment. He did not need to attend to Elizabeth Tudor to know the queen was livid over his marriage and, quite possibly, his Spanish heritage.

In the end, Morgan went to Whitehall, as commanded. He decided he would not endanger others—most notably Kat's family—with his stubbornness. At Whitehall, he learned Sir Christopher Tanner had already tried to intervene on his and Kat's behalf, yet nothing, it seemed, would appease Bess Tudor but an audience with the petty Welsh baron who had defied her wishes.

Despite the fact that Morgan had, in truth, been tricked into marrying Kat, he knew he dared not count upon the queen's sympathies. Bess was ever vigilant against those she believed wronged her or her favorites. She had approved a marriage between Morgan and Mistress Margaret Tanner; the clever substitution of Maggie's cousin was not to be borne.

"I may be an old woman, Trelane," Elizabeth Tudor said, when he was presented, "but I am not a fool. Had you wished an annulment from Lady Katherine, you might have had one by now. Therefore I must concur you a party to treason."

"Treason, Your Majesty?" Morgan stepped forward from the shadows in the receiving room. He made no attempt to conceal his face. He saw the queen blink, as if straining to see him, and realized her eyesight was failing, along with her health. England's Gloriana, though still regal in her ruff, bright tan silk gown and crown jewels, was five and three score now. An auburn wig replaced the thinning hair; white powder and paint smoothed her wrinkles. By contrast Elizabeth's hands remained youthful in appearance and glittered, in her vanity, with half a dozen rings. She used those beautiful white hands to advantage, waving one at him in a dismissing fashion.

"Mayhap treason is too strong a word," Elizabeth granted. She had mellowed in her old age, Morgan decided. But he was not lulled into complacency: Even old dogs had sharp teeth. For over two score, Elizabeth had ruled with an iron fist; she was the only monarch many remembered in their lifetime. Few but the elderly spoke of Henry Tudor anymore: of once watching golden prince Hal ride in the glorious tournaments of yesteryear, and of later witnessing the long, sad succession of the king's wives.

"Y' are uncommon quiet," Elizabeth observed, leaning forward in her throne. "I dislike silence. Methinks it breeds conspiracy."

"Of a Spanish nature?" Morgan inquired. He did not curb the sharp tone in time.

Elizabeth released an unladylike snort. Whatever false-hoods the Earl of Cardiff had whispered in his monarch's ear, at least the queen was wise enough to examine the facts with some measure of impartiality.

"Your heritage does you no credit, Trelane, but I hold no blood against a man who serves me loyally. Even a bastard may appeal to me for mercy."

"I am no bastard," Morgan quietly replied.

"True. Your father was a fine man, who served his young liege with honor during m'sire's reign. 'Tis unfortunate he wed, unwisely, a Spanish harlot, from what I understand."

"No harlot, Your Grace, merely a lady of tortured mind and soul."

" 'Pon my word, sirrah, y'are quick to defend a papist who committed a mortal sin," Elizabeth said, as she observed his flashing eyes. " 'Twas a great scandal, as I recall. There are those who still whisper as to the cause."

"I fear I am the cause, Your Majesty." With sudden humility Morgan came forward and knelt on the steps at her feet, so she might better appreciate the tragic view. He sensed Elizabeth softening even before he lifted his face to the light.

"Ah, so the rumors are true, milord," she murmured. Morgan was surprised at the tender note in the queen's voice, even more so by her next gesture. Elizabeth touched his blemish with her cool ivory fingers.

"This is the bane keeping you from my Court, eh? Such a slight thing it seems on the surface, yet a great chasm indeed to one who is accounted perfect in every other manner."

Morgan felt blood rush to his face. "Your Grace—" he began.

Elizabeth shook her head, stilling any excuses or explanations. "Y'know, I favor a fair countenance, Trelane. In this methinks I am no different than any common maid. 'Tis rare for a woman to love a flawed man without reserve, I trow, lest there is some great fortune to be had. Have you a mighty fortune, sirrah?"

"Your Majesty must know I have not."

"Ah, then. 'Tis the crux of the matter. Pray tell, what impractical demon possessed Lady Katherine to pursue marriage to a lowly baron with unfortunate looks?"

Morgan flushed. "I know not, Your Grace."

"Faith, d'you not?" Elizabeth looked amused by his distress. "I wager, by your high color, Master Humble, that y'know very well. Does the notion of your lady wife's affections sit so ill with you?"

Morgan shook his head. "Nay. However, as Your Grace already observed, even a common maid prefers perfection to a blasphemy upon nature."

"A common maid, aye," Elizabeth replied, "but, I vow, common is too colorless a word for our Katherine. How many women d'you know who sail their own vessels, Treane?"

"Only Kat, Your Majesty."

"And I know but two. Lady Kat, as you said, and her feckless mother, Madam Bryony Tanner." Elizabeth's expression was wry. "Both have sore tried m'temper at times, but I confess they are fascinating females. One cannot count them among my gently bred, courtly lot of ladies."

Morgan had to smile at her observation. "Indeed."

"A likely pair of lady pigeons, whose wings peradventure will not be clipped," Elizabeth mused, seeming pleased by her own poetic description. "Come now, Treane. D'you not count yourself among the most fortunate of men?"

" 'Twould seem I should," he murmured.

"Aye, Master Humble. Methinks you protest too much against the notion of Cupid's dart. Is't so awkward, then, to suppose your face as fair to Lady Katherine as Apollo's?"

"Not awkward, Your Majesty. Nigh impossible."

Elizabeth patted his face in motherly fashion, startling him. "Naught is impossible when I order it, sirrah."

Morgan blinked with surprise. "You would command me to love my wife, Your Grace? I thought you summoned me here to dissolve the marriage."

"I'truth, I did intend it. Methinks there is cause for reconsideration."

"Because of my face?" Morgan's challenge was quiet, though no less bold for the fact.

"In *spite* of it, milord." Elizabeth reclined in her throne

and regarded him coolly. "Yea, one might pity Lady Katherine, but I suspect she has snagged a rare prize. Indeed,
'twould appear so. If the wench is half so canny as her
Irish kin, 'tis a wonder you are still in London."

Morgan was silent a moment. "I had planned to pursue
Kat," he confessed, "but Your Majesty's summons came
first."

Elizabeth snorted. "Aye? Rather I would trow you intended to ignore the royal missive altogether, in a Welshman's dudgeon," she said, and Morgan reddened, since
'twas exactly what he intended. England's domina was far
more perceptive, and sensitive, than he imagined one of
Tudor descent could be. Despite his resentment of Elizabeth's meddling ways, Morgan had to confess he admired
her. Admired a crotchety old queen who simpered like a
young chit one moment and breathed fire and brimstone
the next. Elizabeth Tudor was an admirable foe for
matching wits against, if a man had the courage or incli-
nation. He had neither at present.

Elizabeth's chuckle broke the silence. "Come now, Master Humble. Hast our dear Kat stolen your tongue and
fled with it to Wales? Then I must bade you return to
your modest abode and wrest it from her determined
grip." Her gray eyes sparkled with sudden merriment.
"Marry, 'tis the only solution to this tangled net that I
will consider."

Realizing he was dismissed, Morgan rose and executed
a deep bow. "I would serve your wishes, Your Grace," he
said.

"Just so. Pray God, you will always serve me thus."

"With all my heart, Your Majesty."

Remembering Elizabeth's airy, yet affectionate, dismissal, Morgan was touched anew. He was no less surprised by her perceptiveness. Even the queen realized his
heart's desire resided at Falcon's Lair; Elizabeth had commanded him to settle matters with Kat, however he might.

Their marriage would not be annulled. Not by church dictate, nor royal decree. 'Twas up to Morgan to make amends now. He prayed 'twas not too late.

Twenty-one

"Please, Merry," Kat appealed once again, as her sister readied her departure for London, "I don't want you to leave yet. I understood Mama and Papa's need for haste, but can't you send word to the queen and to Uncle Kit that you need to stay until autumn?"

Merry smiled and set aside the last of her baggage for Jem to attend to later. "I would fain stay, Kat," she said, "but I've overstayed my welcome, and methinks Bess will be growing impatient. I've already risked her wrath by remaining here so long. You will do just fine in my absence. At last the staff is coming 'round to your ways."

Merry recalled the devil's own time she'd had in getting anyone from the village to come work at Falcon's Lair. She'd deduced, during her stay, that the Welsh were far too proud and independent to make decent help and were best left to their own devices. There were precious few choices for servants in the surrounding area; she had to be satisfied with whatever she found. At least she had finally procured a lady's maid for Kat, and a doddering but winsome old man to play valet to Lord Trelane. Merry had arranged for the pair to arrive this evening. The maid servant, Gwen, swore she was experienced. Merry thought the chit seemed somewhat sly, but beggars could not be choosers. Pray dear Kat was not foolish enough to leave jewels and valuable gewgaws scattered about. The elderly valet claimed to be Gwen's grandfather and vouched for the girl's honesty, but Merry was troubled anyway. If only Falcon's Lair was in civilized London!

Well, Merry reasoned, she could at least set about re-decorating Hartshorn when she returned to town and surprise Kat on her next visit. Merry would insist Trelane allow his wife to travel to London, thrice a year at least. Morgan seemed a dour sort of fellow; doubtless Kat would welcome the change of atmosphere. Too much doom and gloom was not good for the complexion, Merry decided.

Meanwhile, she hoped her efforts to improve Falcon's Lair would not go unappreciated when Morgan finally arrived. The lady's maid, at least, should be welcomed by her sister. Kat would soon learn to appreciate all the little niceties of her new position.

Merry sighed at the memory of all she had endured. Kat regarded her quizzically, and she was forced to explain.

"Truth to tell, Kat, I shall be well-quit of this dreary place. I miss Court and all the little civilities I took for granted there. Perhaps Wales suits you, but I fear I find it cold and cheerless. I do wish you happiness, y'know."

Kat nodded. "I know. Bless you for all you've done here, Merry. I believe you're right: the others seem to be warming to me now—except for Winnie." She sighed at the thought of the friendship she had lost.

"The best way to handle subordinates is with a firm hand, dear. I could never make Mother understand the notion, either. She always treated her crew like family. 'Tis a grievous day indeed when a proper English lady must needs converse on an equal plane with commoners."

"Merry! We're both half-Irish."

The redhead ignored the reminder. "You will do quite well, Kat, if you but remember my advice: always dress as befits your station and keep your head high; don't lower yourself to a minion's level by discussing anything but simple business with them; give your orders in a crisp,

clear, authoritative voice. However, you must never raise
your voice, lest you be thought to be losing control—"

"Aye," Kat said impatiently, rising from the settle where
she had sat watching her sister pack. "I've commanded
a whole crew of men at sea, remember? I vow, I shall
muddle through—I wish you would stay, just the same."

Merry crossed the room to embrace her. "You and the
baron must visit Court again sometime soon. By then I
shall be an aunt."

Kat glanced down at her still-slender form, garbed in
claret-colored silk. "Oh, Merry," she whispered, "what if
Morgan doesn't want the babe?"

"Not want his own child? What nonsense." Merry af-
fectionately pecked both her cheeks. "He will be as surprised and delighted as I was when you told me. Faith, I
confess I never imagined you a mother. At least not before me. But I'm well and truly envious of you now."

Kat remembered the day when she and Morgan had
walked together in the fields. The children they encountered screamed and ran as if a demon had sprouted out
of her skirts. What had Morgan called them? Base little
wretches. What if he reacted the same way to news of
their own child?

"Godspeed, dear sister!" Kat called, as she waved Merry
off later that afternoon. Jem looked downright relieved
to return to London as well and hastened the team of
horses onward with a crack of the whip as the coach
rounded the bend in the road. In a moment, they were
gone.

Kat glanced down at her empty palm, still burning with
the image of the raven amulet. Bryony had told Kat she
would know when the time came to part with the clan's
mascot; 'twas today. Somehow it seemed right when Kat
lowered the worn cord over her sister's head. Merry had

protested, of course, pointing out that a pagan amulet hardly favored her primrose and white velvet gown with its elegant embroidery, but Kat persisted. 'Twas important Merry wear it for, some reason. Kat doubted, however, Merry would suffer the amulet for long—not when she anticipated a rich assortment of jewels as Sir Jasper's wife.

After the rumble of the coach faded into the distance, Kat sighed and brushed away a stray tear. She was in no mood to return to the keep and deal with the staff right now. Perhaps a ride would cheer her up. She remembered the intriguing old cave on the mountain, and brightened. There hadn't been time or opportunity to go exploring while Merry and her parents visited, keeping everything stirred up. Kat decided she might slip away now, and no one would be the wiser.

She hurried upstairs to change into her old trews and canvas shirt and frowned when the hooks barely fastened. Her size was increasing rapidly. *God's nightshirt, surely 'twas not twins?* The color drained from her face as she considered the possibility. Her mother was a twin. Bryony had also birthed twins, albeit very different daughters. Kat knew twins ran in families. Sweet Jesu, that's all she needed now. Two demanding little Trelanes. No husband to help.

Kat glanced up at the portrait of the dignified, lovely Elena Trelane, Morgan's mother. Out of respect for her husband's family, she had asked the portrait be hung in her new room. Suddenly she found herself resenting the woman.

"You were selfish, Lady Trelane," Kat said. Even rendered in such life-like oils, the dark Spanish eyes were implacable—like Morgan's when he was angry.

"You did not deserve your son. He never deserved your enmity." Kat trembled with emotion as she stared at Elena's hauntingly lovely face. "Even had you lived, I would never forgive you for hurting Morgan so."

She turned her back on the portrait and went down-stairs. Before leaving the keep, she ordered Winnie to have the portrait removed and put into storage. The housekeeper looked surprised but asked no questions.

At the stables, Kat called for Evan Howell to saddle the gray mare she favored. The stable boy did her bidding with alacrity and steadied the horse while she mounted.

"Will you want a groom, milady?" Evan asked, as Kat settled in place and he handed her the reins.

She shook her head. " 'Tis just a short jaunt to clear my head." She smiled at the towheaded lad. She liked young Evan. He was respectful and bright and kept the stables in perfect order. He'd relieved Lloyd Carey of the heavier chores, and the old man was grateful as well.

Deliberately ignoring Merry's orders to act aloof with retainers, Kat leaned down and ruffled the lad's hair. "Stay out of trouble, Evan. I'll return in less than an hour."

He offered her a crooked, charming grin. "Aye, milady. Enjoy your ride."

Wind whipped and plucked at Kat as she made the slow, awkward ascent over boulders leading to the cave. She was glad she had decided to wear gloves, as the rocks were sharp and speckled with bird droppings in many spots.

She took care to secure her footing before she proceeded upwards. It seemed an eternity before she reached her destination. Cautiously she pulled herself over the lip of the cave, resting a moment to catch her breath. A quick peek down told her what she already suspected: 'twas a sheer, deadly drop to the rocks below. In the distance, the sea swirled and hissed, a vicious cauldron. She fought a wave of dizziness and steadied herself with some effort.

At last, she drew her legs up onto the ledge and stood.

Her shirt and breeks were dirty; she brushed at them while her eyes adjusted to the dim light. Kat stifled a gasp of surprise when a peculiar stone fixture materialized from the gloom. There were other signs of recent occupation, as well. A pile of burned twigs and scraps of what appeared to be material lay upon the makeshift altar. Kat moved forward, extending a gloved finger to lift a piece of the burned cloth. She recognized the blue velvet at once. It belonged to a gown mysteriously missing. Merry ruthlessly questioned each servant about the supposed theft of her blue velvet before she left, but met with no success. The incident had been forgotten—until now.

Kat looked around, disconcerted by a sense of alarm. What was this place? Why did it frighten her so? She did not count herself among the superstitious Welsh, but, despite all her efforts to remain calm, her teeth began to chatter. Cold. She was cold, that's all. She had forgotten to bring a cloak and now shivered like a little idiot. She'd return another time, when she was better equipped to explore the cave further. It appeared to go some distance into the cliff.

Kat shook her head. Who was she trying to fool? If she had her druthers, she would never have ventured into this place again. It reeked of darkness. Evil. Falcon's Lair and the safety it offered seemed very far away.

Morgan had arrived at long last. He was somewhat chagrined by his wife's absence and the dramatic changes his home had endured in the while. He did not deny the ancient keep craved a thorough cleaning, and it appeared to have been the benefactor of a generous hand. Everywhere he looked, the silver shone, the gold plate gleamed, and even the linens were crisp and white enough to feign snow. Gone was the dirt covering the panes of leaded glass; a few had been removed altogether, while most had been cleaned for the first time in years—mayhap centuries.

A tendril of warmth snaked through Morgan. He realized Kat had done this for him, for them. Irritation supplanted the warmer emotion when he was unable to locate Kat within the next hour; not even Mrs. Carey professed knowledge of his lady wife's whereabouts.

Fate was damned capricious. At last he had decided to confront Kat, come what may—and she was nowhere to be found. Furthermore, the servants acted uncommonly subdued in his presence. Even Ailis was not her old bantering self. Morgan wondered what prompted their silence. Did they disapprove of his choice of bride? All seemed to have held Kat in great affection and high esteem before the marriage. All but Gwynneth, if Kat was to be believed.

Morgan recalled Kat's claim that Gwynneth had betrayed her to the soldiers who came to Falcon's Lair on Henry Lawrence's order. He felt shame at the memory of his brief relationship with the maid servant. 'Twas not that he found Gwynneth Owen irresistible, nor even attractive. Morgan had turned to Gwynneth in a moment of supreme agony, a mistake he deeply and profoundly regretted now. There must be no illusions between him and the maid; he would summon the wench and send her packing before Kat returned. Nothing must destroy the precious chance for hope and healing this marriage portended for them both.

"Milady, I was getting worried. 'Twas nigh two hours. 'Tis getting right dark."

"I know," Kat apologized as she swung down from the gray's saddle and faced the stableboy. "I'm sorry, Evan. I lost track of time." Her gaze encountered the stamping

roan in the nearest stall, and she looked at Evan with
surprise.

"Aye, the Master returned today. He rode in whilst I
was off helping Perry load a wagon. Lloyd said the Master
seems in dark spirits."

Kat self-consciously smoothed back tendrils of loose
hair and wiped at her grimy face. She knew she was filthy,
head to toe; Evan was too tactful to say anything, but
Winnie surely would.

Drawing a deep breath for courage, she thanked Evan
and returned to the keep. Thankfully, the long shadows
and rising mist from the sea concealed her approach.
Were Morgan to watch from the ramparts above, she
doubted he would recognize her in such humble garb,
her hair and breasts bound from view. Just to be safe, she
chose the rear entrance through the servant's passage
and slipped past Ailis before she had time or opportunity
to sense Kat's presence. Within minutes, Kat was safely in
her bedchamber, leaning against the closed door with a
pounding heart.

So Morgan had returned home in dark spirits. Why?
Because he must needs present her in person with an
annulment, mayhap a royal command to leave his domain? Kat's hands shook as she unlaced her shirt and
shrugged out of the dirty outfit. She thrust the soiled
clothing into the bottom of her wardrobe and extracted
a gown of flame-colored silk with blush velvet sleeves.
Merry had insisted she wear it at her first formal ceremony as Lady Trelane; what better opportunity than before her lord and husband?

Kat hastily bathed in the cold water left in the basin,
then struggled for almost an hour to dress herself. She
had not realized how much she had come to depend
upon Merry or her tiring woman. Merry's nimble fingers
secured hooks and laces in a matter of seconds; Kat's
trembled, and she almost gave up altogether in a fit of

exasperation and anxiety. She so wanted to impress Morgan with her transformation into a dignified lady. 'Twas difficult to feign dignity, however, when one's bodice was unevenly laced and one's petticoats refused to hang straight.

Kat cursed her own pride. She wished she had agreed to Merry finding her a lady's maid before she left for London. Alack, her stubborn nature assured her defeat when it came to refinement. She tugged at her crooked decolletage and batted at her windblown hair one last time. There was no help for it now. She must find Morgan and plead her cause before he retired for the night.

Suddenly Kat felt nauseous and light-headed, caused by the babe or fear of what was to come. She forced herself to take several deep breaths, then turned from the pier glass and her disheveled image reflected there. 'Twould serve nobody's interests if she dissolved into a whimpering lump of feminine ails. Somehow she must endure.

Kat instinctively knew where Morgan would be found. She was drawn toward Falcon Lair's library as if in a dream, her silk skirts whispering over the plush Turkish carpets. Her hand came to rest upon the door latch. She hesitated before turning the latch and stepping into the library. Warmth greeted her in the guise of a crackling fire. Autumn had come early to Falcon's Lair; already Madoc's Craig sported a mantle of fresh snow. She glimpsed a man in the chair before the hearth, his profile bent over a tome, as the fire reflected burnished mahogany highlights in his hair. Morgan shifted a little in the chair upon her entrance, but his attention remained focused on the book, and he made no move to turn around.

"Has Lady Katherine returned from her ride?" he idly inquired.

"Aye, milord." Kat saw her soft reply gave him pause. Morgan's head rose with a jolt. His shoulders stiffened beneath the white silk shirt he wore. She would have approached him then, yet his formal words held her at bay.

"Kat. I trust you're in good health."

"Yea, thank you." She strained in the gloom for any glimpse of Morgan's expression. His measured speech left no clue as to his thoughts. She saw his hands tighten on the book he held, as if he would fain use it as a shield of sorts. She lingered in the doorway, uncertain of her role. Until he invited her into his private domain of his own free will, she would not presume to go where she was not wanted.

The book slammed shut. Kat jumped at the sound; her resolve shattered in one fell swoop. *Sweet Mother and Mary, Morgan is furious.* Infuriated by her deceit, doubtless angrier still she had returned to Falcon's Lair without his permission. Thus his mild remark startled her.

"I understand you are with child."

Kat swallowed. To her surprise, she detected no emotion in his remark, not even rage. "Aye, milord. I fear 'tis true."

"As well you might." Bewildered by his cryptic remark, Kat saw Morgan tense as if to rise. Instead, he set the book aside and gripped the chair's armrests as if they might lend him strength. He drummed his fingers on the wine-colored leather. "I told you in London we must talk. 'Tis past due such time."

"Agreed, milord."

"Morgan." Absently he reminded her to use his Christian name. Kat felt a flicker of hope just the same.

"I would be honest with you, Kat," he continued. To Kat's chagrin, Morgan addressed the fire in the hearth. 'I know not whether this marriage can or ever will work between us, but the queen has offered her blessing. There is no chance of annulment now, not with a child due midwinter."

"You spoke with Her Majesty?"

"Aye, at Whitehall. I was summoned before Elizabeth and therein lectured quite thoroughly." A trace of mirth entered his sober tone. "Although, I must admit, I admire her blunt approach. In this arena, Elizabeth Tudor could challenge many a man."

"Her Grace can be formidable," Kat agreed. She glanced at the leaping flames Morgan found so fascinating and quelled a tic of irritation. Must needs he address her as a servant who scarcely merited a glance? Devil take him, she was his wife, deserving of more than a cursory comment or two.

Kat expected Morgan to dismiss her at any second, resigned to his dismal marital fate as he seemed, but he rose at last and braced himself with one hand curled upon the fireplace mantel. Surely she only imagined his fingers trembled where they gripped the marble. 'Twas a trick of the firelight, she vowed.

"Kat." Morgan's voice shook. She detected a strange desperation and terrible effort in that simple word, and stepped forward. He bade her remain where she was with a curt motion of his other hand. "Nay, I would continue. Pray do not interrupt me, whatever follows. If I do not face my demons now, perchance I never shall." Morgan drew a breath, and continued in a low voice:

"You know a little of my history, of my mother's death. What you do not understand is why she committed suicide." He was silent a second, absorbed in the past.

" 'Twas shortly after my birth. The tale goes that Lady Elena had me summoned from the nursery and when the midwife placed me in her arms, she screamed, unable to accept the cruel jest God—or Lord Satan—had dealt her household."

Kat wanted to assure Morgan his mother's mental weakness was not a reflection upon his worth, but she honored his request to hear him out. While she ached to go to him, she held her ground.

"Within minutes, Elena threw herself from the battlements. Would to God she had taken me with her." He expelled a harsh breath at the sentiment. His fingers turned white where they gripped the mantel.

"Jesu forgive you both," Kat whispered, shaken by the story but, more so, by the agony in Morgan's wish. She was glad she had removed Lady Trelane's picture from her room; she vowed she would banish Elena's evil countenance altogether from this household on the morrow. What manner of mother burdened her child with blame—Worse yet, blame for a tragic death in which an innocent had no part?

"You'll appreciate her reasoning soon enough." Morgan turned to face her. Firelight glinted on his beautiful ebony hair, shadows caressed his finely sculpted jaw and cheeks—one darker than the rest, curiously shaped like a crescent moon. Yet it did not flee with the other shadows when he moved.

Despite her vow of silence, Kat gasped. 'Twas a gasp of sudden understanding, rather than of fear or disgust, but she saw Morgan's eyes darken to glittering jet and knew 'twas too late to remedy her reaction.

"The Trelane Curse," Morgan announced, with a mocking little flourish, as he stroked the blemish on his left cheek. He confronted her with his level gaze. "Wilt thou not flee?" he taunted her in a Shakespearean vein.

Kat shook her head. "I would fain stay."

"More fool, then. Or mayhap courage lends you foolish ideals. Be warned, Kat. I will not accept pity; nay, not even from you."

She felt her temper flare, and snapped, "I do not offer it. What I would offer, Morgan, is my love and faith. I better understand your past actions now, yet I am no less wounded by your assumption. S'blood, you obviously reckon me too shallow to accept a flawed mate. We are—each and every one of us—imperfect in some way. Especially me: I play at being a great lady, when nothing is further from the truth. Y'see I cannot even lace my gown properly."

"I never noticed."

"As I hardly notice your sole shortcoming," she replied, approaching Morgan before he might withdraw. She took his left hand in hers, pressed it against her own cheek. At this heartfelt gesture, Morgan closed his eyes in pain or denial—perhaps both.

"There is risk for the child," he murmured.

"Our son or daughter will always be perfect in my sight. Fear not, my love."

Morgan shook his head. " 'Tis difficult," he rasped, "too difficult to bear, Kat, the notion of this devil's taint being passed from generation to generation. Although I know of no other ancestors thus cursed, I am not sure."

"Your mother's family—"

"Never acknowledged my existence," he bitterly interrupted. "They blamed my father for Elena's death. I know my grandfather still lives somewhere in Castile; Don Miguel Arruz de Rojas was formerly the Spanish ambassador. He came to London to negotiate with Elizabeth in the days before the Armada. There he met my grandfather Trelane, Griffith. The two old goats schemed to unite the families. Soon Elena was sent to Falcon's Lair, a virtual child fresh from the convent."

Kat felt a pang of sympathy for the sloe-eyed Spanish beauty. "Consider this, Morgan: Your mother found herself far from sunny Spain and her beloved family, isolated in dreary Wales in an ancient keep, married to an older man who was kind but often preoccupied with other matters. Is't any wonder she was unhappy?"

She noticed Morgan's dark eyes gleamed with emotion.

"Mayhap you're right, *Faeilean*. For years, I hated Elena, without consideration for her plight. The convent was all my mother knew before she came. She arrived with her duenna, Donna Inez. I understand the woman was sent back to Castile after Elena wed my father. Elena spoke little English and no Welsh at all."

"I vow nobody bothered to explain the intricacies of marriage or the agonies of the childbed, or took time to comfort Elena in her travail. Mayhap by the moment of your birth, she was so distraught she did not reason. Any imperfection in her child, however slight, was probably enough to shatter poor Elena's fractured mind.

"Your mother was alone, Morgan. In heart and soul and body. 'Tis not so with you." Kat reached up and caressed his face, ignoring the flinch she realized stemmed from years of uncertainty and shame. "I would be your wife in every sense of the word. You need never be alone again."

Morgan gazed into her beautiful green eyes, serene as the surface of a lake, and felt a corresponding ache deep in his chest. Aye, he wanted more than anything to claim Kat as forever his, to brand her lips with desire and fill her sweet loins with his passion each night, but he knew he dared not dream the dreams of an ordinary man.

"Rory." 'Twas hard for Morgan to say the name, much less imagine the handsome Irishman who once held Kat in his arms. His voice wavered with emotion, and not a little worry.

Kat reached up and smoothed his troubled brow. "Rory is gone, my love. He forgave us both, and freed my heart to love again, without reserve." Her gentle smile dazzled Morgan, and his heart leaped in his chest. *'Tis too late for Elena, not so for you.* The unbidden thought startled him.

As if reading his mind, Kat unhooked her bodice and shrugged off the flame-colored silk. Firelight revealed curves lush with promise and painted her ivory breasts with flickers of gold. Morgan trembled with anticipation at the vision of his bride. Her gown slithered to the carpet in invitation, followed by her stays and petticoats. Soon Kat was naked in his arms, drawing his head down to hers. He moaned under the fierce desperation of her kisses, marveling at the texture of her hair and letting it shower over his hands like raven-colored silk. He caressed the faint swell of her belly, ripe with his seed.

Sweet Jesu. How long he had craved this moment, dreaming of Kat and cursing his haunted nights and empty days. This woman held a power over him he neither understood nor denied; 'twas impossible to refuse the succor she offered him now.

"Whenever you ache within, thus shall I comfort you," Kat whispered, rising on tiptoe to kiss him again. "Whenever you grieve in spirit, I vow I shall solace you. If ever you need my body, I will come to you with a glad heart and stay with you until ease is found, but only through my love."

Morgan's embrace tightened around her. His heart cried: *At last, at last!* His lonely vigil had ended; he sensed the curtain falling on a nightmare of nearly three decades. He was awash in a sea of powerful emotions—joy, fear, passion, aye, even a little grief for the wretch he had been, bereft of hope or dignity. Never again would he return to the darkness of yesteryear. Only the light existed now. *Only the blessed light in Kat's green eyes.*

Twenty-two

'Twas time. Soon all would be made right, Gwynneth thought, trembling with excitement. She stroked the rich velvet bed hangings and awaited Kat's arrival. Tomorrow night this room would be hers. Morgan had never permitted her to sleep in the great bed before. He had locked the bedchamber when Kat left Falcon's Lair and refused admittance to any of the staff. Things would change now.

Tomorrow her rival would be gone. Gwynneth would be Lady Trelane. No more a servant, nay, not even a drudge called Gwen. She chuckled at the memory of Mistress Merry Tanner. The little fool never suspected she had engaged a cunning witch to play lady's maid to her sister. If not for Mistress Merry's oversight, Gwynneth would have found it much more difficult to return to Falcon's Lair. She scowled, recalling how Mrs. Carey drove her from the keep while Morgan was in London. The old cow would pay for it someday. She might have poisoned the woman tonight, but anticipation was far sweeter than quick satisfaction. Indeed, Winnie and all the other servants slumbered deeply this night, by benefit of a jug of honey mead Gwynneth had left in the kitchen. She dared not risk being disturbed on this, the single most important night of her life.

Gwynneth glanced at the bed and smiled. Though 'twas fairly dark in the chamber, she saw a faint image of the

two poppets, bound by a ribbon dyed red by her own
blood. It was knotted around the cloth figures nine times.
The poppets seemed but a harmless bit of child's play—
Gwynneth knew differently. She recalled the spell she had
chanted over the pair:

> *Behold they are forever one,*
> *Even as the Dark Lord and Lady.*
> *No more shall they be separated;*
> *No more alone,*
> *But ever fast together*
> *As One.*

A tingle of excitement burst through her. She felt the
power building in her bones. It swept through her belly,
causing her limbs to shake. She glanced at the *athame*
clutched in her fist, stained with the sacrifice of her own
blood. Nay, a few droplets when casting spells was not
enough. This spell might be fixed only by a witch's sword
sated by fresh blood; the *athame* silently howled to be
bathed in the stuff of life; it quivered with the bloodlust
of a predator. It almost frightened Gwynneth herself.

Soon, my dark servant. Be patient.

Gwynneth heard the door open. She slipped behind the
bed curtains, heart pounding, the *athame* held behind her
back. She listened to Kat's soft footfall and steeled herself
for a strike. The steps halted short of the bed, retreating
a pace. Gwynneth heard the creak of a chair. She eased
back a corner of the curtain and peered through the
gloom. Her beautiful adversary had lit a single candle and
now sat before the mirror, brushing out her long dark hair.
She smiled, no doubt, with triumph and satisfaction, sup-
posing she had recaptured Morgan's heart. *'Twill not be,
milady,* Gwynneth silently vowed, her venomous gaze focused on the gracile white throat of her rival.

One quick thrust—'twould all be over. The spell would

fix forever, and Morgan would come to her, bound like the poppet by a ritual as ancient as time, as timeless as the night.

The *athame* screamed to be sated. Gwynneth drew a shaky breath. Why did she hesitate? She longed to destroy the Irish bitch and had craved nothing else for many months. Yet Agatha's words gave her pause:

You cannot destroy the Morrigan, nor her chosen ones. 'Twould be foolish to even try.

No! She had the power. 'Twas hers by birthright. Cairis Owen's evil acts had assured her daughter's fate. Cairis had purchased Gwynneth's place in the dark kingdom with the price of her own soul. Nothing could prevent Gwynneth from claiming her heart's desire now.

She emerged from the shadows, an otherworldly reflection behind Kat. The *athame* rose above her head, glittering in the candlelight. It mesmerized Gwynneth before her gaze fell upon the woman seated before the pier glass. The blade descended. The pale face rose. Their eyes met in the mirror.

"Nay!" Gwynneth's shriek echoed in the bedchamber. Too late. The short blade struck the woman's shoulder, diverted from the vulnerable throat by a quirk of fate. Gwynneth staggered backwards; the bloody weapon spun out of sight.

Agatha Owen calmly rose from the chair and turned to face her granddaughter. The older woman winced from pain as blood gushed from her shoulder, but there was a terrible determination in her dark eyes, and Gwynneth was suddenly afraid. She cried out, stumbling over her own feet in her haste to retreat to the shadows.

"Damme you, old woman!"

"Be still!" Agatha's voice was a thunderclap in the room. Despite her age, she still commanded authority. Her dark eyes blazed with an unearthly light. Gwynneth noticed Agatha's waist-length hair was gray and brittle, not luxuriant and dark as she had supposed. A trick of the light—or the Craft.

Gwynneth's eyes widened in sudden comprehension. "You devious old crone!" she hissed, fists clenching at her sides. "You lied when you said your power was weak! You have the greatest power of all. The art of the malachim: shape-shifter."

Agatha did not deny the jealous accusation. "I foresaw your seeking to destroy Lady Trelane this night, binding the Master to your black heart. I cannot permit it, child."

"You cannot stop me." Gwynneth spat with contempt in her grandmother's direction. "Your power is nothing compared to mine."

"Is't not?" Agatha pressed her palm to the wound on her shoulder, and when she lifted her hand away the blood had vanished. "Will you force a duel of the arts?"

Gwynneth's gaze skittered to the door. Perchance, she might shove past the hag and escape into the night. She knew Agatha would follow, though. If the beldam truly possessed such power . . . Gwynneth bit her lip, violently envious of her own grandmother.

"If I promise to spare Lady Trelane, will you teach me the way of the malachim?"

Agatha gave a hollow laugh at the sly request. " 'Twould be trying to teach the Devil himself to save souls. Nay, child, your reign of terror ends here, tonight. I failed to curb your mother's evil ambitions, to the eternal sorrow of my own cursed soul. I must right the balance now or forever lose the chance."

Kat heard voices coming from her bedchamber and halted, confused, in the corridor. Was it Winnie and one of the maids, turning down her covers? One voice was low, measured, calm, the other an angry whine. A familiar whine. *Gwynneth.*

How dare the wench intrude again into her room, her home. Remembering the girl's previous actions, Kat trembled with fury, a burning knot of outrage in her belly. Darker emotions masked the lingering effects of Morgan's lovemaking. Gwynneth had sought to destroy her once. With a clarity born of female instinct, Kat knew the evil she had encountered in the cave was somehow linked with the creature who tried to invade her life again.

Morgan swore he had banished the girl to the village. When lying with him on the luxurious rug before the hearth, replete with passion, Kat believed her husband— She still did. Morgan assumed the matter was settled once the girl had left. In many ways, men were innocent of the darker dealings between women.

Now was her chance to rid Falcon's Lair of the scourge of Gwynneth Owen. Morgan had gone to find Winnie, annoyed when the housekeeper did not respond to his repeated summons. He intended joining Kat in her bedchamber later. She knew she must act before he arrived on the scene. Morgan would merely banish Gwynneth again, *with no consequence for her actions.*

Kat did not intend to be as generous as her husband. With determination, she grasped the latch and hurled the door open. The crash startled the occupants within— a wild-eyed Gwynneth and an older woman Kat had never seen before.

"What mischief are you planning here?" Kat demanded, her accusing gaze flicking from one to the other. Neither woman answered at once, but she saw Gwynneth smirk a little and her temper flared. She opened her mouth, intending to give the impertinent wench a dressing-down she would not soon forget.

"Milady," the gray-haired woman quickly interposed, with a respectful curtsey. "I am Agatha Owen, Gwynneth's grandmother. I have come to send the girl home."

"She has no home at Falcon's Lair," Kat pointedly replied.

"Aye, milady. I will send her somewhere where she cannot indulge in further mischief."

Kat hesitated. She wanted to trust Agatha, whose clear gaze seemed honest and forthright, yet she feared being too lenient, lest the girl and her kin take advantage of her or Morgan again.

"I will entrust Gwynneth to your care if you can vow she will never return," she said to Agatha. "The village is not far enough to suit. Mayhap Tregaron—"

"Nay." Agatha shook her head. "Where I must send Gwynneth is the province of no man."

At her words, Gwynneth's smirk faded, and she glanced at her grandmother in genuine alarm. "You daren't!"

"I have always done what I must, child, to protect the Master and his family from harm—even as I destroyed your mother, my own Cairis, the night she killed poor Lady Elena."

Shocked, Kat stared at Agatha. "Elena Trelane was murdered?"

The old woman sighed and touched her temple, as if pained by the memory. "There is both a great and sordid history to this place, milady. You must hear it in order to understand the darker dealings here. Wouldst listen?"

At Kat's nod, Agatha continued:

"In the twelfth century, milady, Falcon's Lair belonged to the Owen clan. In particular, Madoc ap Owen, a mighty sorcerer. Through the grace and favor of King Owain Gwynedd, he and his kin ruled Falcon's Lair and practiced the arcane arts in peace. When the *Sassenach*, Henry II, conquered Ceredigion, he banished the Owens and set a loyal Christian lord, Einion Trelane, in their stead.

"Lord Trelane was a kind man. The Owens converted to Christianity and swore fealty to their new lord. They were then allowed to remain. Each did so, at Madoc's command. Yet they all continued to practice the old ways in secret. Meanwhile, Madoc plotted to destroy his usurper. The vision, 'tis said, came to the sorcerer in a dream: Trelane's orderly Christian household must be tainted by pagan blood so the Owens might rule again.

"Madoc appeared to Lady Defena in a dream; Trelane's beautiful bride never suspected the sorcerer worked a spell on her heart, and she went and lay with him in the damiana on Madoc's Craig. Nine months later, she bore a son who was proclaimed heir to Falcon's Lair until his fourteenth birthday. It came about that one of the Owen clan was converted to Christianity and confessed the truth to Lord Trelane. Madoc ap Owen was hunted down and killed; Lady Defena, in her shame retired to a convent; and Trelane took a second wife to mother his five daughters and provide a true heir. He could not bring himself to kill the lad he called his own for so long; the boy was driven from Falcon's Lair and would later mingle his own blood with a Trelane cousin. So it continued between the Owens and the Trelanes, until the year Master Morgan was born."

Agatha grimaced at the memory and quietly proceeded:

" 'Twas a fearful night, milady, when demons roamed free and wolves howled on the Craig. I knew it boded ill when Cairis insisted she tend Lady Elena in her travail. My Cairis was a midwife, skilled in the arts of healing—but also in the arcane arts. When the Master was born, favored as he is by the moon's shadow, Cairis took it as a sign that she was meant to take young Morgan, and the Owens would rule Falcon's Lair again through him." Agatha hesitated, glancing at Kat, as if ashamed. Then she plunged on:

"I foresaw the terrible happenings, milady, but did not want to believe my own daughter was capable of such evil. When I later heard what happened—and gossip said

Lady Elena committed suicide after the babe's birth—I knew I was wrong to ignore the warnings in my dreams.

"Lady Elena did not willingly leap to her death; she was bewitched by my Cairis and coaxed into stepping off the tower so the child might be mother-orphaned. Cairis knew Morgan would be shunned by his own kind. She intended to seduce and marry the widowed Rhys, to raise Morgan herself, and to train him in the dark arts."

"Dear God." Kat looked at Gwynneth and saw the girl was as stunned as she by the tale. Rather than exhibiting repulsion, however, Gwynneth appeared fascinated by her mother's evil exploits.

Gwynneth suddenly spoke in a throaty growl. "Cairis was right. Morgan Trelane does bear the moon's favor. He is destined for great power and arcane leadership. No mere mortal can be allowed to interfere."

As if possessed by some invisible force, the girl turned and gazed directly at Kat. The Gwynneth Kat knew was gone; in her now pulsed a malevolent blackness. At that moment, Kat knew how it felt to stare into the face of Evil.

"Madoc ap Owen!"

Agatha sharply addressed the entity by name. Like a puppet, her granddaughter jerked and spun about. When contact with the malignant gaze was broken, Kat gasped and clutched her throat. She had been paralyzed for those few seconds and 'twas the most horrifying sensation she had ever experienced. No mere sword would conquer such pure evil, nor, she suspected, a flustered priest muttering a few hasty Biblical passages.

Transfixed despite her fear, she watched as Agatha raised her arms and muttered strange, nonsensical words at her granddaughter. Gwynneth, or the entity possessing her, laughed at Agatha's puny efforts to banish evil.

"Silence, old woman," Gwynneth snarled, and a deep male voice suddenly issued from the girl's throat. In two swift strides, she approached Agatha, who continued whispering beneath her breath, despite her obvious fear.

Agatha had addressed the presence as her own ancestor, Madoc. Now she gazed into burning eyes, afire at the cores like the proverbial pits of hell. Nay, 'twas no man or beast, nor even a famed sorcerer, who breathed such foul air against her cheek. Recognition was more terrifying than the fear of losing her life.

"Cernunnos!"

Kat stiffened at the ancient name Agatha uttered. She had heard it somewhere before; its implication was bone-chilling. She stepped forward, intending to drag Agatha from the room, if need be, but the old woman seemed mesmerized by the timeless fiend who now faced her.

"So the Horned One claims his due at last," Agatha murmured, staring into the depths of perdition reflected in her own descendant's eyes. She did not seem shocked.

"The price of great power is also great," Gwynneth silkily replied in her own voice. Her fiery eyes dimmed; she was but a girl again. "Sixty-six Owen souls, over six generations. Is it not worth the dear cost?"

Agatha briefly closed her own eyes, as if ashamed. With an agility born of desperation, she lashed out with her hand and caught Gwynneth unawares. Her palm cracked against her granddaughter's cheek like a bolt of lightning striking the hills. Gwynneth was dashed to the floor, hurled there by an invisible power. Kat heard the girl whimpering with pain and outrage.

"Begone, Diabolus! Your final due was paid with the death of Cairis, at my own hand. You vowed to spare this innocent child." Agatha shook with fury, leveling a finger at Gwynneth whose eyes cleared and then unexpectedly filled with tears.

"Grandmother," she cried, " 'tis I, Gwynneth, your

only living kin." She raised her hands in an imploring gesture. "The terrible darkness . . . has fled. I am free. We are both free of the Owen curse forever." Gwynneth started to rise, wincing as if the motion was painful. She rested a moment, then slid her hands farther back to brace herself. A moment later she rose and approached Agatha, weeping contritely.

"You have saved me again, as you did when Mother died. How can I repay you? Will you ever forgive me?"

Kat saw Agatha was both weary and relieved, as she stepped forward to embrace her long lost grandchild. The old woman was crying, too. "Oh, child, of course I forg—"

A clenched fist materialized from the depths of Gwynneth's skirts. A savage flash of silver, a brutal strike, and Agatha's eyes widened in comprehension and sorrow as the *athame* drove deep and true. Gwynneth impassively watched her grandmother crumple to the ground. Kat tried to scream, but the horror of the moment was so intense, and her terror so great, she did naught but whimper. She stumbled backward over her own feet, striking her shoulder against the doorjamb. As if suddenly remembering Kat was there, Gwynneth glanced at her. The bloodstained knife rose again.

Twenty-three

Kat did not wait for the girl to act. She emerged from her dazed state and whirled, her bruised shoulder throbbing in protest. She ran from the room, fearful of glancing back. 'Twas too late to do anything for Agatha, she knew. The old woman's heart had failed, not from the blade, but rather from the combined shock of Gwynneth's betrayal and her own shame and fear which had been nursed in secret misery for so many years.

Even as she fled downstairs, Kat realized the idea of escaping evil so easily was ridiculous. Her frail mortal mind, however, insisted she try. Her skirts seemed to twist and purposefully trip her as she gripped the banister with one hand and hurtled down the stairs, shouting for Morgan. She never doubted that he would come running or that one of the servants would appear to question her alarming cries. When neither event occurred, Kat tasted fear as she never had before. Not even the burning ship or the angry, unforgiving sea, compared to the horror she felt when she realized Morgan was missing.

Nay, not missing. Gone. The library doors crashed open before Kat and revealed an empty room and a slumbering bed of coals in the grate. The Turkish rug, where they had made love less than an hour ago, still bore the imprint of their bodies. Kat's heart pounded as she stared at the abstract pattern, evidence of their loving conjunction. How could a man and his entire household simply vanish? 'Twas inconceivable Gwynneth possessed such power, yet it appeared the girl was merely the instrument of a much older, greater evil.

A strange sixth sense came over Kat. She glanced up and, for a moment, fancied a large-winged dark bird overhead. 'Twas not the malevolent spirit she feared; rather it was a deep guiding force she did not understand. She closed her eyes and knew with a sudden burst of insight that Morgan was not at Falcon's Lair. Nor anywhere else on Trelane property.

Suddenly *she* was the bird—a raven soaring high above the keep, circling in the darkness. Venturing forth into the depths of night, thrumming and ripe with magic as old as the hills. Her keen bird's eye flicked over the crashing surf below, silvered by the crescent moon. She saw cliffs rushing past, harboring secrets as black as her glistening feathers. She rose on an updraft, wheeling toward the mountain. Even as she neared Madoc's Craig, the yawning mouth of the cave sought to swallow her as it devoured the night.

Kat's eyes snapped open from the trance. The raven's scream lingered in her mind; 'twas one of triumph or perhaps terror. She shivered, envisioning the cave on Madoc's Craig. She knew where her husband was.

Morgan's head throbbed. He felt as if Lucifer's anvil pounded against his skull. He groaned, drawing his legs to his chest and gripping his middle. He ached from head to toe, shivering violently from the cold. He felt like retching. No wonder! His searching hand discovered that he lay naked upon hard, icy stone. Where the hell was he? Morgan opened his eyes and dizzily regarded his surroundings. Darkness, except for a distant flicker of light. For some reason, he shuddered at the notion of fire. He sensed 'twas not a benevolent being who tended those flickering flames.

What had happened? He tried to remember. He recalled the library at Falcon's Lair and he perusing leather-bound volumes with his customary absorption, then selecting a first edition of *Henry IV*. He sat and skimmed Shakespeare's latest play, feeling impatient as he did so. He was aware of waiting for something—someone. He heard the door open but did not glance over.

"Has Lady Katherine returned from her ride?" he absently inquired.

"Aye, milord."

Morgan stiffened at the feminine voice and was subjected to a swirl of intense emotion. Suddenly he neither knew nor cared who Lady Katherine was—mayhap some distant relative come to visit—but the throaty reply of the woman he craved reached out and obscured all else. He rose, tossed down the book, and went to her. Gwynneth welcomed him with open arms, her mouth hungrily seeking his. She wore a fine gown of flame-colored silk. It shredded easily beneath his fierce passion. She laughed at his eagerness, beckoning him to the plush carpet, where she scored his back with her nails while he greedily assaulted her willing flesh—

Nay! Morgan shoved the foul memory away with a gasp, sickened by the obscenity of it. 'Twas his own recollection of the deed, yet it somehow felt wrong. Gwynneth's features seemed strangely distorted in his recollection. Her ordinary brown hair deepened to ebony now and again, her slitted dark eyes turned green. He felt as if he wrestled with a clever demon in his own mind, a changeling from the bowels of hell. Part of him desired Gwynneth with a ferocity so intense, 'twas frightening; the other half was repulsed by the same woman for a reason he did not understand. 'Twas as if he was being manipulated somehow, led meek as a lamb to the slaughter. To surrender

meant loss of heart and soul, to resist entailed certain
death.

Shaking with determination and fighting a pain so intense it made him see double, Morgan rolled onto his
stomach and began to crawl, inch by inch, towards the
light.

Kat hobbled her gray mare at the base of Madoc's Craig
and stroked the animal's quivering flanks. The midnight
wind was fearsome, swirling around them in the little
copse as if to protest their presence. The mare turned
her back to the howling wind, withers hunched against
the brutal onslaught. Kat patted her faithful mount one
last time, then gazed at the brooding colossus looming
above her. Only faint light from the crescent moon paved
her way. She realized she was mad to attempt such a climb
in the dark, especially considering the babe, but nobody
else could help. If she waited until morning, when the
servants roused themselves, she knew 'twould be too late
for Morgan.

She had pursued Gwynneth as quickly as she could,
taking time only to change from her gown into her fencing outfit—the same Kat had worn when she and Lucien
trained in the courtyard. Strapped at her side, the rapier
bumped methodically against Kat's hip as she climbed
the great boulders. Her hair, brutally yanked by the howling wind, flew about like a dark nimbus. It felt as if the
mighty Madoc himself sought to pull her off the mountain, clawing at her with ghostly fingers. Kat's mission was
daunting, but the thought of losing Morgan forever was
worse.

She slipped several times during the steep ascent, her
belly scraping against rock as she gasped and scrabbled
for a handhold. Once, she even dangled by a few fingertips, her right glove ripping as the merciless stone sought

to fling her away. Kat pressed the throbbing fingers to her mouth, tasting salty blood, then grimly wiped them on her breeks. She was forced to assume a slower pace, favoring her left hand. 'Twas not as strong, and she trembled from the effort.

At last Kat reached the cave. She collapsed upon the floor, gasping for air and searching for courage. The light she had glimpsed from below was gone—snuffed out some time during her ascent. An abyss of uncertainty greeted her.

"Morgan?" she called. It seemed her voice echoed timorously throughout the mountain. Kat drew her rapier, using it as a crutch, as she rose to her feet. Then she clutched the weapon double-handed to steady the blade.

Kat was sure she heard a faint scuffling sound in the rear of the cave. 'Twas impossible to ascertain its true depth in the dark. Mayhap it bored into the heart of the mountain itself. Moonlight penetrated only to the altar itself, a few feet deep. She glimpsed a pair of what appeared to be two children's dolls lying on the altar. They were bound breast to breast by a bit of ribbon. Kat's stomach clenched at the sight: more of Gwynneth's witchcraft, no doubt. She smelled charred wood. Then she touched the stone altar, crumbling a few ashes in her fingers. They were warm.

"Gwynneth," she shouted, more bravely than she felt. Only the wind howled in reply. Kat debated on the wisdom of a hasty retreat. After all, there was the babe to think of now. She was hardly qualified to confront Cernunnos, not even with a sword.

Something struck her boot with a dull thud. Kat recoiled and found herself teetering on the lip of the cave. Swiftly she regained her balance, pivoting left and right in a solid fencing stance. Another pebble glanced off her shoulder. She saw where this one fell, and, oddly enough, 'twas painted black.

Laughter rippled through the dead air in the cave. Kat took a short step backwards. She heard a grating noise beneath her heel and felt a fistful of rock crumble and drop. She jumped away from the ledge just in time. She could not go back. She must go forward and face the demon.

"Show yourself," she demanded.

Gwynneth emerged from the abyss. Her balled fists hid something in her bloodstained skirts. Mere pebbles? Or a knife? Mayhap she sought to trick Kat as she had her own grandmother, mewling for pity as she thrust the blade through her adversary's heart.

Kat steadied the rapier. "Close enough," she said. She was surprised when Gwynneth readily halted. Though she already suspected the altar's purpose, she gestured to it anyway. "What is this?"

Gwynneth cocked her head to one side, as if listening to another voice besides Kat's—Cernunnos', perhaps? The Horned One—Kat doubted if even the underlord himself looked so disreputable. Gwynneth was filthy, her hair matted in a frightful halo, lending her the appearance of a mad animal. She put a hand to her mouth and giggled. Her gaze was sly as ever.

"Don't you care for heights, milady?"

Gwynneth emphasized the last word with a sarcastic chuckle. Kat did not react to the taunt.

"I prayed you were wise and had left Falcon's Lair, forever," she said.

Gwynneth tossed her head. "They all wanted me to go. Everyone but Morgan. They should have known I would not leave my love."

"*Your* love?"

"Aye." Gwynneth's eyes narrowed. She confirmed the madness Kat suspected. "Morgan is mine. He always has been, and you will not come between us, now or ever."

She spat on the floor. "You, with the Morrigan's black hair and seawater eyes. He never belonged to you."

"He already does," Kat replied. "I am Lady Trelane."

Gwynneth let out a soft growl, turning to pace like a wild animal in her lair. She halted behind the altar with a mischievous smile.

"Know you what I do here?"

Kat shook her head, not caring to hear the details.

"I weave my spells around Morgan, binding him to me for all time." Gwynneth gestured at the entwined poppets and stared triumphantly at her rival. " 'Tis too late to save him now. Now I can also plan *your* demise." She picked up a scrap of the blue velvet Kat had seen before and fingered it thoughtfully. "How shall it happen, I wonder? Quickly and easily, or slowly and painfully? I've mused upon this for many a night, you see."

"The velvet isn't mine," Kat blurted.

Gwynneth stared at her.

"The blue velvet belonged to my cousin, Maggie," Kat explained. "So your mighty spell is bound to fail."

A snarl sounded in Gwynneth's throat at this revelation. "Then I will have the clothes you're wearing!"

Gwynneth lunged at Kat from across the altar. Something bright flashed in her hand. The *athame* which had killed Agatha pricked Kat's arm in passing. A few drops of blood splattered on the stone altar. Gwynneth shrieked with glee as Kat desperately parried the slashing blade.

Despite its greater weight, and Kat's skill, the rapier was almost ineffectual against Gwynneth's furious attack. Kat's fingers went numb. The *athame* had slashed her dominant hand, cutting deeply. The rapier flew from her grasp, spinning end over end into the darkness. She never heard it clatter to the ground. 'Twas lost.

Kat crumpled to her knees, clutching her injured hand. Gwynneth stepped forward and triumphantly ripped away part of her bloodied sleeve, right above her wound. To

Kat's surprise, Gwynneth broke off the assault and retreated, seeming satisfied with her rival's present position.
Kat watched with mounting horror as Gwynneth tossed
the scrap of her clothing on the altar and moved to sprinkle a white powder over the fresh blood.

"Eternal death to she who comes," Gwynneth chanted,
gloating as she performed the rite, "damnation to she
whose blood here spills—"

"Stop it. Now."

The order issued not from Kat, but from a man labo-
riously dragging himself across the floor of the cave.
Gwynneth dropped the packet with the remaining powder and whirled to confront Morgan. Her expression
transformed from a twisted soul into a simpering angel.

"My love," she exclaimed, "you should not be up and
about. The potion must needs take effect—"

Morgan ignored Gwynneth, and looked to his wife.
"Are you hurt, Kat?"

Kat held up her bloody, useless hand. She was trembling and pale but managed to speak in a whisper. "Be
careful. The girl's mind is unhinged."

Kat noticed something odd on the left side of Morgan's
face when he turned back to confront Gwynneth. She
swallowed an inadvertent cry. The crescent-shaped birthmark was stark white tonight, mirroring the moon.

From the corner of his eye, Morgan saw Kat flinch. He
felt his cheek burning, not with fire but with ice, and his
gut contracted with an invisible blow. Darkness struggled
for possession of his soul. He felt it clawing a foothold in
his heart. In a moment, Kat must turn from him and flee.
The bane coursing through his veins could not be helped.
Madoc rules you now, Gwynneth had whispered in his ear
earlier, while he tossed and fought the hellish fever. If the
witch was right, if he was indeed heir to Madoc's dark legacy, Kat was in grave danger. Still, she was sensible enough

not to scream, realizing 'twould benefit nothing—Or may-hap sheer terror kept her so silent?

The thought sobered Morgan. His gaze fixed on Gwynneth, poised above the altar. Curiously, he felt nothing for the maid now, though he had once sought her bed, a man possessed. Aye, 'twas the answer. He had indeed been possessed, subject to a demon no ordinary mortal understood. This was the legacy of his magical heritage.

"Give me the knife, Gwynneth," Morgan said. Sheer resolve forced his knees to support him at last. He rose from a crouch and approached the white-faced woman.

"But you . . . you are bound to me now," Gwynneth stammered in obvious confusion, looking down at the poppets on the altar. One she had lovingly crafted in Morgan's image, with clippings of his hair and nails, the other represented herself. For the simple price of her soul, Cernunnos had promised they would be together. Forever.

Gently Morgan pried the knife from Gwynneth's shaking hand. He tucked it inside his doublet, out of her reach. Then he picked up the poppets as well, studied them incuriously for a second, and crushed both in his hands.

Gwynneth cried out in protest. Too late! The dolls were torn asunder and lay shredded upon the altar. She and Morgan, by Cernunnos's sacred rites, should both be dead now! She gasped and Morgan regarded her levelly.

"There are some things even black magic cannot guarantee, Gwynneth."

She gazed up at him with bewildered, tear-filled eyes. "I don't understand."

"Love," he said quietly. "Love is stronger than the old ways, Gwynneth."

Kat heard Morgan's words and wept. They were eerily similar to those Rory had whispered in her ear before he departed for a better place. Her entire arm was numb, but her heart overflowed with emotion, a love so fierce and true that it hurt. She wept with relief as much as fear.

Gwynneth gestured to Kat. "She carries your child beneath her heart," she said in a childish voice.

"I know."

"I thought it could be ours. I thought—" Gwynneth bit her lip, staring past Morgan at something else. "I am yours, you know. As Cairis was meant for your father, and Lady Defena belonged to Madoc ap Owain."

Kat never heard Morgan's reply. Suddenly Gwynneth whirled and rushed past them both, hurling herself from the precipice, as if she might fly away on the brisk sea wind.

Kat choked back a cry. There was no thud of a body upon the rocks below, only the distant rush and roar of the sea. She began to tremble.

Morgan went to her. He drew her up into a tight embrace. Released from her vow to be brave, Kat began to sob aloud. He buried his face in her flowing hair.

"Don't ever leave me again," he said fiercely.

She agreed.

Kat finished reading the missive and paled. Concerned, Morgan rose from his fireside chair and went to her.

"What is it, *cariad?*"

"Here." She pushed the paper at him. Her eyes closed as he read the words aloud.

"*. . . regret to inform you neither Merry nor Jem, the family coachman, arrived at Ambergate as scheduled. Rest assured, I have made every inquiry into the matter. Even now the queen considers dispatching a brace of men to scour the countryside. . . .*"

Morgan quickly scanned the rest of the letter from Sir Christopher. He frowned. "Mayhap Merry and her escort were waylaid by bad weather, even as I was."

"Or perhaps Adrien Lovelle found her again. Oh, Morgan, I cannot rest till I know the truth."

He understood his wife's fear. "I'll ride out at once with our own men. We'll leave no stone unturned."

"I would go with you."

"Nay, Kat. 'Tis best you stay here. A mere week has passed since your injury."

Kat sighed and nodded. She reached up to touch his face with her bandaged hand. "Be careful, my love."

Less than an hour later, Morgan and a dozen men left Falcon's Lair in search of Merry Tanner. Lloyd Carey went along, as did Evan Howell. To Morgan's surprise, some of the men from the village had also volunteered to search for his sister-in-law. Even as Kat shared the true story of his mother's death with him, so did his staff spread the word hither and yon, across hill and dale. For once, Morgan was pleased Mrs. Carey was such a well-meaning gossip.

From the window in her bedchamber, Kat watched Morgan and his men depart. She fought off a sudden chill, a premonition of sorts concerning her twin. She closed her eyes and leaned against the window casing. She sensed Merry was not dead. But she also knew her sister was in some sort of danger. Mayhap the raven amulet would protect Merry. She was glad she had forced Merry to take it before she left.

Winnie entered the room. "La, you'll catch your death of cold standing there, milady." She hastily moved to shut and latch the window. "Come over to the fire. You must take proper care, now that there's the wee one coming."

Kat smiled and allowed Winnie to settle her in a comfortable chair with a woolen throw. "I'm worried about Merry," she confessed to the housekeeper. " 'T'isn't like her to be late for anything. I know how anxious she was to return to London and meet her intended, Sir Jasper Wickham."

Winnie paused at the door. "I'm sure she's all right. She seems a hearty girl."

"Strong-willed, perhaps, but Merry's not known for her common sense." Kat sighed, extending her chilled hands to the crackling blaze. "Merry has a sharp tongue, y'know. It has been known to get her in trouble from time to time."

"Fancy that," Winnie tartly remarked, remembering how Mistress Merry had marched around Falcon's Lair, snapping endless orders at the staff. She much preferred Lady Katherine. The realization surprised her. Winnie looked with new respect upon the Master's young wife.

Kat sensed the woman's thoughtful regard and glanced over at Winnie, her own gaze equally warm. "I missed you when I was in London."

"Did you, now?" Winnie inquired. "I'd have thought, with all those fancy affairs at Court, you would be bored here."

Kat shook her head. "Falcon's Lair is home to me now. Here with Morgan and all of you." She paused, studying Winnie a trifle anxiously. "Is it possible for us to be friends again?"

Winnie smiled. "Methinks we already are, dear."

Morgan wheeled his prancing roan about and studied the myriad of tracks in the mud. "This way." He motioned to his men, and they quickly followed his lead northeast.

They rode at a hard gallop, racing the sun and an unknown enemy. Morgan had ascertained that the Tanner coach had been driven from its course by a party of at least four, and his immediate thought was of brigands. *God's teeth!* Once the rogues discovered Merry Tanner was unchaperoned but for an elderly driver, there was bound to be trouble. Knowing Merry, the little dolt was clad, head to toe, in Court frippery for her journey. She probably sported a display of valuable jewelry, beside. Morgan gritted his teeth and dug his heels into the roan. The horse extended its neck for more speed. The horses splashed noisily through huge mud puddles left by the recent rains.

Suddenly, they came upon the coach. 'Twas rocked up on one side, half-buried in the muck. Morgan drew his lathered animal to a sliding stop in the ankle-deep mud and vaulted from the saddle. His men followed suit.

Lloyd Carey arrived, puffing at his side. "What d'you think happened, milord?"

"Trouble," Morgan succinctly replied. He poked his head inside the empty coach, emerging from it with an ominous shake. "No sign of the driver or Mistress Tanner. Most likely the work of brigands."

"Or cutthroats," Lloyd gravely rejoined, accompanying Morgan and the others in a brief, fruitless search of the surrounding area. An hour later, they were no closer to having answers than before.

Young Evan joined his master. "What do you think happened to them?"

"We may never know, Evan." Morgan massaged his aching temples. Another storm was coming in. He dreaded the news he must impart to his worried wife. Just then, he glimpsed a tiny bit of color on the ground. The bulk of it lay battered by hoofprints into the mud.

Morgan bent to retrieve it—A blue silk kerchief unfurled in his hand, fluttering gaily in the wind. Daintily stitched in one corner were two initials: G.L. Morgan thoughtfully regarded the mud stained material.

"What did you find, milord?" Evan eagerly asked.

Morgan was silent a moment. He tucked the kerchief into his jerkin pocket beneath his cloak.

"It remains to be seen, Evan," he said, with a glance at the roiling sky above them. "Pray God 'tis a clue."

Epilogue

Lady Trelane dashed past the great hearth with its crackling yule log. She rounded a corner and peeked back at her pursuer from the other side.

"Come here, wife!" Morgan ordered, lunging after the flying red taffeta with a growl. Laughing, Kat wheeled in the reverse direction, darted through the kitchen, and bowled directly into Morgan on the other side. He had taken a secret short cut to intercept her. His arms closed around her in triumph. She squealed in mock protest as he rained kisses all over her neck and face.

"There, there, and there." He planted kisses on her forehead, nose, and lips with satisfaction. Kat smiled saucily up at her husband. A second later her expression transformed to one of shock.

"What's wrong, *Faeilean?*"

Morgan followed her gaze. He noticed her skirts and his boots were soaked.

"Winnie!" he bellowed.

The housekeeper hurried into the room. "Milord?"

"Lady Katherine's water just broke. We'd best hurry."

Both ignored Kat's protests that she was fine. So did everyone else in the household.

Panic broke loose. 'Twas nigh three decades since a babe had been born at Falcon's Lair. Servants rushed to and fro, crashing into each other in the halls. Evan ran outside to find Ailis. Huffing and puffing and muttering, as she was herded back into her domain, Cook snapped at Evan to help her heft a cauldron full of water over the hearth. Lloyd Carey stepped into the midst of the confusion and was immediately enlisted to find more wood.

In the midst of the chaos, Kat stood and chuckled. Morgan suddenly swung her up in his arms and marched upstairs. She beat her fists upon his crimson velvet doublet.

"Put me down, you blackguard! I'm not some broodmare who must be tied down in her travail."

Morgan lowered her gently onto their bed. "Nay, but you are precious to me, and I won't let anything happen to you."

Despite her ire, Kat smiled at the love shining in her husband's dark eyes. She kissed the fingers cradling her shoulder. She sensed the worry underlying Morgan's words.

"Tanner women are strong, milord," she assured him. A moment later Kat sobered. She thought of Merry again, of the many weeks, now the months, that had passed since her twin's disappearance. There had been no word of Merry's fate. Yet there was no proof she was dead, either.

Morgan smoothed the damp hair from Kat's forehead, as if he read her thoughts. "Merry would want you to concentrate on bringing our child safely into the world, *Faeilean*. She is here with you in spirit, if not in flesh."

"Aye," Kat murmured. She felt her first true labor pain a moment later. Her eyes went wide. Morgan grabbed her hands and held them in his own. When Winnie appeared and tried to shoo him from the room, he wouldn't leave.

"Men," Winnie grumbled but briskly set about her business.

Less than eight hours later, just as dawn peeped above a glittering white Cader Idris on Christmas morn, their first child was born. Morgan stared in awe at the tiny human being Mrs. Carey swaddled and placed in his arms.

"Well, milord?" Winnie asked, beaming as if she had done all the work herself. "What shall we name the wee laddie?"

Morgan was still shaken by the miracle of birth. He could hardly respond for the emotion gripping his heart. He looked at his wife. "The decision is yours, *cariad.*"

Kat smiled tiredly, weary from her travail. "Owen, then, if it pleases you. Perchance 'twill placate your magical ancestors and gain the favor of the mighty Owen clan so they will leave us in peace in future. Morgan and Einion must serve as middle names, of course, and Tanner and O'Neill, to honor my parents."

"God's nightshirt!" Morgan glanced down at his son. "He's surely too wee a mite to bear so many grand names." He paused a moment to reflect. "Aye, I favor Owen Trelane well enough. 'Twill suffice for now."

"Be thankful 'twas not twins after all, milord," Kat mischievously replied. "I chose Madoc for the second born. Mayhap next time?"

Morgan groaned in protest, as he settled the babe in Kat's arms. Their son yawned and snuggled into his mother's warmth, a tiny cheek pressed against her breast. The proud father realized something else. Morgan's gaze had scoured the newest Trelane for sign of anything unusual from the moment Owen was born. He found nothing. Nothing at all.

"He's perfect," Morgan whispered, blinking back sudden moisture from his eyes.

"Of course," Kat replied, sounding sleepy and somewhat indignant.

Gazing upon his beloved wife and son, Morgan smiled

AUTHOR'S NOTE

Dear Reader,

Once again, the myth and magic of the British Isles has captured my heart and kindled my imagination. I hope you were enchanted, too. Kat and Morgan's story is the second book in my continuing Raven series for Zebra. If it struck a chord in you, please write and let me know. I treasure letters from readers and fellow fans of history.

Many of you have inquired if there will be a third full book in the Raven series. Never fear, I won't abandon sweet Merry Tanner to such a dismal fate. In April '98, travel with Zebra and me deep into the wilds of Scotland. Anger and honor rule the mighty Wolf of Badanloch. When love threatens to disarm this passionate warrior, he quickly discovers "pride goeth before a fall!"

You're welcome to write me anytime at: P.O. Box 304, Gooding, Idaho 83330. If you would like to receive a bookmark and/or my latest newsletter, kindly include a self-addressed, stamped envelope (No. 10). Hope to see you in the Highlands next year!

Best regards,

Patricia McAllister

Look for these other Zebra Books by Patricia McAllister:

GYPSY JEWEL
MOUNTAIN ANGEL
SEA RAVEN
"Absolute Angels" *(ANGEL LOVE Collection)*
SNOW RAVEN (April '98)

DANGEROUS GAMES   (0-7860-0270-0, $4.99)
by Amanda Scott

When Nicholas Barrington, eldest son of the Earl of Ulcombe, first met Melissa Seacort, the desperation he sensed beneath her well-bred beauty haunted him. He didn't realize how desperate Melissa really was . . . until he found her again at a Newmarket gambling club—being auctioned off by her father to the highest bidder. So, Nick bought himself a wife. With a villain hot on their heels, and a fortune and their lives at stake, they would gamble everything on the most dangerous game of all: love.

A TOUCH OF PARADISE   (0-7860-0271-9, $4.99)
by Alexa Smart

As a confidence man and scam runner in 1880s America, Malcolm Northrup has amassed a fortune. Now, posing as the eminent Sir John Abbot—scholar, and possible discoverer of the lost continent of Atlantis—he's taking his act on the road with a lecture tour, seeking funds for a scientific experiment he has no intention of making. But scholar Halia Davenport is determined to accompany Malcolm on his "expedition" . . . even if she must kidnap him!

Available wherever paperbacks are sold, or order direct from the Publisher. Send cover price plus 50¢ per copy for mailing and handling to Penguin USA, P.O. Box 999, c/o Dept. 17109, Bergenfield, NJ 07621. Residents of New York and Tennessee must include sales tax. DO NOT SEND CASH.